WOLF
IS A
FOUR-LETTER
WORD

BOOK TWO OF THE ETERNAL SPRING, INVISIBLE FOREST SERIES

CARRIE NEWBERRY

EDGE SCIENCE FICTION AND FANTASY PUBLISHING
An Imprint of HADES PUBLICATIONS, INC.
CALGARY

Wolf is a Four-letter Word
(Book Two of the Eternal Spring, Invisible Forest series)

Copyright © 2022 by Carrie Newberry

EDGE SCIENCE FICTION AND FANTASY PUBLISHING
An Imprint of HADES PUBLICATIONS, INC.
P.O. Box 1414, Calgary, Alberta, T2P 2L6, Canada

The EDGE Team:
Producer: Brian Hades
Edited by: Brian Hades
Cover Design: 100 Covers
Book Design: Mark Steele

ISBN: 9781770532076

EDGE Science Fiction and Fantasy Publishing and Hades Publications, Inc. acknowledges the ongoing support of the Alberta Foundation for the Arts and the Canada Council for the Arts for our publishing programme.

Library and Archives Canada Cataloguing in Publication

Title: Wolf is a four-letter word / by Carrie Newberry.
Names: Newberry, Carrie, author.
Description: Series statement: Eternal spring, invisible forest series ; book 2
Identifiers: Canadiana (print) 20220270619 | Canadiana (ebook) 20220276102 | ISBN 9781770532076 (softcover) | ISBN 9781770532069 (HTML)
Classification: LCC PS3614.E815 W65 2022 | DDC 813/.6—dc23

FIRST EDITION
(20220823)
Printed in USA
www.edgewebsite.com

Publisher's Note:

Thank you for purchasing this book. It began as an idea, was shaped by the creativity of its talented author, and was subsequently molded into the book you have before you by a team of editors and designers.

Like all EDGE books, this book is the result of the creative talents of a dedicated team of individuals who all believe that books (whether in print or pixels) have the magical ability to take you on an adventure to new and wondrous places powered by the author's imagination.

As EDGE's publisher, I hope that you enjoy this book. It is a part of our ongoing quest to discover talented authors and to make their creative writing available to you.

We also hope that you will share your discovery and enjoyment of this novel on social media through Facebook, Twitter, Goodreads, Pinterest, etc., and by posting your opinions and/or reviews on Amazon and other review sites and blogs. By doing so, others will be able to share your discovery and passion for this book.

Brian Hades, publisher

Dedication

To Mom, Dad, and Jen, the best
cheerleaders anyone could ask for.
Love you.

PART I: Before

Chapter 1

A tail brushed across my nose. It wasn't my tail. I knew that even through the bleariness of being mostly asleep. I could smell that it was my dog, Galen's. The long, wiry hair tickled my nostrils and made me sneeze. Galen was like my brother, so even though my sister, Mal, thought it was weird that I shared my bed with my dog when I was in wolf form —

Mal. As I came awake, the name stabbed through me like a giant icicle. I pushed her out of my mind before she could take hold. Thinking about Mal wasn't how I wanted to start my day. Except it was how I started every day, for the last three months. Since she almost killed me.

I stretched myself, front legs first, then left rear leg, then right rear. I raised my nose to the air. The cabin was dark. It was late. No, early. The sun wasn't up yet, but I could smell the impending dawn. It smelled fresh, like ice water on a hot day.

Galen rolled over, glared at me with one half-open eye, and then turned his back to me. Galen didn't like to wake up before the sun. I guess I couldn't blame him.

After shaking myself, I leapt down from the bed. I preferred to shape-shift on the floor. Sometimes, body fluids leaked in the process, fluids that were a bitch to get out of sheets. I bowed my head and tucked my tail close to my legs, before I started the change.

My tail drew back into my tailbone like a retractable leash. It felt like someone was compressing my vertebrae like a sadistic accordion player. My paws unfolded, stretched into fingers, palms, size eight feet. My elbows and knees cracked, hips sliding in and out of joint, as my ribcage opened like butterfly wings, became the flat ribs of a human rather than the folded ribs of a canine. Skin sucked fur back under the surface. My face was the last to change, the bones of the muzzle rearranging themselves to form cheekbones, chin, jawline and nose. It all happened so fast that the pain didn't hit until it was almost over, so my howl was a purely human shriek. Nothing wolfish about it.

Galen raised his head to make sure I wasn't in danger, then settled back on the bed. I stayed on my hands and knees, panting. The pain always seemed worse, going from wolf to human. Changing into a wolf felt like setting myself free. Changing back into a human was like watching the cage door slam shut in my face.

I lowered myself to the cool hardwood, glad that the floor was dry. No messy clean-up this morning. Just as I was beginning to settle into my body, the phone shrilled.

I sat up, my muscles protesting like I just ran a marathon in high heels, and I pulled myself back onto the bed. My cell phone was somewhere in the tangle of sheets. I located it under one of the pillows. "What?"

"Good mornin' to you, too, buttercup." A deep, rumbly bass voice vibrated through the phone.

Annoyance at the stupid name flared and died quickly. I had a hard time staying annoyed at Tony. "Why the fuck are you calling me?" I said. "The sun heard the phone ring and gave me the finger before rolling over and going back to sleep."

The only response was a rumbly chuckle that matched the voice. He was a fairly good guy, relatively speaking, and him being in South Dakota the last three months gave me an opportunity for absence to make the...well, I missed him.

"I'm bored," he said.

I rolled over onto my back and closed my eyes. A breeze drifted through the window over the bed, drying the sweat that shape-shifting left on my skin. "And this is my problem because...?"

"Because I called and you answered."

The simple truth of his statement made it that much more irritating. I grunted and felt sleep tugging at me. Not good. I didn't want to fall asleep. Perchance to dream. The nightmares were always worse in the drifting of almost-sleep. I sat up and leaned my back against the wall.

"You just shift back?"

"No, I'm still in wolf form."

He ignored the sarcasm. "So I didn't wake you?"

"If you woke me, I wouldn't've answered. I can't shapeshift that fast." This wasn't our first meander down this conversational path. Several times, he called while I was still in wolf form, and the call went to voicemail while I shifted. But when he was homesick, he got sentimental and mushy. Which seemed to lead to inane questions.

He was quiet for a while and my head became too heavy to hold up. His voice jolted me awake again. "I think these cattle deaths are the work of some wild animal. I don't think it's anything sinister."

Tony was investigating the death of a bunch of cows. Our bosses thought the cattle were killed by something supernatural. Even demons liked a good mouthful of Angus every now and then. "Thanks for calling me to state the obvious. Next, you'll tell me it's dark at night there."

"Your warmth and charm lack a certain something. Like warmth and charm."

"Yeah, well, lucky for me I'm cute." I paused as the sounds of the morning began to totter around outside my cabin window. I shifted my weight, trying to keep my butt from falling asleep. "Younglings are awake."

"Yeah? What do you hear?"

We had this conversation before, too, but I was more willing to indulge him here. If I was stuck in South Dakota, I'd want to hear about home, too. "Home" was Madison, capitol of Wisconsin and proud home to bike paths, Monty's Blue Plate diner, rabid liberals, invisible forests. On the edge of the city, on the edge of a business park, stood what appeared to be a vacant lot that stretched for several acres. It looked like it was home only to a messy marsh and maybe some rodents. If you wandered very far into that vacant lot, however, you would find yourself in the middle of a forest. And if you continued to wander, you would probably find yourself shot by one of us.

That reminded me of something I wanted to tell Tony. "Gina shot a crossbow yesterday and actually hit a target." Gina was a youngling, one of our trainees, who struggled in nearly everything. Running, hand-to-hand combat, archery, knife throwing, guns. She couldn't even climb a tree, and we were protectors of an invisible forest, for pete's sake. And she was already seventeen years old, which meant she should be ready to graduate in a year or two. For the past three months, I worked with her every day, one-on-one, to help her get up to snuff. Tony was the one who suggested that Gina needed individual help, so he always asked how she was doing.

Tony whooped loud enough to startle Galen, who grumbled and gave me another glare. I reached over and scratched him behind his left ear. He stretched out and gave a contented sigh.

"She hit what she was aiming for?" Tony said.

As I pictured the grin that I heard in his voice, my eyelids slid shut on the image. When I realized what I was doing, I opened my eyes, sat up straighter, and for some reason, pulled up the sheet to cover my breasts. "Uh, not exactly. She hit the target two lanes to the left, but you know. It's still progress."

From outside, I heard a shout and a laugh, then in a deeper voice, a sharp reprimand. One of the Sankhain, making sure the younglings didn't have too much fun. Tony and I were members of the Sankhain, or Secret-Keepers, protectors of the invisible forest and its hidden treasure deep within — a fountain of youth. Well, not really a fountain of youth, more like a fountain of vitality. It didn't make anyone younger, just prevented further aging, increased strength and endurance, and protected against illness and disease. Drink from the Spring and the common cold would be a distant memory, cancer couldn't touch you, and even venereal diseases failed to sink their fangs into you. A human who drank from the Spring could still be killed by an outside force, like a bullet, but her body couldn't turn against her.

Obviously, such a fountain would be highly coveted by humans. When people were willing to kill each other over land or oil, what would they do to control the reins of immortality? Probably not spread their arms wide and practice peace, love and understanding. Not to mention, if the entire world was immortal, we'd have a slight over-crowding problem. The Sankhain protected the secret and the world didn't implode.

The Spring provided perks for supernatural beings, as well. For a shape-shifter like myself, it meant an exponential increase in strength. I, a five-foot-seven female, could bench-press five hundred pounds. I could also heal almost instantaneously, depending on the severity of the wound, and my already-sensitive sense of smell was crazy-good. Good enough that, as I told Tony about Gina and her crossbow, I knew that someone was approaching my cabin door long before the knock sounded.

I recognized the scent that reminded me of damp earth. Finn. He was the Sankhain second-in-command, lackey and confidant to our leader, Janus. And my ex-fuck partner. My teeth clenched when the scent set uncertainty fluttering around in my stomach. Finn was stopping by awfully early. Did they find Mal? "I gotta go," I said into the phone.

"Wait." I waited, because now that my sister was gone, Tony was really my only friend, or my only two-legged friend at least. "How're you doing with, you know, everything?"

By "everything," he meant Mal. But I didn't want to talk about her. I didn't even like that she popped into my head or into our conversation. I sighed and rubbed the heel of my hand into my eye. "I gotta go. Finn's at the door and I'm butt naked."

Tony was quiet. I wondered if I shouldn't have mentioned I was naked. Men tended to take statements like that the wrong way.

Tony said, "Tell him the locals think it's a mountain lion, and I agree." He sounded frustrated. Or maybe he was just hungry. It was really hard to tell. I hated talking on the phone. I much preferred being able to sniff out a person's emotions.

"Okay. Don't call this early again," I said. Even though I was already awake, and even though I didn't have anyone else to talk to at four a.m. I hopped out of bed and struggled to pull on a pair of shorts, one-handed. An ill-fated decision that ended in me falling back onto the bed and landing on Galen. "Oh. Shit. Sorry."

Galen glared at me and jumped off the bed. His toenails clacked into the bathroom, the only other room in the small cabin.

"That's okay, I know you like wakin' up to the sound of my voice." Tony's voice sounded even lower than usual, closer and clearer than a phone voice should've been.

Suddenly, I was aware of my nakedness in a whole new way. Air brushed across my nipples like...Shit. "No. I was apologizing to Galen. I — you know what, never mind, I have to get clothes on. Bye." I hung up, furious with my traitorous nipples.

Finn now pounded on the door and I still didn't have any clothes on.

"Just a minute," I yelled, and, tossing the phone on the bed, managed to put on shorts and a tank top without hurting anyone.

I opened the door and stared at him. He was beautiful, as always. If this was a fairy tale, I would say Finlay Weaver looked like he was spun out of gold by a little troll. Golden hair, golden brown eyes, and a golden tint to his skin that never faded, not even in the dead of winter.

Next to him, I must've looked like the little troll. My long, silver-streaked hair was unruly at the best of times, and post-shapeshifting was not the best of times. Between that and the tattoos that covered over half my body, I probably looked like something a drunk carnie wouldn't touch with a ten-foot pole.

I felt my face heat up and I growled a little as I greeted him. "Good morning, sir. To what do I owe the honor of your presence?"

That was the expected way for a Sankha to address a superior. And Finn was my superior, at least in rank. In pretty much every other category, his superior status was suspect, at best.

Galen finally ventured out of the bathroom. "Some guard dog you are," I said. "He could've been murdering me out here."

Galen didn't even look at me. He did, however, flop down at my feet instead of on the bed, and he fixed his half-closed eyes on

Finn. Galen never liked Finn much. The man's golden beauty was lost on the dog. Dogs didn't like people they couldn't read, and Finn prided himself on his ability to control his emotions.

It used to be that for me, Finn's rigid self-control was exciting. A wall to breach. And when those stones came tumbling down, oh, baby. But Finn wasn't worth it. No fuck was worth putting up with such a colossal douche nozzle.

At the sound of a throat clearing, I tore my eyes away from my dog. I wondered about the proper thing to say and decided that I didn't care anymore. "Why are you here?" I asked.

"In an existentialist sort of way or a current events sort of way?"

Oh, good, he was going to be cute. I growled again. "The only existentialist conversation we're having is to list all the ways you'll cease to exist if you don't get on with it."

Finn let out a sigh. He could make even a tiny exhale sound condescending and dismissive. Reaching behind his back, he pulled out a file folder. I frowned. "Where were you hiding that? Wait, never mind, I don't want to know."

"It was in my back pocket." His scent was dry, like draught-seared earth. "Turn on a light, please."

My gut lurched with trepidation. "Why? What is that?"

"It's a folder." He brushed past me and turned on the bedside lamp. He laid his folder down on the bed. I stepped closer, so I could see. Then he opened the folder, and I took several steps back.

"Jeez. Give a girl some warning next time." The sheaf of papers in the folder was topped by a picture of a mutilated man.

Finn ignored my words. "What does that look like to you?"

I stared at him. "If this is your idea of a Rorschach test, you're even more twisted than I thought."

"Kellan."

A muscle between my shoulder blades spasmed at his tone, but I took another look at the picture. "Hard to tell from a picture, but it almost looks like a pack kill."

"Explain." He sounded imperious, which pissed me off. I resolved to make my explanation as graphic as possible.

I leaned over the photo and pointed to various parts of the man as I spoke. "There, that shredding of the ankle, that's where they cut his Achilles tendon to bring him down. Next they ripped his throat out, there, to kill him so he wouldn't struggle while they dug into his meaty bits." My stomach rumbled. Talk of hunting always made me hungry. I looked up at Finn. "Any chance of continuing this in the mess hall?"

He raised an eyebrow and his mouth twisted like he just swallowed a bug. Humans could be so judgy.

That muscle started spasming again. "Don't judge me. You're the one who played the prey card before breakfast."

"Fine. Let's go." Like my presence was something to be endured.

Right back at you, I thought. "Just let me get my boots." I also grabbed my eight-inch-blade forearm sheathes. Finn led the way out the door. As I cleared the threshold, I closed my eyes and took a deep breath to scent my surroundings.

The smell of the forest formed a sturdy foundation for all the other scents of the Sankhain Academy — the old wood of the cabins, the dry dirt of the training yards, the salt of sweat and iron tang of blood that proved the younglings worked hard the day before. The Academy was located on the side of the forest not occupied by Highland Hills Business Park. It was where I was born and raised, and where my twin sister tried to kill me.

How very circle-of-life of us.

I shook off the clinging morbidity and opened my eyes. Galen waited at my side, but Finn was already halfway to the mess hall. The younglings who were awake headed in the same direction, although a few had already gone for food and were now on their way to jobs like border patrol. One such girl raised a toast-filled hand in a wave. I waved back, smiling. Cat almost looked happy. She was a little taller than me now. Her body started to add curves to the carefully cultivated muscle, much to her disgust. Her ever-present bow was slung over her shoulder, its companion quiver of arrows between her shoulder blades.

The sight of her weapons reminded me to strap the sheaths onto my forearms. Looking down at Galen, my smile widened. He was staring up at me, his wagging tail turning his entire back end into a pendulum. "Let's go do our best to make Finn lose his breakfast, okay, big dog?"

At my tone, Galen's tail wagged harder and he opened his mouth in a wide, panting grin. I buckled the last strap of my sheathes, and thus armed, I waded into the day.

Chapter 2

The mess hall was roughly as orderly as a pack of hyenas ripping apart a lion's leftovers. Following the beacon of Galen's tail, I made my way to the far corner of the room, where I kept Galen's kibble supply.

After I fed Galen, Finn and I divided and conquered. He went to load up a couple of plates, and I went to get coffee. Poking my head through the door that led to the kitchen, I yelled for Gina, the youngling who ruled the kitchens. She popped up from behind the steel-topped island, looking perturbed.

"Coffee, please," I said sweetly. Galen hovered around my feet, his nose up and twitching as he feasted on the scents in the air.

"You're early. I didn't make it yet." Gina and I had an agreement. She needed help with training. I needed a steady supply of coffee strong enough to strip paint. Fate smiled on this little caffeine junkie.

"If you make it now, I'll let you skip squats tonight."

She narrowed her eyes at me. For all her ineptitude on the practice field, she was a right alpha bitch in her kitchen. "If you toss in ab crunches, I'll make pot roast for dinner."

Gina's pot roast was so good, it melted in your mouth. But… "You've used that bargaining chip twice this week. The poultry fans will stage a coup. Besides, you need the core strength."

She sighed. "All right. Coffee's on its way."

"Thanks." I dragged Galen away from the door and went back to the dining area, where Finn secured us a table. The folder sat beside my plate of food. At least, I assumed there was a plate under the half dozen pancakes, three sausage patties, six strips of bacon, and a mound of scrambled eggs. I looked at Finn. "Did they run out of ham?"

"You don't need both bacon and ham." Finn's plate held about one egg's worth of scrambled eggs, two pancakes and two slices of bacon. Honestly, how did humans manage to sustain life on such a paltry diet? I sat down in my chair, while Galen crawled under the table to watch for pennies from heaven.

Finn knew me well — he let me work my way through the eggs and half the pancakes before starting up the conversation again. "So," he said, then stopped as Gina plunked a thermos down at my elbow.

I thanked her. She gave an absolutely insincere curtsy and left. Tuning out the rest of the room so I could give all my attention to the first sip, I poured a mugful of coffee and inhaled. "God, that smells good. Want some?" I only offered because I knew he wouldn't want any.

Finn raised his own mug of sissy coffee. "No, thank you."

"Good. More for me." I closed my eyes and sipped the brew.

"So, can we get on with this?"

At his tone, I forced my eyes open. "It's four-thirty in the morning. You really got someplace better to be?"

"Kellan." He was using his "stop acting like a child and focus" voice. That voice made me want to punch him in the face.

I flipped open the file folder. The mess-that-was-once-man flashed its innards at me. Even though I was better prepared for it this time, the level of gore still gave me a jolt. "It doesn't make sense."

Finn leaned back in his chair. "What?"

I turned the picture over and studied the papers beneath it. "It says here this happened in Madison. So it can't be a pack kill, we haven't had a wolf pack around here for generations." I frowned. "Either we have a killer who likes to emulate wolves. Or..."

"Or?"

"Or they did it on purpose. To grab the attention of someone who might recognize it."

Finn looked entirely too pleased for my taste. "Look at the address."

"I did. Madison. On Fallspring Road. Wait a second. I know that street. It's, like, three blocks from my old apartment."

He took a slow sip of coffee. "It's not like three blocks from your apartment. It's exactly three blocks."

"Thank you, OnStar." My brain slowly turned the facts over in its hands, too distracted by how shiny and new those facts were to be able to make any sense of them. "Not to be egomaniacal or anything, but it seems like someone was leaving me a present."

"Hmm. Interesting thought."

I looked up at Finn again, who wore the same expression my mom wore the first time I beat Mal in hand-to-hand combat. A cross between pride and "what took you so long?" I felt a growl build deep inside me.

"Yeah, you know what's interesting," I said. "Why are you going through this with me instead of Janus? You two usually hash this stuff out yourselves." He didn't respond, confirming my suspicion. "You did hash this out with him already. You just wanted to see if I could figure it out myself."

"No," he said quickly. "We wanted your take on it. You know better than we what the aftereffects of a wolf hunt look like. If I told you our conclusions, your reaction would have been colored by them."

"And you want to know if I figured out what's behind door number three."

He looked confused. Finn was several hundred years old. Fifty-year old game shows were outside of his expertise.

"The third option. One, killer with a wolf fetish. Two, somebody wanting to get my attention with a pack-like kill. And three, the bitch is back in town." I wasn't very hungry anymore, but I shoved an enormous pile of pancakes in my mouth. Nothing drowned painful memories like syrupy carbs.

"There is that, yes." Finn studied me with an unreadable scent.

"She's not," I said. The pancakes were wedged in my throat.

"And you are sure of this because?"

"Because she'd have to be a fucking moron to come back so soon, and Mal's a lot of things, but moron isn't one of them." I swallowed some coffee to try and clear away the pancake dam in my esophagus. "Besides, why would she leave such a public message, in a neighborhood that I'm not anywhere near? It's unnecessarily garish. And it's not like she left it right in my backyard, either. Three blocks away? I don't know. It doesn't make sense."

Finn didn't say anything. Most of the time, Finn was working toward a goal six steps beyond his current position. When I was a wee one in short pants, I tried to see ahead to his endgame. I didn't bother anymore.

I felt tired, and the day hadn't even begun. "Did I pass your little test?" I said.

"Beautifully so." He beamed at me. Like I just made pee-pee in the potty.

I wondered if he would still be impressed with me after I dumped a steaming pot of coffee over his beautiful head. Not my coffee, of course.

Just so I had something to do besides indulge violent fantasies, I returned my attention to my breakfast. While the humans were talking, Galen moved from under the table to inch his nose closer to my plate. I nudged him away. "Think again, big dog. You already had yours." I dipped a piece of sausage in the maple syrup moat that surrounded the remnants of my pancake tower. I didn't put it in my mouth, though. Just swirled it around in the syrup that seemed to thicken with each passing second.

"And in light of our concurring opinions —" Finn's voice jolted through me like the bleat of an alarm clock.

Concurring? Shit. It was way too early to listen to Solicitor Finn. "Could you cut back on the syllables a little? I've only had three cups of coffee."

"I'll try to dumb it down for you," he said dryly.

I gritted my teeth. "Thanks."

"My pleasure. Since we agree that the message appears to be for you, you are being reassigned." Finn's face and scent were blank. RoboFinn. "Janus made it clear that if you reached the same conclusion we did, then you should be reassigned to the city posthaste."

Last week, I spent three afternoons mending holes in the canvas archery targets. While I was a pretty big fan of most sharp metallic objects, the needle-and-thread thing wasn't my scene. But I did it, because doing shit jobs at home was better than doing anything anywhere else. My palms were suddenly damp, and I set my fork down so I could dig both hands in Galen's fur. "But I'm being punished."

Finn blinked. He took a breath to speak, but I didn't want to give him a chance.

"And let's face it, I'm still a pretty big risk. I mean, I won't follow orders. I mouth off all the time. I let an outsider live who knew about the Spring. Who knows what I'll do if you let me out of your sight?"

"Well, actually, you have been doing quite well these past three months. Accomplishing every task we set before you, without complaint." It was true, no good deed goes unpunished. "In light of your compliance, we have decided to reinstate you and give you an assignment off-camp."

Mal enjoyed the adventure of new surroundings, creating new identities for herself and juggling hidden agendas. Frankly, I just didn't have the dexterity for juggling. I liked my forest. "Finn, I —"

"Kellan, this isn't a request."

Galen set his big head in my lap and gazed up at me. Wanting to shield him from my distress, I straightened my shoulders and steadied my voice. "Can I finish my breakfast first or is this an instantaneous order?"

He gave a world-weary sigh. I must've just plum tuckered him out. "Of course you may finish your breakfast."

I remembered something I should ask. "What about Mal?"

Finn set his empty mug on the table. "Still no word on her whereabouts. When we know something, we will let you know."

Not, you'll be the first to know, or even, we'll let you know right away. From another person's mouth, the wording might just be semantics, but from Finn? It meant he'd let me know when it suited him. A few months ago, I might have let it go and told myself to trust him. I knew better now.

I hardened my spine and my voice. "You'll tell me the minute you've heard something. Before you verify your facts, before you discuss a course of action, before you even wipe your nose, you will call me and tell me that you might know something. You will tell me what that something is and you will let me in on the subsequent discussion and planning. Understand?"

I caught a whiff of displeasure, like dirt kicked up by stomping feet. It tickled my nose. "I said I will inform you. But it is hardly your place to dictate —"

My voice slipped out between clenched teeth. "I'll dictate whatever I bloody well please." Galen raised his head off my lap and turned his body so he faced Finn. Placing my hand on my dog's shoulder, I pulled him against my leg and held him there. "She's my sister, and I will be involved in this hunt. And you will involve me, because last time you fucked up and you know it."

"Last time," when Mal betrayed us and almost took my life, Finn suspected something was wrong with her. In typical Finn fashion, however, he didn't tell me anything, opting instead to gather more information before jumping off any bridges. I didn't know if I could have altered the outcome, but really, that was irrelevant. I deserved to know.

All hint of disturbance in his scent vanished. He pushed away from the table. "You can keep that copy," he said, motioning to the file. At the movement, Galen tensed. "When you've packed, come by Janus's office and we will discuss the specifics of your assignment."

He left before I could form a response. For the first time in possibly my entire life, I didn't enjoy the view as he walked away. Instead, I had to swallow my breakfast back down as I wondered how I ever trusted him at all.

Chapter 3

When Galen and I left the mess hall, the sky was beginning to lighten. I frowned. If Finn and Janus wanted me to go to the city, I would have to take the long way out of the forest. It was against the rules to enter or exit the forest between dawn and full dark. Janus's sorcery made the forest invisible from the business park side. We got away with people popping in and out of existence in the middle of the night, because the business park was less populated and humans were more inclined to believe their eyes were playing tricks in the dark. But we couldn't have Sankhain coming and going during the day, visible one moment and invisible the next. We weren't living in a Harry Potter novel, for pete's sake.

If a Sankha absolutely had to enter or exit the forest in broad daylight, we travelled to the far end of the forest, far enough away from the nearest business that someone glancing out a window couldn't really be sure of what they saw. It meant hiking three miles through a marshy mess to reach our parking lot.

Maybe Janus would let me wait until dark to leave. But I doubted it. Finn and Janus weren't known for their patience or tolerance of whims. I suspected Finn came to my cabin so early in the hope that he could usher me out of the forest before sun-up. Then I had the gall to want breakfast, and god forbid Finn tell me that there was a time constraint. What did he care if Galen and I had to walk through three miles of marsh, if my boots soaked through and took a week to dry out? Jackass.

Since it was already too late to exit the forest directly, I took my time packing. I folded clothes that were already wrinkled, I stuck blades without sheathes into socks to protect them from nicks and dents.

While I packed, I dialed Tony's number. When he didn't answer, I realized he might be asleep. He sometimes preferred to sleep during the day, if he was in a bad nightmare cycle. Tony, like most of the Sankhain, came from an abusive past. I left a long message about my new assignment — not the specifics, just the fact that Finn was forcing me to go live in the city again — and only hung up when voicemail cut me off.

About an hour after I left the mess hall, the cabin door banged open. I jumped a little, but I didn't stop folding my underwear and carefully placing it in my duffel. I smelled hot, dry earth. Finn wasn't happy. Oh, well. Neither was I. I glanced up at him. "Yes, sir?"

"Don't yessir me." He kept his tone low, but that didn't lessen the strength of the words. If anything, volume would've been redundant.

A smarter person might've been afraid. Not my style. "Fine. What the fuck do you want?"

He pressed his lips in a thin line. "Your orders were to pack and report to Janus."

"What does it look like I'm doing, taking a bubble bath?" I massaged the base of Galen's neck, placing my hand close to his collar. Just in case he required restraining. "I'm working on it. You never imposed a timeframe."

"The timeframe was implied."

He might be right, but so was I. "And yet, if you want a timeframe to be followed, you should make it explicit rather than relying on implication."

His nostrils flared, and I felt a masochistic urge to smile. I squashed it as best I could, rearranging my features into a scowl. "Very well," he said. "You are to report to Janus in five minutes with your belongings in tow. If you are not at Janus's office in that timeframe, you will be placed in solitary for a minimum of three days. Is that explicit enough for you?"

Solitary? Jeez. Overreact much? "Yes, sir. Five minutes or three days. Very explicit."

Finn turned on his heel. Paused. "Your boyfriend's coming home."

Boyfriend? Before I could ask for clarification, he was gone. I dumped the rest of my socks and underwear into the duffel, and Galen and I double-timed it to Janus's cabin. Smack, the youngling who served as Janus's receptionist this week, raised her eyebrows at me as I dumped my bags on the floor. "He's expecting you," she said in her barely audible voice. Then, even quieter, "Been expecting you for a while."

"I heard that," I said wryly.

"Sorry, ma'am." She smiled beatifically up at me. I rolled my eyes and smiled back. Smack's life hadn't been easy, more pimps and beatings than rainbows and butterflies. A tragically typical story for a youngling, and they each got through it in their own way. Gina survived it by praying to a God who neglected to respond. Smack survived it by ripping the rest of the world to shreds, all hidden under her breath and behind sweet smiles.

Janus tried to rename her when she came to us, but she feigned deafness if we called her anything other than Smack. Personally, I couldn't think of any positive connotation for the word "smack." Why would she choose that for her name? But she did, and eventually, she wore Janus down, a feat of mythological proportions. Hercules and his twelve tasks had nothing on Smack.

I think Janus saw in her the exact same thing I did, the sort of spirit that could dominate the world and convince us that we liked it. And I was pretty sure she had some faery blood in her. Her ears were a little pointy, and I recently got a whiff of her blood when she got a bloody lip in the boxing ring. Her blood didn't smell the same as most humans. Less metallic, more sweet. Faery blood smelled like honey and clover, not iron. The fey were deathly allergic to iron, so it would be counterproductive to pack the blood with it.

Now, as I looked at the door that led to Janus's inner sanctum, I checked her scent for signs of agitation. Nothing. "Is Finlay in there?" I asked.

Smack shook her head. "He left 'bout fifteen minutes ago and didn't come back." Under her breath, she added, "Good thing, too. Damn crab-ass this morning."

As I fought not to smile and lost, I looked down at her. "You're right. So don't let him hear you say that. Got it?"

"Yes, ma'am." And the inevitable muttering, "Like I dumb enough to mouth off to the dude who ate one too many crazy beans today."

"Glad to hear it." I pushed my way into Janus's room.

Janus's cabin was divided into a small reception area and a larger living space. The living space served as both Janus's living and working quarters. There was a large conference table in the center of the room, and the walls to my right and left were lined with filing cabinets and bookcases. The wall opposite the door held a large fireplace flanked by wingback chairs, and in the corner, a small, but comfortable cot. A door by the cot led to a small bathroom with a teeny-tiny shower.

As Galen squeezed through the door behind me, I checked Janus's scent to see if he was as agitated as Finn. Much to my relief, the room smelled like fresh-cut grass. I assumed a parade-rest position — feet hip-width apart, hands crossed at the waist — and waited for Janus to acknowledge me.

He stood in front of the fire. Backlit by the flames in the fireplace, Janus's frame looked much larger than it really was. He was actually a little shorter than me, which made him quite short by today's standards, but pretty normal for a two-thousand year old man. He took up so much metaphysical space, though, that nobody really noticed he weighed ninety pounds soaking wet. And as he turned to face me, his power flowed out from him, washing over me to make my skin burn.

I inclined my head in a mini-bow. Galen sat by my side, as unmoving as I ever saw him. Dogs recognized power when they encountered it. "Good morning, sir," I said carefully. "I was instructed to report to you."

"Over an hour ago, as I understand." His tone was amused, and his scent was warm and cozy. I tried not to be too obvious in my sigh of relief.

"Yes, sir. A slight misunderstanding on my part."

"Not deliberate, naturally." He sounded like he was smiling.

I didn't raise my head to look. "Ah. No, sir. Of course not."

He finally moved, walking to the table and sitting down in the head chair. "At ease, Kellan." He motioned for me to choose a chair of my own. I sat, still closely monitoring his scent. "I would prefer, in the future, if you would refrain from deliberately aggravating Finlay. You may be on your way to the city, but the rest of us still must live with him."

Was he teasing me? I bit the inside of my cheek. "Sorry, sir." But Finn made it so easy.

Janus looked at me like he heard my thought. Which he probably did. Janus could read minds. "Yes, well. I would thank you to restrain yourself in the future."

"Yes, sir. I'll try."

After a brief private smile, he turned serious. I was torn between regret that the moment was over and pleasure at the very leaderliness of him. For a while, a few months ago, he weakened. He lost that air of alpha that he usually radiated. As much as I enjoyed the playful banter, I was willing to set it aside for my alpha.

Leaning forward, he placed his forearms on the table. His shirt shifted and I saw the scar on his shoulder where Mal stabbed him. Yes, my sister not only tried to kill me, she tried to kill Janus as well. A shock of shame burned me from the inside out.

Janus met my gaze. His scent changed, shifting to that of cool linen sheets. Most humans' scents had a theme to them — related to an element of nature or a specific sort of food. Janus's scents had no theme. It took me a long time to learn to read them. This one meant he was worried. That worried me. "What is it?" I asked.

"I do not like this." Janus was allergic to contractions, which often made him sound like a Dr. Seuss book. "This killer knows you. Knows what you are, where you reside. I do not like this at all."

"Yeah, well, I'm not wild about it, either." I leaned back in my chair. "If you'd prefer, I could stay here."

He raised his eyebrows. "Is that what you believe you should do? Hide?"

Well, now he was just playing dirty. Like I could sit by and be called a coward. "No, sir. I don't think I should just hide. But —"

He met my eyes, waiting, while I tried to choose my words.

"With all due respect, sir. But when did we become the monster police? As long as whomever this is hasn't shown interest in the Spring, why is it our problem? You're sending Tony to investigate cattle deaths. You want me to go investigate something that could just be the work of a plain old human psycho. What's with the sudden interest in the rest of the world?"

He tilted his head. He didn't smell angry. Yet. "We have ever possessed an interest in the rest of the world," he said, his tone surprisingly amused. "Have you forgotten how your pack died?"

"Of course not. Sir." My mother and sisters, all but Mal, were killed in battle by a hive of nocturnes, evil shape-shifters. "But nocturnes have always sought out the Spring. They're our arch nemesis, or whatever. But cattle deaths? And this murder?"

"I was under the impression you agreed the murder resembled a wolf's kill."

"Yes, but —"

"And you recognize the address and its proximity to your residence?"

"My —" I wanted to argue that, while I occasionally resided at the apartment, it wasn't as if it were my home. But the look on his face made me stop. The slight heat in his scent made me abase myself. "Yes, sir, I do. And I acknowledge the potential significance, and I certainly acknowledge your wisdom and ability to discern the proper course of action. I just —" I ran out of words.

Fortunately, Janus picked up where I left off. "You do not wish to return to the city." His voice was kind, the heat gone from his scent. Hearing the words shamed me a little. He didn't give me a chance to respond, though. "You were young when your pack died. You were not privy to some of the details surrounding the uprising they put an end to. Nocturnes, when they seek to incite a war, frequently enlist the assistance of other monsters, as you call them. Your pack did not fight only nocturnes that day. They also faced vampires, werewolves, and fey. Rather an insignificant number, but a number nonetheless."

He gave me a minute to absorb. I took five. "So you're saying we have to keep tabs on these guys, especially now that we have evidence of significant nocturne activity."

Janus straightened his shoulders, his chest puffing out slightly. He was proud. Of me. How 'bout that? Now he looked at me, his scent a steady, solid cedar wood smell. "I understand your desire to stay. But you are Hycene, Kellan Alastrina Faolanni. You are the last Hycene. Born for battle. Not mending archery targets."

He stunned me into silence as a softball lodged itself in my throat. The Hycene were a subset of the Sankhain, a sort of Special Forces made up of shape-shifters. And with Mal's defection, I was the only one left. It wasn't the first time I realized it, but the sting of the words didn't fade with time.

"I am glad that is settled." His eyebrows drew together in a frown. "While I agree that you cannot simply stay here —" like it was my idea to leave "— I also wish to extract a promise from you. I would like you to promise to be careful. Care before heroics."

I waited for him to order me to check in with him before I acted on anything. Usually, I needed forms signed in triplicate before I could piss. But Janus didn't tack on any addendums to his request. He just waited for me to promise to be careful. It took me a long time to figure that out, so long, in fact, that he repeated his request. "You will be careful?"

"Uh, yes. Yes, sir. I'll be careful." After a moment's hesitation, I added, "And I'll check with you before I do anything. You know, so you can approve."

"I do not believe that will be necessary." He stood up.

Boy, now I was really confused. Never, ever had Janus given me free rein to do my job. I felt awe. And a little fear that I chose not to examine too closely.

"Oh, and Kellan. Antony has received his orders to return to the Academy. He will no longer be investigating cattle deaths. So you need not fret over his seemingly futile assignment any further. Dismissed."

Tony was returning. Finn's words floated up in my memory. *Your boyfriend is coming home.* Was he talking about Tony? Tony wasn't my boyfriend. He was my friend. That was all. My stomach flip-flopped.

Janus was staring at me. "Dismissed, Kellan."

I tripped over my words. "Yes, sir. Thank you, sir." I clucked my tongue at Galen and we left.

Chapter 4

Walking through the forest, my feet dragged heavier the closer Galen and I got to the end of the trees. To say I grew up here was a gross understatement. I learned to hunt in this forest. My sister and I played our own version of hide-and-seek in those trees.

Hide-and-seek for shape-shifters was much more interesting than the mundane human game. It didn't matter how much of a head start you got, you knew eventually you'd get found because the "it" person could track your scent. When you got found, the real fun began. Combat, running up trees and jumping down on top of your opponent, slashing with nails and knives, rolling around on the ground, grappling for top position. The game ended when one of us was pinned on her back, the other's knife at her throat. Goddamn, but that was fun. Nostalgia squeezed the air from my lungs in a sigh.

The last time I saw my sister, we played a different kind of hide-and-seek. She hid and I sought, but I didn't know it was her I was looking for until the game was almost over. She won that round.

I squared my shoulders and set my jaw. She wouldn't win the next one. But goosebumps coated my skin, as an image shouldered its way into my head. An image I'd been fighting to keep at bay for three months now. Me, on my knees, bleeding and weaponless. Waiting for the final blow, with my sister's scent in my nose.

When something plummeted out of the tree two steps ahead of me, I damn near peed myself. It was Cat, who landed on her feet like her namesake. I hadn't smelled her there. I gave myself a mental head-slap and wiped my damp palms on my shorts. Raking my fingers through my hair, all I could think was, *God, I hope I don't look as fucked up as I feel.*

She didn't seem to notice anything. Galen, of course, wasn't preoccupied by waking nightmares, so he wasn't surprised by Cat's appearance. He wandered over to sniff her. She gave him an obliging pat.

Even as shaken as I was, I couldn't help but smile. She had leaves in her hair, quite possibly on purpose. She looked like a wood sprite on growth hormones.

She gave a little bow. "Sankha Kellan."

"Cat." I felt embarrassingly grateful that my voice was steady. "You're leaving?"

"Is it your duty as border patrol to watch who's going out as well as in?"

"No, ma'am," she said solemnly. "Just nosy." Then she broke into a grin that encompassed her whole face. She looked young. Healthy. Whole. I remembered the girl who came to us years ago, with bones that stuck out at all angles, shoulders bowed under an unseen weight and eyes that looked much too old for such a small face. I rubbed my solar plexus to ease the sudden tightness there.

"In that case, yes. I'm leaving. New assignment." I rested a hand on her shoulder and squeezed lightly. She didn't shy away. Yes, Cat was a long way from that little girl that came to us. "All right, back to your post, youngling. Before someone catches you pestering a Sankha."

"Yes, ma'am," she said again. With an exaggerated salute, she scrambled back up the tree and disappeared.

The exchange with Cat warmed me for about fifteen steps before other thoughts pushed her out of the way. It wasn't just Mal and the nocturnes that we needed to worry about. It was vampires, werewolves. Dark fey. The fey scared me most. Werewolves and vamps were slaves to baser urges. Vampires, of course, just wanted to feed and fuck their way through the human race, which made them fairly easy to track and trap. Werewolves were only really dangerous on the full moon, and on the full moon, they turned into slavering, crazed beasts. Again, fairly easy to either avoid or kill.

But faeries were slippery. And not all faeries looked like Tinker Bell. In fact, even pixies didn't look like Tink — they were scrawny, hawk-nosed little mosquitos with an intense hatred of humanity. Faeries came in all sizes and shapes, and possessed a wide range of natural magickal abilities that a non-fey couldn't begin to imagine. Some of them possessed the ability to perform glamour, which could hide their "otherness" and make them look like normal people. I didn't even know if my nose could sniff out the difference between a faery and a human, if the faery had glamour in place. Anything that I couldn't identify with my nose made me nervous. Like being struck suddenly, selectively blind, like being able to see everything but the color yellow. You probably wouldn't be too bad off until you stepped out in front of that oncoming school bus.

Faeries, like humans, lived in the moral gray areas for the most part. But some gravitated more heavily to the extreme light or extreme dark. Like the difference between Glinda the Good Witch and the Wicked Witch of the West. Except instead of benevolently riding around in a bubble, the light fey considered themselves superior to all other beings — including any fey that didn't meet their measure — and saw the world as their birthright. Their kingdom. The dark fey thought they were superior to humans, too, but they didn't want to rule the world. They wanted to dominate it, control it, make it fear them. Make it weep.

Yeah, give me a vampire any day.

When Galen and I reached the far end of the forest and stepped out into the sun, we stood blinking for a few minutes. It wasn't just the brightness of sunlight no longer filtered by leaf-laden branches. It was the stepping away from the magic, Janus's spell that kept the forest invisible. That spell was a thickness in the air, something we Sankhain got used to, but once we stepped from the trees, we felt its absence. I felt bereft, like someone stole my favorite sweater.

I felt like stomping my foot and bellowing, "I don't WANT to go to the city!"

But I didn't. Instead, Galen and I walked through the marshy muck, swatting mosquitoes and deer flies, to the Sankhain parking lot where my pickup truck awaited us. I think the truck was blue once upon a time. Now, it was sort of grayish in the spots that weren't rusted out. When I opened the door, the hinges shrieked in protest. And when I turned the ignition, the engine roared to life as only an old, my-muffler-is-dying engine can.

While I was stationed at camp, Finn used my truck to teach some of the younglings to drive. It kept the old bucket running, it ensured that the truck moved often enough that the humans wouldn't notice it sitting there for months, and if it got wrecked, Finn didn't care. I wasn't crazy about the idea — I liked my truck — but Finn didn't really give me a vote.

I stuck in a CD. Five Finger Death Punch blasted my eardrums and I heaved a contented sigh. If I didn't really have a choice whether I left the forest, at least I got to pick my own soundtrack.

My apartment was less than ten minutes from the forest. The neighborhood was one of Madison's fringier locales. Some days, I could smell the rage and resentment like a noxious gas, sneaking into all the nooks and crannies of the barely maintained apartment buildings. But today, with the sun shining and the heat index inching toward ninety, nobody had the energy for rage.

People just sat on their porches, drank cold drinks and waited for entertainment to walk past.

I pulled into the parking lot behind my building and turned off the truck. Galen stood up and started waving his tail. This place was home to him as much as the forest was, since I adopted Galen after I moved into the apartment. Ten years ago, Janus sent me to the city so I might better utilize my myriad skills. So he might better utilize my skills. Galen might call the apartment home, but that only made one of us.

Pushing the truck door open required more force than I expected. I felt tired, heavy. I swung down out of the cab and Galen hopped out after me. I grabbed my duffels out of the back of the truck and we headed for the front door.

The building was actually nice. It was old, but that meant the windows were large, the floors solid hardwood, and the walls fairly thick. The door to the apartment was thin and drafty, but that came in handy sometimes. Being able to smell who was on the other side of the door was actually a selling point for a shape-shifter.

Galen and I walked through the door to the apartment, and I instantly cringed at the smell. "Mouse shit. Yummy."

Galen looked up at me, unconcerned. He wasn't bothered by the stench, probably because he wasn't the one who had to clean up the source. I unhooked his leash and he set off to investigate. The first thing I did was open every window in the place, allowing fresh air to mingle with the staleness.

After I found the source of the smell — a cabinet full of turds and a single mouse skeleton — and swept the mess into a plastic bag, I stood and stared at the remains of my only effort to decorate this apartment. The picture, a print of a Pollyanna Pickering painting of two sleeping wolves wrapped around one another, used to hang on the wall above Galen's food and water dishes. The last time I was here, I ripped it off the wall, smashed the frame, and ground my hands into the broken glass in an attempt to reassign my pain. The frame was gone, but the picture remained.

I bought it because it reminded me of Mal and myself. The wolves even looked a little like us. I smashed the picture for the same reason.

I knew I should throw it away, but just the thought made me unutterably sad. Instead I shoved the picture into the mouse-turd cabinet and closed the door. Then I fled the kitchen.

Back in my inauspiciously furnished living room, I looked around. The trash-picked futon looked as sad as ever. The TV, a small, ancient model that missed its rabbit ears, was coated in an inch of dust. The apartment boasted one piece of store-bought, first-hand furniture, an armchair that Finn bought because when he came to the apartment for a booty call, he refused to sit on the futon. Looking at the living room further depressed me. There wasn't a single piece of me in the room.

My dog rescued me, as he so often did. Apparently having completed his tour through the apartment, he joined me in the living room and sat by the front door, looking hopeful. I informed him that, as it was eight hundred degrees outside, we were not going for a run. He heard "run" and swished his tail across the floor. Such were the pitfalls of conversing with a creature with limited English. Now he was expecting a run, and wouldn't give me a moment's peace until I delivered. With a sigh, I changed my clothes, laced up my running shoes, and gave in to my dog. Who was I kidding? I wanted to sweat my way to the mother of all charley horses.

We didn't go very far. It was too hot, and I didn't want Galen to hurt himself. After just a few blocks, I turned for home. My head felt a little clearer, though the broken record of my brain kept skipping back to the last time I was in the apartment. Tony was there with me. He helped me clean up the broken picture frame. He made me stop inflicting pain on myself.

I skidded to a walk, my legs suddenly too heavy to keep running. Galen looked up at me. I didn't try to explain the sudden slowdown. I didn't think I could explain myself in a way anyone could understand. Thinking about Tony took the oompf right out of me. Why? Just one of those weird human mysteries no one could comprehend. Or maybe I just didn't want to comprehend.

When we got home, I fed and watered Galen, then looked longingly at the shower. If I showered now, I would just start sweating again the second I dried off, and then I'd need another shower. I needed to kill time while I cooled down.

I pulled out my phone and started scrolling through my contacts. When I saw "Mal," I twitched. I never deleted her from my contacts, even though I knew she had a new phone number now. She called me from the new number just weeks after she tried to kill me. Called to tell me I made the wrong choice, staying with the Sankhain rather than running off with the forces of darkness along with her.

My skin felt chilled suddenly, though sunlight streamed through the big picture window in my living room. Three months ago, Mal would've been the one I called this morning to complain about being sent back to the city. And she would've been the one

I called now to kill time. She was my only remaining family, the sum total of my pack. And she chose to join forces with nocturnes, the same monsters that killed the rest of our pack two hundred years ago.

I didn't know why. I didn't have a chance to ask, while she was stabbing me in the back. Well, in the side.

My muscles went all boiled noodle, and I plopped down on the futon. Galen stretched out at my feet, panting and enjoying the relative cool of the hardwood floor. That sounded good to me, so I slid off the futon and lay down beside him. I stared at the ceiling and waited for the mental movie to finish. It never really finished, it just started over again, the film of Mal turning on me, the cold sound of her voice, the nocturne stink almost drowning out the scent of her, the scent that I swear I smelled in the womb. Yes, my nightmares came in Smell-O-Vision.

After the first few viewings, the rawness of the memory faded slightly. I came back to myself and realized I was still holding my cell phone. Without getting up off the floor, I hit redial. I listened to the ringing and wondered if Tony was still asleep.

"Hello?" a woman's voice said.

I froze. In my head, I tried to remember if I called anyone else that day. This should've been his cell number. But…"I think I must have the wrong number."

"Oh, did I grab the wrong phone again? Jeez. I tell ya, if it wasn't screwed on…" A deep voice in the background, then the woman's reply. "Yeah, it's for you. Sorry, I just heard the ringing and boom. Automatic, you know?"

"Hello?" Tony sounded amused.

I was still stuck in Jack Frost mode. It took me a second to answer. "Hi."

"Kell? Hey. Can you hang on a sec? No, Mandy, you left it over here. Sorry, Kell. What's up?"

I thawed and sat up. "So tell me. When *Mandy* traded in her brain for a pair of D-cups, did they throw in a free toaster oven, or was her brain not worth that much to begin with?"

"How'd you know she was a D?"

I should've laughed. He was expecting a laugh. But with the day I was having, I couldn't find a laugh with a map. "Sorry. I shouldn't have — I didn't mean to disturb you."

"No, it's fine, she was just leaving. No, Mandy, by your shoes." I heard the woman's voice, but couldn't discern the words. Tony said, "Oh. Sorry. Amanda. Here all this time I've been calling you —"

I hung up. No need to prolong that little bit of torture any further. I looked at Galen. "Why the hell is he with a Mandy? Mandys are so not Tony's type. Not that I care. He can do whatever he wants. Right?"

Galen's only response was to roll over on his back and expose his genitals.

"Men," I muttered, and headed for the shower. When the phone rang as I turned on the water, I ignored it. I couldn't think of a single person in the world that I wanted to talk to at that moment.

After I showered, I dressed in minimal clothing — a sports bra and a pair of shorts — to stave off as much post-shower sweating as I could. I wanted to wait until nightfall to check out the crime scene, so I laid down on the bed, on the sheets that hadn't been washed since May, and, closing my eyes, I waited for sleep. What I got instead was a noseful of Tony's scent, still on the sheets from when he helped me figure out what was happening last spring. He slept in the bed a couple of times. By himself.

Part of Mal's plan to take down the Sankhain involved an outsider, a man named Darcy Jamison. Mal and one of the nocturnes approached Darcy outside his sister's hospital room. The sister was dying of cancer, and Mal gave Darcy some special documents, written in a language Janus invented, that detailed the location of the Spring. She said the documents led to a cure for his sister, but that she couldn't read them. Then she gave Darcy my name and told him to find me, that I could help him find the cure.

Darcy showed up, waving these papers around that he could've only gotten from a Sankha. I was supposed to kill Darcy after wringing every last bit of information from him. But things got complicated. First was the nocturne, the evil shape-shifter, that I discovered was hunting Darcy. The second, and by far more troubling complication, was that I found myself liking Darcy. He was one of those rare birds, a genuinely good person who blushed and cried and said please and thank you. For the first time in my life, I went against orders and refused to kill Darcy.

Mal tried to kill him for me. She failed at that, too.

For the second time in less than an hour, I found myself staring at the ceiling, watching a horrific memory play out behind my eyes. My phone was ringing again. I ignored it again. Through the open windows, I could hear the sounds of summer in a neighborhood where people couldn't afford air conditioning. Feet shuffling, voices calling, kids screeching. When the kids next door started hitting a metal post with a stick, every *poing* reverberated through me like I was the metal post. I sprung out of bed with a roar. "It's bad to kill children, right?" I asked Galen. "Especially with so many witnesses around. Right?"

My dog stood on the bed and waited uncertainly. I sighed and sat down on the mattress, and with a happy wag, he trotted over to me. Digging my hands in his fur, I breathed in his scent and relaxed. "How'd you like to go check out a crime scene?"

He butted his head against my shoulder. I nuzzled his neck. "Crime scene it is. Come on, bud."

The phone rang just as we were walking out the door. I never bothered to check for voicemail from the missed call earlier. When I saw the caller ID this time, I answered with a touch of desperate joy. "Darcy?"

Darcy Jamison could be an irritation, like a bad case of athlete's foot. But there was something about him that I didn't mind so much. Maybe because, when his eyes were opened to the realities of the supernatural world, he didn't just piss himself and spend the rest of his days doing his best *One Flew Over the Cuckoo's Nest* impression. Well, he might've peed his pants a little, but mostly, he fought and he survived. I respected that.

"Hi," he said now. "I was driving past your apartment building and thought I saw your truck. You back in town?"

"So it seems. You know, you're a relatively charming guy. You really shouldn't have to resort to stalking."

"I — I wasn't stalking. I mean, I was just driving past." Or maybe I just liked him because he was really easy to rattle.

I chuckled. "So how are you?" Galen reached the end of his patience. After giving me a dirty look, he began to pull me toward the door. I interrupted Darcy's answer before he really got going. "Hey, Darcy, I have to keep a promise to a dog right now. But, um…" I didn't know how to say what I wanted to say, without sounding pathetic. "If you, you know, wanted to catch up, we could maybe get some dinner or something. Or not, if you don't want to." Oh, sure, that didn't sound pathetic at all.

"Well, I don't know. My social calendar's pretty full, let me check with my secretary. Hold, please." He waited a few seconds. "I guess I'm free."

"All right." I bowed my head in silent laughter. Who cared about Mandy/Amanda? I was going to have dinner with Darcy.

We made plans to meet at a restaurant, then I let Galen drag me out the door.

Chapter 5

Since the temperatures soared from godforsaken to let's-take-a-stroll-on-the-surface-of-the-sun, Galen and I walked this time. If I tore a hamstring because I ran to the point of dehydration, I could heal it before dinner. Galen wouldn't be so lucky.

For a city neighborhood, mine was as good as it got. It was the kind of neighborhood that city planners wanted to buy up so they could kick out the undesirables and build a senior living center. But for now, it was populated by a melting pot of residents. Single parents, just-off-the-boat immigrants, recent college graduates who were too new to the job force to be able to afford the overpriced condo to which they aspired. Of course, there were also the gang members, the drug dealers, and the professional women whose dress code ran more toward Lycra tube tops than linen pantsuits. I liked it here. Nobody was worried about keeping up with the Joneses. Most people weren't even worried about keeping up their pants. It smelled like life — humans, sweat, and a little rotting garbage here and there.

We took a roundabout route to the block where the murder occurred — no need to look like we were rubber-necking. Even if we were.

The scents of the people we passed all blended together in one strong, sweet, sweaty cocktail. But one scent drew my eyes to a familiar face.

Raoul rocked back on his heels and grinned at me. "If it ain't the most beautiful woman I ever saw." He gave me a flattering up-and-down look. From any other man, the look would have earned him a broken jaw. But Raoul smelled like coffee and wacky tobacky, not sex. He might enjoy the view, but he wasn't about to try and touch. Besides, Galen never felt threatened by him, more than enough of an endorsement for me. "How you doin'?" he asked.

"Hangin' on. How 'bout you, Raoul?" After a quick sniff, Galen ignored Raoul and set about peeing on every link of the chain-link fence beside us.

"Oh, you know. Can't complain when the sun's shining." He adjusted his sunglasses. "Ain't seen you around for a while."

"Yeah, I had some family stuff going on. You know."

He nodded. "All right?"

"Will be." I glanced at Galen. He was still busy, but I was itching to get moving again. But Raoul was a friend, or something like it. I didn't want to blow him off.

"You lookin' good, girl. You keep on. Be careful out there — some crazy shit been goin' on."

"Yeah, I heard about the guy that got cut up."

Raoul nodded again. "What's this world coming to, a man can't feel safe at night? You be careful. You need anything, I'm here."

And he was, too. Raoul's feet seemed permanently rooted on his street corner. That was how I met him — Galen and I ran past him every day, and every day, he told me how fine my legs were. One day, I tripped and sprained my knee a few feet from his roost, and he helped me home.

I was pretty sure Raoul was a drug dealer. What other reason would a man have for standing on the same corner all day, every day? But one of the great things about this corner of the city was the measure of a man shifted a little left of center. Raoul might engage in illegal activities. But he also spent his free time acting as the neighborhood watch program, and he was nice to me. That made him a real stand-up guy.

I thanked him, assured him I would be careful and avoid the area where the murder happened, and Galen and I went on our merry way. Straight to the area where the murder happened. I was a liar, but compared to some of my other vices, the lying was practically virtuous.

The yellow crime scene tape draped like crepe paper, remnants of a sad little party held for the gutted man. Who was, unfortunately, long gone. A body could tell me so much more than the sights and smells left behind. Oh, well. I suppose it was too much to ask for, to leave the body in situ for anyone who might want to take a gander.

I paused for a moment, like I was paying my respects. As much as I would've liked to poke around a little, I wasn't there to poke. All I wanted was to get a smell for the place, inhaling deeply through my nose, sorting through the various scents of violence in the summertime. Blood. Feces, urine, and the sour scent of bile. When the man was gutted, the weapon — claws? — sliced open the stomach and intestines. A nifty little fact that Finn's charming photo spread didn't tell me.

The heat of the past few days ripened the scents to an olfactory roar. I struggled not to choke, adjusting the amount of air I took in with each subsequent breath. I searched for that one scent that didn't belong. The scent of the killer. But unfortunately, death's smell was pretty strong. When bombarded with the stench of rancid bodily fluids, even I had a hard time picking up anything else. Especially from ten feet away.

Galen strained at his leash, trying to get closer to the fascinating scent pool. Clucking my tongue at him, I walked away. Maybe I'd come back later, when I had darkness on my side.

——— «» ———

By the time we got back to the apartment, it was time to shower — again — and get ready to meet Darcy. We were going to a little Indian place by his apartment, so I didn't need to dress up.

I chose a pair of cargo shorts, held them up to check for visible dirt, and, upon finding only a small smudge on one hip, deemed them wearable. I completed the outfit with a navy blue t-shirt. I refrained from putting on my forearm sheaths, and snugged my best daggers into the sheaths sewn in my cargo pockets. It's all about the accessories. As I laced up my hiking boots, the phone rang again. I let it go to voicemail, but curiosity got the better of me and I listened to the message as soon as it finished.

There were actually six messages from Tony, each more frustrated-sounding than the last. "Kellan, call me back," he said in the last one. "Why aren't you answering?" Like I was just sitting around, waiting for him to call. "You never told me why you called before. I just — wanted to make sure everything's okay. So either you're okay, but antisocial, or the dust bunnies finally staged that coup they've been planning and you're trapped under the bed or something." He paused, giving me time to smile and wonder how long it took him to come up with the dust bunny line. "I guess I'll talk to you later."

As the mechanical voice informed me that was the end of the message, I felt a strange constriction under my ribs. I shook it off. I silenced the ringer on my phone, not wanting anything to interrupt my evening with Darcy.

When I walked into the restaurant, I instantly regretted the choice of cuisine. I liked the taste of Indian food, but curry played hell with my nose. Not even two steps into the joint and already my sinuses were blocked solid. Then I saw a tall figure walking toward me, and I forgot to be annoyed.

I felt a grin spread across my face to match Darcy's smile. He stopped in front of me. I sniffed, trying to pull his scent through my stuffy nose. I succeeded, and the smell of Bergamot oil and old books drew my eyelids closed. Last spring, I loaned Darcy some clothes — long story involving bodily fluids, but not the fun ones — and our scents mingled to a degree that usually only happened with family or lovers. Even though he was wearing his own clothes now, his scent still brought up that same feeling of connection. He smelled like he belonged to me.

When Darcy cleared his throat, I realized I was standing in a restaurant with my eyes closed, breathing in some guy's scent. Way to blend in with the humans, Kellan. I opened my eyes and cocked my head. "What?" I said.

He studied me like he saw something that I didn't know was there. "Nothing. Nothing at all. Is it all right if I give you a hug?"

A hug? Did I look like a fabric softener teddy bear? But the fact was, Darcy looked a little like the human equivalent of a teddy bear, warm, gentle, and all squishy on the inside. So that was the reason I answered, "Yeah. That'd be okay."

He hugged me, and predictably, he was not one of those huggers who leaned over at the waist and only touched with his shoulders and arms. Nope, Darcy was a full-body hugger. Of course, I hated being restrained like that, so I pretended to like it for Darcy's sake. But I didn't enjoy the warmth and the closeness, or the familiarity of his scent. Not one bit. When I sniffed again, he pulled back. "You okay?"

I nodded. "Curry's a little strong."

Instant frown. "Oh. Well, we can go somewhere else, if it bothers you. Or they have a couple tables out back. They're basically set up in the parking lot, so it's nothing scenic, but if you'd rather..."

He continued to prattle, but I stopped listening. Darcy was the most verbose male human I ever encountered. Maybe because he was more interested in being kind than being macho. Most of the male humans I knew leaned toward macho. When my stomach rumbled, I decided it was time to cut in on his monologue. "Yeah, actually, outside might be good."

"All right." He rested a hand on my right shoulder, hailed the waitress and told her we were going to the patio. She nodded and gave him a little finger wave before returning her attention to the couple she was waiting on. I watched the exchange with curiosity.

"Come here often?" I asked as we walked out the back door.

He shrugged. "I don't really cook much. This place is convenient, and the food's good."

"And the waitress is cute."

His cheeks ripened to a lovely shade of fuchsia. I had a pretty good feeling that Darcy would've patronized this place even if he was allergic to curry.

"So what's her name?" I said in a sing-song voice.

"I — what — who?" His tone matched his squirrel-in-the-headlights expression.

The waitress chose that moment to walk outside. Her gait was confident without that pole-shoved-up-her-ass attitude. Long brown hair in a braid down her back, shiny eyes, and a wide smile. I gave Darcy an approving wink. He turned his deepest shade of red yet.

Her nametag read Sadie Rose. She gave Darcy a big smile before turning to appraise me.

Darcy cleared his throat again. "Sadie, this is Kelly. My —"

"Cousin," I said. "Nice to meet you."

Sadie Rose's stance relaxed when she apparently realized I wasn't competition. "Nice to meet you, too. Your cousin pretty much single-handedly keeps us in business."

As Darcy's blush spread down his neck, I leaned back in my chair. "That's great. Funny, too, 'cause he never used to like Indian food when he was a kid."

"That's not true." Desperation raised Darcy's voice a few octaves. "I love Indian food. Always have."

"No, don't you remember that time your mom took us all to that place on State Street? Your curry was too spicy. You spit it out. Remember?"

Darcy skewered me with a glare. "No. I don't. So. Sadie. What sort of wine do you recommend? Preferably something strong."

Sadie seemed to find our exchange very amusing. "Well, most wines are the same strength, but maybe you'd like a merlot? If you find you don't like the flavor, you can at least do a thorough job of ruining someone's shirt with it."

"A beverage that's also a weapon," I said. "Sounds great. Let's go with that."

Darcy shook his head with a defeated-sounding sigh. "Sure."

Sadie took our orders and promised to be right back with the wine. As she left, Darcy snapped his gaze over to me. "What the heck was that?"

I closed my eyes in mock despair. "Tell me you did not just use the word heck. Are we Amish now?"

"Of course not. If you even went near an Amish person, you'd burst into flames and get sucked right down to hell."

"Don't pass go, don't collect two hundred dollars. Yeah, you're probably right."

He didn't smell angry. Mostly just embarrassed. "She's nice," he said.

I glanced at the door to the restaurant, as Sadie walked back out, carrying our wine and a basket of bread. Leaning forward, I lowered my voice so only Darcy would hear. "I say you go for it."

Now he smelled alarmed. "If you say anything, I swear to god…"

"Don't swear to god, you might burst into flames and get sucked down to hell," I said. I realized I was having fun. After the drama with Finn that morning, I really needed some easy joking. That was why I called Tony earlier, and ended up listening to the world's worst Laurel-and-Hardy impersonation. Suddenly, I felt shrunken.

Darcy must've seen something on my face. "Hey, what's wrong?"

I shook my head. "Nothing."

The joking was gone, as was the blush. Darcy looked at me with the focus of a one-track mind. "How are you, really?"

"That's right, start with the easy questions." I inhaled the scent of the wine, able to taste it before I even took a sip. Alcohol played a different sort of tune with my system, since I metabolized things much faster than humans. I could get buzzed really fast, but I couldn't get drunk because the alcohol never stayed in my blood long enough. I rarely bothered with alcohol, choosing to get my buzz from coffee instead. But that floaty, disconnected feeling sounded absolutely wonderful. I gulped down the contents of my glass and poured myself a second.

Darcy's eyes were narrow. "What's going on? Where have you been the last three months? What happened to your sister? Why haven't you called me?"

My glass was empty. How did that happen? I was suddenly very thirsty, so I poured another.

"Do you always drink like this?" He sounded worried. Why was he worried?

"No, I don't drink much. This is really good."

"Yeah, so's the bread. Have some bread." He pushed the basket my way.

I ate a piece, then looked at him, my head cocked to the side. He looked a little like Marlon Brando from that angle. The young Brando, of course. "Hey, do me a favor. Yell Stella for me."

He frowned. "Have some more bread."

The bread popped my metabolism into high gear, and the buzz started to wear off. I sighed, slouched in my seat, and studied him. I tried to remember the questions he asked me, but the machine-gun delivery caused his words to blur together. I asked a question of my own. "You healed up okay?" You know, from when my sister threw a knife at you.

Darcy took a piece of bread from the basket and began to pick it apart, a habit I recognized. He liked to shred things when he was nervous. "Yeah, I'm okay. No big deal."

"She hit you in the lung. Your lung collapsed. Pretty big deal." A ball of heat lodged itself behind my solar plexus, as I remembered that night. The look on Mal's face as she threw the knife. The look on Darcy's face as he struggled to breathe around the blade lodged in his chest. I reached for my glass.

"How'd you know all that?" His heart sped up. I could hear it. I ate another piece of bread before my wolfy side decided it would be fun to make his heart race.

"When I went to visit you in the hospital. When you were all hopped up on painkillers. Your neighbor, the soccer mom, told me."

Sadie Rose brought our food, and, upon noticing how much wine we — I — consumed, she asked if we wanted a second bottle. I said yes, Darcy said no. I was faster, so she smiled and said she'd be back with more.

"You never answered my questions," Darcy said when she was gone.

"No, I guess not."

He stared at me for a moment. "Well?"

"Well what?"

"What happened with your sister? Where have you been? Why didn't you call?"

Oh, yeah. Those were the questions. "Um, she tried to kill me, too. She failed. She got away. I've been at the forest. I didn't call because I guess I figured you wanted to forget all about me. Since all our times together were so fun-filled and shiny."

His scent turned peppery. He was angry. "Well, you figured wrong. Even if I wanted to forget you, which I don't, I couldn't. For better or worse, you were there during the most awful days of my life. You took my mind off my sister's death for a little while. And you convinced me to survive. Then you just dropped off the face of the earth. What's up with that?"

It was my turn to stare. It never occurred to me that those days might mean as much to him as they did to me. That I might mean as much to him as he did to me. "Um. I'm sorry?"

He harrumphed and picked at his food. He glanced up at me. "You're not eating."

I stuffed an overflowing forkful of spicy chicken curry in my mouth. My eyes started to water, and I washed the food down with wine.

"Did you get in trouble? For not killing me?"

Trust Darcy to ask all the questions I didn't want to answer. I drank some more wine, feeling floaty again. Should I even be talking to him about these things? Darcy knew about the Sankhain and the forest, the Spring, because my sister told him. He even drove Tony and me to the forest when we were attacked by a nocturne and badly wounded. He saw the Academy and spent some time in one of our solitary cells. But just because he knew, didn't make him one of us. It didn't give me the right to discuss Sankhain business with him.

And yet, who cared? Finn wasn't here, looking over my shoulder to make sure I was a good little girl. Nobody was going to know what I told Darcy unless I 'fessed up. I needed a friend, and Darcy seemed dumb enough to volunteer for the job.

I took a deep breath and started talking. "I got in a little trouble. But mostly, I got in trouble for what my sister did. After we left you in the parking lot, we went back to the Sankhain Academy. To Janus's office. Janus is our leader, remember? Well, she pulled out another knife..." I told Darcy the whole sordid tale, how Mal helped me break out of a solitary cell, how we were about to run away together when her lies finally tripped her up and I realized that she was the traitor. I told him about the fight between us and the way Tony and Cat came to my rescue. And then I finally answered his question. I told him that Finn still wanted me to kill Darcy, but I used Finn's guilt over keeping Mal's suspicious behavior a secret from me to buy Darcy's pardon. And Darcy listened to it all with his mouth hanging open slightly, reminding me a little of Galen staring at a hamburger.

I shrugged. "She's a crazy bitch, but what is it the Jesus folks say? We all bear crosses?"

"We've all got crosses to bear," he corrected me absently. I raised my eyebrows. "My mom was Catholic."

"Your mom, not you." My question was implied.

But he seemed to hear it. "Let's just say, I'm in the middle of a crisis of faith. A very long, no-end-in-sight crisis. That I'm perfectly content to stay in." He took a sip of wine. Possibly the first he'd taken all night.

"If you're perfectly content, how is it a crisis?"

He tossed me a smile. "It's not, I guess. It just sounds better than saying I decided God sucks."

I gave that some thought. "I guess that depends on your definition of 'better.' I prefer the God sucks version." I smiled the broad, sloppy smile of one who couldn't hold her liquor.

Darcy pushed my plate closer to my breasts. "So, your sister."

I needed to change the subject. "Yeah, speaking of sisters, how are you doing with yours dying and all?" Fuck, fuck, fuck. I should never drink alcohol. I apparently lost what little tact I possessed. Darcy's sister died because I couldn't let her drink from the Spring. No outsiders drinking from the Spring. No exceptions. So his sister died, and mine tried to kill him. That was a really shitty week for Darcy.

"Super." Darcy's voice was careful.

"I'm sorry. God, Darcy, I'm sorry. Please call me an ass. Most people find it makes them feel better."

He smiled wanly. "No, thanks. But you know what would make me feel better? You, telling me why you're back in town. And if you're staying for a while."

Again, my Sankha training kicked in, trying to prevent me from talking. But whether because of the wine or because I just really needed someone to talk to, I ignored the little voice in my head that sounded like Finn in falsetto. I poured another glass of wine to ease the way, then I told Darcy about the murdered man.

"Why would that be your problem? I mean, awful things happen and they have nothing to do with the Sankhain. Right?"

"Right, but —" I hesitated. Darcy knew about the Sankhain, but he didn't know I was a shape-shifter. If I started talking about wolf kills and bite marks, he'd want to know why that made it my problem. Suddenly, my head started pounding, not just aching, but almost vibrating with each beat of my heart. I managed to make it to the bathroom before I got sick.

After I threw up everything and the kitchen table, I sat on the floor of the one-seater and waited. The bathroom smelled like Pine-Sol and toilet bowl cleaner. It smelled amazingly little like vomit, which I took as a sign that they cleaned it more frequently than people puked in it.

I might have stayed all night if the knock on the door hadn't come. I reached up and turned the knob, but I didn't stand. I knew that if I stood up, my head would explode, and that would make a big mess. Brains were surprisingly sticky and really difficult to clean up off cheap linoleum. It was with that thought ricocheting through my head that I faced Sadie Rose.

"I don't drink much," I told her.

"That's probably a good thing," she said. "I appreciate you making it to the toilet."

"My sister is evil."

She raised her eyebrows. "As good a reason to get sloppy drunk as any, I guess. Think you can stand up?"

I accepted her hand and slowly stood. She steadied me while I waited for my head to stop pulling an Exorcist and resettle on my shoulders. Finally, she walked me out to Darcy, whose scent was a beguiling combination of concern and irritation. I switched from leaning on Sadie Rose to leaning on Darcy, and we left.

I apologized. Darcy waved my apologies away and insisted on giving me a ride home. I made a token protest, but I was in no condition to drive and we both knew it. I accepted and prayed I wouldn't puke in Darcy's car.

"You're never going to speak to me again, are you?" I leaned my head back against the seat and closed my eyes so I wouldn't have to look at him while he answered.

"Oh, please." His tone made me open my eyes and turn my head much too fast.

"What?" was all I could manage.

"Kelly. You really think I haven't had my share of drunken stupors over the past few months? Jeez. Granted, I don't usually lose it until I get home, but I've had to call in sick with the 'stomach flu,' like, three times now."

That didn't make me feel better. Instead, I felt like there was something I should be saying, some bit of wisdom that a human woman would have genetically programmed into her brain but that I obviously lacked. The best I could come up with was, "You didn't tell me."

"Yeah, well, it's not something I brag about." He sighed. "I'm telling you now so you know." He smelled like cold sweat. I turned my face ever so slightly in the direction of the open window, because I didn't want to smell that smell on him.

"So I know what?"

"That I know. What it's like. What you're, you know, going through."

I had a little difficulty keeping up with all that knowing. "Um, thanks. Good to...know."

He chuckled, a hard sound that I didn't like hearing from him. It came from the same place as the cold sweat smell, and probably the same place that prompted him to come down with the "stomach flu" three times this summer. It made me want to beat up the bastard that decided to give his sister cancer.

I didn't feel right, letting Darcy lump my sister in with his. "Except, well, it's different for you, isn't it?" I said. "Your sister didn't go all axe murderer on you. She was a good person. And for better or worse, my sister's still alive. You get to grieve. Your loss is…more."

He snorted. "Who told you that you don't have a right to grieve? My loss is different, but at least my sister didn't choose to leave. And besides, we're both alone now, right? No family left." His hands were so tight on the steering wheel, I heard the squeak of skin on plastic. Darcy was alone now. I still had the Sankhain. I vowed that I wouldn't go more than two days without calling Darcy ever again.

When we got to my apartment building, Darcy insisted on walking me to the door. I shivered in the muggy, eighty-degree air. "Thanks for the ride."

"No problem. It was nice to see you." He made no move to leave.

I nodded and instantly regretted the motion as pain exploded behind my eyes. "Hey, how much of that wine did you drink?"

"About a glass and a half."

"Yeah. Sounds about right. Fuck, if Mal finds out about this, she'll give me so much shit about being such a lightweight —" I stopped myself, my stomach lurching for a reason completely unrelated to alcohol. I forced out a laugh. "Stupid wine. Usually, it doesn't take me so long to remember."

Darcy reached out his hand, hesitated, then reached the rest of the way until he held my hand in his. I hadn't realized how cold and clammy my hand was until it was enveloped in his warmth. He didn't say anything, just held my hand.

Finally, I pulled away. "Thanks. For dinner. And stuff."

"Thanks for the company."

"Boy, you must be pretty desperate if you're grateful for my puke-breath." I didn't like his scent, the way his shoulders sagged under some unseen weight. I saw, smelled, the grief he wore like a spandex leotard. I needed to change that, end the evening on a different note. "Although I guess we did bond over barbecued nocturne."

I watched him remember that night, watched his head pop up, his eyes widen, his mouth tip with the beginning of a smile. His scent brightened, and, for possibly the first time all day, I felt good about something I did.

"Good night, Gracie," I said, and started to go through the door.

Darcy grabbed my hand again, pulled me against his body for another hug. Chilled as I was, his body heat felt like stepping into a warm house after walking ten miles through a snowstorm. I sank against him, relaxing. He was warm, he smelled good, and he had yet to discover that I was a pain in the ass.

Or maybe he already discovered it and hugged me anyway. "Good night, George," he said, and let me go. I shivered and walked up the stairs to home.

Chapter 6

After taking Galen out to pee, I collapsed on the futon and managed to sleep for a few hours. At midnight, the cell phone, which I'd unwisely turned back on, rang loudly. I woke up with cotton-mouth, a raging headache and serious homicidal urges. "Who the fuck is this?" I snarled into the receiver.

"Hello to you, too." My sister's voice made me drop the phone.

I stared at it for a moment, considering whether or not to pick it back up. This wasn't a dream — my head hurt far too badly for this to be a dream. Which meant that if I picked the phone back up, I would end up talking to Mal. I wasn't sure I could handle that. And yet curiosity didn't just kill the cat. It took down the wolf, too. I picked up the phone. "As if I didn't have enough reasons to want to kill you," I said.

"What crawled up your ass and died?"

This conversation was playing out exactly as it would've four months ago. Before. The whole thing felt very surreal. Like I was watching a movie. While being struck in the head with a tack hammer. "Why are you calling? Where are you?"

Her laugh sliced through me like, well, like the sword she stuck in my side. "I'm not a moron. I'm not about to tell you where I am."

"The moron part's debatable, but whatever." My heart lodged itself in my throat, and every beat wanted to trigger my gag reflex. "You could share why you're calling. At midnight, for chrissake." My voice sounded so normal. Not at all like I was gagging.

"Maybe I missed my sister. Is that so hard to believe?"

"Yes." The word just hopped out, like a toad.

She was quiet for a while. I considered hanging up, but she still didn't tell me what she wanted. "I heard there was a murder up by you."

She said "up." Was she down south somewhere? Of course, most of the country was south of Wisconsin. And some people said "up by you" regardless of their relative location. My head hurt way too much to be thinking this hard. "Did one of your little friends leave that present for me?"

"My - ?" I heard the question mark in her voice, despite the fact that she lopped off the rest of the sentence. "No. You're going to have to find a new villain this time, little sister."

Because she was born first and never let me forget it. "Don't call me that." I lost control of my voice. It turned loud and harsh and ragged.

"You are my little sister. Remember?"

I did remember. My skin felt so heavy, I thought my bones might buckle under the strain. "No. My sister's gone. So go fuck yourself, or go fuck one of your nocturne buddies. Because you chose them over me. And don't call me again."

It wasn't until I hung up the phone that I realized I still didn't know anything about how to find her. I stared at the phone, wondering if I should try to call her back. I picked up the phone and checked caller ID. "Number unavailable." So I couldn't call her back. But probably I should at least call Finn and report that she made contact. Definitely, I should do that. Instead, I walked into the kitchen and stuck the cell phone in the junk drawer. I put on a pot of coffee, wrapped my arms around my dog, and stared out the window at the yellow glow of streetlights.

———— «» ————

I turned the TV on for company, but hours later, I had no recollection of what was on. I drank coffee and waited for the sky to lighten. I replayed the events of those few days last spring leading up to Mal's defection. I never suspected for a moment that she was the person who gave Darcy those documents, the Sankhain documents that detailed the history of the Spring. I knew that my sister didn't like Finn, that she thought Janus was an old man who didn't care about the people he led. But betray us? Betray me? Never.

She was my pack. My littermate. Not that shape-shifters were usually born in litters. We came out as babies, not cubs. But our mother liked to joke that after giving birth to ten daughters, all single births, she finally gave birth to a litter of two. Twins, Kellan and Amalea. Inseparable since the womb.

Even now, part of me wished she would call back. So I could hear her laugh again. Remember her scent and the way her dark eyes would grow darker, like they were drawing the night into them, the opposite of my eyes that glowed like molten gold.

I wondered if I took a blade and started cutting off bits of my flesh, if I could cut out that part of me that wanted her back.

It was that thought that made me dig my cell phone out of the junk drawer. I almost dialed Tony, then remembered the horrid conversation the day before with What's-Her-Name. No way would I risk a repeat performance. Even though Tony left three more messages since last night. So I dialed Darcy instead.

He answered on the second ring. "Hello?" he said, his voice riding a yawn.

I glanced at the clock. Four-thirty. But I didn't apologize for waking him up. "Hi. It's me. Kelly."

"Oh." He suddenly sounded more alert. "How are you feeling this morning?"

"Okay, I guess. Wanna come over?" My leg began to jiggle as I waited for an answer. I wasn't sure what I would do with myself if he said no.

"Um, now?" I heard the doubt.

I hesitated. It was early. Too damn early. But my lungs were too tight to breathe, waiting for him to say yes. "Um, yes?"

He was quiet, and I pictured him listening to all the things I wasn't saying. Maybe he heard the cracks in the foundation. Maybe he took pity on me, or maybe he really meant it when he said he missed me. "Do you want breakfast?" he asked.

Relief flooded me, a wave of warmth that made the August air seem frigid by comparison. My stomach growled, surprising me. My head still hurt, but apparently, my body wanted food. "I'll take a sausage and egg sandwich. No, make that two. And hash browns." Potatoes sounded good. "No, fries."

"Okay." He yawned again.

I felt a pang of guilt for waking him up. But my leg was jiggling again. I didn't want to be alone. "When do you think you can get here?"

He was quiet for a moment. "Are you sure you're all right?"

"All right is relative," I said. The artful dodger, that's me. "So I'll see you soon?"

"Within an hour." He hung up.

What the fuck did he have to do that could possibly take an hour?

I decided I could probably use a shower, so I took one. It did not take me an hour. And I had a lot more hair than Darcy did.

When I was clean and dressed, Darcy still wasn't there, so Galen and I went outside to wait. As Galen lifted his leg on the bushes by our front steps, I took a deep breath of the morning air. And almost gagged. Somewhere nearby, there was something dead. And I didn't think it was a squirrel. Dead animals smelled musky, like fur and skin oil and dirt. This smell was human, with a hint of decomp. I closed my eyes to gather my strength. I didn't want a dead body this morning. I just really, really didn't want that.

I remembered my conversation with Mal, her comment about a corpse. What if she wasn't talking about Finn's dead guy? What if she was talking about a new corpse, yet to be discovered? But maybe not. Maybe this was just some homeless guy, or a junkie. Maybe it was a normal, garden-variety murder victim. And maybe a pink unicorn would fly out of my butt.

I followed the scent around the building to the parking lot. Whoever killed the man was kind enough to pull him into the grass, the long stuff by the back fence that my landlord never bothered to weed-whacker. So nobody noticed the dead guy. Yet. But soon, he would start smelling bad enough that humans would pick up on the stink. And that would bring police, and questions, and all sorts of headaches to my door. I already had a headache. I didn't need any more.

I looked around. I didn't want police here. I mean, sure, the police investigated crimes in my neighborhood all the time. But the second dead body in less than a week, and it's right in my backyard? Too close. Too close.

If my truck was parked in its usual spot, I would've just dragged the dead man over to it and stuck him in the covered bed, closed the tailgate, and enjoyed a nice breakfast with Darcy before I found a place to dispose of the body. But my truck was parked next to the Indian Restaurant from Hell, right where my drunk ass left it last night.

When Galen started sniffing the dead guy, I came to my senses. Maybe I didn't have my truck, but I didn't have to stand there like a big neon arrow pointing at the body. I rolled my shoulders back, pulled my dog away from the body, and looked around. I saw a tarp over by the trash cans. I grabbed it and started to lay it over the body.

As I worked, I noticed several red marks on the man's neck and face. I glanced at his arms. More there. Burns? I rubbed a hand over the back of my neck, feeling the similar scar there. An acquaintance of my mother's, a faery whose saliva burned like acid, spit on me there when I was a kid. His face popped into my head, and I wondered. No, it couldn't be Aza. My mother got him to leave town. Burns happened all the time, for all kinds of reasons. Maybe this guy burned himself at work. Or maybe he was an arsonist. There was no reason to think this guy's burns — all of them fresh-looking — came from the same jackass mine did.

Dead Guy wasn't gutted and he was covered in burns. He didn't look like the last neighborhood corpse. Except for one thing. His Achilles tendons were severed, just like the last body. Just like a wolf pack ran him down. This was the same killer. I shivered. A present, left just for me.

And if I could make the connection between the two bodies — severed Achilles tendons was a pretty specific signature — so could the police. A random dead body was one kind of investigation. Gang violence, a mugging, all kinds of possible motives. But the investigation of a serial killer was a whole other beast, more manpower, more spotlight. I didn't do spotlight. I had a tail, for fuck's sake. I needed to get rid of this fucking body.

But first, I needed to examine it. I once again looked around, trying to engage my sense of smell as well. Once I was sure we were well and truly alone, I knelt beside the body and breathed.

I appreciated that he wasn't gutted. That minimized the fecal smell, which allowed me to pick up more scents than I would've been able to on the first body. He smelled like old booze, a little like pee — not surprising, since many people soiled themselves when dying — but he also smelled like something sweeter. Like cologne.

My breath stopped, my heart stopped, my vision went black around the edges as I remembered another body, another scene in tall grass. When Mal attacked two of our Sankhain last spring, she doused herself in heavy perfume so I wouldn't recognize her scent. It must've been hell on her sinuses, wearing that much perfume. But that's dedication for you.

This cologne was different. It wasn't overpowering. It was faint and smelled expensive. This wasn't Mal. I would've been able to smell her scent under this cologne. I had to tell myself that several times before I started believing it. This wasn't Mal. This wasn't Mal.

I snapped some pictures of the body, taking close-ups of the ankle wounds and the burns. Then I rolled the body over and checked for any other oddities. Nothing, not even any burns. Like the killer only bothered to sear one side of him. I rolled him over onto his back again, feeling absurdly like he would be more comfortable that way, and returned to positioning the tarp.

Darcy pulled in just as I finished tucking in the dead man. After turning off his rusted old hatchback, Darcy got out and gave me an appropriately odd look. "What are you doing?" he said.

"Covering up a dead man" didn't seem very diplomatic. But diplomatic really wasn't my thing, so... "Covering up a dead man."

Darcy's mouth drooped open slightly. "Did you kill him?" he whispered.

"No. I don't even know him." I glanced down at the lumpy plastic, then looked away. I wondered if he wore the cologne. I wondered who he put on cologne for. "I don't suppose you'd let me load him in the back of your car and take me to dispose of him, would you?"

He stared at me. "I brought breakfast."

"Thanks and all, but I think I better take care of the dead guy before I eat." Galen was sniffing the tarp. I pulled him away again. "Maybe we could eat in the car while you drive me to Diesel's farm."

"In the car, with a dead body. In my car."

I frowned. I knew I was asking a lot, but I really needed him to say yes. The longer the body sat there, the worse I felt. Like electricity coursed through my body, burning my veins and charring my bones. "Well, I'd take my truck, but it's still at the restaurant."

Darcy swallowed, a big swallow that forced him to stick his chin out in order to get his spit down. Like maybe spit wasn't all he was swallowing down. "I — I don't — we should call the police. Who is he?"

Didn't I already say I didn't know? "We can't call the police. I can't talk to the police and answer questions about my life. Please, Darcy."

"Why not? What do you have to hide? You said you didn't kill him. The police will be able to see that."

His naivety was almost cute, but my blood's electrical charge was getting worse the longer we stood and debated. I clenched my fists, digging my fingernails into the flesh of my palms. "Please, Darcy." I ground out the words from between clenched teeth.

He looked down at the dead guy's shoes, the toes sticking up out of the grass. "You're sure he's dead?"

"Yes." I didn't explain. I had a sneaking suspicion any complex sentences would be lost on Darcy at the moment.

Slowly, he raised his head to meet my eyes. "Okay."

"Thank you." I studied him. He looked pale and sweaty, like he was the one with a hangover. "Do you want me to drive?"

He shook his head, looked down at the body and stuffed his hands in his pockets. "Do you need me to help you lift him?"

"No, I can handle that. Just do me a favor and keep watch. And pop the back open, will you?" I glanced around — we were still alone so far. It was probably about five-thirty now. Sweat began to pool in some very unpleasant places when I saw a light flicker on in a second-story apartment next door. I bent down to gather the dead man in my arms. The tarp slipped as I picked him up.

"OH, GOD!" Darcy's moan was loud enough to wake the dead guy.

Chapter 7

I looked up. "What?"

"That's Rick. That's Dolly's ex," Darcy whispered. Dolly was another librarian at the branch where Darcy worked. "He — they got divorced last year. He — oh, my god."

I didn't know what to say. Darcy seemed really upset, so I went with, "I'm sorry."

He looked at me with eyes too wide, showing too much white around the edges. "He was a jerk. He cheated on her and he used to hit her, too."

"Oh. Then I guess I'm not sorry. Darcy, pop the trunk. This guy's heavy and he smells."

Darcy was back to staring at what's-his-name. I would've snapped my fingers in front of his face, but my hands were occupied with the dead guy who was really way too big for a woman of my size to hold onto for very long. Even a supernaturally strong woman of my size.

I kept my volume low while increasing my vehemence. "Darcy! Pull yourself together. He's dead. No amount of staring is going to change a damn thing. But I have to move this fucking body. I can't leave it here. This is the second body this week. I can't afford police attention, even peripheral attention. Please."

He rubbed the back of his head, causing his hair to stand on end. "What do you want me to do?"

I felt my face grow hot, which meant I probably looked like I was about to have steam come out of my ears. At least, if we were living in a cartoon. Sometimes, it sure felt that way. "Open. The. Trunk."

"It's a hatchback, it's not really a trunk, it's a —" Darcy finally seemed to see the look on my face. He opened the trunk. I dumped the body inside and arranged the tarp once more so it covered the dead guy.

I turned to Darcy. "Give me your keys."

"What? Why?"

Because you look like you just wet yourself, and maybe a little extra. "I'll drive. You look...upset." I was very pleased with my restraint.

Darcy wasn't as impressed. "Of course I'm upset. There's a dead body, a dead man that I know, that I saw at the July fourth party four years in a row. And now he's dead in my trunk!"

He was making too much noise and we were no longer alone. A guy, wearing a polo shirt and carrying a small cooler, glanced over at us as he walked to his sedan. Just a glance, so either he only heard Darcy's tone, not the words, or he lived in this neighborhood long enough to abide by the see-no-evil-hear-no-evil-live-to-see-another-day way of life here. Still, I needed to get a handle on Darcy, or the next person would end up calling the police.

"Darcy, he beat your friend. He cheated on her. Not exactly Time magazine's Man of the Year here. If you don't want to help me, you could just drive me to my truck and let me transfer the body, and I'll take care of it. But each time we move this body around, the odds that someone will see what we're doing and call the police increase by about a thousand. So I would really prefer to just use your car to take it to Diesel's farm."

"Will we have to burn him?" Now his voice was small, the voice of a little boy.

The last time Darcy accompanied me to Diesel's farm, we burned a nocturne carcass. Burning was an efficient way to obscure remains, but it did take a long time. "We can bury him, if you'd rather."

"If I'd rather?" The six-octave jump of his voice told me that my choice of words was poor. "I'd rather I never met you, sometimes."

It surprised me how much that hurt. I couldn't blame him, really, but it still made my skin turn numb for a moment. "Most people who know me come to that conclusion eventually. But before you write me off completely, will you let me use your car?" Because I was a little worried he was going to back out, even though the worst part was over. The body was in the car. Out of sight, out of mind, I figured.

He scowled at me and handed me the keys. "I'm not going to write you off. I said sometimes. And really, can you blame me for being upset? There's a dead body in my trunk."

"It's not a trunk," I couldn't help saying.

Darcy climbed into the passenger seat and slammed the door. "Your dog rides in the back seat."

Darcy knew Galen's name. I thought it was just plain rude to refer to him as *your dog*, but I decided to keep my mouth shut for once. I held the door open for Galen, then I slid behind the wheel and turned on the car. "Thank you," I said to Darcy. I braved a look at him, even though I wasn't sure I wanted to see the revulsion that must be all over his face. Revulsion at me, at my way of life. Surprisingly, I didn't see any of that. Darcy looked sad. The corners of his mouth were turned down and his eyes were squinting as though the light was too bright. "I'm sorry. I wish you didn't have to see any of this."

Darcy looked at me. His lower lip trembled ever so slightly, but his eyes stayed dry. "You, either."

I stared at him. He wished I didn't have to see this? Did he know how many things, much more awful, I'd seen? More awful things I'd done? Darcy had a way of doing this to me, treating me like I was a human being, worthy of compassion. It shocked me every time.

As I backed out of the parking space, I finally noticed that the radio was tuned to NPR. "NPR? What are you, eighty-five?"

He made a sound almost like a growl. "I like the voices of the commentators. They're soothing. Besides, my parents used to listen to NPR while we all ate breakfast every day. It's like starting out my day with my family."

I almost told him he was lucky and I wished that I had a similar link to my family. Fortunately, before I spoke, I remembered that his family was all dead, whereas I still had one living sister. A psychotic stalker of a sister, but still. She was alive. "Sometimes I wish she was dead. I think that would be easier."

I didn't realize I spoke out loud until Darcy said, "What?"

My words horrified me. I didn't want Mal to be dead. Because even though she was creepy and evil, she was my only living pack. No matter what, I still wanted to know she was out there. "Uh. Nothing. Sorry. Just thinking out loud." I pointed at the bag that sat between us on the console. "Could you pull me out a sandwich?" It was going to taste about as good as sand, but maybe if I stuffed my mouth full of something, I wouldn't say any more stupid things. Considering how much I ate and how many stupid things I still managed to say, I wasn't too optimistic. But it was worth a try.

Darcy handed me a sandwich. "Who do you wish was dead?" Because of course, he couldn't just let it go.

I unwrapped the sandwich and took a bite to stall my answer. Unfortunately, chewing and swallowing didn't bring any insight into how to respond. "Mal. My sister."

"I know who Mal is." He sounded a little annoyed. That was probably healthy.

"Yeah, I know, I just…" I glanced in the rearview mirror and caught sight of Galen. He didn't look worried. That was comforting. "I'm sorry. Your sister is…and mine…"

"Tried to kill me." A rustle told me Darcy was unwrapping a sandwich of his own. I saw from the corner of my eye that he didn't eat it though. Just cupped it in his hands, like he was relishing the warmth.

"Yeah." I wondered if he had nightmares about when my sister stabbed him. Like I did, about when my sister stabbed me.

"Why do you wish she was dead?"

I felt a tremble start inside me, as the knowledge settled in my bones. Just as a part of me missed my sister, part of me wished for a grief that was simple. Like Darcy's. Dead sister equals grief. Traitorous sister equals…? "Why not? She's evil. She's a murderer. Well, attempted murderer. She didn't actually kill anyone she set out to kill, we all survived, but just because she sucks at it doesn't mean she has any redeeming qualities."

"She killed your friend. At the farm. What was her name?" Darcy set the sandwich, which was probably cold now, back in the bag without taking a bite.

"Trini," I said, remembering. "Her name was Trini." But Trini's wounds weren't really life-threatening. She might have lived, if we found her sooner. By the time we got to her, she lost all that blood and…I felt my stomach twist like a Bavarian pretzel. Mal didn't actually suck at killing people. Mal was very good at killing people. So why did Darcy and Janus and I all live? "She called me this morning." I didn't know I was going to say it until I heard it come out of my mouth.

"Mal? She called you? Why would she do that?"

"You haven't been listening. She's psycho." I turned right into Diesel's driveway. The Sankhain owned the farm. Diesel didn't live here anymore, he moved to Nova Scotia or someplace like that. But he used to run a mechanic's shop and, well, basically a chop shop, on the farm. Now it just served as a convenient place to dispose of bodies. Darcy accompanied me to the farm twice last spring. The first time, the night Trini died, we told Darcy that we were taking him to the forest, when really, we took him to the farm to use him as nocturne bait. The second time was when he helped me burn a nocturne. All kinds of happy memories here.

"She's your sister." Darcy sounded troubled by the fact that I called my sister a psycho.

"She's — well — I don't know what she is." I stopped the car and looked at him. "Look, I'm sorry about what I said, about wishing she was dead. I didn't even mean to say it out loud. But she's a traitor. She chose the monsters over me. I guess, if she were dead, then it would be done with. I wouldn't have to think about her anymore."

Darcy looked at me, then turned to stare out the window. "It doesn't work like that. You'd still think about her. That doesn't go away."

How many times could one woman get her foot stuck in her mouth in a twenty-four hour period? "Darcy —"

"We should take care of the body." Darcy sucked in a deep breath. "I think I'm going to need another shower before work. I feel like I have corpse cooties."

"Corpse cooties?" I laughed. "You didn't even touch him. How do you think I feel?"

"Why didn't you just leave him for someone else to find?"

I studied Darcy and decided to tell a little more of the truth. "Kelly O'Connell's not my real name. I don't want to find out my alias doesn't hold up under scrutiny because the police decided I'm a person of interest in the death of Dolly's schmuck of an ex."

"So don't call the police. Let someone else do it."

I didn't want to explain about the possible serial killer hunting in my neighborhood. Humans tended to get anxious about possible serial killers. But I knew Darcy's tenacity, and so I explained. I added, "Besides, he was in my backyard. You really don't think the police would at least question the tenants in the building?"

"Maybe." He didn't sound satisfied, which bugged me.

I huffed. The big bad wolf. "Maybe I'm a little stupid sometimes and don't think things through, but I managed to stay alive for two hundred years. I must be doing something right."

"I didn't say you're stupid. I would never say that." Darcy finally unbuckled his seat belt and got out of the car. He stuck his head back in and looked me in the eye. "I just wanted to know why you chose to move the body instead of leaving him be."

He looked so calm, so nonjudgmental, that I actually believed him. "Well, that's why."

He nodded. "Okay," he said. "Now can we get Rick out of my car, please?"

We buried Rick the Wife Beater in a wooded area, about fifty yards from the farmhouse. Well, I buried him. Since it was my idea to move the body, he was my responsibility. Darcy watched in relative silence, only muttering a few things under his breath. I didn't ask him to repeat himself so that I could hear him.

I mounded dirt on top of the grave. One of the things they didn't tell you when you bury a body was that after decomp, the dirt settled and left a little grave-shaped crater, a sure sign that a body was buried there. The extra dirt helped counteract that.

After I dragged some branches and dead leaves over the grave to hide the body-sized freshly dug spot, Darcy finally spoke loud enough for me to hear. "We should put some sort of marker there. Like a cross. Or maybe a nice rock."

I stared at him. "Right. Because I went to the trouble of dragging the body into the woods and carefully burying it, just to leave a nice symbol that screams, Here lies a dead guy that I don't want anybody to find."

Darcy's cheeks reddened, but his jaw firmed into an expression of stubbornness. "Nobody should be buried in an unmarked grave. Even a jerk like Rick."

Not for the first time, it struck me how different my world was from Darcy's. How many unmarked graves did I have in my past? I never bothered to keep count. Some things, if you tried to carry them with you, would just drag you down. "Fine. But no crosses, for chrissake. Find a rock, preferably a small rock, and place it wherever the hell you want. Then let's get out of here."

Darcy didn't take long finding a rock. Apparently, he didn't want to linger any more than I did. He looked at me. "Which end is his head?"

Darcy was a decent guy. A sense of decency must be a real pain in the ass in awkward situations like this. I wouldn't know. I couldn't remember which way I laid Rick in the grave, and I decided Darcy probably didn't care. He just felt he needed to do things the right way. So with no moral qualms, I took a guess. Darcy placed the headstone, I called for Galen, and we all walked back to the car.

"Do you think we should've said something?" Darcy asked as I wiped the sweat and dirt off my face with the hem of my t-shirt.

Were we back to the police conversation again? "About what?" I said, letting Galen into the back seat, opening the driver's door and sliding behind the wheel.

Darcy got in the passenger seat. "About Rick. About who he was, and you know, may he rest in peace or something."

I knew that whatever I chose to say, I would sound like a bitch because I was tired, dehydrated, and covered in corpse cooties. So I didn't try to rein myself in. "You did say something. You said he cheated on and beat your friend. This was a backyard burial of a ginormous dickweed. The only thing left to do is breathe a sigh of relief and go home to take a shower."

Darcy's scent flashed hot and angry. "You can't really be that horrible. He was a human being."

His words hurt, but I refused to buckle under the ache. "The fact is, deep down, you're glad he's gone. You're glad he's never going to show up at another Christmas party, or whine his way back into Dolly's heart. You're glad you don't have to worry about him waiting for her in a dark parking lot with a knife, because that's what guys like him do. Maybe he was somebody's son, but he was also somebody's nightmare. You're not sad he's gone. You can hate me for pointing it out, but you can't say I'm wrong."

Darcy glared at me for several heartbeats, looked away and inhaled. The kind of breath that usually follows a good bout of sobbing, a breath full of catches and snags. "No. I can't say you're wrong."

He looked so young. So innocent. Most of the people I spent my time with, even the younglings, looked more world-weary than Darcy. There was a lightness about Darcy that made me want to wrap myself around him, shield him with my body from the blows that would change him into something bitter, something a little bit dead. "I hope he rests in peace," I found myself saying. "It might be more than he deserves. But if it'll give you peace, then I hope he finds some."

When Darcy looked at me, I saw a pain in his eyes that had nothing to do with Rick the Wife Beater. And I wondered if maybe Darcy didn't need me to shelter him. If Darcy would never turn dead inside. "I'm sorry I called you horrible," he said. "You're not."

I envied him. I knew that I was already a little dead inside. I turned to face the steering wheel and started the car. "Oh, I don't know. I can be pretty horrible sometimes."

"We all can. But your heart's in the right place."

I didn't argue. I wanted someone to believe that about me, even if it wasn't true.

———— «» ————

I drove to the lot where my truck was parked. I said good-bye to Darcy, almost hugged him, but stopped when he turned his shoulders away from me. That subtle shift in body language hurt me in the center of my chest. He managed to hurt my feelings twice in one morning. Fuck.

Something must've shown on my face, because he said, "Sorry. I just — I know it's stupid, but you were carrying around a dead body."

I could smell the sincerity on him. It smelled like huckleberry tea. I let that sincerity soak in, let it ease the sting of his rejection. He wasn't rejecting me, he was just grossed out by Dead Guy Rick. I was so relieved, I just smiled and nodded and told him to call me soon. I immediately regretted it, hearing the girly neediness in my voice and hating it with the fire of ten thousand suns. Darcy didn't comment on the girliness or the neediness, just promised he would call. Galen and I watched him drive away before we climbed into the truck. I rolled down the windows once I got a whiff of myself. Why did hangover have to smell like pickled beets? Who made that judgment call? Like the headache, nausea and cottonmouth wasn't bad enough, you had to smell like something that just crawled out of a swamp.

When we got home, Galen went straight for his water dish and I didn't even take the time to start a pot of coffee before stripping and stepping under the hot spray of the showerhead. My apartment didn't boast a lot of amenities. For example, the bathtub drained slow, no matter how much drain opener I used. But the water pressure in my building was superb, and the hot water nearly endless. So I got to stay in the shower until I felt clean rather than being chased out by a dwindling hot water supply, even though the slow-draining tub was almost overflowing when I was done.

When I pulled back the shower curtain, I found Galen staring at me. As soon as I saw his expression, I realized I forgot to feed him breakfast. I knelt down and apologized profusely, then without even grabbing a towel, I filled his bowl and watched him eat. There was something comforting about watching Galen inhale his food. He licked the inside of the empty bowl, sniffed around the bowl to make sure no strays managed to escape. Then he looked up at me, his big dark eyes clearly asking, "That's all?"

I ruffled the top of his head and went back into the bathroom to dry off.

A short time later, I sat at the kitchen table with a cup of coffee, my phone and the file Finn gave me with the first dead man's pictures. I studied the pictures. On both men, the burns looked fresh, like they died before the burns could begin to heal. Again, I rubbed the mark on the back of my neck and remembered Aza. An ugly fucker, inside and out, who burned me because I saw him without his glamour and I laughed at him.

Faery glamour was a type of magick. Not all faeries were gifted at glamour, but the ones who were used it to alter their appearance. It was a passive form of defense, a way to hide in plain sight. Change your hair color, your eye color, your skin color. Change the shape of your facial features. Hide pointy ears or extra appendages. Not all faeries had pointy ears, but some of them did, and some of them had more arms than an octopus or an extra eye in the middle of their chest, or ten fingers on each hand. Some wore their differences with pride, but most faeries were vain and wanted to be seen as beautiful. Or to pass as human.

Aza, for example, loved to live among humans, because humans made the best prey. Aza liked men, womanizers. He'd choose someone — and Aza had a talent for picking man-whores out of a crowd — and follow him, stalk him. This was his foreplay, watching and waiting until he felt desire come upon him, until need burned through him like a fever. Aza would kill the man. Bloody, showy.

I overheard my mother talking to Janus about Aza's latest kill when I was around five years old. And while I was too young to understand the sexual component to Aza's behavior, I understood the thrill of the hunt. But I also knew that hunting humans was never, ever allowed. Well, unless our alpha ordered us to do it. But never without permission and never for pleasure. This creature who dared to violate the taboo fascinated me.

Janus wanted my mother to eliminate Aza, but she didn't want to. She worried about starting a war with the fey if she killed one of their own. No, she said, better to convince Aza to move his hunting grounds elsewhere. A bigger city, perhaps, might be more suited to his needs. Janus didn't want to start a war with anyone, so he agreed to try my mother's plan.

I begged my mother to let me watch her talk this man (for lack of a better word) into leaving town. She was my alpha, I told her, and I wanted to learn from her. She agreed and told me to keep my mouth shut. I don't know why she thought I would, or why she thought I wanted to learn anything. I just wanted to meet the faery that Janus called the Horror.

My cellphone rang, making me jump and dragging me back into the present. My heart started racing and coffee churned in my stomach. Part of me hoped it was Mal. Part of me hated that part of me. I checked the caller ID. "TONY," it read.

Not Mal. The disappointment was so intense, I wanted to drop my head onto the table. I silenced the ringer and pushed my chair away from the table, but I didn't stand up. My hands were shaking and I couldn't seem to take a deep breath. Galen stuck his head between my knees and gazed up at me. I plunged my shaking hands into his thick fur, and buried my face in his neck until my breathing steadied.

As I pulled myself upright again, I wiped off the dog hair that stuck to my face. I wiped my sweaty palms on my cargo shorts, and forced myself to stand up. I started singing Five Finger Death Punch in an attempt to avoid thinking about how I felt. But that didn't work, because without the bass and guitars and drums, Five Finger Death Punch couldn't drown out my thoughts.

Would I have answered if it was Mal on the phone? What did I think would happen? I'd like to say I thought to discover some clue as to where she was hiding, but I knew in the pit of my chest that wasn't true. The feeling when the phone rang, the excitement, the happy jolt, that wasn't the anticipation of a hunt. That was hope. Stinky, traitorous, no-good-ever-comes-from-that hope. I missed my sister, and I wanted her to call me.

There's only one way to deal with emotions like that — try to outrun them. It was too damn hot to actually run without putting Galen's health at risk. I cursed the weather for a few seconds; ignoring the nagging light on my cell phone that told me Tony left a message, I harnessed Galen and we went for a long walk. I kept a close eye on Galen and we stopped frequently so he could sip water from the bottle I kept in my pocket.

No matter how far we walked, I couldn't escape the thoughts that pinballed around in my skull. The thoughts were still there, fragmented and all the more tormenting because with every step, I seemed less and less capable of logicking my way out of anything.

Why did she call me? How did she know about the body? When she called, was she talking about the body in the police file, or was she talking about Rick the Wife Beater, before I even knew there was a second body? Could she have known about Dead Rick? Did she know who killed these men? Did she kill them?

Suddenly, my legs gave out, and I hit the sidewalk in a skin-scraping sprawl. My vision dotted with black spots that grew larger every time I tried to pull in oxygen. Stupid, stupid Kellan. When did I last eat? Not since that early-morning sandwich in Darcy's car. I was going to pass out, and Galen would be unprotected. Someone might steal him, he might get hit by a car. I couldn't pass out.

Galen started licking my face, and a breeze brushed across my sweat-soaked skin — my skin felt hot, not the damp chill that preceded loss of consciousness. That was good sign. I focused on the breeze, focused on the feel of Galen's tongue on my forehead, and stopped working so hard to breathe. My muscles relaxed, my heart slowed, and oxygen worked its way to my brain.

Galen stopped licking me, and I heard a growl deep in his throat. He moved to stand over me, but I pushed him out of the way and sat up. A man was walking toward us. I didn't recognize him, not at first. Not until he held out his hand and asked me if I was all right. When I heard his voice, I knew him. Aza. The Horror.

Chapter 8

An involuntary growl started in my chest before I swallowed it down. His glamour was firmly in place. His skin appeared a deep tan, when I knew it actually looked sickly gray. Rather than its current blond, in reality his hair was white and grew in tufts around his head like something out of a Dr. Seuss cartoon. And I knew his human-looking ears were actually pointy with hair growing out the top, and his eyes were actually black, rather than the brown his glamour created. He didn't put the energy into changing his thin, tight lips, although he made his jagged teeth appear Hollywood-perfect. He wore a suit despite the heat, and he wore glasses, a new accessory. I never heard of a faery who needed corrective lenses, and Aza's eyesight was just fine the last time we met.

I ignored the offered hand, pushing myself to my feet. I wavered a little, but I tried not to let it show. A couple of joggers approached, and they slowed, looking at me with concern. I forced a laugh. "Clumsy. But I'm okay." They jogged on, and Aza looked at me with his lips pressed together. He smelled heated, like he was angry.

"You should be more careful," he said. But without any inflection, like he was reciting a memorized phone number. "You might injure yourself."

The scrapes on my knees were already healing, and I brushed the blood and dirt away. "Thanks for the tip, Aza." He smiled when I said his name, like he was pleased that I recognized him. When I met his gaze, my insides started squirming, so instead I studied the dirt on my palms and looked at him from the corner of my eye. I couldn't kill Aza now. Not here, not in broad daylight on Fish Hatchery Road with cars zooming past and a kids' softball game playing on the field behind us. Besides, faeries could only be truly injured with iron, and I didn't have any iron blades on me. I didn't have anything but a small switchblade in my pocket. Stupid, stupid Kellan. "What brings you back to town? I thought you moved away."

"Well, we all must come home again at some point in our lives, mustn't we? I missed the climate. Though I must say, the city has grown significantly, and not necessarily for the better."

Then go back to where you came from. "Yeah, well, that seems to be the way humanity does things." I felt like a little kid, avoiding his eyes, so I forced myself to look at him. "Why go blonde? It's so cliché."

He bared his teeth at me. "I think it's rather becoming."

"Well, as long as you're happy with it." I fiddled with Galen's leash, unable to look at Aza and stand still at the same time. Suddenly, I realized what he was doing, and my spine stiffened. "Stop that. What is it, some sort of discord spell? Trying to make me uncomfortable in my own skin?" I didn't know he could work magick on other people, and the knowledge that he was playing with me made me want to kick him in the groin. It also made me wonder if my fall a few minutes ago was really blood-sugar-induced, or if he did some sort of spell to make me clumsy, too.

Looking almost genuinely sheepish, he rubbed the corners of his mouth with his thumb and forefinger. "My apologies. It was a childish tactic."

"Yeah? So's leaving a body in my backyard." Maybe, just maybe the murders weren't his work. Maybe this was all a big coincidence, Aza coming to town the same time two dead, burned males show up in my neighborhood. Or maybe it was all the work of the tooth fairy, and I'd go home to find a quarter under my fucking pillow.

"No, I don't believe that was at all childish. I wanted to announce myself, if you will." He adjusted his glasses on his nose and looked down at me. He wasn't too much taller than me. Two or three inches. But he still managed to look down his nose at me.

"Yeah. I'm glad, seeing as we're such great friends. Why are you here?" Did Janus know he was here?

My skin went cold. Did Mal know he was here?

"I'm hurt. Haven't you missed me?" He spat, barely missing Galen's nose. The grass smoked where his spit landed.

Fuck it. I'd rip him apart with my bare hands. Even a faery would struggle to survive having his spine torn out. I punched him in the face with every ounce of strength I had. I felt his nose cave in, and he fell to the ground. Galen tried to lunge for him, probably hoping to help finish Aza off, but I pulled my dog tight to my side. I heard a shriek, and when I turned, I saw two soccer moms — softball moms? — pointing and staring at us, with more rushing in our direction. I looked down at Aza, whose skin looked gray and eyes black. Glamour was slipping. "Go back where you came from. Or I'll do a lot worse than fuck up your glamour job."

"Your mother's truce," he said, with the thickness in his voice that meant he was swallowing down blood and other, thicker things.

I snorted. "Your truce with my mother consisted of the Sankhain allowing you to hunt, as long as you did it elsewhere. You broke that truce, not me."

"No! You interfered with my hunt. You and your sister and her disgusting nocturnes. You stole my prey. You broke the truce."

"My —" The gaggle of soccer moms was descending on us. I didn't want to deal with questions or hovering or 911 calls. I glared at Aza for a moment more, then tugged Galen's leash and took off for home.

I must've done something to my ankle when I fell, because I couldn't really run without shooting pains running all the way up my hip. I didn't want the soccer moms to catch up with us, though, so I forced myself to jog for a few blocks before I slowed to a gimpy walk. Galen didn't mind the change of pace. He marked every tree we passed. I limited his leg-lifting to trees, because if I stopped every time he wanted to mark something, we'd never get home.

Unfortunately, the ankle pain wasn't bad enough that my brain stopped working. I had plenty of time to think about what Aza said. How did Mal and I interfere with his hunt, steal his prey? The only time I saw Mal in the last two years was this past spring, and the only man we both were in contact with was —

Darcy. Aza was hunting Darcy. Fear, cold and sharp, dragged me to a stop. Not Darcy. I couldn't lose anyone else.

"Wait a minute," I said to Galen. "Darcy's not a womanizer. Darcy's a gentleman. Why the hell would Aza target Darcy?"

Galen took advantage of my confusion to sniff-and-lift on a clump of weeds.

"And besides, if he was hunting Darcy, he was already in violation of the agreement with Mother. So it's not my fault at all."

Galen wagged his tail. I wasn't in a waggy sort of mood, though. The fear was fading and now I was pissed. It was bad enough having to own up to all the screw-ups that were actually my fault. No way in hell was that fugly faery prick going to pin his indiscretions on me.

"And what the fuck's up with all these supernatural creatures hunting Darcy?" When Galen heard the "f" word, he seemed to know wagging wasn't the appropriate response. He looked up at me with big eyes instead. I tried to moderate my tone. "First the nocturnes, now Aza. He's a librarian. Not the fucking ark of the covenant."

We started walking again. My ankle was healing, so I could walk a little faster, but the healing took precious energy that I simply couldn't afford to lose. By the time we got to our block, I was weaving like a drunkard and my vision was starting to get spotty. I needed to get home. I needed food, coffee, fuel to replace what I'd burnt up. I could heal any wound except something instantly fatal — like beheading — but not without a cost. And even though I was two hundred years old and even though I lived in this body that entire time and even though this wasn't the first time I injured myself while exercising and ended up almost passing out, I still couldn't seem to remember to stuff an energy bar in my pocket before heading out on a run. I wasn't about to let anything happen until Galen and I were safely inside our apartment. So I forced my feet to keep moving forward.

I was focusing so much energy on one foot in front of the other, I didn't even look up. I wasn't scenting the air. I might as well have been wearing a t-shirt saying, "Victimize me, please." So I didn't smell him until I almost bumped into him.

"Kell? You okay? What's wrong?"

I looked up. And up and up. My eyes were slow to register the visual — never my strongest sense — but my nose recognized him right away. His scent reminded me of fresh baked bread. Not that he smelled like bread, it was just the image his scent brought to mind. A warm smell. One I could wrap myself up in.

That thought more than anything pulled me out of my daze. No way was I wrapping myself up in anything Tony had to offer.

I dug my fingernails into my palms to wake myself up, took a step back to put distance between me and his scent. Then I took in the sight of him, and much to my chagrin, I smiled.

Tony was six foot four, and his shoulders were broad enough that he'd have to turn sideways to walk through the Arc de Triomphe. His hair was cropped close to his head, and his two-shades-darker-than-white skin made you look twice at his green eyes. His mom was an addict who sold herself to buy drugs, so even if I had the guts to ask who was swimming in his gene pool, he couldn't tell me.

He looked like an honest-to-goddess cover of a romance novel, with his worn jeans and faded black t-shirt, his sunglasses and what looked like two days' worth of beard. He looked tense, though, like he was holding himself back from doing something. God, I hoped he wasn't going to hug me.

Suddenly I remembered where I was, what just happened, what I must look like. I remembered him asking me if I was okay, and me not answering. "I'm fine."

"Uh-huh." Those two syllables were so saturated with sarcastic doubt, it's a miracle they didn't fall to the sidewalk with a splat. But he didn't do anything obnoxious, like try to take my arm or help me up to the door. Instead, he knelt down and greeted Galen. "Hey, there, big dawg. You been running her ragged?"

I watched Galen's muscles melt as Tony rubbed him vigorously from head to tail. Galen wagged, snuffled a little and looked up at me as if to agree with Tony that I looked like shit.

"It's not Galen's fault," I said. "I blame the wine. And the faery."

Tony stared up at me for a second before he burst out laughing. "Not even gonna ask. At least, not until we get you some food. And maybe a shower?"

"I just took a shower."

"And then you went for a run. Smart."

"Shut up. Why are you here?"

He stood up, looking like Jack's beanstalk sprouting magically to the sky. Then he sneezed, which ruined the magic. I took a closer look at him, noting how red his nose looked. I was willing to bet that behind those sunglasses, his eyes were bloodshot and red-rimmed. Wisconsin flora wasn't kind to the allergy-inclined.

"Ragweed?" I asked.

"Or something." He turned his head away from me to sneeze again.

"Want to come upstairs?"

"Naw, I'd rather just stand out here."

I narrowed my eyes. "I'm having a bad day. Is that sarcasm or did you really just choose my front yard to work on your tan?"

"No one would choose your front yard to do anything in."

"Galen loves my front yard. Every inch of it."

Tony chuckled, and it turned into a cough. Suddenly, I was less inclined to stand and chat. He needed to get away from the great outdoors for a while. Not that I cared. But I still needed food.

"Come on. I want coffee. You interested?"

"Coffee or sludge from the Black Lagoon?"

As I passed him, I caught the scents of warm plastic and other people's sweat. "Bus or plane?" I asked as I led the way up the stairs.

"Bus," he said.

"You rode a bus from South Dakota?" Horror pinched my voice.

We reached my door, and he stood very, very close to my back as I unlocked it. "Yeah. The POS that Finn gave me finally choked to death on its own exhaust fumes."

I felt light-headed and floaty. I set the keys in their spot on the table by the door and bent over to unbuckle Galen's harness. The room tilted, but I didn't fall over. I glanced at the clock. No wonder I was a wreck. It was almost five o'clock. Almost twelve hours since I ate. Shit.

"Kellan, what's wrong?" Tony's scent took on a sour tinge that I recognized as worry.

"I wiped out on our run. Sprained my ankle. And I haven't eaten for a while." I stumbled toward the kitchen, determined to start a pot of coffee before I died. Which I was fairly sure I was going to do, soon.

"Why don't you sit down and I'll get the coffee?" Tony came up behind me and laid a hand on my shoulder. I jumped like he slapped me on the ass.

"Because it's my fucking apartment and it's my fucking coffee. And I'm not some damsel in distress." The smells he picked up on the bus hit me hard. They were sickly smells. The wolf in me perked up. Not as much fun to hunt as something that smelled like the cold sweat of fear, but sickly made easy prey.

There was a reason I never took public transportation.

"Do you have a change of clothes?" I said.

"Why? You plannin' on ripping these off me?" His mouth curved in his cocky grin, the same one he wore when I first met him, when he came to the Sankhain as an eleven-year old youngling. Eleven-year old Tony told me to call him T-Bone. I told him that unless he wanted to be grilled on a pile of charcoal and slathered in A-1, he should pick a real name. That was the first time I knocked that cocky grin off his face. Now that smile made me pause, made me want to take it in. Damn, I must be more loopy than I thought.

"You smell." I pulled a package of lunchmeat out of the fridge and started munching. Stuffing my face helped curb the craving to hunt.

He raised his eyebrows. "No, you smell. Your scent's probably just rebounding off me."

"No, it's — you —" I couldn't tell him he smelled like prey. Most people didn't react well to being told they smelled tasty. Frustrated at the lack of verbal options available to me, I gave up and returned my attention to Mr. Coffee.

"Do you need me to take a shower, too, or just change clothes?" Tony's voice was soft and gentle, all teasing edges gone.

I thought for a moment. "Do you have your own soap?"

I wasn't as OCD as I sounded. When Darcy borrowed my clothes and our scents mingled, he also showered with my soap and shampoo. It made the sensory experience much more intense. I didn't need to go through that all over again, with Tony this time.

Of course, I never told Tony about the thing with Darcy, the scents and the instinctive response they evoked. So he stared at me like he was offended. "Because you don't want me contaminating your best-the-dollar-store-has-to-offer soap?"

Yup, offended was a safe bet. Apparently, it was one thing to tell someone he smelled, another to tell him you didn't want him to use your soap. Things that seemed so simple to me made humans react so strangely sometimes. "No." Sometimes, I got tired of explaining wolf shit and reminding people just how different I was. "It's just — I'm not sure — um — you know what, never mind."

Tony glowered at me. He leaned against the fridge and crossed his arms over his chest, which made his t-shirt work just a little bit harder. No matter how he smelled, it was very nice to see him. Especially in that t-shirt.

That thought made me scowl, because I didn't even like muscle-bound men. I finished prepping the coffeemaker and hit the little button, making the happy green light turn on. Finn was lean. Broad-shouldered, but not bulky. Tony was...I found myself staring at him too long as I tried to find the right word to describe him. He quirked an eyebrow and his mouth softened into a sort of pre-smile.

"What? I got a milk mustache or something?" he said.

I shook my head and turned away to glare at Mr. Coffee. Mr. Coffee was not Mr. Speedy. "No. Of course not."

"You sure? 'Cause you were staring at me pretty —"

"Well, if you're not going to shower, I will," I said, almost shouting with a sudden, desperate need to tune out his voice. Then I fled the room, leaving behind Galen, Mr. Coffee, and all the other males I simply couldn't deal with at the moment.

Chapter 9

Sometimes when I shower, I realize just how disgusting I allowed myself to get, because of just how good it feels to suddenly be clean and odorless. And sometimes when that happens, I feel bad for subjecting the humans around me to my stink. Then I see my dog wag his tail at me, and I think, fuck 'em. Galen likes me no matter how bad I smell. Of course, Galen also likes to eat goose poop, so, you know, consider the source. But only if you want to.

This was one of those showers where I realized just how rude it was for me to complain about Tony's scent. At least for Tony, no other humans could pick up on the scents he was carrying around. Nobody with nostrils could've missed my malodorous presence. Hell, it was probably one of those where nobody with tastebuds could've missed it.

When I finally turned off the water, even before I stepped out of the tub, I could hear Tony. Sneezing, coughing. That's when I realized I never turned on the air conditioner. The windows were wide open, letting in all the pollen. I wanted to rush out and remedy the situation right away, but I was wet and naked, and men tended to misinterpret such situations. So I dried off quickly and inadequately, and I put on the same dirty clothes I wore before my shower, because they were the only clothes I had in the bathroom and I didn't want to take the time to grab a fresh outfit. I walked casually out into the living room, where Tony sat in Finn's comfortable chair, his head tilted back, presumably to facilitate breathing through blocked passages.

He looked up when I entered. "Why'd you shower and just put your dirty clothes back on?"

I hate it when people ask questions like that. Wiggling their fingers around in the holes in my plan. I recovered quickly. "I wanted coffee."

He sneezed three times in rapid succession. He pressed the heels of his hands against his eyes and rubbed. Something inside me clenched up, seeing him like that. I wanted to touch him. Lay a hand on his forehead, or maybe the back of his neck. The want scared me. I wasn't the laying-on-of-hands type. Instead I started closing windows and turning on the window A/C unit. By the time I returned to the living room, Tony's head was once again resting against the back of the chair and his eyes were closed.

He looked tired, and in the oversized chair, somewhat vulnerable. I couldn't stand it. "Look," I said. "Why don't you call Finn? Tell him the bus broke down somewhere, and you won't get there until tomorrow. You can sleep here tonight."

He opened one eye and peered at me. "You don't have to put me up. I just stopped by to say hi. You weren't answering your phone."

I went into the bedroom to change clothes and so that I wouldn't punch him. On the way back, I stopped at the kitchen to get a cup of heaven. I stood by Mr. Coffee, purveyor of heaven, for a moment, and saw Galen at my side. I didn't even notice him there. I never failed to notice Galen. He was my touchstone. But I didn't know where he'd been. While I was in the shower, while I was closing windows. While I was standing tongue-tied in the living room. Where was Galen that whole time? Shit.

I heard the scuff of boots on hardwood, heard the heavy footfalls that gave me a moment's warning before Tony joined me in the kitchen. "Seriously," he said. "I know how much —" He stopped to sneeze. I went to the linen closet and belatedly retrieved a box of tissues. He accepted them with a mumbled word that might've been "thanks," and took the box into the other room before I heard him open it and blow his nose.

I finally managed to pour myself a mug of coffee. The pot was completely full, which meant Tony didn't help himself while I was in the shower. "You want some?" I said, loud enough for him to hear me.

"Yeah. Sure." Another powerful nose-blow. I winced and hoped he used a fresh tissue. He had a tendency to reuse. I'm all for green living, but some things just shouldn't be recycled. Especially not the way Tony blew his nose.

I took him a mug and sat down on the futon, cradling my mug to warm my hands. I felt chilled, now that my hair was soaked and the AC was blowing. The aroma of the coffee distracted me, the feel of the ceramic in my hands. The coffee was strong enough that the scent raised the hairs on the back of my neck. Who wants to live forever, Kansas asks? I do, as long as Mr. Coffee remains my friend.

When I looked up, Tony was watching me with a smile on his face. That smile made me blush and adjust my posture. "What?" I said.

"Nothin'," he said. "Anyway, you don't have to put me up. I know how much you love houseguests."

He wasn't wrong. Though I was a pack animal, I didn't relish having random people in my living space. But it wouldn't be the first time he stayed with me, and he wasn't bad company, really, all things considered. I watched him quickly set down his coffee mug, just in time to sneeze.

I clenched my jaw. "Your call." I leaned back and forced a sip of coffee past my teeth. "I may not provide all the amenities that Miss D-Cup had to offer. But I've got clean sheets, a queen-size bed, and, with the air on, I've got relatively allergen-free air. Or you could go to camp, sleep on a tiny cot with a fifty-fifty chance of getting sheets, and be stuck in the middle of the great outdoors, also known as Allergens-R-Us. But it's up to you. Just offering you a room at the Ritz instead of the roach motel."

He frowned. "I'm sorry, but just to clarify — which one is the roach motel?"

"I hope you sneeze so hard your head actually falls off."

He laughed, but his face quickly turned serious. "You really don't mind?"

"If your head falls off?"

"Yes, Kellan, that's exactly what I meant." He rested his elbows on his knees and started rubbing his eyes.

I was having a hard time breathing. I wondered if it was possible to have sympathy allergies. "If I didn't want you to stay, I wouldn't have made the offer. I'm not that kind of girl."

He looked up at me. My stomach clenched again when I saw how bloodshot his eyes were. I decided that if he tried to leave before morning, I'd hit him over the head with a rock. If it was good enough for the cavemen. "All right, great, so it's settled, I'm stuck with you. Good. So you go ahead and call Finn, and I'll change the sheets on the bed. If you want to shower, you can..."

I kept babbling. I couldn't seem to make myself stop. Tony watched me with an amused look on his face, which made the babbling worse. "You better call Finn," I finally said, and made my escape.

Even though the sheets were barely slept on, I put fresh ones on the bed. I pulled towels out of the linen closet and went back into the bedroom to shoo Galen away from the bed. Fat lot of good it would do for Tony to stay here if Galen got pollen all over the clean sheets. By then, Tony must've finished his phone call because he wandered into the bedroom.

"So, um," he said, and my nostrils flared at his careful tone. Adrenaline dominated his scent, but when I listened, I could hear that his heart wasn't beating abnormally fast. Ready for a fight, but not there yet. Why? What was going on? I turned to face him.

"What've you been up to?" he said.

"What do you mean?" That acrid adrenaline scent made me tense up. I forced my hands to stay open and loose at my sides, no matter how much I wanted to clench them. Sensing my tension, Galen took up position on my right flank. It took more concentration than I cared to admit to reach out and stroke him reassuringly.

Tony's gaze flicked to Galen before returning to my face. "The last day or so. I've been trying to call."

I didn't want to tell him about my evening with Darcy. I didn't want to know what he thought about that. And I sure as shit didn't want to tell him I refused to answer the phone because I didn't want to hear more about the Mandy Escapades. "Have you? I've been around."

"Really? Didn't you hear the phone?" His voice still sounded neutral, but his scent was inching toward angry. I could understand being annoyed that I ignored his calls, but the tension in the room seemed disproportionately high.

"Guess not. So, I got out clean towels. You can go ahead and use the soap —" Maybe I could distract him with the old soap argument.

"Forget the soap. How can you not keep your phone with you? What if Finn or Janus tried to reach you?"

I was starting to get annoyed. And maybe a tad bit defensive. "They didn't. Not that it's any of your business."

"How would you know if they tried to reach you, if you haven't answered the phone or checked your messages? Unless you have, and you just ignored my calls." Tony's heart rate accelerated, and his scent heated. The urge to shape-shift choked the air from my lungs.

I didn't want to go into the whole thing with Darcy, the dead body and Aza and Mal. I took a deep breath and realized Tony's scent had a different nuance to it. Something both sweet and sour at the same time. I wondered at it, but didn't have time to puzzle it out before he spoke again.

"I was worried about you," he said. "You hung up on me."

"You seemed a little busy." The sarcasm just snuck up on me.

"Well, I wasn't busy the thirteen times I called you. Where were you?"

His pugilistic tone snapped my brittle control. "I was with Darcy. We went to dinner, I drank way too much wine, and ended up sick as a — well, probably with alcohol poisoning." I hated the phrase "sick as a dog." Dogs were nowhere near as prone to illness as humans.

All the heat left his scent. He was flash-frozen, like they do to strawberries. "Darcy. Got you drunk." Why did that seem to bother him so much?

He didn't look like he was breathing, and I was awfully glad that I could hear his heartbeat without pressing my ear to his chest. I knew he was still alive. "Yeah, Darcy. You remember him. Tall. Pale. Likes books. And then this morning, we found a dead body in the backyard, and he helped me bury it." I didn't mention that Darcy went home to sleep in his own bed, in between the alcohol poisoning and the dead-body-discovering.

"You —" He paused, holding his breath. "You found a what? Where?" Tony's voice was still cold, but far from empty. His scent was a curious combo of heat and sourness. Like grilled pepper jack cheese on thick sourdough bread. Damn, I was hungry. "Care to explain?"

I thought he was talking about my current train of thought — grilled cheese. "I really need to eat something." He looked at me funny, and I remembered what we were talking about before images of sandwiches started dancing in my head. "Oh. Sorry, I was — never mind. Yeah, there's a faery named Aza who's taken to leaving me dead things. The way a cat does. Except instead of mice and chipmunks, Aza leaves dead men."

"Aza. So you know who he is? Why's he still breathing?"

"It's harder to kill a faery than you might think. They're quick, and smart, and they can't be killed with guns or steel blades. Just iron. I wasn't carrying any iron when I saw him."

"When you — you saw him?" With each question he asked, Tony's voice got a little bit higher and a little bit louder. It was getting on my nerves, this barrage of question marks. Then he turned away and sneezed. "Fuck!"

Galen twitched, and I felt his chest vibrate with a soft growl. He liked Tony, but like didn't buy forgiveness for cardinal sins like yelling in Alpha's presence. Wrapping one hand around Galen's collar, I backed toward the door. "Towels're in the bathroom."

Tony sniffed, rubbed his face just above his cheekbones — sinuses? — and refused to meet my eyes. "'Kay. Thanks."

I dusted off my hostess hat. "I think I'm going to order pizza. And maybe wings. And maybe some pasta. You want anything?"

He finally looked at me, the look in his eyes almost sad. It made me wish he held eye contact with the dresser. "Whatever you order is fine."

I turned to leave, pulling Galen with me. Just before I closed the bedroom door, I stopped. Without looking back at him, I spoke. "Tony? Good to have you home."

I shut the door between us and went to the living room. The apartment was quiet — maybe Tony decided to take a nap before he showered. I found my cell phone, ordered three pizzas, four orders of wings, and a pound of chicken alfredo. I loved the evolution of pizza places. Pizza was good, but pair it with tiny chicken wings drowned in buffalo sauce? I'm pretty sure that if there is a heaven, they cater along those lines.

I picked up my dumbbells and started bicep curls. Sitting still and waiting like a good little wolf wasn't on the menu.

———— «» ————

I didn't know how much time passed. Enough for the pizza to arrive, for me to eat my fill and box up the leftovers. Enough to get through a Metallica CD and a half. Enough for darkness to fall. Just as I was thinking I should go check to see if Tony was still breathing, I heard the screech of the shower turning on. His shower lasted for three songs, then two more songs passed before the bathroom door opened and I heard footsteps heading to the living room.

I was sitting on one of the folding chairs from the kitchen, with my arm braced against my inner thigh as I tried to lift too much weight with biceps that were just too tired to curl anymore. I was sweating, my arm shook like a virgin visiting death row, and I knew my face was an unpleasant shade of mottled red. The dumbbell was going to win. My bicep just wasn't up to the task.

Tony knelt beside me and put his hand under one end of the dumbbell, steadying it and taking some of the weight. Spotting me. I glared at him, wondering if he was going to revive the weird argument about the phone calls. "I don't need help," I said.

"Oh, stop it. Maybe just once you don't have to turn every little thing into a pissing contest. You've been lifting pretty much this whole time, haven't you?" He put his other hand under my forearm and started applying pressure. Helping me complete the rep.

I knew where he was going, and I knew he was right. That pissed me off enough to finish the rep and lay down the dumbbell with a tiny bit of control. "I stopped to eat."

"So aside from the fifteen minutes it took you to wolf down some food, you've been lifting this whole time?" He sounded smug.

"Maybe. I guess."

"So your muscles are tired and need a rest. Maybe need a little help. That doesn't make you weak, Kellan. Just makes you human."

He must've seen something in my expression, because he grinned. "Well, kinda human."

I struggled to find some dignity in my annoyed you're-right-and-I'm-wrong state of mind. "Fine. But I didn't ask for help, so if you're waiting for a thank-you, you can just go suck an egg."

He pushed to his feet. He was wearing a different t-shirt, a deep green one that said, *I'm not arguing, I'm explaining why I'm right.* "Where's the food?"

"In the fridge."

He was already heading toward the refrigerator. "Mind if I help myself?"

"I said you could have some, didn't I?" I heard the pettiness in my voice, and I clenched my jaw, closed my eyes, and told myself to buck up. "Of course, you can help yourself. While you're at it, bring me one of the boxes of wings. And put on a pot of coffee."

He looked at me. "You didn't say the magic word."

"I don't see how 'fuck' applies here, but if it'll make you happy — fuck."

He chuckled as he dumped the old coffee grounds and started scooping more into a fresh filter. "You found a situation where you couldn't work in the word 'fuck'? Never thought I'd see the day." He poured water into Mr. Coffee and pressed the button. "So tell me about this dead body. That you and Darcy buried?"

Exhaustion swept over me like a hot summer wind. When was the last time I slept? Really slept. Without dreams that chased me into wakefulness. My shoulders sagged, but when Tony placed the cold chicken in front of me, I revived a little. "Is the coffee done?"

"No, seeing as I just started it three seconds ago, it's not done." Tony sat across from me and dug into his pizza. I saw that he chose the one with vegetables on it. He was the only reason I ordered pizza with vegetables. Tony told me once that he never saw a vegetable before he came to the Sankhain Academy. He said he loved veggies and everything they stood for. I didn't think he was talking about fiber. I was pretty sure he meant that vegetables symbolized his new life. But I didn't ask. If he offered, I would listen, but some things you just didn't ask. He finished the first slice. "Are you okay?" he asked.

I blinked several times and chose a piece of chicken. "Fine. Just a little tired."

"Cause you look like you could try out for the zombie chorus on *Walking Dead.*"

I glared at Mr. Coffee. Maybe I should get an espresso machine. Maybe that would be faster. Then I felt bad for considering cheating on Mr. Coffee. "I think I must've missed the debut of Walking Dead, the Musical."

"I meant — you know what I meant."

"Yeah, I know what you meant." And probably, if I stood up and tried to walk anywhere, I'd shuffle around and bump into things, just like a zombie. "You asked me a question before. What was it?"

"About the dead body." Tony took another bite of pizza, but his eyes were glued on me.

"Right, that." I glanced at Mr. Coffee, still taking his sweet-ass time. "I'll give you a thousand dollars to go interrupt the coffee and get me a mugful."

He snorted and stood up. "If you have a dollar fifty on you, I'll be shocked. But I'll get you a cup, if you start talking."

"The body's name was Rick."

Tony stopped halfway to the coffee and stared at me. "Did he tell you that?"

I gave him what I hoped was a withering glance. "No. Darcy told me."

Tony paused as he was pulling a mug from the cupboard. "Darcy knew him?"

"Yeah, he was the ex-wife-beater of one of Darcy's coworkers."

"He was the what hunh?" Tony finally delivered my coffee.

I took a sip. It wasn't strong enough. Probably a shock from a car battery wouldn't be strong enough to make me feel completely alive at that point. "Darcy's friend Dolly's ex-husband who beat her and cheated on her."

He had an unusual look on his face. Like he was thinking really hard while trying to swallow something too large for his esophagus. "Did the faery know the guy had a connection to Darcy, and therefore you?"

I was way too tired for therefores. "Gee, I forgot to ask him. Maybe you should make a list for me, and pin it to my shirt so I don't forget next time."

"Kellan!"

I was also too tired for exclamation points. "What time is it?"

"What?"

I pulled my cell out of my pocket and saw it was only nine-thirty. "I really am old."

"You're not making sense." Tony smelled less frustrated and more concerned. I opened my eyes — when did I close my eyes? — and studied his expression. When he was worried, his mouth turned down at the corners. I didn't like that. Like I made him sad. My hand extended toward him, like I was going to touch him. The surprise of that almost-touch gave me a jolt of adrenaline, waking me back up. "You need sleep," he said.

"That's what the coffee's for."

"No, that's what the bed's for." Tony stood up and walked over to me, like he was going to help me to my feet. That annoyed me. I could stand up all on my own. And even if I couldn't, I'd be damned if I was going to let some man help me.

I deliberately picked up my coffee and took a sip. It tasted sour, or burnt. My stomach rebelled against it before the coffee even arrived. "You're taking the bed. And maybe I'd already be asleep if you didn't keep yakking at me. Ever think of that?"

"Right. It's all my fault you're sleep-deprived and half-dead. I suppose it's my fault that what's-his-name keeps leaving you corpses, too?" He didn't smell mad. He smelled amused. Bastard.

"Aza. What's-his-name's name is Aza."

"Wait a second. Aza. I know where I heard that name. Your mom knew him, right?"

My mouth dropped open a little. Fortunately, it was empty, otherwise I'd have been dribbling all over my shirt. "How the hell do you know that?"

"Faerie lore 101. Ophelia was the instructor."

My mom's association with the acid-breath faery was part of the youngling curriculum. Lovely. I was going to have a talk with Ophelia the next time I saw her. "Fine. Yes. My mom knew him." My shoulders were sagging again. Adrenaline didn't seem to be taking me as far as it used to.

Tony squinted at me and took away my coffee mug. "No more coffee. I'm going to finish my pizza, you're finishing your wings, then I'm going in the bedroom and you're going to the futon, and everybody's going to sleep. Okay?"

I wanted to argue, but I could barely hold my head up. So I picked at one last chicken wing while watching Tony eat his pizza. He ate funny. Not tip-to-crusty edge like most people ate pizza. And not crusty-edge-to-tip, either. He surveyed the slice, then seemed to eat around the bit that had the most toppings on it, saving that for last.

He glanced up as he stuffed the last prized bite in his mouth, and when he saw me watching him, he wiped his mouth like he was worried he had sauce there. "What?" he said around his food.

I didn't want him to feel bad for eating like a little kid. Tony never got to be a little kid when he was a kid. So it was only fair that he be allowed a few eccentricities now. "Nothing. You really do like vegetables, don't you?"

He swallowed. "Yeah. What about it?"

"Nothing," I said again. "I'm going to bed. If you need anything, come get me. Unless I'm asleep, in which case leave me the hell alone and get it yourself."

As I put the remaining wings back in the fridge, Tony squeezed behind me on his way to the bedroom. His front brushed against my back, sending a jolt through me. "Good night," he said.

"Um, yeah. 'Night." I didn't want to feel jolts around Tony. I had too few friends as it was. I couldn't afford to go losing some because I gave into a few good jolts.

Chapter 10

Tony went back to the bedroom, and I opened the futon and laid down. I didn't want to shift into wolf form, not with Tony in the apartment. It just felt funny, like sleeping nude. So unfortunately, I dreamed human dreams.

When I woke up, heart racing in the dark apartment, I thought it was the dream that woke me. Though I couldn't remember specifics, I knew it was a running dream. Running from something. Someone. Running for my life. Plenty of those dreams dragged me awake in the last few months.

I heard the soft scuff of bare foot on hardwood and knew it wasn't the dream. I reached in my pocket, pulling out a blade and rising to a crouch before I recognized Tony's scent. I set the blade on the floor and laid back down, wrapped my arms around my torso to hide the trembling from the overdose of adrenaline. "Didn't I tell you to let sleeping wolves lie?"

"Sorry," he mumbled thickly. He laid down beside me. "I can't sleep."

"So you thought you'd share the wealth?" I rolled over on my side to face him. Galen settled himself against my back, a wall of warmth to lean on. My trembling began to ease.

"Sorry," he repeated. When he started to get up, I considered letting him go. I didn't want to risk any more jolts.

"Oh, who am I kidding?" I reached up and grabbed his arm, pulling him back down on the futon. The wood frame groaned under our combined weight. "It's not like I'm going back to sleep anyway. Wanna watch a movie?"

He held himself very still. "For real?" His voice was hesitant, and I was glad that I couldn't see the look in his eyes that went with that voice.

"No, I'm offering as a cruel joke. As soon as you settle in, I'm gonna light you up with a taser."

"Okay, as long as I know up front." Now, his voice sounded more sure, more Tony. "What do you want to watch?"

I got up to get him a pillow, nabbing the knife from where I left it on the floor and instructing Tony to pick out a movie. I figured if he chose something I didn't want to watch, I'd exercise my veto power. He held up Star Wars. The original, of course, not some crappy-ass digitized wannabe. With a grunt of approval, I took the movie from him and put it in the DVD player.

"You don't have the new ones," Tony commented as the opening tones signaled the start of the best movie trilogy ever.

I stretched out on the futon, this time with Galen curled up against my stomach and Tony behind me. We weren't touching, but I could feel the heat radiating from him and my lungs filled with his scent. I shuddered with the last of the adrenaline shakes. He rested his hand on my shoulder. I froze, then said belatedly, "Star Wars isn't Star Wars without Han Solo. Classic Solo, not the one where they killed him off."

Tony chuckled, and I relaxed into the sound. "Figures you'd like him."

"What are my other options? That fish-headed guy's not too bad, he's got a nice voice. Otherwise, there's just Skywalker, and he's a whiny little bitch."

"He's a great Jedi warrior."

"He's a kid who doesn't have the stones to help his family. He just wants to go out with his friends. Whiny little bitch."

Tony laughed again, cut short by a muffled sneeze.

"Try not to snot in my hair, okay?"

Silence. Then, "You should have mentioned that before."

I raised myself up to gently elbow him in the ribs, and settled back down to watch the movie.

"Hey, Kell?"

I hit pause. Something in his voice told me this wasn't just a request to turn up the volume. "Yeah?"

"Can I tell you something?"

I had the juvenile urge to reply, *I don't know, can you?* But I didn't. "Sure."

"I'm not asking for a new Outside assignment."

"What?" Every youngling wanted an Outside assignment when they graduated. Out in the world, away from the forest. Where the action was.

Cinnamon-sugar filled the air. "I just — that shit in South Dakota was boring. Made a Disney cartoon look like a Tarantino flick. And I missed — home."

I tried to digest what he was saying. "So you want to stay here? What do you want to do? Because I gotta tell you, scut jobs suck."

He snorted. "I'm not looking to clean toilets." After a long hesitation, he continued. "I want to teach." A pause. "Don't say it."

I was relaxing, starting to feel sleepy as the adrenaline left the building. "What? I didn't say anything."

"Whatever you were going to say. Don't say it."

"All right. I won't." Why did everyone always assume I would say something mean? "Don't worry, I would've been lying when I said I thought it was a great idea, you'd be really good at it."

He held very still, barely even drawing breath. "You were gonna say that?"

"Yeah, but like I said, it would've been a lie."

The cinnamon scent grew stronger. He was really embarrassed about something. But he didn't speak. And I knew he wasn't asleep. His breathing was too irregular.

I went on. "I mean, nobody wants an instructor who's engaging, smart, funny. And on the same maturity level as the younglings themselves. None of those things are assets."

More silence. "I thought you were going to give me shit."

"Hmm. I thought I just did."

"I meant —"

"Tony. Don't be a dumbass. You know you'd be a great teacher. But if you ever tell anyone I said any of this, I'll deny it and maim you in your sleep." I picked up the remote and asked, "Was that it?"

"Thanks, Kellan. I mean it." His voice sounded deeper, like he swallowed something very cold. I wasn't sure I wanted to continue the expedition into uncharted emotional territory between the two of us, so I hit "play" and floated away on John Williams' score.

I didn't sleep for very long at a stretch, as Tony kept sneezing and waking me up. In between sneezes, though, I slept better than I had in weeks. I wasn't sure if it was the combined warmth provided by him and Galen, or if their combined scents had a soothing effect on me. But when I thought about it later, I had a feeling it was all of the above and yet something else all together. When I was a cub, my mom, my sisters and I would hunt together. After we gorged ourselves on deer or whatever the prey of choice was, we curled up in a big pile and slept. Mother and my eldest sisters always made a ring around the rest of us. I never felt so safe before or since. Sandwiched between Tony and Galen, I felt safe. I didn't have to be on guard, not completely. That pack thing is the only excuse I have for what happened next.

When I woke up, the movie was over and the DVD menu played the same chords over and over again. The rising sun lit the room with a creeping glow, and my back was pressed against Tony's chest. He was asleep, snoring softly, his chin resting on the crown of my head. One of his arms pillowed his head, while the other was thrown across my middle and his hand laid next to mine in Galen's fur. This should feel weird, I thought. I should get up, go — somewhere. But it didn't feel weird. Instead of feeling trapped under Tony's arm, I found the weight, the solidness, a comforting presence. Like a heavy blanket. The chest at my back didn't block my exit. Instead, it felt thick enough to protect me from anything.

That thought gave me pause. I didn't need protecting. I was not that girl. So, as much as the part of me that was still half-asleep wanted to stay there and breathe in his scent, the rest of me started to freak. I pushed Galen off the futon, which fortunately wasn't a very long fall, and tried to move to the floor without disturbing Tony. I failed.

He opened his eyes and peered at me blearily. When he rolled over on his back, his t-shirt rode up to reveal his abs. Those abs deserved an entire decade of Michelangelo's life devoted to them. I clamped my mouth shut before I started to drool.

"Hi," he said.

"Hi. You overslept." I pointed at the window. Daylight meant Tony couldn't go to the forest. Not until it got dark again. Well, he could walk around the long way, but Finn wouldn't tell him to do that. He'd tell him to stay in town for the day. After all, there was no urgent need for Tony to report to the Academy.

The warm feeling of *pack* pooled just behind my sternum again. I didn't want that. Look at what happened to my pack. Most of them were killed in a battle when I was just a kid. The last member left me so she could join the nocturnes. Friend Tony was safe. Pack Tony was…something I couldn't even understand.

Tony looked at the window and made a noise that sounded like "mmpfft." He glanced at the TV. "Oh, damn. How'd it end?"

No more attachments. No more attachments. For chrissake, why couldn't he pull down his t-shirt to hide those bloody abs? "This time, Luke biffed it. Totally missed his mark, the emperor destroyed the entire galaxy and is now on his way to conquer Earth. They figure he'll be here in another millennia or so, so we should probably start preparing."

Tony turned his head to look at the ceiling, but I could still see his grin. Would it even help if he covered his abs? "If the emperor destroyed the galaxy, how'd he manage to escape?"

No, the abs weren't the problem. Something else, something bigger — metaphorically bigger — was the problem. "Well, the emperor knew it was coming, so he made the jump to light speed at the last second."

"Ah, I see. Makes perfect sense."

"Of course, it does. George Lucas always makes sense." Nothing else did, but you could always count on Star Wars. "Want some coffee?"

He yawned and closed his eyes. "Sure. Wake me up when it's ready."

I stared at him a little too long, then I shook myself and pushed to my feet. "What're you talking about? You're making it. I gotta walk Galen." At that combination of words, Galen perked up, apparently forgiving me for shoving him off the futon. He followed me to the door.

With a soft groan, Tony sat up. "Sorry about last night."

I frowned. "Why? Did you cop a feel while I was sleeping?"

"God, I hope not, because if I did, I don't remember."

I snorted as I snapped Galen's harness in place.

"No," Tony said. "I'm sorry about all the sneezing. I must've kept you up. I shoulda left you alone."

"Actually," I began, then stopped. I wasn't sure I wanted to tell him how good it felt, having him there. I didn't want him to know. That might give him more power over me than I was willing to hand him. "It's okay," I said instead. "If I got drunk off my ass and couldn't manage to sleep soundly, I don't think last night would've been all that restful whether you were out here or in the bedroom."

He stood up and stretched, treating me to another peek of his abs. Damn him. I gave Galen's leash a tug and we left before Tony could get in another word.

It wasn't until I was halfway down the block and heard pounding footsteps behind me that I remembered my encounter with Aza yesterday. And realized I left the apartment without an iron blade. Again. Shit. Quickly, I tried to read the scents in the air as I whirled around.

Tony skidded to a stop beside me, and annoyance bubbled up. Not only had his running up behind me gotten me in defensive mode, but currently, I was blaming him for the vulnerable position I put my dog and myself in. And besides, I was kind of counting on him making coffee before Galen and I got home. He beamed at me, oblivious to my ire. "You guys walk fast."

My breathing was too fast and I couldn't seem to unclench my right fist. "Yeah. It gets us home to the coffee that much sooner. Don't suppose you put on a pot before you crashed our party, did you?"

He trotted out in front of us, turning so he jogged backwards. The goofy grin on his face softened my mood, but only a little. "If you run, the endorphins replace the need for caffeine. Unless you can't keep up?" He turned and took off.

Galen looked up at me. I hadn't intended to jog, but I also couldn't resist the bait. We double-timed it to catch up with Tony, then set a pace just a smidge faster than his. Not that I was competitive, but I made a stadium full of hockey fans look like hippies stringing daisy chains.

Poor Galen's run didn't last very long. Tony's allergies hit hard after about twenty minutes, so we slowed to a walk and turned back toward the apartment. I wasn't sorry to stop running. Walking allowed me to keep an eye out for Aza, and besides, all three of us were pretty well out of breath by that point, as we increased the pace anytime one of us gained a stride on the other. When I banked up enough oxygen to form words, I spoke, although I didn't have enough air to cram everything into one question. "Why'd you come outside? With us, if your allergies are so bad?"

He was having a harder time regaining his breath. He coughed before he spoke. "I wasn't done talking to you."

I shook my head. "Right." I took a short, deep breath. "Since we were never coming back."

"Didn't want to wait." We walked in silence for a while. Tony coughed again before he spoke. "I wasn't just apologizing. For the sleep thing."

It took my O2-starved brain a minute to pick up the long-dropped conversational thread. "Wow. I get two apologies...in one day? Cool."

"You're...easy to please."

"Most men like that."

He laughed, which prompted another cough. I slanted a glance at him, concerned. He didn't look at me, didn't acknowledge my glance, but the embarrassment that tainted his scent with a cinnamon-sugar flavor prevented me from asking if he was okay. Instead, I told him we needed to stop so I could check Galen's feet. The embarrassment grew thicker in the air, so Tony probably knew I wasn't worried about Galen, but he didn't protest.

After I examined Galen's pads, taking long enough that Galen started fidgeting and trying to pull his foot out of my hand, Tony spoke again. "So, anyway." He sounded a little less winded, and a tension that gripped my shoulders, unnoticed until now, slowly let go. "I'm sorry about the, um. The thing. About the phone calls."

The tension in my shoulders returned threefold. I bent farther over Galen's feet, trying to drown out everything but the scent of dog. "The thing?"

"Yeah." Even Tony's hesitation had a smell, an intoxicating cross between the sourness of anxiety and the hot sweetness of embarrassment. "The fight. Thing. Last night. It's none of my business if you want to get drunk with some guy you barely know."

It didn't really sound like much of an apology by the time he got to the end of it. "As opposed to screwing someone whose name I don't even know? At least I didn't exchange fluids with Darcy."

"Exchange — what are you talking about?"

"With Mandy/Amanda — what name did you two decide on in the end?"

He still smelled confused. "Her name's Amanda."

"Hmm. Too bad. I liked Mandy. Especially if she spelled it M-A-N-D-I. Very now."

"Okay," he said slowly. "I'm sure she'd appreciate the feedback."

"Well, you can tell her when you talk to her." My shoulders were tense again. Jeez. I needed a massage.

As he turned his head to look at me, the shift in the air wafted his scent my way. My lungs gulped thirstily. Stupid lungs. "I'm not going to be talking to her," he said, his voice odd.

"Why not? You seemed to like her." Why did I say that? The guy didn't even know her name.

"Yeah, she was nice, but why would I talk to her?"

That made me mad. "So what, you just use women and throw them away? You don't even do that with Kleenex! Fuck. You know what that makes you?" I paused. Tony tried to cut in, but I started talking again, just to monopolize the conversation. "That makes you a, a big giant creep, is what it makes you."

Ooh, yeah, that'll show him. If our last name was Brady and Alice just walked in to break up the fight.

He seemed as cowed as the insult warranted, which is to say, not at all. "We didn't have sex. We just sat next to each other on the bus. She was by herself, she was kinda freaked out by this guy who kept staring at her. So she asked me to pretend to be her boyfriend."

I couldn't process the shift in direction. "But she answered your phone. And she had her shoes off."

"She was trying to sleep. You ever sleep on a bus? It's impossible to get comfortable, even if you're wearing comfy shoes. And she was wearing these high-heeled thingies. So of course, she had her shoes off."

I didn't know what to say. Words completely failed me, so I turned away and started walking again. Behind me, I heard Tony sneeze four times. Four. Who the hell sneezes that many times in a row? My stomach was tight. It wasn't as if I never saw him this way before. Drinking from the Spring ensured he never caught another cold, but apparently, it had no effect on seasonal allergies. And he hated taking pills of any kind, so Simone, our healer, usually had to strap him down to force antihistamines down his throat. So this wasn't a new thing. The difference was, before now, I never cared enough to pay attention.

Not that I cared.

Except I kinda did.

I shook my head violently, buzzing my lips in a cartoonish noise that made Galen's tail wag. By then, Tony caught up with us again. "You sure you're okay?" he said. His voice sounded lower, thicker, with a more pronounced rumble.

Something other than my stomach clenched. I swallowed hard. "Peachy keen, jelly bean." We'd been talking about something. If only I could remember what. When a loud ringing sounded suddenly, I jumped. Tony pulled a phone out of his pocket and I stared at him in disgust. "You brought your phone on a run?"

"Never know who might call." He gave me a pointed look and answered his phone.

"Right," I said to Galen. "Who knows, her name might actually be Mandi this time."

Tony made a choking sound and placed his hand over his other ear to drown out extraneous noise. Like my voice. As he talked, I did what any normal person would do. I listened.

"Yes, sir."

As I listened to Tony lie to Finn about how the bus was fixed and he was almost to Madison, I reflected that if he insisted on talking on the phone while he was with me, the least he could do was give me good eavesdropping material. Bored, I started humming a Godsmack tune and focused on stepping in time with Galen. I heard Tony hang up the phone, but I continued to hum.

Tony interrupted my musical review. "That was Finn."

"Hmm." I'd gotten out of step with Galen, and I did a little hop to get back. Add a tuba and we'd have a parade.

"He said, since it's light out, he doesn't want me to come straight to camp. I'm supposed to wait til after dark."

"Fascinating." I finished my song and switched to The Offspring.

"Sorry to bore you," Tony said dryly. He broke into a run. I stopped, stared in disbelief, before putting on the speed to catch up with him. Thrilled at the happy turn of events, Galen ran at my side with his tongue lolling out.

I grabbed Tony's arm and dug in my heels, dragging him to a stop. Galen hit the end of the leash, almost dislocating my shoulder. "What the fuck are you doing? You wanna stop breathing all together? Because I'm not about to do mouth-to-mouth, you know."

His scent spiked with the peppery heat of anger. "Nobody asked you to."

"So when your lungs seize up and you fall over, I'm just supposed to leave you there?" I was shouting now, stretching my spine to stand as tall as I could without actually rising up on my toes.

He raised his voice to match mine. "I'm not gonna fall over. I'm fine!"

The catch in his voice revealed the lie. "You're not fine, you big dumb-ass! Jesus, get over yourself. The only thing that sets you apart from everyone else with allergies is you're stupid enough to go fucking jogging in the fucking middle of fucking allergy season!"

We were both breathing hard, sweating in the burgeoning heat of the day. And suddenly, looking at him, all big and annoying and vulnerable, I wanted to touch him. If I touched him, would he jump? With all that sweat, would his scent rub off on me? I froze, because I didn't just want to know what he'd do if I touched him. What would he do if I wrapped my arms around his neck, or maybe hooked my leg behind his, so I could feel all that warmth pressed up against —

Galen bumped up against my leg, breaking the spell. I tore my eyes away from Tony, to look down at my dog. He pressed himself against my legs, while giving Tony the evil eye. I forced a lungful of air down my throat, and let it out in jagged gasps. "Come on, big dog," I said. "Let's go home."

Against every instinct, I turned my back on Tony. I resisted the urge to look back at him. By turning my back and ignoring the threat, I sent Galen the signal that I wasn't concerned about our safety. In reality, I was concerned about a lot of things, but I was more than happy to turn my back on those, too.

That was when I saw Aza. A block away, watching us. Aza met my gaze, then pointedly turned his attention to Tony. The threat was clear. I could practically hear Aza's whiny voice. *So this human is special, eh?*

I was so shocked, I dropped Galen's leash. I grabbed it again before my dog could run off, but my hands shook badly. I think part of me held onto the hope that running into Aza yesterday was just a horrible coincidence. But denial was no longer an option in this case. Aza's presence was because of me. And now he knew who Tony was.

I couldn't breathe. My whole body started to shake. Just as I was about to pull a blade and run Aza down and cut him into little bitty pieces — faeries could regenerate if cut with a noniron blade, but just because he could grow it back didn't mean it wouldn't hurt like a son of a bitch — Tony stomped over to me.

For a lot of people, anger pinched their voices, made them high and painful on the ears, but not Tony. Anger forced his voice into such low registers, it was almost inaudible. "Hey. We're having a conversation. What are you doing?"

Fear slid so easily into rage, I almost forgot the fear was ever there. I barely looked at Tony, unwilling to take my eyes off Aza. I dug my house keys out of my pocket and pressed them against Tony's chest. "Go. I'll meet you back at the apartment."

"Like hell. Who is that?"

The stubborn curiosity in Tony's voice made me glance away from Aza. And by the time I looked back, Aza was gone. "Fuck!" I whirled on Tony, too full of adrenaline and emotion to even think about reining myself in. "Why the hell can't you follow directions? Stop distracting me. Go!"

"Sorry to be so *distracting*." His suggestive tone made my fist clench. I actually started to raise my fist, pull it back to punch him in his stupid nose, when the look on his face penetrated my rage-induced haze. He flinched. Because he thought I was going to hit him.

I dropped my arm to my side, suddenly and thoroughly ashamed. "I'm sorry. I — I'm sorry." I couldn't find any other words. The English language was unable to erase the look that came into his eyes for that split second.

Now, his eyes were hooded, his face blank. Even his scent was empty. It was like Tony disappeared, and what stood before me was a hologram. He looked at me for a moment before he walked away. In the opposite direction of my apartment. He opened his hand and dropped my apartment keys on the ground as he went.

I felt sick, actually physically ill. I didn't know how, but I had to fix this. I had to get him to come back. "That was Aza!" I yelled. I winced as I realized that Aza probably wasn't that far away yet, and he probably heard me. But it was too late. And Tony stopped walking and turned around to look at me.

My knees almost went out from under me, I was so relieved. I didn't dare think about where that relief might be coming from. I didn't want to know. I tried to move, to close the distance between us, but I tripped over my feet. I heard Tony's sigh from several feet away, then he was beside me. "Come on," he said. "I think we both need some coffee."

We moved in the direction of the apartment again.

Chapter 11

We didn't speak much on the walk home. When we reached the apartment, I fed Galen while Tony started the coffee. I showered first, and while Tony showered, I stared at the fridge. The pizza and wings from the night before were the only items even remotely fresh. Would Tony want to eat cold pizza for breakfast? Even I didn't find the idea of cold pizza and high-octane coffee very appealing this early. I searched the freezer and found toaster waffles encased in only a thin layer of ice. I scraped off the ice before toasting the waffles. I was out of lunch meat, but I found three yogurts that were only a couple weeks past date. I set the food on the table and waited for Tony to join me.

I pulled out the photos of Finn's dead guy. That was one way to differentiate the two bodies — Finn's dead guy and Darcy's dead guy. Since I didn't know the name of Finn's dead guy.

When Tony came into the kitchen, smelling like his shaving cream, he looked over my shoulder before sitting down. "Is that one of your friend Aza's?"

"Don't call him my friend. And yeah, it is." I shuffled the photos, the world's most macabre deck of cards, piled them neatly and turned them over. I figured the mature thing would be to focus all my attention on the conversation that Tony undoubtedly wanted to have. About feelings and shit. And I felt like I should say the first words, since I was the one who almost hit him. Who made him flinch. "I'm really sorry."

His scent shifted slightly, unreadably, like he was trying so hard not to feel anything and that effort was the only thing I could smell. "It's okay." He didn't ask why I was sorry. He didn't even pretend not to know. I wasn't sure if that was a good thing or not.

"No. It's not okay." I forced myself to look up at him, but the way he was studying my face, the cool set of his mouth was too much. I closed my eyes, so I could say what I needed to say. "I was a bitch. And I'd like to say I wouldn't have hit you, but the fact is, I don't know. I wasn't thinking. About you. I was just — I'm sorry."

He didn't say again that it was okay, which I appreciated. Instead, he said, "What were you thinking about?"

Aza hunting you, I thought. "Aza."

"Uh-huh. Why was he there this morning? Is he stalking you?"

"I don't think so. He usually stalks men." I picked up a toaster waffle. It smelled like wet cardboard.

Tony picked up a yogurt. "This is expired," he said.

"Yeah, but not by much."

His mouth twisted in a disgusted S, and he set the yogurt back down. "We need to get groceries. So what's your plan?"

I scowled. "I don't have a plan, per se. But I'm working on it."

"Could you be more vague? Because I almost have faith in what you're saying." Tony set his mug down heavily on the table, sloshing a little coffee over the side.

The sound made Galen jump, which made my temper flare. "Maybe you could just start doing my thinking for me. Like Finn feels the need to do."

The scent of Tony's frustration was hot like anger but not as dry. "A faery is stalking you and leaving dead bodies as welcome home presents. I shouldn't be concerned?"

"Why should you be? What's it to you?" Maybe for some women, the thought of a man concerned for her welfare might make their hearts skip a beat, or some other romantic bullshit. But to me, it sounded like he thought I couldn't take care of myself. And that made me want to gag.

He stared at me, like a reply was trying to burst out of his mouth and only his clenched teeth kept the words inside. He took a deep breath and was quiet for at least six Mississippis. Finally he said, "You're my friend. I care."

Oh, crap. Why couldn't he spout some sexist shit so I could snarl at him? Instead, his simple words disarmed my righteous indignation. I took a big gulp of coffee while I tried to think of something appropriate to say. Eventually, I decided appropriate was just aiming too high, so I spoke out of my ass instead. "I just found out yesterday that the killer was Aza. And then you showed up and started sneezing all over everything, and I got distracted. So I'm working on a plan. All right? So fuck you."

He cocked one eyebrow. "So it's my fault?" But he didn't smell quite so testosteroney anymore. He smelled sweeter, more amused.

I didn't really like being a source of amusement any more than I liked being something the big, strong man needed to protect. "Yes. So fuck you," I said again, because apparently he missed it the first time.

He picked up his mug. "All right. Sorry."

I didn't know why, but the argument seemed to be over. And I hated not knowing why. I didn't know who won the argument. It was like it just dissipated, like a cloud of exhaust. I felt lost. So I did the one thing that made me feel better when nothing else did. I pulled a blade from my pocket.

The great thing about being in my own apartment was, if I needed to indulge in this particular self-soothing technique, nobody was around to see it. Humans, even younglings, tended to overreact when they saw me holding a knife. Like if I was holding it, that meant I had to use it? Sometimes, it was just for fun. It wasn't like I ran naked through a tent full of Pentacostals or something.

Knowing me as well as he did, Tony didn't freak out. He studied me, his eyes slightly narrowed as if in concentration. "The flinch was just a reflex, ya know."

I hated this conversation, so I started twirling the knife between my fingers.

"I mean, how many times did you beat my ass to hell on the practice field?" he went on, like I wasn't playing Russian roulette with my fingers.

I didn't bother trying to think about it. "I didn't keep count."

"Yeah, well. It was a lot. And I know Finn told you to back off, but you didn't. Why?"

"You pissed me off."

"And you thought I needed to learn something. And you know what? I did." He took a deep breath, like he was fortifying himself. "I learned that violence wasn't just for making people feel small. And that power isn't just for the big and strong."

I didn't point out that, despite my size, as a shape-shifter I was stronger than he could ever be as a human. I also didn't point out that he carried about a hundred pounds of extra muscle on his frame. For once, I just listened. I wanted to know what he said next.

"You don't hurt people for the sake of hurting them. You threaten to a lot, but you never do. You only use violence for a reason. So maybe I flinched, but it wasn't because I thought you'd hurt me. Sometimes, my muscles just remember shit that happened so many times that I can't help how I respond."

I couldn't breathe. I stared at the knife in my hand like I didn't know what it was. He gave me more credit than I deserved. I was pretty sure that some of the times I knocked him on his ass, I did it because he annoyed me. And I was also pretty sure that must put me on the same shelf as the people who hit him before. I didn't know I was going to speak until I felt the words vibrate out of my throat. "I'm still sorry."

It was like he read my thoughts, which creeped me out a little. "Kellan. If I flinched like that on the practice field, you never woulda hit me. You're nothing like Them." I could hear the capital letter in his voice.

My throat was closing. Pretty soon, I wouldn't be able to swallow, and drool would start running down my chin. That image, more than anything, pushed me to my feet. I picked up my coffee mug and carried it to Mr. Coffee for a refill. I might not be able to swallow the coffee, but at least it got me away from the table and the gentleness in Tony's voice.

"So. What kind of guy is this Aza?" Tony came up behind me, reached around me, and helped himself to Mr. Coffee.

I scowled and extricated myself from the threesome. Standing by the fridge with a nice thirty six inches between Tony and myself, I decided I didn't want to talk about Aza right now. "You said something about a food run?"

Thankfully, Tony let me change the subject. "Yeah. Freezer-burned waffles aren't going to hold you for long."

"All right. Any requests?"

"Yeah. No fast food."

I frowned. "So, what, leftover pizza? I figured you wouldn't want pizza for breakfast. Even the kind with vegetables."

Tony rolled his eyes. "No. We're going to the grocery store."

"We?"

"Yes. If I send you, you'll see the golden arches on the way and take the easy way out. All I've been eating the last two months is everything the hot plate has to offer. I want real food."

"What's a hot plate?" I watched him head to the door. As far as I was concerned, this conversation wasn't near over.

"Nothing that should be seen outside a dorm room or a bomb shelter. Come on, let's go."

"No."

He stared at me. "Aren't you hungry?"

"I am."

"So?" More staring.

Stores were horrible places. They were full of people, with all their cacophony of raucous smells and shrill voices. All those people made it difficult to move, almost impossible to run or escape. Add to that the layout of your typical grocery store, with its row upon row of tall, crowded shelves, and the whole spectacle that was the shopping cart...My palms started to sweat and my vision went spotty. I swallowed, tasting bile.

Suddenly, Tony was next to me and his hand was under my elbow. "What's wrong? You sick?"

I swallowed again. "Not yet. I don't do stores."

He was quiet for a moment. The soft scent of his concern burrowed through the pile of anxiety I'd built. I could feel his breath on my cheek as he said, "I'll take care of the shopping. But you need real food. Okay? Kell? Gimme a sign here."

I tried to breathe a little deeper. Gradually, I detected Galen's scent mixed with Tony's. Only then did I notice the pressure against my leg. How long had Galen been leaning against me? I forced myself to pull back from Tony. "I'm okay." I choked out a laugh, dragging my fingers through my hair.

Tony reached out and caught my hand. "You're shaking."

"Well, I'm hungry." I was so not hungry, anorexia sounded like a decent lifestyle choice.

He studied my face with narrowed eyes. "You better come along. No, not in the store," he added quickly as I tensed up again. "We'll stop for fast food along the way, you can eat in the car while I shop." After another moment, he said, "We should bring Galen along, too. Wouldn't want him to get lonely here, all by himself."

I was torn between gratitude that he saw exactly what I needed and unease that he saw exactly what I needed. "Um, okay. I guess that sounds all right."

Before we left, I put on one of my latest creations — a Hawaiian-print shirt with a sheath sewn into each of the side seams. I put my only two iron blades in those sheathes. Most of my blades were steel, because steel stayed sharp longer and pure iron rusted too easily. But when wounded by iron, a faery healed almost human-slow. After seeing Aza twice in as many days, I didn't feel fully dressed without some iron.

After the promised drive-thru pitstop, Tony found a grocery store and parked far away from the door. He pulled the key out of the ignition and looked at the untouched egg sandwich in my hand. Galen was looking at it, too, but I was pretty sure their stares were motivated by different things.

Tony reached out and started tracing circles on the top of Galen's head, then letting his hand drift lower to give him a scratch behind the ear. When he finally spoke, all he did was ask what groceries I wanted. I was so busy watching his hand, expecting him to ask why I wasn't eating my sandwich, I took a minute to change channels. "I don't know. This was your idea." My voice was a little harsher than I intended.

Tony met my eyes with a half-closed gaze. "Okay. Tofu and zucchini it is."

The last time he stayed at my apartment, he also went grocery shopping. He bought zucchini, along with fake crab and other weird things I never would've touched, much less bought. He made a wonderful pasta dish with the zucchini and fake shellfish. I remembered it fondly. But I couldn't just let that comment slide, for fear he might actually return with tofu.

"Jesus, if you want to kill me, just shoot me, please." When he didn't smile, I forced my way past my pride. "I'm sorry." I had to clear my throat before continuing. "This is a very nice thing you're doing. To be honest, I haven't been inside a grocery store for years, so I wouldn't even know where to start. I guess I'm trying to say I trust your judgment."

Surprise lightened his scent. "Where do you get your food?"

"The kitchen at camp."

"Do they know this?"

"Probably somebody does. It's not like I can sneak out of there with a baked ham under my shirt."

"But you never asked for permission, either."

I shrugged. "It's there to eat. What difference does it make if I buy my own food with their money or if I take stuff from the communal kitchen?"

A small smile teased at his mouth. "So all the signs about not stealing food?"

I waved the question away. "Those're for younglings. Not me."

He shook his head. "Must be nice, being you."

"It doesn't suck. So you gonna go buy food or what?"

"What do you want?"

I cocked my head to one side. "I thought we decided on tofu and zucchini."

"Okay." He opened his door and started to get out. Panicked, I leaned across Galen's body, grabbed Tony's arm and pulled him back. He looked at me. "Yes?"

"I just remembered. Tofu's outta style. It's so last year. Let's try real food, okay?"

"If you're sure." When I nodded compulsively, he grinned. "All right. Lots of meat, plus some other stuff so you don't get scurvy. Sound good?"

"Great."

He waited a moment. "You gotta let go of my arm before I can go."

I looked down. Sure enough, my hand was still wrapped around his wrist. "Right. Well, I guess I can let go now. Thanks." Thanks? What the hell?

His eyes were laughing at me, but at least he didn't do it out loud. "You're welcome." Then he was gone. Galen looked up at me.

"What, like you're better at this stuff? You think I'm the cream of the crop. Your credibility's shot, big dog."

He thumped his tail against the seat and gave me a tongue-lolling grin. I leaned over and blew a raspberry on top of his head. He twisted around and planted a slurpee kiss on my cheek. I laughed, and the steady thump of his tail told me he did, too.

———— ‹› ————

Tony took a very long time in the store. As the adrenaline faded, my appetite returned, and I scarfed down the sandwich. Galen and I got out of the truck to stretch our legs. I looked around the parking lot, searching for Aza. Or anyone else who might cause trouble. That was a broad category and, in my neighborhood, included just about everyone. But at least I didn't see Aza.

I knew that the Aza conversation was simply postponed. Tony would want to talk more about him, which wasn't a bad thing. Tony had a good head on his shoulders for a twenty-something male. He made a good sounding board and usually had helpful ideas.

I was beginning to wonder if I should go in the store after him. Make sure Aza didn't corner Tony by the grapefruit. Then I saw him walk out the automated doors. As I watched him walk across the parking lot, clutching three bags in each hand, I discovered a whole new concern. My mouth went strangely dry at the sight of his biceps. And his forearms. Forearms tended to get overshadowed by showier muscles like pecs. But well-muscled forearms evidenced strong hands and wrists, and Tony's forearms were as well-developed as the rest of him.

Galen stopped peeing on a scraggly weed growing through a crack in the pavement, and joined me in Tony-watching. When Tony stopped in front of us, he greeted Galen first. "Hey, bud." He turned to me. "How 'bout giving me a hand here?"

I considered telling him he looked like he was doing *just fine* all on his own, but decided against it. Tony did a nice thing for me without asking anything in return. I took three of the bags, stepped back and let Tony load his three bags first. If I thought it was fun watching him carry the bags, watching him lift them and place them carefully in the truck bed was downright delicious. As

I loaded my own bags, Tony leaned against the side of the truck and looked at me. Like he expected me to say something. Hmm. "Um, thanks."

He didn't say anything, just kept staring at me.

I tried again. "Thanks a lot? I'm really grateful?"

Apparently, I hit the jackpot with that quarter. A smile crept slowly across his face, setting the neon WARNING sign in my brain to flashing. "Yeah?" he said. "How grateful?"

I managed to snort at the innuendo, even though the rumble in his voice made my pulse pound. "You could save my dog from a burning building and I wouldn't be that grateful. But thanks for the food."

He pushed off from the truck and started for the passenger door. "You drive. I'm exhausted. And something tells me you'd rather go into a burning building than a grocery store."

"True. And don't tell me you're so out of shape that a simple trip to the supermarket wears you out."

"It's Senior Double Coupon day." Tony glared at me as he climbed into the truck and started scratching Galen behind the ear. "A guy tried to run me over with his power chair when I took the last box of raisin bran."

I couldn't help but laugh at that visual. "Well, then, you should've just gone for the Cocoa Crunchies."

"Nope. Those were being guarded by the little old lady with the two-ton purse."

I laughed harder. "I'm so sorry. Never realized grocery shopping should come with hazard pay."

"You better believe it." He leaned his head back against the seat and closed his eyes. Then he peeked at me through one cracked eye. "So what sort of compensation do I get?"

I looked up at the ceiling, feigning deep thought. "Well, I would say I'd perform some sort of sexual favor, but since you're so exhausted, I guess that's out."

"Aw, man, I knew I shouldn't've laid it on so thick."

I started the truck. "Live and learn."

"Maybe just let me cop a feel."

"Try it and you'll be pulling back a bloody stump."

With a chuckle, he closed his eyes again. "Home, Jeeves." I growled, and he laughed again. Then he sneezed. "I hate summer. And spring. And fall." He sneezed again.

I glanced over at him before throwing the truck into gear. My chest felt suddenly, suspiciously tight. "All right, sir, as you wish. To home."

On the drive home, I felt frustration build over the fact that Tony wouldn't take care of himself. I parked the truck and turned in my seat, to glare at him over Galen's head. "You know that they make drugs for this sort of thing, right?"

He sneezed. "Kellan, we talked about this. Back off already."

The tightness in my chest exploded. Fine. He wanted to be miserable, I would leave him to it. I didn't have to care if I didn't want to. I leapt out of the truck, waited for Galen to hop down, and left Tony to carry the groceries. I heard a "Hey!" behind us, but I ignored him. I felt like a wretched bitch. But I didn't stop or go back.

I stood by the front steps, letting Galen mark the bushes, while waiting for Tony the Blockhead to make it around the corner. When he did, he didn't look happy. That seemed to be going around. "Took you long enough," I said, and gave Galen's leash a gentle tug. He abandoned his sniffing and trotted up the steps with the contented gait of a thoroughly empty dog.

"You could've helped. This is your food."

I looked at him. His eyes were red and looked itchy. *Don't have to care*, the voice in my head said. *Wretched bitch*, another voice said. And no matter what the voices told me to do, I couldn't seem to alter my heading. "I'm holding the door for you, aren't I?"

The air filled with the nostril-singeing scent of his anger. Maybe not anger, but only about two chili peppers shy.

Galen assumed his defensive position in front of my body. I told him to sit and I looked at Tony. "You coming or what?"

He glowered at me, the force of his glare diminished only slightly when he sniffled. The blasted man even made a runny nose look masculine. *Don't have to care, don't have to care.* I reviewed my options. I could maintain the staring contest, and probably win. But, I told myself, the longer we stood there, the greater the odds that Tony would sneeze and drop the groceries, and I really didn't want to go back to the store.

With a heavy sigh, I released Galen from his sit-stay before moving to relieve Tony of half his burden. His voice held surprise as he said, "Thank you."

"Wow, you almost manage to make that sound sincere," I said as I opened the front door again.

"Sorry, didn't mean to." Coming up behind me, he reached over my head and took the weight of the door from me. His scent was cooling, but a little spice still lingered. It was kind of nice, that little bit of heat. Unexpected flavor, like biting into a croissant and finding it was filled with chocolate. Caught up as I was, I jumped when Tony placed his mouth next to my ear. "Is something wrong? You smell something?"

I swallowed. I could almost hear my mom admonishing me. Stop acting like a cub newly out of the den, Kellan. Getting lost in a scent was kid's stuff. Stepping through the doorway, I cleared my throat to ensure vocal steadiness. Unfortunately, no amount of throat-clearing could solve my sudden lack of vocabulary. "Um, no. I, uh, thought. Well. No."

We went upstairs. When the door to the opposite apartment opened, I jumped again. The ten-years-past-frat-age-but-still-kegging-it guy who lived there glanced blearily at us before squeezing past Tony and going downstairs. "That's your neighbor?" Tony asked, smelling amused.

"Yup." I unlocked the apartment door and dropped Galen's leash as we crossed the threshold. Leash trailing, Galen followed me to the kitchen and, as soon as I set down the grocery bags, stuck his head in the nearest sack. I shooed him away. "Pretty sure there's not a chance in hell Neighbor Bob could pick me out of a line-up, but that's not a bad thing."

"Anonymity has its perks," Tony agreed as he helped me put away the groceries.

"It's less my efforts at anonymity than his fondness for cannabis."

"Whatever it takes."

"Yup."

Abruptly, Tony left the room. I heard a muffled sneeze followed by the sound of very forceful nose-blowing. With clenched jaw and tightly closed eyes, I counted to ten and back down to one. I lost count twice.

Heavy footsteps pulled my eyes open, although not soon enough — Tony was looking at me like I was suddenly orange. "You okay?" he asked.

I opened my mouth to say yes, but his eyes were red and his nose looked raw. "You're miserable."

Immediately, his scent flipped from the warmth of concern to the freezer-burned chill of defensiveness. "If it's bugging you so much, I'll just go."

"Tony." As he tried to move past me, toward the living room and the door, I grabbed his arm. He tried to pull out of my grip, but I latched onto his wrist. Shape-shifter strength was a nifty thing — my grip was awfully hard to break. Galen helped — he planted himself in Tony's path and sat down, eyes glued to the two of us.

Apparently realizing he wasn't going anywhere, Tony stopped struggling and looked at me. "What?" He sounded for all the world like I just denied him his ice cream cone.

Petulance was my wheelhouse. I was very comfortable here. "Overreact much?"

He barked a bitter laugh. "That coming from you. That's funny."

"I don't overreact that much." Even Galen looked disbelieving. "Okay, fine, but that just makes me a better judge of the situation. And you, my friend, are overreacting."

His hands formed fists. I wasn't worried — clenched fists were Tony's equivalent of me holding a blade when I was uncomfortable. He wouldn't hurt me, not over this. I knew what "this" was. But I couldn't pretend his misery didn't bother me.

"I don't need drugs," he said. The way he said *drugs* made me pause. So much pain in that little word.

His jaw was clenched, and the muscles under my hand almost vibrated with tension. I could hear his heartbeat, pounding so hard from the adrenaline that drenched his scent. I took it all in, and the strangest thing happened. From some place that I would have sworn didn't exist, an impulse rose up. I let go of his wrist and reached up to touch his cheek. He jerked, making me jump. When he looked down at me, I saw all the things I expected — fear, surprise. What I wasn't expecting was heat. The adrenaline hid it from me, that dark, rich scent of desire. But it was there, and oh, god, did it smell good.

Chapter 12

Desire smelled like chocolate. When Finn was horny, he smelled like chocolate so dark and bitter that it feels chalky on your tongue. But Tony. Tony's scent made my knees weak, my pulse jump, every bloody cheap romance novel cliché. He smelled like chocolate cake, not a mix from a box, oh, no, chocolate cake from scratch, deep, dark, only able to eat one piece per sitting because it was so rich kind of cake. But not just that. The cake was topped with dark chocolate frosting, and drizzled with thick, dark chocolate sauce. It was the greatest smell in the history of time, and it scared the bejeebers out of me.

Because this was Tony. *Tony*. And it was obvious and made perfect sense and made no sense at all, because this was Tony. Obnoxious, infuriating, deep-pain-in-my-ass Tony. Gentle, insightful, good-to-my-dog Tony.

I didn't know how to have sex with someone I liked. I spent the last two hundred years fucking Finn. Our relationship only worked if neither of us spoke. But Tony? I was going to fuck this up in so many ways. It was a question of when, not if. And then I'd lose Tony forever.

I backed away so fast that I rammed into the doorway, smacking the back of my head on the corner. Pain blasted through my skull, clearing away any and all thought. Thank the goddess for sharp-cornered doorways. Except, after that one blissful moment of mind-numbing pain, I was still stuck in that kitchen, and now Tony was touching me, examining the back of my skull for leaking brains. I tried to take a deep centering breath, but deep centering breaths work better for people with normal olfactory receptors. All I got was a nose-full of Tony's scent, which still smelled like chocolate cake, but his concern made it warmer, like somebody warmed the cake in the oven to make it all the more sweet.

I had to clear my throat twice before I managed words. "I'm okay." He didn't back off. I needed him to back off. "Tony, I'm okay."

"You're bleeding." His gently probing fingers made me whimper. That, finally, made him pull back. "Sorry. Did I hurt you?"

"No, you poking around my bruised scalp felt good." Actually, I kind of enjoyed it, but that was only because I was twisted.

"Sorry," he said again, so softly, it was more of a rumble than a word. He was looking at me, and I wanted to look away, but I was caught in his tractor beam. That gaze pulled me toward him, when everything inside me screamed, RUN AWAY! Women in my family had sex for procreation and/or pleasure. We never slept with men we were in any way attached to. I half-broke that rule with Finn, making him a habitual partner, but I could justify it because once he zipped it back up, we didn't like each other. But Tony...

"Do you have a small penis?"

I had no idea where the question came from, and apparently, neither did Tony. He squinted and cocked his head to one side. "What?"

Shit, now I had to explain myself. So I went with the tried-and-true method of open your mouth and see what comes out. "Well. It's just that, you know, you hear all these stories. About steroids and what it does to your, you know. And so I just was wondering." Oh, yeah. That worked really well.

Tony pursed his lips. He smelled amused and — oh, joy — still turned on. "I won't take a Benadryl. You really think I'm juicing?"

My cheeks were on fire. Silence would definitely be the better part of valor. So, of course, I spoke. "Well. No, but since I already asked. Do you? Have a small, you know."

He leaned toward me. "No. From what I've been told, my 'you know' is pretty nicely sized."

He was so close, filling my senses, overwhelming me with sheer presence. I tried to keep my consciousness upstairs instead of down. "Ah. Well. They might've just not wanted to hurt your feelings."

His shoulders shaking with a silent chuckle, he placed his lips on my temple. "Thanks for the vote of confidence. Now please shut up."

"Why?" Never before did I want to hear the answer to a question and also sincerely hoped he wouldn't answer at all.

He didn't answer. He just kissed me.

It wasn't the first time I kissed Tony. But the first time, we did it to play a role, not because we wanted to. Much. This time, this was different. This time, I didn't want to punch him afterwards. This time, I didn't want there to be an afterwards. I wanted to kiss him until I dropped dead of suffocation. I wanted...

To be taller. Breaking contact as little as possible, I hooked my fingers in the waist of his shorts and pulled him back into the kitchen. I backed myself up to the counter and hopped up, freeing up my legs so I could wrap them around his waist.

Even as I put my legs around him, though, I sensed Tony hesitate. He was too still, and a little bit of that gooey chocolate scent faded away. I frowned at him, tried to get him back in the game by letting my hand wander toward his crotch. He caught my hand before I got close, and my frown deepened. Had I misread his scent? I didn't misread that kiss. Not even possible. But Tony just stood there, looking at me. He raised his free hand to touch my face, brush my hair back and tuck it behind an ear. The softness of that touch paralyzed my lungs. I felt something like fear at that touch. "Don't do that," I said.

He ran his thumb down my jawline and brushed my lips. My lips parted of their own accord and wrapped themselves around the thumb, and I felt a pulse thrum through me like I stood too close to a bass drum. "Don't do what?" Tony said.

Huh? It took me a second to remember what I said. "Don't do the gentle thing. Wolves like it rough." To illustrate, I tightened my legs around him and scooted to the edge of the counter so I was pressed against his groin. I pulled his t-shirt up to expose one of his nipples, which I took between my lips while making a grinding motion with my hips. I worked both nipple and groin until, with a groan, he relaxed against me.

Finally getting into the spirit, Tony placed his hands on my butt and repositioned me against him. With a firm hand under my chin, he pulled my head up to kiss me. Not for long, though. Tugging my lower lip between his teeth, he pulled away and moved his mouth to my neck. With tongue and teeth, he worked the sensitive spot where my jugular met my jaw. That was my spot, *the spot*, that sent me reeling. The cross between pleasure and pain, the danger of, with just a little too much pressure, breaking the skin and spilling my blood. I trembled and wrapped my legs tighter. Unable to stand it, I ducked my head to find his mouth with my lips.

I yanked off my Hawaiian shirt and tossed it away. The blades in the shirt made a clanging sound as they hit a folding chair in the dining area. Tony helped me pull off my tank top, and I heard seams ripping. Next came my sports bra. "Jesus, you wear too many layers," he said. Every once in a while, he would pull back, sniffle, rub his nose. But his allergies seemed to be fading into the background. Watching me, he lowered his mouth to my breast, gently pulling the nipple between his teeth and biting down.

"Oh, fuck," I said, more of a prayer than anything I uttered in over a century. My hands went to his t-shirt, trying to pull it up over his head.

His hands pushed mine out of the way and so I went to work on my shorts. Damn, I was going to have to pull away from Tony to take the shorts off. "Here," he said, and placed his hands under my armpits to lift me up.

I pulled my legs from around his waist and slid my shorts and underwear down, letting them fall to the floor before wrapping my legs around him again. I helped, with impatient hands, to free him from his shorts and guide him toward me. "Now. God, now."

He placed his hands on my wrists, forcing me to be still. "Well?" he said.

I stared at him, confused. He glanced down at his penis, then back up to my face, his eyebrows raised expectantly. Finally, I remembered my earlier question. "Lives up to the hype. So far. Now fucking put it inside me."

Scent musky with masculine pride, he yanked on my waist, closing those few inches so that we were pressed against each other. He pulled his hips back so he could maneuver. I started to lower my head, to run my tongue over those much-admired pecs, but he gripped my shoulders, drew my gaze back to his face. His voice was as dark and husky as his scent. "I want you to look at me. I want to see your face."

I couldn't breathe. I tried again to look away, to focus on his body, that beautiful, sculpted body. But it was too late — I'd been reminded that it was Tony. And with that came complications I didn't want to be saddled with. Wiggling my hips, I tried to force him inside me. If he would just fuck me, then everything would be normal.

Tony wouldn't let me force it. He held fast, and I lacked the leverage to override him. "Kellan."

I closed my eyes, trying to get back to where I'd been. Heat, passion, sex. I didn't have to look at him. But he wouldn't let me do it my way.

He let go of my waist, and he raked his nails down my back. They ran over the bumps of my scars, bringing up remembered pain to mix with the new. It stole my breath in a new way, and my eyes flew open, flew to his face. He smiled a softly satisfied smile. "Thank you," he said, and thrust inside me.

I cried out in surprise. He was big, big enough to stretch me. But before I could get bored of the feeling, he pulled back out. He waited, on the edge, touching me, but not entering. My hips worked, trying to get back to him. Once again, he held me still. I started to tighten my legs. If I just used a little more strength, I could...

He grunted. "Try not to break my back."

I stopped moving and looked down at my legs. Shape-shifter strength. "Well, hurry the fuck up." I angled my pelvis, brushed him against me. Without releasing my hips, he dipped his head down to intercept my gaze. When I was once again looking at his face, he pressed himself a little harder against me. Desperation drew a whimper from my throat. "Fuck," I grunted, and reached down and grabbed him.

He gasped. I watched him breathe, watched his eyes glaze, knew that I was the one who made him feel this. His grip on my waist weakened, and I moved, taking him inside me, hard and fast. He tried to pull out again, but I wasn't having any more of that. My show, now. I tightened my legs and held him inside me, the tip of him so deep, it hurt, my body so full, there was no room for air. Now I made him meet my gaze before I allowed him to move. And when I finally loosened my legs, we worked together, finding a rhythm. And when I came, it was so strong, I almost passed out.

When my vision finally cleared, the top of my head was pressed to Tony's chest. My legs were still wrapped around his waist, and the edge of the counter was making a permanent indentation in my butt cheek. His hands pressed down on the counter, the remaining strength in his arms the only thing between us and the floor. Semen leaked all over my legs, and a slight tremor took hold of both of us, making movement seem unwise. However, that tremor also told me that he couldn't hold my weight much longer, so I carefully raised my head. "I don't think I can move my legs."

He laughed, a hoarse sound that sent another bass-drum vibration through me. "If I move, I'm gonna fall over."

"Okay." I thought for a moment. The gray cells took their time. "I'm gonna place my hands here, like this." I set my hands on the countertop, bookending his. "I'll unwrap my legs, and you can move. Sit down, fall over, whatever. Okay?"

It worked. I leaned back against the cabinet behind my head, and Tony moved to stand beside me so he could lean against the counter. "Next time, we're doing that in a bed," he said, his voice still deep and hoarse.

"Next time? My, my, somebody's optimistic." I was teasing — I was already wondering how long it took humans to recover from something like that. I figured I'd be ready again in about fifteen minutes. But first — "I'm hungry."

He swung his head to look at me. A tired half-smile quirked his lips. "Well, we just kinda made a mess of the kitchen, so..."

"Damn. You're right. You're gonna have to clean the kitchen now."

"I'm gonna? How do you figure?"

"Well." I slid down off the counter, pleasantly surprised when my legs took my weight. "First of all, I wasn't the one who spilled goo all over the place. Second, I need to shower and get said goo off me before it dries too much. And third, it's definitely to your advantage to get the kitchen cleaned and get me fed." I moved to stand in front of him, trailing my fingertips down his chest and stomach to stop just above his groin. "You want me to keep my strength up. Don't you?"

He caught my hand before it wandered any further south. Then he lowered his mouth to mine and kissed me, biting my bottom lip before he pulled away. I ran my tongue over it, tasting blood. My heart started to pound again.

The satisfied look on his face told me he knew exactly how that kiss made me feel. "Yeah, wolf. I guess I do."

"Don't start something you're not ready to finish." I ran one finger down the shaft of him, pulling a choked laugh from him. I turned and walked away, almost tripping over Galen. He was lying half-in, half-out of the kitchen, where he could keep an eye on me without being underfoot. He didn't even bother to raise his head, simply tracking my movements with his eyes.

I stopped suddenly, all hints of playfulness fleeing. When I had sex with Finn, I always had to make sure Galen wasn't around for the finale. He'd start barking, or try to get in between us as soon as we pulled apart. I think the fact that we usually started fighting the minute the orgasm faded put a bad taste in Galen's mouth. But now, not a peep, not a movement, not so much as an ear twitch. The fact that this wasn't just another lay didn't hit home, it got power-driven into my solar plexus with so much force, I felt a physical ache. This was bad. Maybe not right now, maybe not today, but someday, this whole thing was going to blow up like a man who just ate two pounds of brussel sprouts.

"Kell?" Tony was there, his naked body brushing up against mine. The air-conditioning raised goosebumps on him as the sweat dried on his skin. I could feel his goosebumps. Jesus. I jumped away from him like he hurt me. He cocked his head to the side, looking at me with all kinds of naked concern. He reached out his hand, maybe to touch my face, but I jumped away again. His scent changed then, went blank and cold like the air right before a January icestorm. He looked the same, but his scent told me something shifted inside him. "You okay?" he said.

No. The bellboy just brought up my baggage and buried me under it. But thank you for asking. "Yeah. I'm fine. Better go shower." And I walked away before he could call me out on the lie.

——— «» ———

I couldn't believe I just fucked Tony. Except it wasn't fucking. That was the problem. He made me look him in the eye. And I made him do the same thing. And it was Tony, who was the closest thing I had to a best friend, now that Mal was gone. If I fucked this up, who did I have left?

Galen knew it wasn't fucking. And Galen was happy about that. So why wasn't I? Because like I said, fucking was my normal. This — whatever it was — wasn't normal at all. As I rinsed the last of the soap off my legs, I heard the bathroom door open and caught Tony's scent. I felt a mix of anticipation and anxiety. Would he join me in the shower? Did I want him to? I ducked my head under the stream, turning my face upward so I had to focus on not inhaling water. With a resigned sigh, I turned the water off.

Tony was leaning against the closed door. He was fully dressed — he must have cleaned himself up in the kitchen. "You could've taken a shower," I said. My words felt and sounded lame, like a boneless limb.

His eyes roamed over me and I almost reached for a towel. That glance, combined with his scent, a combination of desire and something darker (self-disgust?), made me feel self-conscious. Exposed. "Even better wet," he said.

I looked down at myself. I didn't have a complex or anything — I knew I had things to offer a partner — but beautiful, I wasn't. I was skinny and angular, with breasts that were smaller than most of my muscles. Tattoos covered a good portion of my shoulders and arms, and the scars outnumbered the tattoos two to one. I was a badly-put-together voodoo doll. "I didn't know allergies caused blindness."

His mouth twitched with a sickly smile. "It's not always about what you see with your eyes."

I never heard a human say something like that. Another shifter, sure. I could even imagine Janus saying something along those lines. But not a human. And not about me.

He pushed away from the door, opening it to let the steam escape. "I should get going," he said. "There's a pasta dish in the oven, it'll be done in about twenty minutes. Don't eat it straight out of the oven. Let it cool first."

He was leaving? Did he sense my little freak-out after I noticed Galen's non-reaction? Of course, he sensed it. Tony was as intuitive and empathetic as I was insensitive and sarcastic. And now, he was leaving. Part of me wanted to speak, to tell him not to go, but I didn't. Inside my stomach, the butterflies were rather frenzied, and they got worse every time I looked at him. I wasn't the fairy tale girl. I was the monster that Grimm found so compelling. And monsters didn't have nice, pretty relationships. We had monstrous ones.

Tony walked away, and, despite my best efforts, my feet insisted on following him. I caught up to him two feet from the apartment door. Grabbing his arm, I stood there, naked, staring up at him, dripping large amounts of water on my hardwood floor.

He looked down at me, eyebrows raised. His gaze flicked to the floor. "You're making a mess." He might've been talking about the water. Then again, he might not.

I wanted to tell him to stay. Instead, I said, "If it was blood, I'd be worried. Blood on hardwood's a pain in the ass. It stains."

Raising his gaze to the ceiling, he shook his head. "You ever wonder what normal people talk about?"

"No. From what I've overheard, they're boring as hell." I watched him stare at the ceiling for a few beats too long. When he looked back down at me, his scent was empty, bland. Just skin and sweat and the scent of his laundry detergent, nothing personal. Tony was standing right in front of me, but he was really somewhere else. He was already gone. I stopped trying to talk, stopped trying to stop him.

"I gotta go." As he spoke, I just nodded. Nod, nod, nod. "Sorry I can't stay for dinner. Lunch. Whatever. I'm gonna head to the forest, take the long way around. The sooner I get there, the sooner I can get my next assignment." He reached out and tugged my hair before he walked out.

I stared at the door. Then I looked down at Galen, who was at my side, alternating between looking up at me and looking at the door. Waiting. Waiting for Tony to walk back in.

I started to take a deep breath, stopping short when I got a nose-full of Tony's scent. He had the capacity to be the most vital human I ever met. Full of life. But sometimes, all that life drained away. No, not drained away. Fled, hid behind a door that he locked tight to keep it safe. Safe from me, and the pain I might cause him. That was why he smelled so empty. Because he forced himself to feel nothing at all.

I rubbed my breastbone, trying to ease a sudden tightness there. Tony chose to walk through a mosquitoey marsh rather than stay here with me. Fine by me, I told myself. Sex without strings. Like Doctors Without Borders, except less socially conscious. "A beautiful thing, right?" I asked Galen. He gave up on the door and gazed up at me. "That's right. You and me, kid. That's the way it is."

I rubbed him up and down, thumped his ribs and made his tail wag. That's the way it is. So why did I feel like I had more strings attached than Pinocchio and his whole unhinged family?

After I dried off, dressed, and ate — Tony's ziti with meat sauce and at least four different kinds of cheese was delicious, damn him — I took Galen outside. Maybe I didn't know a relationship from a battleship, but I had bigger problems. Aza was out there, wandering my neighborhood, popping up in my life like the world's deadliest zit. I was sick of surprise visits. Surprise visits, like Tony showing up yesterday. No. I shook my head violently. I refused to think about him. Aza. Aza was an important thing. Maybe if I walked around the neighborhood long enough, Aza would find me and I could kill him. Killing something almost always made me feel better.

Focus on the positive.

First, Galen and I walked to the spot where the first dead man was found. The crime scene tape was gone. The only visible sign that something violent happened was a small cross made of Popsicle sticks held together with band-aids. I smiled. My neighborhood had heart, if you bothered to look for it. Of course, that little cross would fall prey to a band of roving teens who would amuse themselves by stomping on it, but still. Heart.

The smell of blood still lingered, as did the smell of excrement. They'd stick around for a while, until they finally got buried under snowdrifts this winter. Even in spring, this area would smell different to me. Richer, more earthy. Blood makes the grass grow, long live the king and all that.

Maybe I could add Aza's blood to the collection and turn this into the healthiest grass in the county. The thought made me smile as I smacked my lips to get Galen's attention and started walking again.

The trouble with walking a dog was it didn't require full use of a person's brain. If you needed an activity to stimulate thought, dog walking was always a good option. If you were looking to avoid thinking, dog walking was a shit option, every time.

Why did Tony leave? I knew I was acting weird when I left the kitchen to go shower. But Tony knew me. He knew I had intimacy issues, didn't he? Did he? We never really talked about that. But come on. Anyone who could spend over a century fucking Finn the Fink had to have major intimacy issues. You didn't get into bed with someone like Finn because you loved yourself. You did it because you couldn't separate beauty from pain, and because some small part of you thought you deserved to be treated like an idiot.

You did it because you were damaged. Tony was smart enough to figure that out, right?

I asked Galen. He looked up at me while he was lifting his leg on a lamp post. I got the impression he was a little annoyed that I was disturbing his moment. I sighed. Maybe it wasn't about Tony's smarts. Maybe even someone as smart as Tony had baggage heavy enough to distract him from his brain. Of course, he had baggage. I knew he had baggage. But he made living look so effortless, sometimes I forgot just how heavy that baggage must be. Maybe me pulling away from him after the world's most amazing orgasm triggered something for him. Or maybe just having sex, having an experience like that triggered something. Or maybe I did something or said something during sex that gave him a flashback, and even now he was tormented with memories and —

A huffing sound and a cold nose against my leg pulled me out of my head. I realized we were standing still in the middle of the sidewalk, and I was panting like we just ran a long way. Because we did — I was standing in front of my apartment building again. I looked down at Galen. He was staring at me with too-wide eyes, like a horse about to kick. I forced a deep breath down my throat, and knelt beside him, massaging him to calm us both. I started at his ears, and worked my way down his spine, over his ribs and back to his rear end. I felt the bone and muscle and deep, thick fur under my fingers, and began to breathe naturally again.

A sudden breeze wafted a scent to me, and I stood and turned to face Raoul. I was grateful for a familiar face, a chance to step outside my own thoughts. "Hey," I said.

Raoul stopped a foot away and waited for Galen to approach him. It was a familiar dance, and one I always appreciated. As soon as Galen sniffed Raoul's hand and leg, and Raoul greeted him with his usual, "And h'lo to you, too, sir," the shady gentleman turned his attention to me. "You all right?"

My stomach lurched. If Raoul noticed I was rattled, anyone could've noticed. Anyone, like maybe Aza. I needed to get a grip. I rolled my shoulders back and put on my most dazzling smile. "Yeah. Why do you ask?"

"You just ran past me like the hounds of hell were on your ass."

And he followed me over here? To make sure I was okay, or to do something else? Chivalrous or creepy? It was amazing how close the two concepts could appear. I forced a laugh. "Just realized I forgot to pay the electric bill. I wanted to get home to pay it before they shut off my power."

The carefree flirt façade cracked to show something underneath. "So you decided to stop short outside your apartment and give your dog a rub-down?" His voice was different, not the slow easy drawl of Raoul, but a clipped, slightly lilting cadence. "You should be more careful."

My hand twitched toward my pocket and the knife hidden there.

"No need for that," he said, his voice once again Raoul, but I wasn't soothed. "All's I'm saying is, a woman like yourself should watch her back."

Maybe I imagined it. Maybe the change I saw wasn't real. But something in his demeanor set my hackles on end, and I couldn't force my voice to be as casual as his. "I got my back covered, thanks."

Raoul took a step closer to me, and my tension increased tenfold. Galen picked up on it and started to growl, a low rumbling sound that belonged in a Stephen King novel more than in my dog's throat. Then something happened that almost made me pee my pants. Raoul's eyes, his dark brown eyes, flashed bright, glowing green as he looked down at Galen. "Hush now, friend," he said in a voice that sounded like wind chimes.

Galen met that gaze, stopped growling, and plopped his butt on the ground. I stopped breathing for just a second before pulling one of my throwing knives. I hid all but the tip in my hand as I reached up and placed my hand on his neck. To a passerby, it might've looked like a loving caress, but in reality, I held the edge of the blade poised to slit his throat. My voice was a mere breath. "What the fuck are you and what did you do with Raoul?" He raised his hand, and I moved the blade, nicking his skin. "That's your one and only warning. Next time —"

I broke off as the scent of his blood hit me. Honey and clover. I knew that scent. It was the same smell as Aza's blood when I punched him and broke his face. It was faery blood. My breath caught as reality slid into place with a heavy click. Raoul was a fucking faery. Shit. My steel knife — not iron, why the fuck wasn't I carrying an iron blade? — wouldn't do a damn thing to help me.

Chapter 13

"Yes, little wolf," he said, his voice a disturbing cross between the familiar Raoul and the windchimey fey. "Now, since we both know that baby pigsticker won't do you any good, how's about you give us some breathing room?"

I stayed where I was, debating. I could still slit his throat. That would cause a scene and allow Galen and me time to get away. But where would I go? Back to the forest, to hide in the tree branches and let faeries do whatever they wanted with my city? Fuck that. And if I wasn't going to run, I might as well gather some information. I stepped back and stared. God, his glamour was good. Not only did he look one hundred percent human, he even smelled human, on the outside, at least. He smelled like the ugly parts of humanity — sweat, cigarette smoke, hot dogs. I couldn't imagine a faery actually smoking cigarettes, much less deigning to eat hot dogs. As I looked at him, I just had to know. "Was Raoul ever real, or was it always you?"

"What is real? But as you ask so nicely," he said smoothly, placing a hand to the already-healing cut on his neck, "it was always me." He smiled that obnoxious, arrogant smile of the fey. Faeries believed they were better than humans, the superior race. Humans were like the nifty little statues in the Monopoly game, a source of entertainment to be used, played with, sometimes even fought over or taken home to add to the collection. But always lesser. Hence, their obnoxious, arrogant smiles.

I felt cold and nauseous and a little like I wanted to cry. I didn't like a lot of people, but I liked Raoul. I felt like my favorite uncle just died. And what if he was lying? What if this faery killed Raoul and took his place, to help Aza with his vendetta against me? What if this faery was Aza in disguise? He didn't smell like Aza, but he didn't really smell like Raoul anymore, either. His scent was cleaner, sweeter. Like cherry blossoms. And Aza's scent was more like the dry, brittle smell of fall leaves crunching under boots. No, I didn't think this was Aza. But that didn't mean they weren't working together.

As I panicked, the Thing That Wasn't Raoul kept talking. "He wants your blood." He? Was he talking about Aza? "He always has. You —" The Thing That Wasn't Raoul stopped as a pair of teenagers shouted their way past us. "Now, I s'pose that's enough talk for t'night. You just be careful, girl." He flashed his teeth at me and started to walk away.

"Wait! Are you helping him? Are you in cahoots with him?" I didn't think I ever used the word "cahoots" before. It felt like just about the stupidest thing I ever said, and that's a pretty stiff competition.

The Thing That Wasn't Raoul turned around and looked at me, his head cocked. "How could you ask me such a thing, girl? You know I only ever been on your side."

He left, and I let him go. I couldn't stop him, not without iron and not with my mouth hanging wide open. I didn't move, I didn't even breathe until he reached his corner and struck up a conversation with another man. I found myself staring at the other man, wondering if he could be Aza with a new face. Or if he was yet another faery, if my whole neighborhood was infested.

When I finally gave up my pointless wondering and tore my gaze away, I skewered Galen with a glare. "Thanks for nothing." He stood, shook himself, and started pulling me toward our front door. But I wasn't done with the lecture. "You know, I take you in, I feed you, I give you shelter. But a few sweet words from a freaking faery and you leave me hanging. Thanks a lot."

On the way up the stairs, I continued to grumble, but I couldn't really blame Galen. Some fey had power over animals, and obviously, Raoul was one of them. It made me wonder about my interactions with him in the past. After all, I was as much animal as I was human. Did he play me as easily as he played Galen? Was all that charm and likeability nothing more than faery bullshit? The thought shook me, more than I cared to admit. I didn't want to be played anymore. I'd been played my whole bloody life. By Janus, by Finn, by my own twin sister. I wasn't about to be played by an overgrown pixie.

Damn it all, I liked Raoul better when I thought he was a drug dealer.

I should go to the forest, tell Janus and Finn of this revolting development. But it was light out, and I would have to take the long way around to the far end of the forest, and that sounded like torture. Feeling disheartened, I was suddenly so exhausted that I decided to take a nap. I didn't even take the time to shape-shift. I stuck the first disc of the *Lord of the Rings* extended edition in the

DVD player and lay down on the futon, Galen stretched out against my torso so that when I rolled over on my side, I had my face in his fur. I fell asleep before Bilbo finished his musings on hobbits.

I dreamed, of course, but this time, instead of Mal and an army of nocturnes chasing me down, it was Tony and an army of hobbits. It might've been funny, except Tony had bloody fangs and the hobbits all had red eyes, and it was surprisingly terrifying, all those little people with hairy feet bearing down on me with their glowing red eyes. I jolted awake to find the apartment dark and the LOTR theme song playing on the DVD player, helping to cement the image of Demon Hobbits in my mind.

I sat up. "This is probably why they say never to fall asleep watching TV," I told Galen. "You end up with demonic hobbits dancing in your head."

Galen yawned and hopped off the futon. I turned off the TV and wandered into the kitchen, where Galen was slurping up water. That sounded like a good plan, so I filled a glass for myself. My hands only shook a little from leftover adrenaline. Yippee.

I needed to talk to Janus about Raoul. I needed some advice, some perspective from someone who knew more about faeries than I did. After feeding Galen and eating some cold ziti out of the Tupperware, I checked myself to make sure I was adequately armed and dressed. I put the Hawaiian shirt back on, since that had the iron blades in it. I grabbed Galen's harness, slapped it on him, and vamoosed out the door.

I pulled into the Sankhain parking lot at two minutes to nine. The forest itself had about as much air movement as you would expect a forest older than Methuselah to have. The air was so humid and close, I felt it pressing against my skin, squeezing more sweat out of my pores.

When the arrow zoomed from the darkness to land with a shush at my feet, I knew that Cat must be on border patrol. Most of the younglings fired their warning shots high, so the arrow hit a tree or sailed off to land harmlessly in the brush. Only Cat actually aimed at people. She was damn good, and I was proud of her and her skill. But her arrow landed dangerously close to Galen. "Cat, if you shoot my dog, I will cause you pain. So much pain. Stop showing off, youngling."

I heard the rustling of leaves, followed by the creak of a branch and finally, the thump of her feet hitting the ground after she swung down from her tree perch. Next I caught her scent, like strong, black coffee. Finally, I was able to pick her paler form out from the surrounding shadows.

"Sankha Kellan, welcome home." She glanced down at Galen. "My apologies, Galen. I would never hit you, you know."

Galen wagged his tail and nudged her hand. All's forgiven as long as you pet me. I shook my head. "Look, Cat, I really need to talk to Janus, so if we could just move this along."

Cat straightened her shoulders, and her scent strengthened. This was the scent of good coffee, the kind that's bitter at first, but if you sit with it, other flavors rise up, spices and sometimes even sweetness. It was a mature scent, and fairly new. Kids grow into their scents like puppies grow into their feet. Cat was sixteen, or maybe seventeen now. She fought hard to be as good as or better than the boys her age. Now, she was at the head of her youngling class. The best archer, the best sharp shooter, the best at knife throwing. She was small, which made hand-to-hand combat difficult, but she knew the techniques cold and she managed twice to beat Ryder, a youngling who outweighed her by almost a hundred pounds. Not bad for a girl who used to be her uncle's punching bag.

"As you wish, Sankha Kellan." She dropped into a bow.

"Thank you, youngling. You're dismissed."

Cat rose but didn't leave. I took a closer look at her. I knew my eyes would be glowing, as they always did when my night vision kicked into high gear. Her shoulders looked slumped and the corners of her mouth turned down. She didn't look like she just made an impossible shot in the dark with her bow. She looked like someone just kicked her.

"Cat, what's wrong?"

She hesitated, then said, "Nothing, ma'am."

"Bullshit. Tell me what's wrong, youngling. Did someone hurt you?" I felt anger start to warm me at the thought of someone taking advantage of Cat.

"No. Nothing like that. I just — I heard that Tony might be coming to teach here, that's all."

Now I was confused. Cat liked Tony. Everyone liked Tony. Except maybe Finn, but Finn didn't like anyone. "You don't want Tony to be a teacher?"

With a look that said I was about as smart as one of those moths that keeps banging into a window screen, she said, "No. I do want him to teach, but he's not going to. I guess he changed his mind."

I felt suddenly cold. Tony changed his mind? Without really seeing her, I looked at Cat. "Oh. Um, okay. Look, I have to go, but I'll — I'll see you. Bye."

I forced myself to walk for ten steps. My self-control broke and I started to run. Where would he be? One of the cabins? Janus's office? I heard a sneeze coming from the direction of the archery range and changed direction. The range was an old horse paddock, with a fence designed more to define its boundaries than to keep anything in or out. Just wood rails stretched between posts. I stopped outside the fence. There he was, longbow raised, preparing to take a shot. I waited until he loosed the arrow before I called to him. "Tony!"

He jerked and turned around. "What're you doing here?"

"What're you doing, using a bow when your allergies are bad? You wanna kill somebody? You could hurt yourself. What the hell are you thinking?" My heart was pounding too fast, like I ran much farther than I actually did.

"What are you doing here?" he said again, enunciating each word like I was too stupid to understand the first time. He didn't move toward me, didn't even set down the weapon.

Fine, if he wouldn't come to me, I'd go to him. I wasn't going to have this conversation shouting halfway across camp, damn it. I vaulted over the fence and advanced on him. "Cat said," I began, then stopped. He looked at me, his scent heated and strong. "I —" Two centuries of vocabulary building, you'd think I could manage a declarative sentence. "You —" Or even just a verb or two. But standing before him, wondering if he really told Finn he didn't want to teach after all? That he didn't want to stay, that he'd request another off-camp position that would take him far away? I had absolutely no idea what to say. Except — "Don't."

He was very still. Damn it, why wouldn't he move? "Don't, what?"

I swallowed, gulped audibly like a cartoon caricature. God, he was going to make me say it. "Don't. Don't...go."

He still didn't move for the longest moment in the history of time. He said, "Why?"

Oh, god, really? More? I whimpered in genuine pain. "I — because — you — aargh!" I spun away, jamming my fingers in my hair and yanking on it, trying to pull it out by the roots.

Tony was there, his hands on my wrists, forcing me still. He looked down at me, and I saw his mouth twitch.

My eyes narrowed. "You. You did that on purpose. You enjoyed that, you sadistic bastard."

He laughed. "I learned from the best."

He kissed me. I might have jumped him right there, if not for two things. One, he still wore the quiver of arrows on his hip, and it was in the way. And two, Galen gave a warning bark.

Since Galen barked about as often as Jim Carrey succeeded in a dramatic role, I instantly broke off the kiss. I didn't even say anything to Tony — my entire focus was on Galen and what caused the uncharacteristic sound. What I saw when I turned around made me go cold. Finn stood there, staring at us like he just caught us disemboweling a goat. Even though he was several yards away, I could smell the dry heat of his anger. I grabbed onto the sides of my shorts, gathering the fabric in my fists to keep from drawing a blade.

I felt Tony's body heat behind me. He kept his hands to himself, but I knew he wanted me to know he was there. Judging from the musk of testosterone radiating from him, he wanted Finn to know he was there, too.

I rolled my shoulder back so it bumped Tony's chest, acknowledging him without showing affection. I stepped away and started for the fence. Galen had been trained not to enter the practice yards unless I gave permission, so he was on the other side of the fence and I didn't want to leave him alone with Finn. I wasn't afraid for my dog's safety — I wasn't sure Finn even noticed him there — but I did know that Galen only tolerated so much from Finn before taking action. None of us wanted to see what kind of action Galen would take. So, with careful, controlled movements, I climbed back over the fence and stood beside my dog. Once I had a hand on his head, I breathed a little easier.

"Hello, Finn," I said. Until I knew which road he was going to take, I figured "hello" was the only safe thing to say. I did promise Janus I would behave, after all.

Apparently, Finn hadn't bound himself by the same vow. He chose the low road. "Sorry to interrupt such pressing business. I was not aware that the archery range was newly designated as lover's lane."

If Finn's language sounded a little 1950's, that was because the last time he took a course in slang was right around the time Kennedy was shot. Finn was a little past due for a refresher, but I wasn't about to point that out to him. "Look, just because you can't manage to fit pleasure into your schedule doesn't mean the rest of us have to play monk along with you. Not that it's any of your business."

A shift in his scent, to something other than anger, was so fast and short-lived I couldn't be sure of its meaning. But I had a pretty good guess. The conversation telling Finn I slept with Tony was guaranteed to be awkward, but I certainly could've chosen a gentler way to break the news than this. Of all the things our relationship lacked, like depth and affection, Finn and I were always exclusive. Mostly because the sex was good and we were both too damaged to go looking for someone normal to have a relationship with. But whatever the reasons, that was our agreement. I broke that agreement, and now I was rubbing it in his face.

Tony's scent filled my senses, and I looked over to find him leaning on the fence. The last thing I needed was a macho showdown at the Sankha corral. So I spoke up. "Actually, Finn, I'm glad you're here." Now I just needed a reason to be glad he was here. The idea lightbulb lit up over my head. "There have been some developments in the case. I'd like to talk to you and Janus in a little bit. Are you guys going to be around?"

Finn's scowl turned haughty. "You mean you can pull yourself away from your tryst to actually do your work?" He tilted his head back so he could look down his nose at me. "Perhaps Janus has put too much faith in your abilities."

"And maybe he put too much faith in yours," Tony said, but I threw him a silencing glare. Tony might outweigh Finn by a good fifty pounds of muscle, but Finn was a sorcerer. He had skills that would allow him to overpower a room full of Tonys. I didn't want to be stuck in the middle of a knock-down-drag-out between the two.

I growled. "The tryst is scheduled for tomorrow night, just let me dig out the parchment with the wax seal." I dug around in my pockets, causing Finn's angry scent to reappear and thrum through the air with each heartbeat. "Huh, guess I must've left it in my other petticoat. Anyway, unless you two are going to whip 'em out and start measuring, maybe you could tell Janus I'd like to see him? Otherwise, I'll just show up unannounced, which he loves, and act all surprised that you didn't let him know I was coming."

Finn stared at me, his lips pressed together and the vein in his forehead pulsing so hard, I could hear it against his skin like a conga beat. "Very well. I will alert him."

"Fantastic. Thanks for the fun, boys. Come on, Galen." I left them there, trusting that they'd either walk away from each other or wind up in a fight to the death that, if nothing else, would simplify my life exponentially.

I should have gone to Janus's office. But the cabin would be too brightly lit, too hemmed in. I experienced too much humanity in too small a time. I needed dark shadows and fresh air. With barely a thought, I stepped into the forest, stripped out of my clothes, knelt on all fours, and shape-shifted.

Chapter 14

Seeing Human grow fur made most dogs lose control of bodily functions. But from the very beginning of our friendship, Galen, having seeing enough Bad Shit to know it when he saw it, didn't bat an eye. Not when my hands curled in on themselves to form paws. Not when my ribcage folded in half like closing a book, as my torso realigned itself. When my tail popped out from the base of my spine and my jaws and cheekbones rearranged themselves into a muzzle, Galen's only reaction was to join me in my jubilant howl. He knew I was still me, and he knew I was happy. He didn't care about the rest.

And he knew that the fun part came next. After a salutary butt-sniff, Galen and I set off at a run, whipping through brush and kicking up leaves in our wake. We chased each other, doubling back and nipping at haunches, grabbing ears. I was bigger and faster than Galen, but I didn't use my full speed because part of the fun was getting caught. The night air was so rich with scents that at first, I didn't bother trying to separate them out. I just let them wash over me. Even with my special sense of smell, the difference between human form and wolf form was like the difference between being dead and being alive. I never realized just how much I was missing until I got the chance to experience it all.

Before long, one scent caught my attention and wouldn't let go. A deer passed by here, and the scent trail was strong enough that I knew it was still close. I froze. Janus liked it when I hunted the forest animals. Because they all drank from the Spring, the animals didn't age or die of natural causes. The cooks used the rabbits and deer that the younglings hunted, but one buck could feed the camp for a week. It just wasn't enough to keep the animal population from overflowing into the city and revealing our existence. So hunts were always sanctioned here.

Galen skidded to a stop, instantly on alert. His ears pricked, his tail curved over his back in excited joy. Now? his body language asked me. I snorted, stayed frozen for a few seconds, pulling the scents into my nose and keeping my brother guessing. He huffed and wagged his tail. Just before he ran out of patience completely, before he made a frustrated sound that would alert our prey to our presence, I took off.

We stopped running long before we reached the deer. We let it see us. We let it smell us. Then we slowly started to approach, Galen flanking to one side while I went to the other. We didn't want to catch it yet. We didn't want the fun to be over.

The deer stared at us, nostrils flaring and fear-scent screaming. I paused, meeting its gaze. Across from me, Galen stopped moving, too. For several breaths, we stared at each other, the three of us. I threw my head back and howled, and the deer took off.

Galen and I chased and played, letting Prey think it was getting ahead of us, letting it think that maybe it would get away. Then we closed in. I dove for its leg, tore its tendons, and it fell. Galen moved as if to rip out its throat, and I growled. I was alpha. The kill was my privilege. I almost didn't want to end it. The scent of Prey's fear was like a drug, a delicious delicacy, but it was more than that. Part of my brain knew that soon, I would have to go back. Back to the two-legged cage. If I put off the kill, I could stay here, stay wild and free.

I waited too long. My brother lost patience and stalked toward me, toward Prey. I snarled and snapped my jaws together, and he lowered his head in submission and stepped back. I looked down at my prize, and hunger took over. I tore out the throat, hot blood filling my mouth.

We ate side by side. Human brain reminded me that deer liver could make dogs sick, so I kept my brother away from the organs, only allowing him access to the flank and rump. We lay down for a short nap, barely even enough to move the moon in the sky. When I woke, I heard the skitter of scavengers gathering, waiting for my brother and I to leave what was left of our kill. My brother raised his head to look at me, his eyes questioning. Did we have to go back? I knew that was his question, because it was mine, too. If I shifted back now, I would probably lose my lunch, so to speak. Raw deer in wolf form was fine and dandy, but the human stomach didn't handle it so well. I sighed. Shame to waste a perfectly good meal. But I needed to deal with human business yet tonight. I rolled to my feet, shook and stretched, and began to pad away. I didn't wait for him, because I knew he would follow. I was alpha. He would always follow.

Back at the spot where I left my clothes, I shifted back to human form. My legs wouldn't hold me at first, and I just lay there, naked, leaves and sticks poking into my back and butt. Shifting beat up my body pretty good, leaving my muscles the consistency of watered-down pudding. But it was worth every weak and aching bit.

Before long, I had to roll over on my side and vomit. Second time around, the deer was a lot less appetizing. But what's a wolf to do? Trying to restrain myself from digging in would be like trying to go vegan. Maybe better for the body in the long run, but it just wouldn't feel near as good.

Grabbing my clothes and dragging Galen with me so he didn't clean up my vomit, I scooted like an almost-ready-to-walk-baby over to a tree, settled in against the trunk, and reveled in the bite of the rough bark against my back. I dressed and wrapped my hand around Galen's collar to keep him with me. He curled up at my right hip, panting hard and tossing occasional glances in the direction of my vomit, but otherwise obviously blissful. I pity people who can't run with their dogs like that, I really do.

I needed to get up and get on with my night. Instead, I leaned my head back against the trunk and closed my eyes, drifting off into a doze when I heard the sound of feet rustling through leaves. In an adrenaline-charged moment of disorientation, I pulled the blade from my left cargo pocket. Aza, I thought, but of course it wasn't. Galen hopped to his feet and stood stiff, waiting for the intruder to show himself. I caught Tony's scent, and I relaxed. I let my head fall back against the tree trunk and closed my eyes again. "Hi," I said.

Tony's scent flowed over me as he sat down beside me. "Hey." His voice sounded congested, but at least he wasn't sneezing. "Good run?"

My lips curved. "How'd you guess?"

Galen's scent filled the air. Tony must've been rubbing him down. "Honey, they heard those howls at the capitol. The governor pissed himself."

I struck out with my elbow, which, since my eyes were closed, he easily blocked. My smile broadened at the sound of his chuckle. "I wasn't that loud," I said.

"The Weekly World News is on their way here to report on the werewolf sightings."

"Must be a slow week for UFOs, then."

"No Elvis sightings, either." He was quiet for a while, and I enjoyed his relaxed scent mixing with Galen's. "Hey, I'm sorry I forgot a condom earlier."

I frowned. "Why?"

I felt his shrug, a rolling of his shoulder against mine. "I should've remembered. I'm sorry. If you — you know, got...I don't even know if that's something you'd want."

Even though he never said pregnant, we both knew that was the missing word. "Don't worry about it. I can't. Get pregnant, I mean. I'm sterile." I never went into heat, as my mom liked to call it.

"Oh." He fidgeted, like he was suddenly uncomfortable.

My stomach rumbled, turning my focus to more important things. Shape-shifting took a lot out of me, and I just threw up my dinner. "You got any food?"

"No."

I was going to be sick again. Too much acid in my stomach with nothing to work on. I started to stand up, placing a hand on the tree behind me for support, but my vision went all spotty and I fell back to the ground. I swore as Tony touched my arm.

"Shit, you're all clammy. When was the last time you ate?"

It took me a scary-long time to process his words. It took even longer to find an answer. "I had some deer —" oh, shit, I wasn't going to tell him that "- um, some stuff earlier. But I threw that up."

I was hoping maybe he wouldn't hear my slip. But of course, he did. "Some deer —" I heard the revulsion in his voice as he apparently realized that I wasn't talking venison stew. I would've tried to make him feel better, reassure him that I wasn't as big a freak as he thought. Except I was every bit as big a freak as he thought, and there was no point in denying it. "Shit. Come on." He started to gather me up in his arms.

"Oh, hell, no. You're not carrying me." I pushed myself back on my feet. It wasn't pretty, and I was about as steady as a ninety-pound coed after two dozen jello shots. But I did it, and I kept my feet.

Tony glared at me for a minute before he let me walk. Camp was quiet as we made our slow, plodding way to the mess hall. Outside the door, Tony pulled a set of lock picks out of his Mary Poppins back pocket and got us in the door. He walked with me to a table, waited until I was safely seated in a chair, and went into the kitchen.

"Don't know why Janus bothers locking the door," he called back to me. "Younglings learn how to pick locks in their first year."

"Principle." I was pretty proud of managing a one-word answer, since the room looked suspiciously polka-dotted. I really needed to start carrying energy bars in my pockets. I really needed bigger pockets. Between the knives and energy bars, I was going to run out of pocket space.

I was pulled out of la-la land when Tony pressed a granola bar in my hand. "Here, start with this. Coffee's brewing and I'm looking for more substantial food, but in the meantime." He stepped back and looked at me a moment before heading back to the kitchen. "You really should start carrying energy bars with you."

It scared me a little, that he knew me so well. But the foil-wrapped bar in my hand beckoned and I downed the glorified candy bar in three bites.

The granola helped steady me, but I wasn't sure I wanted to walk anywhere just yet. So I just reached down to pet Galen's head, and waited for Tony to return. When he did, he was carrying a mug of coffee and a bowl of stew. I frowned. "Gina made stew? Why the hell would anyone want stew in August?"

Tony stopped and glared at me. "You're practically in shock. Just eat the fucking stew."

My cheeks warmed with a cross between anger and embarrassment. "I am not." I accepted the mug and bowl, and promptly almost dropped them. Tony grabbed them from me and set them on the table. I thanked him awkwardly. I guess I wasn't feeling as good as I thought, with muscle control that poor.

His mouth twisted in a smile. "How hard was it to squeeze out that thank you?"

I picked up the coffee and took a sip. "I'm a little rusty."

"Hmm." He pulled up a chair and sat down on the other side of Galen. "So. I talked to Janus."

I set down the coffee and pulled the stew closer. It was pretty simple fare, just potatoes, carrots and stew meat, and it smelled like heaven. The act of eating distracted me sufficiently that it took me a moment to react to Tony's statement. "Janus? About what?"

"Teaching. I asked if he would still consider me for a position."

I waited for him to elaborate, but my prodigious impatience got the better of me. "And? What did he say?"

"Don't rush me," he said softly. "I'm having fun."

I swallowed hard. He could have said he was going to plunge the toilet and I would've wanted to jump him, but to say that? In that voice? I scooted my chair closer to him and nudged his knees apart. He laughed, a deep masculine sound that warmed me better than any coffee ever had. He began to radiate that gooey chocolate smell again. "I guess you're feeling better," he murmured, still gazing up at me.

I nodded and kissed him. He met me hungrily, his hand gripping the back of my neck, digging into my hair. After a moment, I pulled away, nipping his lower lip as I did. I said in a low, seductive voice, "What did Janus say?"

His smile relaxed into a lounging half-smile. "He said yes. I'm a teacher."

I stood and pulled him to his feet. "I get to be on top," I said.

"Mmm." He reached out and hooked his hands in the waistband of my shorts, pulling me to him.

"Mostly because if you come and collapse on top of me, you'll crush me."

"Fortunately, you heal good." He lowered his head.

"Still," I murmured, right before his lips met mine. "I get to be on top."

He pulled back, a familiar mischievous smile on his lips. "Then I get to be in a bed."

I narrowed my eyes, pretending to consider. I nodded once. "Deal."

"Bout time." We put our tongues to other, more aerobic uses.

———— «» ————

We never made it to a bed. We never made it to a horizontal position, or even a no-pants position. "Oh, shit," I said suddenly, interrupting Tony as he trailed his hand down a wonderful path around the curve of my hip, to my butt, to my thigh, and around front to... "Janus."

He pulled his mouth from my neck to look at me. "No." He thumped his chest. "Tony. And might I say, of all the names you could've said just now, that's probably the most creepy."

"What? No. I have to talk to Janus."

He just looked at me for a second. "I'm doing some pretty good work here, and you're thinking about Janus?"

To illustrate how ungrateful I was being, he completed his pilgrimage to my holy land, and my knees went weak. "No," I said in a voice uncomfortably close to a pant. "I just, I have to talk to him about Raoul."

Tony raised his hands in surrender. "Fine. Who the hell is Raoul?"

"Raoul, you know, the guy in my neighborhood. Shit, I'm all wet, I can't go see Janus like this, he'll know what we were doing."

"Darlin'," he said, and rubbed the stubble on his cheek. "I hate to break it to you, but you look like you took a power-sander to your face. He's gonna know what we were doing long before he looks at your clothes."

"No, no, that'll heal." After a few moments of fruitlessly examining my shorts, I gave up. "Whatever. Too late now. Damn. Your hands are much too good at...that."

He tugged my hair. "No such thing as too good at that."

I grinned goofily as I looked up at him. "No, I guess not."

He smiled down at me, the heat in his gaze mingling with the scent of his desire to make my knees weak all over again. Jesus. When did I become such a girlie girl? Shaking my head, I stepped away from him and patted my leg to get Galen's attention. "I gotta go. You gonna be up for a while?" I asked over my shoulder.

A slow grin with just a touch of lechery. "Looks like it," he said, his voice rough.

Just the sound of his voice made me want to tackle him and fuck him back to the Eisenhower administration. I swallowed hard and reached out to Galen for support. "All right," I said, and my voice cracked. I cleared my throat. "Which cabin are you staying in? I could swing by after talking to Janus."

"I'm in the cabin you stayed in this summer." Janus and Finn were the only Sankhain who had permanently assigned residences on camp. Most of the Sankhain were on assignment in the outside world, and when we came back to the Academy for an overnight stay, we bunked in whichever cabin was vacant. I was pretty sure Tony was the first Sankha, other than me, to request a permanent assignment at camp. Most of the younglings' instructors just filled in, while in between assignments. "I'll wait up for you," Tony told me.

With more willpower than I cared to admit, I turned away from his smile and led Galen through the door. And walked right into Cat. "Whoa!" I said.

Cat and three other younglings stood before me. The three boys took a step back, averting their eyes, but Cat held her ground. "You guys about done in there? We're starving."

"Kitchen's closed," I said, my tone a warning. Younglings could take as much food as they wanted from six a.m. to ten p.m., but once the kitchen closed for the night, they were supposed to wait until morning.

"We just got off a six hour shift," the smallest boy — I think his name was Lucky — whined. Then he cleared his throat and deepened his voice. "Sankha Kellan. Ma'am."

I chewed the inside of my cheek. If I laughed, it would make him feel bad. "Next time, take extra at dinner to eat while you're on duty. This time, and this time only, you can go in. Tony might even help you fix something. He's a soft touch."

Cat's mouth twitched as she bent slightly at the waist in a half-bow. "Yes, ma'am. He's the soft touch."

I arranged my features in a scowl. "Get inside before I change my mind and send you to your dorms."

If four people could constitute a stampede, they did, tripping over their feet and each other to get through the door.

I shook my head and looked down at Galen. "All right, big dog. Let's go see a man about some faeries."

———— «» ————

When we got to Janus's cabin, I wasn't surprised to see lights blazing inside. The man never slept.

I entered the outer office and smiled at the sight that greeted me. Smack, her head on the desk, sound asleep. As perfect as the picture was, if Janus caught her, she'd be scrubbing bedpans with her own toothbrush. Forget that it was the middle of the night. He would only say that she had plenty of time off to sleep the previous afternoon.

I cleared my throat loudly and her head jerked up. She reached behind her, presumably for a weapon, and her eyes were wide to match the sudden fear in her scent. They looked so innocent when they were asleep, I sometimes forgot. Think it's bad to wake a sleeping wolf? Try waking a sleeping teenager whose "rise and shine" used to come from her pimp.

"Stand down, youngling," I said softly.

Her fear slowly ebbed as her eyes focused on me. She cleared the sleep from her throat, bringing her hands back around front to show me they were empty. "Apologies, Sankha Kellan."

"Not necessary." I inclined my head toward the door to the inner room. "He around?"

She nodded, adding under her breath, "He ever leave?"

I raised my eyebrows. "Yeah, he does, and if he found you asleep out here, he'd give you a wake-up call in more ways than one. So drink more coffee."

Her mouth twisted as she chewed the inside of her cheek. The air filled with the warm scent of her embarrassment. "Yes, ma'am. Thanks. I, um, I ain't — I haven't been sleeping much lately."

Join the club, was my first thought. But Smack was young. She needed more rest than an old hag like me. "What's going on? Nightmares?" Not uncommon for younglings. In fact, it was more uncommon for them to sleep peacefully.

She hesitated, the scent of embarrassment souring into shame. Her voice was as quiet as I ever heard it. "Yeah."

I hated the smell of shame. It was a completely worthless emotion that made me want to hunt down and kill the people who put those nightmares in Smack's head. I'd play with them first. Teach them what fear felt like. The violent fantasies felt so good, I wanted to stay with them rather than focus on the girl before me. So I had to force them out of my head, because me pulling an Incredible Hulk wouldn't help Smack. I breathed deep, took in her scent, and studied her face, all to help me focus on the here and now. "You should talk to someone. Simone's pretty good at listening. Or one of the other younglings. But holding it in will just make the nightmares worse."

Her breathing was fast and shallow, fear drenching her scent. "I don't need to talk about nothin'." Again, she caught her grammar slip. "About anything. You gonna go see him, or not? I don't have time to sit here yakkin' with you all night." She picked up an English textbook and let it fall open. Though she bent over it like she was reading, her fingers tapped a manic rhythm on her thighs, making me think she wasn't seeing anything except the scene playing inside her head.

I let it go. Obviously, she wasn't ready to talk. But I was still going to say something to Simone later. "Go to the mess hall. Tony should be there, tell him I requested coffee for my meeting with Janus. He'll let you in the kitchen. Make it strong, and take a big old mug for yourself." Without waiting for an answer, I knocked on Janus's door and stuck my head inside. "Sorry to bother you, sir. You got a minute?"

He was standing by the fire, holding a file folder in his hands. Without bothering to turn and look at me, he shook his head. "Perhaps I should not have sent you out into the world. Your grammar suffers."

I sidled into the room, holding the door for Galen before I shut it behind us. "Never too late to change your mind, bring me back here."

He shook his head again, and I caught a whiff of warm vanilla. He was amused. Good. I didn't intend to piss him off tonight, but I never set out with that goal. It couldn't hurt to start out with him in a good mood. He turned to face me, and I relished seeing his face creased by a smile.

Did Janus know that Finn and I were done? That I was with Tony now, and Finn knew it? Would Janus be mad at me for hurting Finn? Would Janus notice that my shorts were wet? I reminded myself that Janus could read minds and shut down that train of thought. After several moments of anxiety-ridden silence, I forced myself to speak. "Um. Finn's not here?"

"He was rather…upset. He did not wish for anyone to see him that way." Janus sighed. "He is too proud."

I couldn't help it — I snorted. When Janus looked at me with raised eyebrows, I shrugged. "Sorry. Sir. But you gotta admit, coming from you, that's kinda funny."

"Kind...uh?" I knew he understood the word, he just found it distasteful.

I shrugged again. What could I say? If I was going to be a resident of twenty-first century Madison, I couldn't talk like I was born in Jane Austen's heyday. "You're right, he's too proud," I said instead. "And as much as I enjoy enumerating Finn's faults, that's not why I'm here."

Before I even heard the knock on the door, I could smell the coffee. Now, that was some good brew. Strong enough to make its own entrance. Smack opened the door, balancing the tray in one hand without spilling a drop. Instantly, Janus draped formality over his shoulders. "Why do you presume to bring us this, youngling?"

"Ah, that's my fault," I said, motioning to Smack to lay the tray on the table. "I asked her to get some coffee. It's been a long night."

Smack edged toward the door while keeping her head lowered submissively.

"Dismissed," Janus said, and she was gone almost before he completed the word. Janus turned to me. "Did you intend to inform me of her impromptu nap?"

I clenched my jaw to keep my mouth from dropping open in surprise. It shouldn't surprise me — Janus could read minds. It wasn't polite, and he refrained from doing it unless it served his purposes. Unfortunately, mind-reading almost always served his purposes. Never stopped me from trying to lie, though. "Yes, of course, sir. I just, well..." My voice drifted off as I caught the scent of his amusement again. People were just finding me all kinds of funny tonight. Fine, I could play that game. "No, actually, I wasn't. In fact, I also wasn't going to tell you that your fly is open."

His eyebrows drew together. "I do not understand. Fly?"

It was no fun trying to pull someone's leg when they didn't get the joke. "Sorry, sir. You want some coffee?"

"Perhaps if you drank less coffee, you might sleep."

"It's been suggested." I poured myself a mug. "But everyone keeps assuming I want to sleep."

His eyes narrowed as he gave me that I-can-see-through-your-skin-and-straight-to-your-soul look. "If you continue to avoid your nightmares, they will begin to intrude on your waking mind."

It irked me, having my own advice to Smack thrown back at me. "Thanks, Confuscious. Any other fortune cookie wisdom you'd like to impart? About my soulmate, or maybe lucky lottery numbers?"

Maybe there was something to be said for well-rested. Maybe well-rested people didn't compulsively trip over their own tongues.

Fortunately, Janus found me amusing tonight instead of obnoxious, and he simply raised an eyebrow and ignored my sarcasm. "If I am to understand, you need no assistance with the search for a mate."

My cheeks warmed to a point that the heat overflowed to the rims of my ears. "You should know better than to listen to the youngling grapevine."

"I did not hear it from the grapevine. Young Antony was here this evening."

Tony wasn't a youngling anymore, but Janus was old enough to remember Jesus's first birthday party. He still called me young sometimes. "Yeah, I heard," I said carefully, my earlier worries about my love life surging forward again to wash me in nervous sweat. Was this when Janus lectured me about my callous treatment of Finn?

"When I mentioned your name, he colored."

He wasn't being racist. "Blushed, Janus. The term is blushed." At his expression, I added, "Sir."

"And you *blushed* as well."

Even as my face flamed, I shrugged. "Fine. But for the record, Finn and I were done before Tony and I got together. Now can we please talk about this case? Because some weird shit — I mean, weird things are happening, and I'd really like your input."

But only one person in the room possessed the privilege of deciding when a topic got dropped. "Your relationship with Finlay is your business. To be frank, I have never understood why the two of you insisted on pairing with one another. You are very ill-suited. But tread with care, little one." His tone brought a lump to my throat. "Antony is a good man, but he has nightmares of his own."

I so did not want to be talking about this. But if I had to... "Tony's more than capable of slaying his own dragons, Janus. I'm not offering. I just really like the way he wears his birthday suit." The frown lines between his eyes told me the euphemism was beyond him. I clarified. "The man looks good naked."

Even though his mouth smiled, his voice was still serious. "Tread with care."

"Speaking of which. I found out a couple things today. Yesterday? What time is it?" I didn't add, What day is it? because that would worry him. It probably should worry me.

This time, Janus let me fumble my way to a new subject. "It is past midnight. Continue."

"So, yesterday. Or well, the first thing happened the day before." I was getting really annoyed with my attempts to impose a timeline on recent events. "Aza is back. The dead bodies are his work."

"Bodies?" Any trace of amusement was gone. The boss was all business now.

I told him about the second dead body, leaving out Darcy's involvement. Last spring, Janus agreed to allow Darcy to live, but that didn't mean he would approve of my maintaining a friendship with him. I told Janus about meeting Aza on my run, and seeing him again on the morning outing with Tony. Then I remembered that Tony was supposedly still on the bus to Madison at that time, and I felt myself blush again. But if Janus picked up on the inconsistency, he didn't comment. Truly, there were more disturbing elements to the story than one little lie about Tony's arrival time. Especially when I told him about my discovery of Raoul's true identity.

He absorbed the info with a look on his face that reminded me of Mal when she was processing. Similar to Finn, too, now that I thought about it. Funny, I never made the connection before. It made me wonder: if Mal possessed the same gifts with magic that Finn did, would Finn still be Janus's protégé? Or would Mal have taken his place? She certainly had the mental capacity for plotting and subterfuge. Maybe if Janus had taken her on as his second, she wouldn't have felt the need to run away. Suddenly, I felt cold, and I wanted to warm myself. I wanted contact, body heat. I wanted pack. Faces flashed through my mind. Galen. Janus, Tony. Mal. But the one that was most persistent surprised me. It was Darcy Jameson.

I reached out to Galen. Pulling him against my leg, I leeched off his warmth and vitality. Still, I was so shaken by my thoughts that when Janus spoke, I had to struggle to arrange the sounds in the air into something that made sense. "It is curious, the way this faery's revealing himself to you coincides with the Horror's return."

"Uh, yeah." That was all the response I could muster. Picturing Darcy and Mal so close together meant that now I was replaying Mal's greatest hits from last spring.

Janus didn't seem to notice my Neanderthal vocabulary. "And odd that this — Raoul? — chose such an urban place to dwell. So much iron, so much machinery. And you say he seems to thrive there?"

Galen wasn't enough to ground me in the here and now. I dug my fingernails into my palms so hard my knuckles turned white, and the pain finally caused my thought-train to change course. "He's been there the entire time I've had that apartment. Since you first sent me into the city, what, ten years ago? If he was going to fade, he would've by now." Faeries liked rolling hills, lots of green and wild things. Cities tended to drain the energy of the fey, causing them to fade into a hollow shell, devoid of magic. Raoul's ability to live in the city and retain his power was, as Janus said, odd.

"Hmm. Now, tell me again everything the Horror said to you." Apparently, oddities weren't at the top of Janus's priority list tonight.

I repeated the Aza parts of my story, and Janus listened with eyes that looked far away. His scent reminded me of rainwater, which usually meant deep thought, too deep for actual emotion.

"He refers to the outsider, does he not? The librarian."

"Yeah. Yes. I think so." My stomach fluttered at the confirmation that Janus still remembered Darcy. Remembered that he let him live. As if remembering might cause him to reconsider the wisdom of that decision.

"So this man attracted the attention of both the nocturnes and the Horror, in roughly the same time period?" Janus's eyes were suddenly focused and intense. He studied me with the look that made me think he was reading my mind.

I resisted the urge to squirm. "It would appear so." Spend enough time with Janus, and Snoop Dogg would start talking like him. "And no, I don't know why. Darcy's single and probably the most straight-laced guy in the world. I doubt he would cheat at solitaire, much less cheat on a partner."

"And yet, he did attract the attention of the Horror." Janus never used Aza's name. Like he was afraid the name would conjure the faery, like Beetlejuice. Why did Aza want Darcy? I didn't know, and it bugged me. It seemed important. Janus seemed to think so, too. "You must find out what happened if you are to understand why the Horror believes the treaty is null and void."

"Can't I skip the why and just kill Aza? I mean, he's scum, and he's stalking me now, too. And he —" I stopped, remembering that moment on our morning run when Aza saw me with Tony and gave me that knowing look. I felt an overwhelming need to pull Galen's too-big body into my too-small lap.

"He saw you with Antony." Janus's voice was kind, which I hated.

"It's rude to read people's minds," I said, my lip curled in a snarl that would've made Elvis proud.

"It is also rude to leave a sentence half-finished."

"So you decided you'd finish it for yourself? Did it occur to you that maybe I would've finished it myself, in my own time?

That maybe, just maybe I wasn't withholding information but trying to pull myself together? Jesus. Must be nice to have so much fucking magickal power that you don't have to care about things like empathy or compassion."

Even before I caught the change in his scent — from the peace of fresh rain to the ominous scent of metal sparking in the microwave — I knew I crossed a line. "Kellan Alastrina Faolanni." That's all he said, my name, and I wanted to crawl under the table and hide.

"Sir. I'm — I'm sorry. I — I never should've —"

Just as fast as it came on, the burning smell disappeared. "I enjoy sharing moments of familiarity with you. Yet I would appreciate if you refrained from treating me as you do everyone else with those outbursts."

"Yes. Of course. My humblest apologies, sir." I felt shaky, like I teetered on the middle of a rope bridge over the Grand Canyon.

"Very good. To answer your earlier question, no, you cannot simply kill the Horror. If we can find a way to repair the treaty, we should do so."

"Why?" It just leapt out of my mouth without my consent. "I mean, if you don't mind giving me a reason, I would appreciate it. He's a bad guy. I don't see why the world is a better place with him in it."

Janus smiled, and I relaxed a little. "It is not about making the world a better place. It is about maintaining the world that we have. The peace we enjoy."

That wasn't much of an explanation, but I refrained from griping about it. "Yes, sir. But he wants to kill me. I'm pretty sure he wants it pretty bad. I'm just supposed to let him keep walking around? I'm supposed to let him win?"

He sighed. So did Galen. Everybody in the room was exasperated with me. "Kellan, the Horror is, as you say, a bad guy." His mouth twisted on the word "guy." "However, in the faerie court, specifically the court of the dark fey, he is nobility. I believe he falls third in the line of succession. Killing him would ignite a war."

Of course, it would. Just once, I'd like to be able to kill the villain without any complications. A nice, simple murder. Was that really so much to ask?

Chapter 15

"I guess war would be a bad thing," I said.

"Yes. You guess correctly."

It was my turn to sigh. "So then, what? My next move is to find out why he's interested in Darcy, and how I broke the treaty so that I can repair it. Oh, and meanwhile, I should avoid killing or getting killed."

"Yes. That sounds acceptable."

"Super." I poured myself another cup of coffee and leaned back in my chair. The chairs around the table in Janus's office were wonderful. Big, wooden monstrosities that would've looked right at home around Arthur's table. The backs were tall enough to act as a headrest. Of course, they were also hard as a rock, but you can't have everything.

I didn't realize my eyes were closed until Janus spoke and I had to open them to look at him. "You ought to be returning to the city."

No, please let me stay. I managed to keep the thought to myself. I knew there was work to be done. Somehow, my brilliant traitorous sister and I managed to piss off the third-in-line Big Faery on Campus. That needed to be dealt with before Aza dumped more bodies on my doorstep. But it was so nice here. So quiet, so clean. So earthy and familiar. I have no desire to return to the womb, but I always long to return to the forest. Always.

But staying wasn't my job. And Darcy needed me. "All right. Is there anything else? Sir?"

"No. I believe our business is concluded. Will you be seeing young Antony before you leave, as well?"

I didn't bother answering. The blush that heated my cheeks was answer enough, and if he wanted more of an answer, the old bastard could just read my mind. I drained my coffee and pushed away from the table. "Thanks for the coffee. And for the talk." I looked him in the eye, trying to say, without actually having to say it, how much I enjoyed those moments of familiarity, too.

"You are most welcome." He stood, walked over, and wrapped his arms around me. I was so shocked, I didn't return the hug at first. "Be careful, little one."

"Yes, sir." Touching him was one of the only times I realized just how tiny he was, physically. If he weighed more than ninety-five pounds, I would eat my boots. But he called me little one. "Careful's my middle name."

He barked a laugh, a rare, special treat of a sound. "No. It is most definitely not any part of your name. But thank you for humoring an old man."

It was starting to creep me out, this warm-fuzzy-sentimental Janus. Not that it was unpleasant, just that it was against the natural order of things. Like a bull moose wearing fuzzy slippers.

Before the scene could devolve into actual sappy syrupy vomit-inducing sweetness, I made my exit. I said goodbye to Smack. She didn't look up from her book or say anything even remotely audible, although her lips moved and I heard a sort of hum. I stood and stared at her until she made eye contact. "Good night, Smack. Do yourself a favor and talk to someone. Whether you need it or not." I didn't wait for her to answer, although morbid curiosity left me wondering what would've come out of her mouth.

The air outside felt cool after the fire-heated interior of Janus's cabin. I breathed deep and relished the miniscule breeze on my bare skin. August in Wisconsin wasn't prone to breezes, but every so often, one would sneak up on you.

I reevaluated my plan to talk to Simone about Smack. Daylight was creeping closer, and I still needed to say good-bye to Tony. Instead of heading to the infirmary, I pulled out my phone and sent Simone a text. There. Now someone who was actually good at helping people could work with Smack.

Galen's tail started wagging. I looked up to see Tony walking toward us. "I got tired of waiting in the cabin," Tony said.

For a moment, I just breathed in the scents of Tony and Galen layered over the scents of camp, and felt happy.

Tony leaned in to kiss me. I pulled back. If we started kissing, we wouldn't stop and I'd be late leaving. Janus didn't like the Sankhain to take the long way around if we could avoid it, and I felt like I used up enough of my alpha's goodwill for one night. "I — I shouldn't. It's getting early." I glanced up at the sky, still dark but not as dark.

Exasperation smelled like bread that rose too long. Tony sighed. "How about I walk you to your truck then?"

He smelled so good, so warm and male. "Screw it. I'll take the long way around." We took off for the cabin. Galen figured out where we were headed and beat us there. The three of us piled through the door, and I laughed breathlessly. Tony kissed me, and I didn't come up for air for a long time.

———— «» ————

We both dozed off for a while and when I woke, sunlight crept through the window. Tony rolled over on his back, sneezed, groaned, and rolled off the bed while reaching for his jeans. I watched him with a big, dopey smile on my face. As he zipped his fly, he glanced over and caught me looking at him. The instant heat in his eyes made me both delighted and uncomfortable at the same time. I looked away and started gathering my own clothes.

"What's wrong?" Tony asked. Galen lay in the middle of the floor, and I almost tripped over him. My bra was all the way on the other side of the room.

"I can't find my underwear," I said. "Where'd it go?"

Tony grinned at me. "I was too busy payin' attention to where it wasn't to worry about where it was." Slowly, his grin faded and he studied me. "Now what's going on?"

"I'm trying to find my fucking underwear."

"Yeah, got that part. You're acting weird. Why?" He crossed his arms over his chest — his entirely bare, yummy chest — and got that stubborn look on his face that meant we were about to have a Talk.

"Tony, it's late. I'm already way past the time I should've left. And I can't walk through the mosquito-infested marsh to my truck without my underwear on." My voice was rising, but I couldn't help it. I felt something close to panic, and I knew it didn't have anything to do with my lack of undergarments.

Tony glanced under the bed, grabbed my wayward underwear, and handed it to me. "Now what else is bugging you?"

"I — nothing. Nothing." But I could barely draw a breath, my chest was so tight.

He sat down beside me, sneezed three times, and reached for a tissue from the bedside table. He set the used tissue on the bed behind us. I glanced at it and looked up at him skeptically. He sighed, his scent heating with exasperation. "I'll throw it away in a minute. But I'm not moving until you tell me what's wrong with you. I might not be able to smell your emotions, but I'm not stupid. Something's wrong."

I dug deep for words. When none came, I dug deeper. I was going to hit China before I found what I needed. "Fuck," I said, starting with the easiest word. "I — this —" I pointed to him, pointed at me, then motioned back and forth a few times. "Is so…good."

He blew his nose again and cocked his head to one side. "How come you say good like it means malignant?"

I sighed and rubbed my eyes. "I'm no good at good." I glanced up at him. "And you're — so good."

His mouth twisted in a way that made me think he was trying not to laugh. "How 'bout we find a different word?"

"I'm tired, all right? Sorry if my vocabulary is lacking."

"No, I mean, stop thinking of what we have as good. Just come up with a different word, one that doesn't scare the shit out of you."

I growled. "That is an offensively simplistic way of approaching the problem."

"Look at you and your vocabulary." Now he was definitely laughing.

"Fuck off." I stood up and stalked over to where my bra lay. The fact was, I was sloppy, noisy, I ate too much, and I had a fucking tail. This whatever-it-was between us wouldn't last. Couldn't last. And the thought made me so incredibly sad that my shoulders bowed under the weight.

He came up behind me and it took everything I had not to elbow him hard enough to crack ribs. He seemed to sense my efforts, because he opted not to touch me. "Kell, I'm not as good as you think I am. But it's nice that you think that. Whatever this is, it's gonna be messy, and that's good. I mean," he hastily said, "that's all right. We figure it out as we go. Okay?"

Despite my annoyance, despite my absolute certainty that I would fuck this all up, I felt myself relax slowly as he spoke. "You don't have to avoid the word good. It's not actually malignant." I leaned back, knowing that he would be there to lean against.

"If you say so." He kissed the back of my neck, and I shuddered. "You need to go, right?"

"Uh-huh." I reached up, found the back of his head, and pulled him down to my neck again. As he sucked on the pulse point below my ear, my knees went weak and I felt my whole body throb. I turned, wrapped my arms around his neck and my legs around his waist. I had to untangle myself to once again remove the blighted underwear.

———— «» ————

Later, I hobbled into the shower. I was fairly sure I pulled a muscle. But it was worth it. When I got out of the shower, Tony was waiting in the bathroom. I felt an ugly déjà vu, remembering the last time this happened. This time, though, Tony's smile was genuine and relaxed. "Don't leave without me," was all he said, and stepped into the shower.

I felt a now-familiar flutter of fear. I meant what I said earlier —
I wasn't any good at good things. I was very good at sarcasm,
exceptional at knife-throwing. Pretty damn good at hand-to-hand
combat. But goodness? Not one of my skills. Relationships, honest
communication, and healthy emotions — not so much those, either.

But as I dressed in yesterday's clothes — complete with
underwear, thank you — I knew that I didn't have a choice in the
matter. I would probably fuck up this thing with Tony. Probably
fuck up the friendship with Darcy, too, for that matter. But walking
away from them wasn't an option, either. I was too greedy and
selfish to miss out on whatever happiness I might be able to hoard
before the inevitable fuck-up.

———— «» ————

When Tony emerged from the bathroom, I felt uneasy but not
panicky. Progress. I watched him pull clothes out of his duffel bag
and get dressed. And I noticed something strange. Under the scent
of soap, I caught a whiff of something chemical. Even mild drugs
like anti-histamines left trace scents, although not the knock-you-
over-the-head smell of the hard stuff — alcohol, cocaine, heroin.
Holy shit. Tony took some Benadryl. Not enough for someone his
size and with his allergies. But something. Wow. I wanted to cheer.
I wanted to do backflips and hire a skywriter to proclaim the good
news. Probably that would embarrass him to the point that he
never took anything again. Carefully, I took all that good will and
wrapped it up in a tiny, tiny smile. Then I turned away before I
could ruin the moment.

"I'll walk you to your truck," Tony said.

"The long way, through the field, with all the wildflowers and
pollen? Don't be a dumbass."

"I took something." The whine in his voice, combined with
the fact that he was rubbing his eyes, gave him the appearance of
an extremely overgrown child.

The confirmation of what I already knew made the desire for
backflips surge up all over again. And since he brought it up, I
figured I could offer some positive reinforcement. "You did? Wow.
That's — unusually fabulous. Thank you."

He gave me a look like I spoke in tongues. "Thank you?"

I smacked him upside the head. So much for positive
reinforcement. "Yes. Thank you. For being man enough to take care
of yourself. Dumbass."

Despite the head-slap, he eyed me like he suspected a trick.
But he didn't say anything, just sat down and laced up his boots.
"To your truck?"

He was wearing a green shirt that accented his eyes. I wondered if it was on purpose, if he knew how striking his eyes were. Yeah, I was way too tired.

———— «» ————

There is absolutely nothing pleasant about walking through a marshy area in the middle of Wisconsin in the middle of summer. It didn't matter how blue the sky was, or how good Tony smelled. The choking cloud of mosquitoes completely negated any potential for enjoyment. By the time we reached the truck, I was covered in bites and worried that even Galen's heartworm preventative wouldn't be enough to save him from that many mosquitoes. Usually, August was dry and therefore relatively mosquito-lite in this part of the state, but we had enough big thunderstorms the last few weeks that the mosquito population was booming.

"I'm sorry, big dog," I told him. He was too busy licking his feet to bother acknowledging my apology. Galen hated getting wet, and in some weird canine realm of logic, believed that he could lick the water off his fur. I smiled and stopped caring about my itchy skin while I watched him. Then a mosquito flew at my eye, and the moment was over.

"Why's he doing that? Did he hurt himself?" Tony was watching Galen's ministrations, too, but he smelled concerned.

"No. He's just wet."

"So he's licking himself to dry off?"

"He's a dog. Just because it doesn't make sense to you doesn't mean it's not helping him." I noted that Tony had several bites on his scalp. "You should've stayed back at camp."

"Naw." He rubbed the back of his head. "No big deal. What're you going to do today?"

"Um, good question." Sleep, hopefully. "I've got to come up with a plan to convince Aza to resume our truce and go away. Preferably one that doesn't include serving up any humans to him on a silver platter."

"Why? What happened to the 'kill him' plan?" At a series of fast beeps, Tony pulled his cell out of his pocket. "Finn's wondering where I am," he said after glancing at the text. He looked at me. I smelled the sweet tang of concern, a slight heat like cinnamon. "Don't get dead, okay?"

"I'll do my best."

"Kellan. I'm serious. Be careful." He dipped his head and kissed me. I pulled away before he could really get into it. The whole "you're my woman now, so I'm going to treat you like something I need to protect" vibe was really irritating, and I needed to put a stop to it.

"Tony, I'm always careful. And believe it or not, I'm actually really difficult to kill. So lose the macho protective attitude, okay? I'm not that girl."

He stepped back. "For someone who's always careful, you sure get attacked a lot. And I'm sorry if my attitude offends you. But I'm not gonna just wham-bam and walk away. I'm not that guy." His nostrils flared and his jaw clenched, and I suspected he needed to sneeze, but pride wouldn't let him.

I softened. I had a weakness for pride.

I reached up and touched his cheekbone, under his eye, which I figured would either help ease the need to sneeze or force him to go through with it. Sure enough, he jerked away and turned before he sneezed. "I better go," he mumbled.

I hugged him. After a brief hesitation, he hugged me back. "You're right," I said. "I have a tendency to run into other monsters' claws. But my main goal for today is to get some sleep. I promise I'll do everything in my power to not get dead before we have a chance to fuck again. Okay?"

He kissed the top of my head. "All right. See you later."

I opened the truck door and let Galen jump in before I swung into the driver's seat. Despite the stuffy heat of the truck cab, I left the windows rolled up until we were moving, hoping to avoid allowing any more flying intruders. The a/c didn't work in the truck when I bought it. That only bothered me during bug season.

The warmth of the truck cab, the rumble of the engine, the motion of the vehicle all combined to drag me toward sleep. When my phone rang, I almost jumped out of my skin in that just-pulled-from-the-edge-of-dreamland adrenaline rush. I swore and answered, just so I could stay awake until I got home.

It was Darcy. "Hey, you busy?"

I blinked rapidly to make my eyes focus. "Driving."

"Oh. You want to call me back?"

I forced life into my voice. "No. No, I'm glad you called."

"Really?" He sounded pleased, and I felt a little squirm of guilt in my stomach, because I was mostly glad that talking kept me from driving into a telephone pole.

"Yeah. Absolutely. What's up?"

He asked if I wanted to have breakfast. Ordinarily, I'd say of course. I always wanted to eat. But what I really needed was to pass out in my bed. I told him I hadn't slept yet.

"Oh. Sure. Well, you should get some sleep. I'll see you some other time."

The disappointment in his voice inflated that little squirm of guilt into an overwhelming guilt trip. Darcy was alone. Presumably, he had other friends that were less freakish than I was, but he didn't seem to want to talk to them. He wanted to talk to me. And, I told myself, maybe seeing Darcy would help me figure out a solution to the Aza problem. He was a key piece of the puzzle.

Jesus god on a toaster waffle, why the hell didn't I think of this before? Aza was hunting Darcy. Aza was going to kill Darcy. I needed to find a way to stop this. I needed to protect my friend. Because if this thing with Tony went south — when this thing with Tony went south, I was going to need a friend.

Maybe if I figured out why on earth Aza wanted to hunt Casper the Friendly Librarian, I could find a way to pacify Aza while saving Darcy's bacon. Again.

Mmm, bacon. And coffee. What was breakfast, really, if not an opportunity for fresh coffee? My mouth started to water. "You know, I'm starving, and I don't think I have any bacon in the house. I know I don't have anyone who'll cook me bacon in the house. Do you know a good place?"

After a token protest where he expressed concern over my sleep deprivation, Darcy named a restaurant, a little family diner on the north side of town. I promised to meet him there after I dropped Galen at home. While Galen ate his kibble, I took a quick shower and changed clothes. Attired in an almost identical outfit of shorts, tank top, button-down shirt and iron blades — I might not be creative, but I was always comfortable — I gave Galen a kiss and left.

To keep myself awake while I drove, I listed off all the food I was going to order at breakfast. Omelet, with ham, cheddar and swiss cheese, and jalapeno peppers. Pancakes. Bacon and sausage. Links, not patties. I'd try every kind of syrup they offered except the sugar-free kind, even if I had to order extra pancakes to accommodate the syrup.

I probably wouldn't order that much food. It tended to alarm the humans, seeing a skinny chick pack away more food than a football team. But the thought exercise kept my brain from freezing up. Unfortunately, it also had me all but drooling by the time I walked through the door of the diner.

Darcy stood a few steps from the cash register. When he caught sight of me, his tense face relaxed into a smile. He crossed to me in two strides. Without a moment's hesitation, he enveloped me in a hug. I let out a breath I hadn't known I was holding and drew in another breath, letting his scent smooth away the rough edges of the morning.

If I were human, the moment might have bothered me. The fact that I just began a sexual relationship with one man and was now thoroughly enjoying the embrace of another. But I had enough wolf in me to simply accept that I was with a key member of my pack. The fact that this human I barely knew somehow became a key member of my pack, on the other hand, would probably cause me a few sleepless nights. Like I needed more excuses not to sleep.

Darcy released me and I almost toppled over. He frowned. "You are tired. Are you sure you don't want to just go home and go to bed?" His breath smelled sour. The scent hit me so hard, I could taste his hangover on my own tongue.

I snorted. "I'm more likely to fall asleep at the table than in my bed." The words were out before I had a chance to censor them.

"I hear you," he said. It bothered me that Darcy understood the travails of insomnia. He was a nice guy. He deserved to sleep peacefully. "If you nod off, I'll try and make sure you don't fall in your food."

"Thanks."

We walked over to the hostess, who gave us a smile so high in wattage, it couldn't possibly be sincere. She led us to a booth and agreed to send our waitress over with coffee.

Darcy leaned forward and started playing with his napkin. I watched his hands with trepidation. Fidgety Darcy was a bad sign. Then the waitress brought the coffee, and the rest of the world faded away for a while. There was only me and the hot, bitter brew. After drinking most of the meager mugful, I refocused my eyes on Darcy.

He slid a laminated menu in front of me. "You said you were hungry." He went back to playing with his napkin.

Before I addressed his obvious anxiety, I glanced at the menu. It took me all of two seconds to find the lumberjack-style platter. Now I was free to assess Darcy. He was even paler than his normal shade of pasty, which accented nicely the puffy, dark blue circles under his eyes. Those eyes were bloodshot, and his hair looked like it hadn't seen a bottle of shampoo in at least a week. I saw Darcy the day before yesterday, and he didn't look nearly this shitty. What changed?

Coffee burbled in my stomach as I put a name to the emotion I was feeling — worry. "You gonna order food, or just a stack of napkins?"

Darcy glanced up at me, then down at his hands. His scent was tense and rich with adrenaline like Earl Gray tea with extra bergamot and lemon. He met my gaze and opened his mouth, but the waitress interrupted us before Darcy could enlighten me. When

Darcy tried to order just toast, I intervened and tacked oatmeal and fruit onto his meal. "I'm not that hungry," he said.

"You look like something Galen swallowed and yakked back up. Toast is not going to help you. You need hot food."

"Toast is hot. And fruit isn't." He sounded like a child.

Because I was getting pissed off, and because my coffee mug was now completely empty, I just blurted out the first thing that popped into my head. "Fruit makes people happy. Nobody gets upset when they're eating fruit. So either thank me or shut the fuck up."

Darcy let out a startled laugh, and his scent relaxed a little. Less lemon, more of a sweet vanilla. I stopped scrutinizing him long enough to raise my mug at our waitress, who nodded and brought over the coffeepot.

She filled my mug and started to walk away again, but I said, "Wait!" I drained the mug in three gulps, scalding my esophagus. "Refill, please."

"Why don't I bring over a pot for your table?" said my savior.

"Yes. That would be lovely." A small voice inside my head told me that I needed sleep, not coffee. I told the voice that unless it had a plan to drive home while asleep, it should shut up and let me caffeinate. I took a sip before starting in on Darcy. "So not that I'm not happy to see you, but I get the feeling you're not just looking for the pleasure of my company. What's up?"

"I — I think someone's following me." He avoided my gaze as he spoke, once again starting up with the napkin.

Suspicions confirmed, beautiful denial tossed out the window with the bathwater. I knew Darcy was right, that someone was following him. Knew, like you know that you're not going to be able to stop the car in time, that you're going to smash into the car in front of you. The Horror was hunting my friend. My pack. "When did you notice someone was following you?" My voice came out rough, and I took a sip of coffee.

"You — you believe me?"

I nodded, as his scent once again became the citrusy sour scent of fear. Funny. A few months ago, the scent of his fear awakened every hunting instinct in my being, and it took all my self-control to avoid seeing him as lunch. But the instinct rising up now, filling my chest, wasn't the thrill of the hunt. It was a desire to protect. To close ranks around my pack.

Still, his fear was getting a little out of hand. His breathing was so shallow, it almost wasn't there at all. His eyes were wide and yet didn't appear to see anything. When faced with someone so obviously troubled, some people might react with concern and reassurances. Some people apparently liked to waste valuable time. I took his hand and gripped tight, to a point just shy of crushing bone. He yelped, but I saw a presence and clarity in his eyes that wasn't there before. I let him go.

"That hurt," he said, rubbing his uninjured hand over the back of the other.

"Yeah. Sorry about that." I wasn't the least bit sorry. "Take some deep breaths. And maybe a drink of water."

He straightened in his seat, his chest puffing out. I wondered if he realized he was trying to intimidate me with his size. Bigger wolves always thought they would win just because they had more weight to throw around. But Darcy Jameson didn't know how to use his size to his advantage, not really. His display didn't concern me. "You know," he said, "you can't just go around beating people up all the time."

"Sure, we could talk about that." I leaned back as the waitress delivered our food and my pot of coffee. When she left, I went on. "We could invite Billy Graham up here and set up a tent and sing fucking hymns and maybe I'll see the error of my ways. But see, I'm betting you've got plenty of people you can call when you need a little compassion. Instead, you called me, which tells me that maybe there's something you need from someone who goes around beating people up."

I began to methodically work my way through my plate. Eggs first, because they were the worst when they got cold. Then the meat, leaving the pancakes for last. When dealing with platters full of food, it was important to prioritize. I was being cruel to Darcy, but I needed him to stop being scared and start being pissed off. Being pissed at me could act as his gateway drug, and lead to being pissed at Aza and anyone else who might want to hunt him.

Darcy glared at me for a moment before succumbing to the lure of hot food. I tried not to smile as he dug into the bowl of oatmeal. I failed and went for the gloat. "So, not hungry, huh?"

He didn't acknowledge the question as he spooned some of the fruit onto the oatmeal. I used the silence to consider my options. Even if I succeeded in getting Darcy pissed off, I couldn't leave him to defend himself. He was a librarian, for chrissake. Granted, a librarian whose father was a cop and taught him to shoot a gun, but still. He was more bookworm than coiled snake. When Aza chose to strike, Darcy would be easy prey. I really, really needed to kill Aza. Except that was *verboten* because it would start a war with the fey. So I needed to give Aza something he wanted more than Darcy. The only thing I could think of that he wanted more than his prey was, well, me.

Chapter 16

Oh, good. That was a brilliant alternative.

Maybe more information would help me find a better Plan B. "Darcy, have you ever been married?"

He stared at me, obviously — and understandably — flummoxed by the question. "Uh, no."

I debated how much to tell him. After all, he was a human and maybe it was better he retained some of his naivety. Except I needed to know why Aza chose him, and the best way I could think of to figure it out was to lay all the cards on the table. "I do believe you, Darcy. And I think I know who — what's following you. It's a faery named Aza."

Darcy frowned. "That term is incredibly offensive."

"What? No. Not — not that kind of — no, a faery. A member of the fey." I watched this sink in before I went on. "He's also a serial killer, I guess you'd call him. He likes to kill cheaters. Men who cheat on their wives."

He got a funny look on his face, like he just threw up a little in his mouth. "Oh."

"And you're not married, never been married. But have you ever cheated on a serious girlfriend? Or, um, boyfriend?" I didn't want to be accused of discrimination again.

"No, I — not exactly."

Jesus, this was an awkward conversation. I didn't want to pry any deeper into his personal life. I didn't want to see behind the curtain. But since when did what I wanted matter a damn bit? "But there's something? Something that might fall into the realm of cheating?"

He hesitated, then nodded.

I was going to die of old age before he elaborated. "Darcy, I'm sorry. Really. You have no idea how badly I want to end this conversation. But if I'm going to help you, I need to know what happened."

He seemed to shrink before my eyes. His shoulders slumped, his head drooped. "I slept with my neighbor."

"Okay."

"My married neighbor."

I worked very hard to keep any reaction out of my voice. "Okay."

"Who has a little baby."

Was this really Darcy saying these things? "Okay."

"And it wasn't just the one time."

"Okay."

His head shot up. "Would you say something else, please? Anything else?"

If I tried to string more than two syllables together, I was afraid my shock would show. I never in a million years would've thought Darcy would sleep with a married soccer mom. Well, probably the kid didn't play soccer yet. "Is the baby yours?"

"No! God. Of course not." His head hung down again. "But the baby was right in the next room, when we — well. And Brian found out. I think Sarah actually has feelings for me. But — I just needed to feel better. To forget things for a while. It was right after my sister was diagnosed, and it was stage four, they said she maybe had six months, and I had to be strong for her, but I felt so alone. I felt lost. And Sarah was right there, and she was so nice, and one thing led to another, and..."

I bit my tongue to keep from saying okay. "Uh-huh."

He glanced up at me through his eyelashes. "You think I'm a terrible person."

I snorted. "Don't be a dumbass, Darcy. You could kill a bus full of nuns and I would still know you're a great person. You made a mistake. Over and over again, but, well. When it comes to mistakes, I have absolutely no stone-throwing room. All right?"

"How is it you say these things that sound just awful, and yet, they make me feel so much better?" Darcy sounded truly dumbfounded.

"I don't know, it's probably proof you're demented."

"If this — this guy —" apparently, Darcy couldn't force himself to say "faery" even in this context — "kills cheaters, why is he after me? Sarah's the one who's married."

"He doesn't kill women. He likes to kill men." When Darcy opened his mouth to ask the next question, I held up my hand. "And don't ask me to explain why. I have no idea why he likes to kill anyone. He's twisted. All I know is, he has a type."

"Why do — people — keep wanting to kill me?" Darcy sounded almost as forlorn as when he confessed to doing the nasty with the neighbor.

I didn't have an answer for that, either. "Some of us are just lucky, I guess."

He scowled. "That doesn't make me feel better."

"Well, fortunately for you, you know someone who's fairly experienced in solving these sorts of problems. We'll figure it out. Okay?"

"How?"

I stared down at my pancakes. It would be a crime not to eat them. They looked fluffy and beautiful and perfectly brown. But my appetite was gone, crowded out by all of Darcy's unanswerable questions. "I don't know. But we'll figure it out." I poured syrup on the pancakes, deciding to eat them despite my lack of appetite.

Darcy watched me eat, his face a little paler and sweatier than it looked a moment ago. "If he wants to kill me, why not just kill me? Why drag it out?"

My eyes lost focus as I remembered last night's hunt with Galen, when we batted the deer between us like a cat playing with a half-dead mouse. "Because the chase is half the fun." The words came out slow and soft, my voice caressing each syllable. "Because your fear is almost better than the kill itself." The scent of fear brought me back to the present moment. I found Darcy staring at me. Clearing my throat, I forced my body to slump back in my seat. "Or at least, that would be my best guess. Can't say for sure."

My attempt at casual didn't appear to reassure him. I knew he saw something in my face, heard it in my voice, an intimate knowledge of that which I spoke. I couldn't take it back. So I didn't try. I went for bald honesty, instead.

"Darcy, listen. Maybe I'm a little left of center. Or a lot. The story is too long to go into right now, and frankly, I don't think you want to know it. But the best way to fight a nightmare is with another nightmare. I might not be Nobel Peace Prize material, but I can keep you safe. I will keep you safe."

He studied my face. Slowly, the fear ebbed, and his scent regained some of its warm, sweet normalcy. "I thought maybe it was a nocturne." He sounded wistful, like he was hoping he didn't have to find out the world contained more than one type of monster.

Little did he know, he was sitting right across from another one. "Not this time. You sure are a popular guy, for someone who doesn't really live a video-game type of life."

"Video game life?" he said.

"Yeah, you know. The sort of life where you throw yourself onto moving trains and shoot bad guys with RPGs. You're a librarian. From Wisconsin."

"You don't know what I do in my free time. Maybe my weekends are all about jumping onto moving trains."

I laughed, and he laughed with me, and it felt good. For a second, we were just two friends teasing each other. Then the second was over, and we had to get back to the business of saving Darcy's life. "I'll figure out a way to protect you."

"Last time you 'protected' me, I ended up with a knife through my lung." It took all my self-control not to flinch at the reminder. His tone still sounded teasing, and his scent never changed. But there was a tightness at the corners of his eyes that made me think deep down, he was more serious than he wanted to commit to out loud.

I set down my fork very carefully, lining it up exactly an inch away from the left side of my plate. I straightened the spoon and butter knife, too, making a perfect place setting while I tried not to think about anything at all.

"I'm sorry," Darcy said. "I shouldn't have brought that up."

I laughed humorlessly. "No, actually, you make an excellent point. I fucked up big time that day. The difference is, this time, I know who the bad guy is. I know who's hunting you. I just need to keep you safe while I figure out how to get him to give up."

Darcy squinted at me. "Give up? Aren't you —" He looked around, making sure no one was listening before finishing in a whisper, "Aren't you going to kill him?"

"Look at you, getting all blood-thirsty. I'm so proud." My voice sounded dead. "That's really why you called me, isn't it? Because you have other friends who would tell you that alcohol poisoning must be making you paranoid. You called me in case you were right and needed someone who's good at killing."

He leaned forward. "I called you because I knew I was right, and I was scared, and I didn't want to talk to someone who would tell me I was paranoid. I wanted to talk to someone who would take me seriously. I knew I could count on you for that. And for the record, no, I really don't have any other friends. I did, sort of, before my sister died. But I don't talk to them these days. People stop knowing what to say when your whole family has dropped dead. I'm like the last guy left standing in the leper colony. And I don't know what to say to them, either. They don't get it. They're so interested in dating and having kids and getting a raise or a promotion. It's like we don't even speak the same language anymore."

I didn't want to know this. I didn't want to know that I was Darcy's life raft. I thought I was scared of losing Tony? The pressure

Darcy's statement put on me and my social ineptitude stole the air from my lungs. "So who do you talk to?"

A blush crept up his neck, reddening his ears and cheeks. "Bartenders, I guess. The women who sit next to me. It's actually turned out to be a great pickup line. My parents and sister are dead and I'm all alone. Women eat that up."

I tried to reconcile the Darcy I knew with the drunk Darcy picking up chicks in bars. And using his sister's death to do it. My head started pounding long before I could marry the images. "That doesn't really seem like you," I said finally.

He laughed, and it was a horrible, wounded sound. "It's not me. But every time I try to stay home, try to read or watch a movie or any of the things I did before, I can't focus. Can't sit still. I have to get out of the house, go somewhere noisy and dark that smells like alcohol. Then I drink until I feel better. Or don't feel at all. And sometimes, I meet someone who wants to sleep with me, and that feels good. At least, it feels good while it's happening. Not so much after, but, well. If that's the only time I get to feel good, why should I stop doing it?"

"STDs, for one thing," I said before I thought about it. Gradually, thought forced me to process all the things Darcy said, not just the icky indiscriminate sex thing. "Sorry." That was the only thing I could think of to say, so I said it again. "I'm sorry."

He stared at his empty bowl. "I didn't mean to say all that out loud."

"Yeah. Happens to me all the time. My mouth is constantly saying shit that my brain didn't agree to." My words made him look up at me and smile, and I felt on more familiar ground. "Your place or mine?"

"What?"

Now that my brain was working on a concrete plan, I felt relaxed, almost happy. "I can protect you by staying at your place. Or you can come to mine. But I can't protect you from across town."

"I — wow. You're a good friend, Kelly."

I was almost positive that no one ever said that to me in my entire life. Two hundred years was a long time to remember on the spot, but I was pretty sure this was a first. I didn't know what to say. Bypassing the "good friend" part, I focused on the fact that my friend didn't even know my real name. "Yeah, about that. My name's actually Kellan."

"Oh." He cocked his head to one side, as if he were listening to music I couldn't hear. "Kellan. That suits you. You're not much of a Kelly."

"Um, thanks, I guess." I studied him. I wanted to tell him that I was a shape-shifter. The urge to say it was so strong, like the urge to pee after drinking sixty-four ounces of Gatorade. But I just told him about the existence of faeries. Sure, his head didn't explode, but he did have a lot on his plate right now. And, well. What if he decided that it was one thing to know such creatures exist, and a whole nother can of worms to sit across the table from one? I chickened out. "So your place or mine?"

"I don't know. I have to go to work."

"Work?" I didn't want him out of my sight. I didn't want to take any risks. I didn't want to go sit in the library for eight hours and watch dust float through the air. I wanted to sleep, and sleep could only happen in my apartment, where I could let my guard down.

"Yes. Work. Where they pay me, so I can have fun things like food and shelter."

"But —"

"It'll be fine. Nobody ever got killed at the public library."

I hung my head. "Jesus, do you not watch movies? Have you never heard of famous last words? Don't say shit like that. You're begging Fate to prove you wrong."

He smiled at me, like I was a little kid who just said something adorable. "I don't believe in fate. But thank you for your concern."

"Fuck concern. You're a moron." I stood up and pulled some cash out of my pocket, tossing two twenties on the table. "That should cover it. Fine, let's go take you to the library, where nobody ever could possibly die."

"I didn't say that, I said no one ever got killed there."

It was too early in the morning to argue semantics. "Oh, well, then. I'm sure you'll be fine. Just get in your damn car, so we can go to work before Aza picks you off here in the parking lot."

Darcy's smile vanished as we walked outside. "You think he's here?"

"You'll live longer, always assuming that answer is yes." I tried to sniff the air without being obvious. It would make things easier to just tell Darcy about my special talents, a small voice in my head pointed out. I told the voice to shut the fuck up and returned to my discreet sniffing. No unusual scents, but just because I didn't smell Aza didn't mean he wasn't there.

"So you're going to follow me?" Darcy sounded hopeful. And his fear scent filled my nostrils, blotting out all other scents.

"Yes. I'll go with you to work." I tried hard to sound like I didn't dread the prospect.

His fear scent faded as he frowned. "You're not going to stay, are you? You look like hell. You should go home and get some rest."

Did he want my help or didn't he? I felt a snarky response rise up my throat like bile. But snarky would make him defensive, and possibly cause him to resist my help later. I swallowed down the snark and tried to think of a compromise. "Okay. How about I follow you to work, make sure you get there in one piece, and then I'll go home and sleep, since nothing bad ever happens at the library?"

He shook his head. "You're never going to let that go, are you?"

"Trust me, I'm hoping you're right. But if you're wrong, I'm carving it into your tombstone. 'Nobody ever got killed at the library. Until he did.'" Some of the snark snuck out anyway, I guess.

We arrived at his car. He leaned down and kissed my cheek. "You really are a good friend."

"I'm starting to think you don't actually understand what those words mean, but whatever." I waited until he got in the car and started it, before trotting over to my truck and pulling into traffic behind him.

The drive to the library was uneventful. I followed him inside and took a quick walk through the stacks, making sure nobody smelled like a faery. Of course, faeries didn't smell like anything special until you made them bleed, which I couldn't do to any of the library patrons without getting arrested. But I did my best to make sure Aza wasn't there before I left for home.

As I drove back to my apartment, I considered the situation. If I wanted to save Darcy's life, I didn't have a lot of time. Aza had been waiting for this kill since spring. Of course, he found other people to kill in the meantime, but I was sure the desire to kill Darcy festered in him like an ulcer. Darcy wasn't just the one who got away, he was the one who was snatched from Aza's jaws by me. I was the salt ground into that wound.

Wait. I was the salt. Which meant my existence probably stung a lot more than Darcy's. My head started to ache again as I tried to follow the metaphor. Raoul said Aza wanted my blood. He didn't mention Darcy. Maybe Raoul didn't know what he was talking about, but I suspected he knew exactly what Aza sought. Aza wanted to kill Darcy since spring. He wanted to kill me since I was a little kid. A few months versus two hundred years.

What was that thought I had earlier? The only thing Aza wanted more than his prey was me.

So what if I gave him what he wanted?

Chapter 17

As soon as I got home and was greeted by my dog, I felt horribly guilty for even considering handing myself over to Aza. Not that I intended to trade my life for Darcy's. I liked living. But if I could find some way to get Aza to agree to not kill me, just play with me for a while — and I tried not to think too hard about what Aza might consider "play" — maybe he would be happy enough to leave and never come back.

But what would happen to Galen while Aza had me?

Maybe Tony would watch him for me. Shit, Tony. He wouldn't be thrilled with this plan. Well, different problem for a different day. Right now, I needed to figure out some way to leverage the agreement I wanted from Aza. If I couldn't find a way to do this without getting killed, the plan wasn't an option. But I knew someone who might be able to help me get what I wanted.

I harnessed Galen and we took off down the block. Raoul stood on his corner.

When he greeted Galen, he refrained from the faery glamour routine, so Galen merely wagged his tail instead of turning into a puddle of pudding. When Raoul greeted me, he didn't hold back. I found myself smiling shyly, hoping, wishing, needing him to look at me, to speak to me...

I shook my head and took a step back. "You're playing dirty."

"Only way I play, beautiful." His tone was light, but his scent and eyes were cool, like he was waiting to see whether I pulled a blade.

I sighed. "Look. The guy you warned me about yesterday. You said he wanted my blood."

He seemed to lean, as if against a wall, settling into his stance. "Uh-huh." He drew out the first syllable, uuuuuh-huh, and cocked his head to one side.

"What do you know about him?"

"More than some. Less than others."

I almost gave up. Almost cussed him out and walked away. But Raoul made up the entirety of my faery resources. The fey didn't go around making themselves available for questioning to any curious soul. It was Raoul or nothing. "Look, could we talk straight? A little less of the vague obscurity? I need some help."

"And how is that my problem?" Raoul's drawl faded slightly.

Maybe if I laid my cards out, he would feel obliged to open up to me, too. "It's not your problem. Except you went to the trouble of warning me about him. What I know about fey tells me that your kind doesn't do shit like that. Which makes me think you like me a little. Or at least, you like me a little better than you like Aza."

He studied me for a moment, while my heart pounded in my throat and threatened to gag me. Then Raoul started to laugh. "Oh, honey, you crack me up. You're not wrong. I do like you better than that psycho sack o' shit. How 'bout you tell me what kind of help you're looking for, and I'll decide if I can provide it?"

That was probably the best offer I was going to get. "He wants to kill a friend of mine. Frankly, I'd like to kill him, but apparently, that would start a war."

"Mmm-hmm. He's got family high up in the Shadow Court." Of course it would be the Shadow Court, where the dark fey worshipped their queen and entertained themselves torturing humans that they lured into their clutches. Or so the bedtime story goes.

I plunged ahead. "My thought is, I'll offer myself up to him in trade."

Raoul went absolutely still and silent. He ceased blinking and breathing. He just stared at me.

"Not for him to kill me," I said. I explained my idea. "But I need to convince him that it's enough just to torture me, and stop short of killing."

Raoul was quiet for so long, I thought he must have decided not to help. Then he spoke. "That's easy enough. You see, if he were to kill you, he would start a war of his own."

I frowned. "No, the Sankhain wouldn't go to war over me. Janus is too smart to risk that kind of shitstorm."

"Not the Sankhain, little wolf. The Court of Light."

My frown deepened into a scowl. The fey were divided into two courts, the Shadow Court, where the Dark Fey hid their ugly, tortured selves. And the Court of Light, home of the beautiful and reportedly snobbish Light Fey. And when I said divided, I meant it. The Dark and the Light hated each other. The Dark Fey were jealous of the beauty of the Light, and the Light treated the Dark like something smelly they just stepped in. The two courts were continuously squabbling over something. And I was supposed to believe the Light Fey would start a civil war if Aza killed me? "What the fuck are you talking about?"

Raoul looked around. People were around, but no one paid attention to us. No one paid attention to anyone in this neighborhood. "You are the daughter of the Sun Prince."

I couldn't make that make sense. "Uh. Come again?"

"Your father is the heir to the Court of Light. When the Summer King dies, your father will reign, and you and your sister will be the heirs."

I didn't know which part was tripping me up. The fact that I was part fey, that Raoul knew this when I didn't, that my father was royalty rather than some stableboy, that my mother fucked a faery prince...It was all stop-your-brain-in-its-tracks material.

"So you see, you already have all the leverage you need." Raoul didn't look happy about this. He didn't look like he wanted me to know any of it.

"Are you — are you part of the Court of Light?"

He smiled a distinctly sardonic smile. "You could say that."

We were back to vague obscurity. That pissed me off. "Sure, I could say that. I could also say supercalifragilisticexpialidocious, but what I want to say right now is —"

"I am the Sun Prince."

I blinked several times in rapid succession. He was the Sun Prince? That would mean — "You're my father?"

He dipped his head in an annoyingly haughty nod.

"You — shit. I thought you were a drug dealer, for chrissake." A few more seconds. "You wolf-whistled at me! You complimented my legs on multiple occasions. You're sick."

"You would have preferred I introduce myself? As your father, the faery prince?" He looked like he was finally enjoying the moment.

"Fuck you." It was all I could think of. "I have to go."

"Kellan." His voice rang out and riveted me in my spot. I didn't know why his voice did that to me, and it pissed me off even more. "Despite these revelations," he said, "your plan is ludicrous. No human is worth the pain that Aza would put you through. Let him have the human, and find yourself a different friend."

I tilted my head back until I looked down my nose at him. "You're wrong. Plenty of humans are worth it. And it's sad, if you've stood on this corner for this long and still don't see that. I pity you." I didn't feel as bold as my words. Instead, I braced myself for a blow. But I tried really hard not to let it show.

He didn't hit me. He smiled, a private half-smile that looked like he was remembering something from long, long ago. "Your mother was right. You are more like her than any of her other daughters."

I couldn't have heard that right. "My mother didn't think that. She thought I was weak."

He shook his head. "You preferred to hide in the shadow of your sister. Your mother tried to provoke you into the spotlight, if you will. But you were quite stubborn."

"Check your verb tense, buddy. I still am."

He studied me, and gradually I realized I could move my limbs again. But I didn't leave. As much as I hated to admit it, I wanted to know what he said next. "Wording is everything when making a deal with one of us. Especially one of the Shadow Court. They will twist your words to mean things you never dreamed."

"What would you suggest I say?" I wasn't sure I trusted him, but if anyone could broker an ironclad faery deal, a faery prince could.

He grinned a Raoul grin at me, and the air filled with the scents I associated with Raoul the drug dealer — cigarettes, hot dogs, sweat that smelled a little too sweet. "I ain't in the business of martyrdom, honey. You wanna go down that road, you do it on your own."

I wasn't surprised. I was pretty sure that I already got Raoul to reveal more than he wanted to. And besides, Janus and Finn were plenty experienced in the art of twisting words. I tugged on Galen's leash, pulling him closer to me. "See you around?"

Raoul — I couldn't think of him as my father, I didn't have a father and anyway, he smelled like Raoul — dipped his chin in a nod. "Yep. See you."

I couldn't get home fast enough.

———— «» ————

After giving Galen fresh water and chugging some myself, I shape-shifted and we curled up on the futon. I felt like my whole sense of self just shifted a hundred miles to the left. My mother slept with a faery prince.

My mom wasn't crazy about men. I suppose she was probably a lesbian, but sexual identity wasn't really something people declared two hundred years ago. When she wanted to create another daughter, Fionna Faolanni would find an eager male and sleep with him. Then she'd wait a while to see if she got pregnant. If not, she'd find a different male and start the process over again.

Why would she deviate from that pattern and choose to fuck a faery prince?

Were any of my other sisters fathered by fey? Did this mean I was susceptible to iron? What else did it mean?

And why would Raoul hang around in my neighborhood? Was he keeping an eye on me? Was that paternal or was it creepy? How the hell could I know the difference? I never had a father. Much less one who took an interest in my well-being.

With a grumble, I stood up, turned in a circle several times, and laid back down. This time, I fell asleep almost before my tail settled across my nose. When I woke, the room was growing dark.

After shifting back, I glanced at the sunset out the window, then at the clock. Darcy's shift at the library started at nine-thirty this morning. It was now almost eight-thirty p.m. Where was he?

I dialed his cell, which went straight to voicemail. Adrenaline began to build, making my hands so shaky, I fumbled Galen's harness. I put it over his head the wrong way, was forced to take it back off and start over. He gazed at me with bald concern in his too-wide eyes. "It's okay, bud," I said, even though I was terrified that it wasn't okay at all. "It's okay."

I was jonesing for some coffee, but didn't dare make a stop on the way to the library. Darcy's car was still in the parking lot. I tried to tell myself that was a good sign, but why was he still here? I pulled one of the iron blades from its sheath and slid it into my pocket, where I could grip the handle while looking casual. Promising Galen I would be right back, I slid out of the truck and closed the door softly, not wanting to announce my presence.

It was eight forty-five. The library closed at nine, and the parking lot was drained, only a few cars left. I sniffed the air as I walked to the front doors, but knowing what I knew about Raoul's glamour abilities, I didn't hold out a lot of hope that Aza would still have his familiar scent. I gripped the hilt in my pocket and pushed through the doors into the library.

Immediately, I spotted Darcy on one of the computers. I was so relieved, my knees started to shake. But relief was a transient emotion, one that faded almost as soon as it appeared. In its place was rage, the flipside of fear, the strongest of the strong. I stalked over to Darcy and barely stopped myself from yanking his chair out from under him. "Where the hell have you been?" I said. I mentally cringed when I heard the words and realized how stupid they were, but outwardly, I kept my glower in place.

Darcy blinked up at me. "Um, hi. I've been right here. Remember? You walked in with me. I wasn't sure if I was supposed to call you when my shift was done, but I knew you needed to sleep. I figured you'd call me when you were awake."

His concern for me was sincere, I could smell that much. But I already hopped a ride on anger, and I couldn't just hop off again.

"I did call you. It went straight to voicemail. Do you know how worried I was?"

"Oh, I'm sorry." And again, I could smell his sincerity. He dug in his pocket and pulled out his phone. "I turned it back on when my shift ended, but I set it on vibrate. Must not've felt it in my pocket. I'm so sorry."

Maybe I could've maintained my rage through one apology, but the second one with the "so" thrown in was my undoing. I wilted as all adrenaline left me, and I slumped into a chair. "Whatever. I'm — I'm glad you're okay."

Soft footsteps on carpet and a cloud of perfume brought a fraction of adrenaline back to my system. I leapt to my feet and whirled around, and the librarian Dolly, who I met last spring and whose ex-husband I buried two days ago, jumped. She pressed a fluttery hand to her chest. "Oh, I didn't mean to startle you," she said in a sugary, Minnie Mouse voice. "I just wanted to let you know it's almost nine o'clock. Darce, you might want to wrap up."

"Right. Thanks, Dolly. We're headed out right now."

As we walked outside, I said, "Darce? Are you sleeping with her, too?"

He scowled at me. At least, a Darcy version of a scowl. His annoyance still managed to have a gentleness to it. "No. For pete's sake. I'm starting to wish I never told you all that."

I snorted. "Only starting to wish? I would've been wishing it from the moment the story left my mouth."

"Yes, well. You're my friend. Friends tell each other things. And when friends respect and care for each other, they don't use those things to mock each other."

"Are you sure? That doesn't sound right at all." Meanwhile, I suspected he would say that friends would tell each other when one friend was planning to swap her life — temporarily — for the other friend. But I didn't want to tell him yet.

We reached his car. "Would you mock Galen if he revealed something shameful to you?" Darcy pulled out his keys and unlocked the driver's door.

"I have to watch him lick his dick on a regular basis. If he managed to come up with something shameful, you better believe I'd use it against him every chance I got."

"Which may be why you don't have more friends," he said.

"Watch the stone-throwing, Mr. Glass House. Look, something's come up. I have to go to the forest. So I'll follow you to my apartment, then once you're inside —"

Darcy interrupted me. "In that case, why don't I just go to my apartment? He left a dead body in your backyard, not mine. My apartment may be less of a risk. I'll stay with you while you're home, if you think it will help. But if you're not around, I'm no safer at your apartment than at mine."

It sounded reasonable. But somehow, I felt like my apartment would be safer. Maybe it was the collection of knives in the dresser, but my reasoning was probably less logical than that. "He knows where you live," I said.

"He knows where you live, too. If he comes for me, then I'll call you. But he can't walk through walls, right? So I'll be safe as long as I stay inside and don't open the door."

"Sure, because nobody in the history of time has managed to bypass a fucking door." I felt anger bubble up, but Darcy's stubborn jaw wouldn't budge. "All right. But I'm still following you to your place."

Back in the truck, I rolled Galen's window down all the way so he could stick his head out and let his tongue loll in the wind. I needed somebody to be happy for just a little while. Galen had the best shot of any of us.

I went inside the apartment with Darcy, ignored his protests, walked through the place to make sure it was secure. Then I went back out to the truck and Galen, and we drove to the forest.

The area was pretty abandoned when we arrived, so I decided to forgo the ordeal of forcing Galen to get his feet wet. Since nobody was around to see the improbable spectacle of little ol' me carrying big ol' Galen, I picked him up and carried him through the marshy field. He squirmed and grumbled, but I ignored him. "Lesser of the evils, big dog, trust me." When the trees appeared around us, I set him down. He shook himself and turned his back on me, shunning me. "Fine. Next time, I'll drag you through the puddles."

Approaching footsteps brought Galen to stand protectively by my side. Galen accompanied me to the forest countless times, and every time, he encountered the border patrol, and every time, everything was fine. Didn't mean it would be this time. Galen was a pessimistic boy scout at heart. Always be prepared for the absolute worst.

It wasn't Cat this time, which explained why the patrollers were walking toward us instead of shooting arrows at us. Dirk and a young girl appeared out of the shadows. I wracked my brain for the girl's name. She was fairly new, and it surprised me that Finn assigned her to border patrol, a job that required both skill and the ability to sit very still for long, boring periods of time. She arrived two or so years ago with her younger sister. The younger sister's name was Tia, and this one's name was…Valentine.

"Sankha Kellan, we weren't expecting you." Dirk spoke and Valentine watched me without moving. She didn't blink, didn't fidget, didn't even seem to breathe. Suddenly, I understood why she'd been given this particular assignment.

"No, you weren't. But I really need to speak to Janus and Finlay. May we pass?" I hated that I had to ask permission, but it was expected. Failing to ask would only prolong the exchange.

"Very well. We won't accompany you." Dirk stepped back, making room for Galen and me to pass. Valentine didn't move. Dirk prodded her. "Vallie."

I blinked, surprised. Dirk didn't strike me as a guy who would use nicknames. But it worked. Valentine blinked, stepped back and bowed her head. "Welcome, Sankha Kellan," she said in a voice that was actually much bigger than her size would suggest.

"Thank you." Galen and I stepped between them, and I kept a hand on Galen's collar. I didn't know how Valentine felt about dogs. A few of the younglings were scared of Galen. Fear made people behave strangely around dogs, and strange behavior was one of Galen's triggers. I held on tight, and we passed without incident.

When we reached the edge of the forest, a breeze kicked up, and I closed my eyes and turned my face toward it like a caress. We — the Hycene, the shape-shifting warriors in Janus's little army — believed that the spirits of the dead were set free to ride on the wind after we burned them on a pyre. Every once in a while, the wind came along just when I needed a friendly touch. I breathed it in now, let it soothe me. It carried the scents of the forest, pine needles and decaying leaves, the August-dry earth and dying grass of the paths between cabins. I wanted to curl up in a ball with Galen and rest, surrounded by those smells.

I dragged my eyes open and rubbed my hands up and down my cheeks, trying to perk up. I caught a new scent on the wind and felt all my courage and certainty flee.

"Hey," Tony said. "What're you doing back here already?"

I hesitated. I wasn't ready to tell him my plan. "I need to talk to Machiavelli and his Mini-Me."

He smiled and threw an arm across my shoulders. "What's up?"

Well, I wanted to tell them about my idea to offer myself up to Aza as chum. "I need to brainstorm about Aza. He's after Darcy. There's got to be a way to stop him that won't put us at odds with the entire faery community."

Tony shook his head. "That poor guy. Darcy's having a hell of a year."

"Thank you, O Master of Understatement." This earned me a snort from Tony and a wag from Galen. "So anyway, I should probably —"

"I'll come with you. If that's okay. The more brains storming, the better the odds we can come up with something."

No. I wanted to get Finn and Janus on my side before I started telling people who actually cared about my well-being. Well, Janus cared, but not in the same testosteroney way Tony did. But how could I leave Tony out of the meeting without showing my hand? I couldn't think of anything. "Um, okay. Yeah. Why not? Unless you have someplace else to be. I wouldn't want to keep you."

He bent down and brushed his lips across mine. "Nowhere else I'd rather be."

"Oh. Okay. Great."

Tony squinted down at me, while Galen looked up at me with an eerily similar expression. "If you don't want me to sit in on the meeting, just say so, Kell."

This was it, my opportunity. But suddenly I knew he would be hurt if I told Finn and Janus my plan before I told him. I took a deep breath. "Actually, before we go to see them, I want to tell you something."

We went to his cabin. He listened to my plan, or the beginning of it, anyway. And he didn't say a word. Not one single word. Not a grunt or a sigh. He didn't even sneeze. He just sat there. But before I could tell him the key element of the plan — that I was the daughter of a faery prince and therefore too valuable for Aza to kill — Tony abruptly stood up and walked out.

Chapter 18

I stared after him, wondering what I should do. What would the Emotionally Mature Handbook say about this situation? Fuck, I was about as likely to qualify as emotionally mature as I was to qualify for Wimbledon. No, I had a much better shot at Wimbledon.

I allowed myself one self-pitying glance at my dog. "That went well." Galen returned my gaze with wide eyes. So wide that a foolish part of me wondered if he understood what I just told Tony. The thought of abandoning Galen, even temporarily, made me queasy, so I worked very hard to avoid thinking about it. And I couldn't do much to soothe my poor dog right now, because I needed to go talk to Finn and Janus. Who usually didn't have a high opinion of my ideas even when those ideas didn't sound like the plot of a Harry Potter novel.

I shook my head and squared my shoulders. My mother wouldn't have asked permission. She would've marched into Janus's cabin and told him what she was going to do. So that was what I would do. Just as soon as I was certain my voice wouldn't quiver.

Galen and I took the long way to Janus's cabin, walking around the outskirts of camp, around the paddocks and the ammunitions barn. It was late enough that most of the younglings were in bed. As quiet as the Academy ever got. I loved it here this time of night. Hell, I loved it here anytime. But now, with the stars overhead and the warm breeze and the soft rustling of leaves the loudest sound, this was home. The only thing that could improve the night air would be a chorus of howling wolves. Something inside me, that part of me that usually relaxed the second I stepped across the boundary of the forest, finally let go.

Maybe it was the fey in me. The unwelcome thought made me scowl, though it might have some truth to it. Faeries preferred open countryside to the dense intensity of the city. And no matter how long I lived there, no matter how many Darcy Jamesons I met, the city would never make me feel like this.

When we arrived at Janus's cabin and I caught a whiff of Tony's scent, all serenity fled. Did he arrive here first to break the news to Janus and Finn before I did? Obviously, his version of my plan wouldn't be nearly as appealing as my version. I felt a flutter of panic, and then a warm rush of anger. How dare he — but no. He was waiting for us by the door. He wouldn't have had time to talk to Finn and Janus and still be waiting outside when I arrived. He must not have gone in yet.

Oh, the rage in his scent. I almost felt scared of him, and I never, in all these years, had a reason to be scared of Tony. I didn't say anything, because I knew that anything I said would probably make everything worse.

"I told you I'd go in with you," he said to my unasked question. "To brainstorm." He spat out that last word like it was a poison dart aimed at my eye.

I would never get Finn and Janus on my side with rage-blind Tony in the room. But he was kinda big and difficult to stop from doing something he obviously felt strongly about. A low rumble sounded in the vicinity of my knee. I looked down at Galen, whose eyes were glued to Tony. Well, I definitely couldn't have both Defensive Galen and Rage-Blind Tony in the same room. Bloodshed, anyone?

I pulled Galen's leash out of my pocket. I looped it around a sapling and snapped the leash on Galen's harness. Then I wasted a few precious seconds trying to figure out a way to do the same to Tony. I could always hit him over the head with a rock, knock him out. But in the long run, that would probably make things worse, not better. Still, it was tempting.

While I was thinking, Tony stood glowering at me. I gritted my teeth. "Fine," I said. "You can come. But I'm not going to change my mind."

He held the screen door open for me. I saw his knuckles were bloody and torn. Little bits of bark stuck to the drying blood. It looked like Tony spent the last several minutes taking his anger out on some poor tree. The tightness of the tendons in his forearm made me wonder if he too was fighting the urge to bash someone in the head with a rock.

"And try to get a grip on the rage, would you?" I said as the screen door slapped shut behind us. "It's really not your thing."

"Oh, honey," Tony said in a voice that sounded both harsh and seductive. "You sayin' that just proves you don't know half as much about me as you think."

I swallowed hard. I shouldn't have been turned on. But I was.

The youngling at the desk — a boy whose name I couldn't bother to dredge up — took one look at Tony's face, let out a little squeak, and scuttled into the inner room to announce us. "You're scaring the children," I said under my breath.

Tony stiffened. I heard him take a deep, noisy breath and let it back out slowly. His anger went from a level eleven to, say, a five-and-a-half. I slanted a glance at him out of the corner of my eye. His mouth was set in a thin, hard line, his gaze fixed straight ahead. He looked pale. The pallor was what got me. Was it because of my plan? Or because he thought he frightened a youngling? Either way, it all came back to my plan. Tony was only scary-angry because of me. Maybe this wasn't the best option. Maybe something that could drain Tony of color was just too awful to really be considered.

Then I thought of Aza. I thought of more bodies popping up like fucked-up flowers. I thought of Darcy's lifeless eyes. Of Galen's body twisted and ripped open. Of Tony, burned and broken. How pale would he be then, when his insides were all on the outside? This was what would happen, if I didn't find a way to rid myself of Aza. He would take away everyone I ever cared about, everyone I ever said hello to, just because he could. I didn't want to cause Tony pain. But I couldn't let Aza make any more corpses.

I raised my chin and fixed my own gaze straight ahead. The long run. In the long run, this would be best. Even if Tony never forgave me. My chin faltered as the door opened and the youngling told us we could enter. But I picked my chin up and walked into Janus's room.

As soon as I saw Janus's face, I knew he read my thoughts and knew what I came here to say. But Finn didn't read minds, and he looked from Tony to me, back and forth over and over, before finally settling on me. His curiosity smelled like dried moss.

Tony moved to lean against the wall, or at least, that's what I thought he was doing. I didn't dare look at him. I was holding onto my will with the weakest of tethers. I couldn't allow outside stimuli to break me. "Hello, sirs." I heard Tony snort, and I faltered slightly. "Um, do you have a moment? I need to tell you something."

Finn glanced at Janus, who said nothing. In fact, Janus was as silent and still as Tony when he found out about my plan. Bad sign. I focused on Finn. If I could sway him, maybe I had a chance at winning over Janus, and then Tony wouldn't be able to stop me.

Mother would just tell them what she was going to do. Just say it, like it's a foregone conclusion, because with her, it was. Raoul said I was more like her than any of her other daughters. Maybe this was a good time for Fake It Til You Make It. I looked

Finn in the eye and said, "Aza, the Horror, is growing more and more dangerous. More and more conspicuous. He can't be allowed to continue so close to our door. We cannot allow attention to be drawn to the forest, or to the Sankhain. And he will continue to harass us. He despises me. But he can't kill me, for the same reason I can't kill him, so he'll find other ways to hurt me. To make me pay."

Finn's scent grew more and more dry, an indication he was thinking hard. Could be a good sign. At least he was listening.

"So I'm going to offer myself up to him. Let him have me, to do what he wishes, for the span of two months, provided he stops short of killing me." The words surprised me. I just came up with the time limit on the spot. In the life of an immortal, two months was nothing. But I had a feeling that in the hands of an evil faery who hated me, two months would be a pretty good-sized chunk of hell.

I shut down the fear and doubt that threatened to creep in. I could do this. Darcy was counting on me.

"And in return," I went on, "Aza will leave, go far away, and never return to Wisconsin. If he returns, or if he kills me, he will be in breach of contract, and we will be able to kill him without fear of retribution."

"We?" Tony said. "If you're dead, there's no we."

"I meant it like the royal we," I snapped. "Anyway, that's what I'm going to do."

Finn finally spoke. "So you are merely informing us?" The air wavered slightly, as he raised a little power.

Shit. He wasn't going to help me. I clenched my jaw, refusing to let my anxiety show. "Yes. This is my decision, and it's the best option we have."

"It's a shit option," Tony burst out. Finn and Janus both turned to look at him, their faces a silent rebuke for his language. He crossed his arms and looked down at his feet.

Finn turned back to me. "Have you forgotten you are a Sankha, and therefore subject to our orders?"

My hand twitched. I wanted a blade. Just to hold, not to throw at anybody. "No, sir, I haven't. But I am also the last Hycene. I am my mother's daughter, and it's up to me to clean up my mother's mess. She forged a lousy agreement with the Horror. He found a way to come back to Madison, and not only that, he's flaunting his kills, dropping them literally on my doorstep. What's to stop him from coming here? From picking off the younglings, one by one? This agreement will work. He'll be gone. For good."

Janus still didn't say anything. It was making me sad, his total lack of support. Not that I was surprised, but I was hurt. Finn, however, considered me. "What did you mean when you said he cannot kill you, for the same reason you cannot kill him?"

I took a deep breath. "He won't kill me, because my father is the Sun Prince, heir to the Court of Light. Mal and I are next in line for the throne. So if he killed me, Aza would start a war of his own between the Light and Shadow Courts." I snuck a glance at Tony. His jaw was scraping the ground. I tried to feel a little bit good about the moment, like it was a victory. But it still felt shitty, like it had since Tony got up and walked out of the cabin before I even finished telling my story.

"Well," Finn said slowly. "That changes the situation considerably." Finn looked at Janus, and kept looking at him until the old man returned his gaze. Janus's lack of reaction made me wonder if he already knew about my royal parentage. I pushed the thought away. This wasn't the time.

Tony charged forward. "You're not actually considering this?"

Finn's eyes flashed. "Antony, you are dangerously close to insubordination. Mind your tone."

Tony shook with the apparent effort to check his temper. "Sir, my apologies." His voice sounded strangled. "But this is insane. Kellan can't deliver herself into his clutches. He's nutballs." Tony closed his eyes, clenched and unclenched his jaw. "He's a madman. You can't let her do this. Please, sirs."

"Kellan is Hycene. She can heal any wound he might inflict," Finn said. I was starting to get annoyed at being talked about in the third person, like a coma patient or a particularly stupid child.

"She only wants to do this," Tony said, "because Aza is hunting Darcy Jameson, the outsider that Kellan saved last year. Against your orders, I believe, sirs." Apparently realizing he was losing, Tony decided to fight dirty.

I couldn't believe Tony brought Darcy into it. And after I worked so hard to frame my reasoning to sound like I wanted this for the good of the Sankhain. I clenched my fists and held my breath to keep from breaking Tony's nose. "Sirs," I began, but Finn held up a hand. So there it was. All my cultivated confidence and careful wording, for nothing.

"Leave us," Finn said. He looked at me and held my gaze very deliberately. As if he was trying to tell me something. "We will discuss the matter and inform you of our decision."

I was being dismissed. I trembled, but not from anxiety. "Sirs," I said coldly. "I am doing this. As you so astutely observed, this is merely an informative meeting. If you feel it's necessary to punish me after the fact, so be it. But I'm not asking permission." Then I turned and walked out, leaving all of them to whatever bitchfest they felt they were entitled to.

"Kellan!" I expected the footsteps behind me to be Tony's, but they belonged to Finn. He caught up to me outside. "Must you do everything so abrasively?"

"Have you met me?"

He smiled. "Sadly, yes. I was attempting to give Janus time to adjust to the idea. He — you're very important to him, you know."

My indignation seeped out of me like air from a balloon. "I have to do this."

The door opened and Tony stepped out. He brushed past us without a word, disappearing into the night. Finn sighed. "What will you do with Galen?" he asked unexpectedly.

"Uh. I sorta hoped Tony would watch him for me."

Finn nodded. "I would offer, but Galen's never particularly warmed to me."

Massive understatement. "Thanks anyway."

"I'll work on Tony. Or perhaps Gina and the female younglings could take on Galen's care. He knows several of them quite well."

I stared at Finn as realization dawned. "You're really going to let me do this?"

He gave me a cynical smile. "What happened to the Hycene warrior who told us what she would do, and consequences be damned?"

I bared my teeth. "She got blown away by the Twilight Zone experience of having you on her side." At his puzzled expression, I said, "The Twilight Zone was a TV show —"

"I'm familiar with the show. Or at least the concept, though I have never watched an episode." He cocked his head to one side. "I've been on your side many times."

Many seemed like an overestimation, but I told myself not to look too hard at the gift horse's teeth. "Yeah. Sure. It's just a little weird having you support me, and Tony — well."

"Tony is unable to see the logic of your words. He fails to appreciate that he would likely be the Horror's next target."

I goggled at Finn's divination of my nightmare. He didn't seem to notice.

"Very well," Finn said. "You should go. You've given me much to do." He paused, then laid a hand on my arm. I stared at it, not sure what to do with it. "Be careful, Kellan."

"Uh, yeah. I will." I didn't know how to end this increasingly awkward encounter, so I just walked over to my dog and started untangling him from the tree. Finn went back inside, and Galen and I were alone.

I sank down to the ground and let Galen climb all over me. He knew something was horribly wrong and showed it by trying to crawl inside my skin. The familiarity of his scent brought home what I was going to do, and for possibly the first time ever, I tried to stop breathing it in. To wean myself off of my doggie security blanket.

I didn't smell him or hear him until he spoke. "I'll do it." Tony's voice made me jump and reach for a blade. I didn't pull one, but only barely. "I'll take care of him."

My breath came too shallow for too long, and my vision began to go spotty. "I — thank you," I finally managed to say.

"I'm not doing it for you." Tony left.

Galen would be safe. I tried to tell myself that made it better. Easier. I wasn't fooling myself, but the lie helped me push to my feet and start walking toward the trees. Before I made it three steps, my cell phone rang.

It was Darcy. "I think someone's here," he whispered.

I stopped, my skin going cold. "What? What do you mean? In the apartment?"

"No. But it's like I can feel him watching me."

"But he's not in there with you?"

"No, I just checked the whole place. No one's here."

I was out of time. I started in the direction that Tony went, knowing Galen would follow. "Darcy, stay inside. Don't open the door for anyone, including me. Do you understand?"

"Why? Is he — a shape-changer, like the nocturnes?"

I didn't want to take the time to explain faery glamour. I didn't even know if Aza could make himself look like me. The way I understood it, glamour was more about subtle changes to the appearance, not a full-body-and-gender makeover. But I couldn't risk it. "Something like that. Just stay there, and call me back if he breaks in. Okay?"

"Okay." He sounded steady. He was being brave.

Darcy was worth it. Galen and Tony would be hurt by my leaving, but they would survive. Darcy wouldn't if I backed out. I felt calm. "I'm going to take care of this. By the end of tonight, you'll be free. Bye, Darcy."

I followed Tony's scent trail to the weight room. He was the only one inside. At least, I didn't have to do this with an audience. "It sounds like Aza's at Darcy's place. I have to go. Will you take Galen now?"

Tony's eyes went wide, and his scent was a jumbled-up mess of fear, anger and sadness. "Now," he said, like the concept was slow to sink in. "Yeah. I told you I'd take him."

"I know, I just —" I really hoped to have time to convince you to be a little less mad at me before I handed over my brother to you. I shook my head. Just do it, Kellan. Hand him over and don't look back. "One cup of food, twice a day. No more than that. He thinks he needs more, but he doesn't. It's really good food and he only needs two cups a day." I didn't want to be talking about Galen's food. I wanted to say something meaningful to Tony, something that would help him forgive me.

"Yeah, I get it. One cup, twice a day." Tony took the leash from me, and his hand brushed mine. His expression shuttered and his scent went blank. He didn't want anyone to know how he was feeling.

"I'll be back in two months." I begged him to look at me, to show me something I could hang on to.

"Yup. All right. See ya. Come on, big dog, better let her go." Tony focused all his attention on my dog, and Galen focused all his attention on me, straining against the leash that Tony held tight.

I turned away, unable to breathe and a little grateful I didn't have to take in the scents.

Don't look back.

I didn't.

I ran to the truck, and while I drove to Darcy's apartment, I thought of the things I didn't take the time to do. I didn't tell Janus and Finn I was going. I didn't work out the wording of the faery contract with Finn. While I drove, I dialed Finn's cell and left him a voicemail, telling him I was sorry I didn't say good-bye, and asking him to please come and retrieve my truck. I liked this truck. I should've been worried about how to word the damn contract with the wily faery, but all I could think about was the stupid truck.

I pulled up in front of Darcy's building and saw Aza walking toward me. Out of time.

I opened the door.

"Have you come to thwart my hunt again?" Aza asked.

Thwart? Seriously? "No. I've come to offer you something even better than some skinny-ass librarian."

Aza smiled a smile that showed way too many teeth. "Really? And what could you possibly offer me that would interest me in the least?"

I spread my arms and held out my hands, palms out. "Me."

He laughed, the fucker, a loud belly laugh that was kind of insulting. "Oh," he said, as though catching his breath. "I apologize.

But you took me by surprise. You aren't my type, dear. Thank you, but I shall pass."

"Trust me, you're not my idea of Mr. Saturday Night, either. But I think it's more than a fair trade. I'll give you two months of my life to do with as you please, provided you don't kill me." The second the words left my mouth, I wondered what loopholes he would find. Too late now. I bit the inside of my cheek and reminded myself to breathe every minute or so as I waited for his response.

He cocked his head to one side, the poster boy for Intrigued. "And in return, I allow the human to live."

I snorted, proud at how easily I was able to pull off derision. "Yeah, that, but not only that. You're also going to leave and never return. Never come back to Madison, to Wisconsin, to the states known as the Midwest. Never again hunt on our lands. If you do, if you return or kill one of our people or if you kill me, the Sankhain will kill you. No retribution from your folks, either, because you'll be in breach of contract. Those are the terms." I was sweating profusely, certain that I left something out, something that would lead to our doom.

"It seems you get the better end of that bargain." But I could smell how he salivated. I had him. I won.

"Two months to bleed, torture and rape the daughter of the Sun Prince." His eyes widened, like he didn't expect me to know who my father was. "Oh, yeah, I know about that, and I know you do, too. All you have to do is agree to leave the Dairyland behind you? Seems to me I'm not asking for enough from you. But if you'd rather say no, I guess you could just go kill the librarian. He's only human, so he can't heal half the shit I can. I bet I'd be a lot more fun. But hey, if you want to stick to your type."

"Now, wait. I didn't say no." Of course, you didn't, you fucking fuck. "If I agree to your terms, our time together begins now. No long good-byes. No wheedling out of the deal."

"I don't wheedle." I felt oddly offended.

"And no blades. Leave the iron in the truck."

I emptied all my hidden sheathes, then patted myself down to make sure I didn't forget any. Wouldn't want to get a reputation as a wheedler. I slid them under the driver's seat of the truck and said a fervent prayer to anyone willing to listen that Finn would send someone to retrieve my truck. I could get a new POS, but good blades were hard to come by. "So. Do we have a deal?"

Aza smiled a cold, satisfied smile that scared me more than just about anything I'd ever seen. "We do." He took my hand and we disappeared.

I never teleported before. Not sure if that was what it was called, and pretty sure it didn't matter what you called it. It was like jumping headfirst into a frozen lake, paralyzing and when you emerged, excruciating. Except I had a feeling that I didn't know what excruciating truly meant. Not yet.

The room was large, dark, echoey. I didn't understand quite how it echoed, since the walls were made of earth. Like Aza dug himself a cavern deep in the dirt. It was all I could smell at first, the dirt. But other scents came to light as my senses adjusted. Aza's cologne. Leather. Blood. Lots of blood.

I won. Yeah, right.

PART II: After

Chapter 19

TWO MONTHS LATER

The sunlight was horrible. So bright, it frightened me. When Aza
whizzed me back to Madison, I felt sure he picked the middle of
the day on purpose, to shock my system the most. I barely left his
little terra torture chamber in two months, and on the rare occa-
sion that he did take me out, it was only to the Shadow Court. No
sunlight allowed there. Images began flashing through my brain. I
shut them down, digging my fingernails into my palms. One foot
in front of the other. One breath at a time.

Aza left me at my apartment. Just left me, not a word, not a
parting shot or a good-bye smack. Our playdate was done, so he
had no further use for me. I didn't have a phone or my keys, no way
to go inside. I knew Janus and Finn would expect me to report in
as soon as possible, so after a brief, longing look at my apartment
and the shower inside, the shower with its endless supply of hot
water, I started to walk. The forest was only a few miles from my
apartment. I didn't feel the sun, didn't smell the rich, warm scents
around me. My mind couldn't make sense of these things. But I
walked. I moved. I didn't think. Just moved.

It took me hours to reach the Sankhain's empty lot. It was still
broad daylight but with a definite chill in the air. In a dirty tank
top and cargo shorts that were torn up one leg, I was dressed for
August, and it wasn't August anymore. I looked at the length of
the field, the distance I would have to walk if I went the long way.
I was already so tired. During my time with Aza, I barely moved.
Barely used any muscles. I was weak. Maybe I should try to sleep,
I thought. But there was no way. This place wasn't safe. Too open,
too exposed. Deciding on the best bad option, I started walking
toward the far end of the forest.

I knew the border patrol must've seen me. Probably spread
the word that I was back. Someone would be waiting to receive me
inside the forest. Inside, rather than coming out to meet me. Not

worth risking exposure. I told myself I was glad. I had some peace. No need to rush into any face-to-face encounters just yet. That's what I told myself. But I knew I was a liar. Peace didn't exist. Quiet was just an opportunity for your thoughts to scream louder.

As I entered the forest, I caught his scent and began to shake. I didn't let myself think of him until now. Don't look back, that was what I told myself every time I wanted to remember him. Don't look back. But now, his scent hit me, and I had to bite the inside of my cheek and clench every muscle in my body to keep from sobbing.

My dog. My dog was here.

I didn't register the hand that held, then dropped the leash. I didn't care. All that mattered was Galen. I dropped to my knees and let him bowl me over. He shook just as bad as I did. We sniffed each other, his snuffles of doggy excitement and my snuffles of human emotion mingling until I couldn't tell one from the other. I had snot running down my face, I could taste it in my mouth, along with the dog hair that now covered me. I didn't care. All that mattered was Galen.

Finally, we subsided and just leaned against each other. He felt shockingly solid. I felt like I could float away, but my dog was made of iron.

"Kellan." The voice made me jump. It took me a minute to recognize it. At first, it was just male, and the only voice in the world for so long was Aza. The last one million times my name was spoken, it was Aza. But this was Tony. Of course, he was here.

I didn't want to see Tony. Didn't want to hear his recriminations. If I could've run, I would have. Run anywhere that he wasn't. But I wasn't even entirely sure I could pull myself up off the ground. Don't think. Don't feel. Just move. I pushed up, dragged myself to my feet. I tried to look at him, but it was too hard. I tapped my fingers against my leg in a random rhythm, focused on the sound of fingertips brushing cotton, and waited for whatever he might say.

"You look like shit."

The blunt, cold words shocked me out of numbness. Rage filled me like an old lover, and I liked it. I felt alive, powerful. I could look at him. And I could speak. "Go fuck yourself. Who asked you?" I started to walk. My legs threatened to give out, but I kept walking, thanks to stubbornness and lovely, lovely rage. Galen stayed glued to my side.

Unfortunately, Tony kept pace as well. "What? You expected me to throw my arms around you and tell you how much I missed you?"

He brushed up against me, and I jumped like an electrocuted cat. I was suddenly ten feet away and staring at him, my breath coming in short, fat bursts. He stared back at me, apparently startled by my response. I didn't care. "I don't want your arms around me," I said. "You can do whatever the fuck you want. Just don't touch me."

We stood there for a few seconds, or maybe minutes. But my legs were shaky, and the rest of me wasn't feeling real great, so I started walking again. Tony didn't say anything else, and he stayed a little ways back as he followed us to camp. I wondered if I hurt his feelings. I wondered if it mattered.

The air felt so heavy.

I went straight to Janus's cabin. I knew they would be waiting for me. If Tony and Galen knew I was back, Janus sure as shit knew. Tony didn't come inside with us. Smack sat at the desk. When she saw me, her eyes widened, but for once, she didn't say a word. She just did her duty, announced my presence to Finn and Janus, then told me I could enter. The whole scene struck me as being incredibly stupid and pointless, since I could hear the entire exchange between Smack and Finn. But it had very little to do with me, so I went along with it.

Galen and I entered the inner room. It was warm, and it smelled like Janus and like Finn and like the wood burning in the fireplace, and my legs gave out. Finn caught me and I let him. I didn't know why it was okay for Finn to touch me, but not Tony. It bothered me, so I pushed Finn away once I was on my feet again.

"You should sit," Finn said. So I did. Finn blinked, like he was surprised I obeyed. That bothered me, too. Like I was forgetting something important. I stood up again and started to back toward the door. Then I changed direction, not wanting to have my back to the door, so I stood with my back to the wall, but close enough to the door that I could make a break for it if I needed to.

That was better. I leaned against the wall, allowing myself to relax slightly.

Finn and Janus stared at me. I wondered vaguely just how bad I looked. "You have returned," Finn said.

Of all the dumbass things to say. And for once, it wasn't me who said it. "Very observant," I said. "I'm just here to check in. Where am I going?"

Finn studied me with that gaze that saw everything, even the invisible parts. Then he glanced at Janus before saying, "We think it best if you stay here for now. You may have the cabin next to mine. That one is vacant."

Next to Finn. They wanted to keep an eye on me. That made my skin feel too tight, and that pissed me off. I spent far too much time under scrutiny lately. "I'd rather go back to my apartment." My stereo was there, and my television, and my big cushy armchair that was almost big enough for Galen and me to curl up in. I wouldn't have to listen to quiet ever again.

Janus finally spoke. "No. You will stay here in the cabin assigned you." He smelled angry, so angry. Not his usual angry scent, but a different one, colder, like frostbite.

Apparently, Janus was still pissed at me for giving myself to Aza. "Fine. Whatever." I started for the door.

"I have not dismissed you." Janus' voice was soft, but I felt it like the crack of a whip. I flinched, my shoulders crowding up around my ears and my head dipping down.

I forced my voice out. It sounded tinny. "My apologies, sir." Then I stood and waited, my head down and eyes averted. If I kept my head down, he would lose interest in me. It was only when I fought that —

I shuddered, closed my eyes, held my breath. With my eyes closed, I couldn't see him coming. That was neither better nor worse. It just meant I didn't have to see him.

Finn's voice, not Aza's. "Kellan, thank you. You are dismissed. Here." He took my hand, and I jumped. I clamped my eyes more tightly. "Your phone." Finn's voice was so soft. I didn't know it could be that soft. He pressed the phone into my hand.

I didn't move. Janus was the one that told me I wasn't dismissed.

"Go." Janus. So angry.

I forced my eyes open. I started walking. One foot in front of the other. One breath at a time. Just keep moving.

———— «» ————

After I showered, I stared at my reflection in the mirror. Tony was right. I looked like shit. I'd lost weight off my already skinny frame, and the new scars were horrible. And those were just the ones on the outside.

Lots of new white lines littered my face. He liked to use his fingernails, sharp as razor blades, to slice my skin. A small mass of scar tissue hunched over the spot where my carotid artery met my jaw. He liked to rip the skin away with his teeth and draw designs on my body with my blood. I rubbed a finger over the calloused skin on my neck, where the collar chafed its own sort of tattoo. That might fade, or it might turn into another scar. I wondered if I should start wearing a scarf, to spare people from having to look at my throat and neck. No. Let them stare. Let them see the marks. Then they would know. That one's broken. Give her a wide berth.

At least, I felt cleaner now. Aza allowed me to wash almost every day, because he didn't like the smell of bodily fluids like sweat and cum. But washing with cold water from a basin wasn't the same as a hot shower. The hot, pressured stream felt so good, I cried a little. Galen was the only one who heard.

And for once, I didn't smell like perfume. He liked me to smell like flowery, chemical scents. Not like wet dog, he said. I would use perfume liberally after washing. But now, I smelled like bar soap and mint shampoo. I used unscented lotion. I put on clothes, real clothes that someone put here for me, jeans that were too big and a hoodie I could drown in. And socks, thick woolen hiking socks that were so luxurious and warm. You don't realize how special socks are, until your feet are ice cold for two months. Those socks almost made me cry again.

I looked at my phone. It was fully charged. Finn charged my phone. I put that thought away, because I didn't know what to do with it. I checked my voicemail, even though the little icon said I didn't have any new messages. I even checked the incoming and missed call logs. Nothing. Did Mal know what happened? Would she care if she did? I pushed that away, too.

This was when I would shape-shift. I knew that. Shed humanity and sleep as a wolf, as nature intended. Just the thought sent fear shivering through me. No. Not again. No more. I curled up on the floor, curled my body around my dog's, and waited for whatever was coming. Because something always came.

What came was a sneeze. Or rather, the sound of one, right outside my window. The sound, like all sounds, made me jump, made my adrenaline surge and my pulse race. And that pissed me off, because I got out, it was done and I didn't have to be afraid anymore.

I threw open the door and lit into Tony. "What the fuck are you doing here? I didn't ask you to sit outside my fucking window. And take a fucking Benadryl, for fuck's sake!"

He rubbed his eyes and peered up at me, like he just woke up. He glanced at the sky, which was beginning to shift into dusk. "Musta fallen asleep. What time's it?"

I wanted to kick him. "I asked you a question! What the fuck are you doing?"

He sneezed again, pulled two small pink pills out of his pocket and popped them in his mouth. After swallowing, he said, "I was answering you. I fell asleep and missed taking my next dose. Sorry if the sneezing woke you up."

Next dose? What fresh rabbit hole was this? "You didn't wake me up. What are you doing?"

"Sleeping." He pushed to his feet, and I took an instinctive step back. He watched me and took his own step away, putting a more comfortable distance between us. I didn't like that he did this for me. I didn't like that he saw what I wanted. "You seemed kinda jumpy earlier," he said. "I thought maybe you shouldn't be completely alone. But I didn't want to crowd you. So I sat outside your window. I know you didn't ask me to. If you ask me to leave, I will. But if it's okay, I'd rather stay."

I opened my mouth to tell him to leave. And to spread the word that nobody else should take up residence outside my window. But no sound came out. I went back inside and closed the door and tried to pretend that nobody was sitting outside, waiting for me to flip out. Because that's what he was waiting for. The screams, the night terrors, the complete mental breakdown. He was waiting for me to start bawling, so he could come in here and play the big man and wipe my tears and comfort me.

Fuck that.

I pulled on the brand-new pair of running shoes that someone so thoughtfully placed in my room. Stubbornness and rage got me this far. Let's see how much farther they could carry me. I opened the door and Galen and I started running.

I could hear Tony's footsteps behind us. This was too much. If the moron wanted to hide under my window, that was one thing, but this was stalking, pure and simple. I skidded to a stop and whirled around. "Why are you following me?" The volume of my own voice made me jump.

Tony just met my gaze with an infuriating lack of distress. "You look like you're about to fall over dead. I didn't want you to end up lying in a field, decomposing or something."

The anger was an elephant sitting on my chest, crushing and suffocating me at the same time. "I can't fall over dead. It's physically impossible for me to have a heart attack. Trust me."

When I realized what I said, I expected him to ask questions. Like, are you speaking from experience? Or maybe, what exactly happened to you these last months? But he didn't say anything, just looked at me with eyes that told me he heard what I said and was thinking about all the implications of that "Trust me." I remembered the smell of burning flesh and the jolt of electricity coursing through me. I needed to run. I needed to move. If I could just move, the memories couldn't catch up with me. I started running. And for the second time in one day, my legs gave out from under me.

Tony didn't try to catch me the way Finn did. He just stood there, watched me fall on my ass, then watched with no expression as Galen nuzzled me. "When was the last time you ate?" Tony said. "How 'bout we go to the mess hall and get you some food?"

Time to eat. The singsong voice rang through my head like He was standing next to me. I started panting, fast, short, hard breaths. "No. I'm not hungry."

"You're always hungry."

"I don't want to eat, okay?" I sounded hysterical. Maybe I was.

Tony squinted at me. Then he sat down and started pulling blades of grass from the ground.

"What are you doing?" I said.

"I don't know. What are you doing?"

I made a sound that was part growl, mostly roar. "What the fuck are you doing? Don't you have someplace better to be? And what did that grass ever do to you?"

He glanced up at me before returning his attention to the grass. "I don't have anyplace else to be. I'm waiting to see if you pass out or if you try to get up and start running again. Morbid curiosity."

I didn't believe him for a second. This was Tony. He made a practice of being nauseatingly good. "Why are you being nice to me?" I said.

"I didn't think I was being all that nice."

I shook my head and it wobbled a little bit in the motion. "No, I mean, why don't you hate me? When I left, you hated me. When I showed up at the forest today, you didn't seem to like me all that much. But now, you're being...you. Why?"

The muscle in his jaw stood out as he clenched it. He took a deep breath and looked at me straight on. "I saw that look in your eye when I brushed up against you. I know that look. I couldn't stay mad at you."

He saw. I felt so cold. "Don't pity me," I snapped.

He shook his head and smiled a humorless smile. "I don't. So why aren't you eating?"

"I — I'm not hungry."

"Bullshit. Why aren't you eating?"

"He — I —" Bile rose in my throat. Memories tried to crowd my brain. I pushed them away the best I could. One breath at a time. "He liked to feed me...weird shit."

Tony studied me. "You gotta eat, Kell. Or you're going to keep falling over."

"I — I don't — I can't eat meat. Don't make me." The whine in my voice shamed me. My cheeks grew hot.

"All right," he said slowly. "No meat. What about eggs? Some scrambled eggs?"

I considered. The mental image didn't make me gag. "I think that would be okay."

"Great. You able to walk to the mess hall?" He didn't take the question to the next step. He didn't ask if I wanted help. I was grateful I didn't have to say again that I didn't want to be touched.

"I think so." Actually, I had no idea if I could even stand up, but if I didn't want to be touched, my options were limited. Not like I could ride Galen to the kitchen.

"Okay." He stood up and waited for me, but didn't offer me a hand. He listened. It was so nice to have someone listen to what I said.

I managed to stand up and walk. We made our way slowly to the cafeteria. Galen looked bummed that we weren't running anymore. I felt a stab of guilt that I let him down again. That one little stab of guilt spread through me like poison, until my limbs were too heavy to lift and my face felt alien. I was worthless. Pointless. Weak. Couldn't even take my dog for a damn run without falling on my face. What good was I anymore? What good was I ever?

I didn't realize I stopped walking until Tony said, "You okay?" Galen was looking at me too, asking me the same question with his eyes.

I closed my eyes, because I didn't want to see them. Didn't want to see the moment that they realized just how not okay I was. Just how weak I was. Not physically. A blind man could see how physically weak I was. But they would see how weak I was inside. *You like it. See? You like it.*

"Hey!" Tony clapped his hands right in front of my face, shocking my eyes open. "Don't do that. I don't know where you went, but don't do that. You're here, now. All right? You gotta take care of your body. Your mind will get better, but not if you starve yourself. So we're going in there and we're going to make you some eggs. Maybe an omelet. Huh? Put some peppers and onions in there, maybe some mushrooms? Some cheese?"

My mouth started to water. I couldn't look him in the eye, but I nodded.

"Good. Now come on." Tony didn't lead the way. He waited for me to start walking, then he walked a little behind me. To a human, that might not mean much, but to a wolf, it was everything. I wasn't the submissive here. Even if I felt like the bottom of all bottoms. Tony waited for me to lead. He believed I could. The voice in my head started to laugh. He isn't doing it because he believes in you, that voice said. He's probably just waiting to see if you fall on your face again. My stomach churned, but I pushed the voice away. Told it to shut up.

Then we entered the kitchen and I smelled the smells of meat cooking. Not currently, but for past meals. My legs didn't give out. I was proud of that. But I did throw up a little in my mouth.

Chapter 20

Something must've shown on my face. "You can smell it," Tony said.

I nodded, afraid to open my mouth.

"Okay. Outside." Once again, Tony waited for me to start walking before he joined me. We left the mess hall and I took deep, gulping breaths of the fresh autumn air. He didn't speak until I stopped gulping. "You wait here. I'll bring the food out."

I sank down in the grass, feeling pathetic and miserable. I used to be a warrior. Now I could be laid low by the smell of baked ham. I might've drowned in my self-pity if not for Galen. Obviously thrilled that I was once again on the ground, he scoured my face with his tongue and then crawled in my lap like an overgrown Shih tzu. I buried my face in his fur, trying to obliterate the memory of the smells in the mess hall.

I didn't raise my head until I heard the slap of the mess hall screen door. Tony walked toward us with three protein bars. "We're out of eggs. I don't believe it. I'm so sorry, Kell."

It didn't matter. Nothing mattered. "That's all right." I tore open one of the protein bars. It smelled strange. I couldn't remember the time I ate processed food. Chew. Swallow. Food is fuel, nothing more.

"You need anything from your cabin?" he said.

Instant suspicion. I hated it, because he was Tony and Tony was good, but I needed to know what he was planning if I was going to keep breathing. "Why? What are you going to do?"

"We're going to order pizza."

I stared at him. I didn't care what pizza place you called, none of them delivered to the secret invisible forest. "I think Janus and Finn wouldn't appreciate you giving the delivery boy our address."

"Not here," he said. "At your apartment."

I considered. Pizza sounded good. It wouldn't smell anything like the things Aza fed me. A flash of raw meat clouded my vision for a moment before I stomped it down. "Janus said I couldn't leave. That I had to stay here."

Tony's eyes fluttered shut. "He didn't say that."

His disbelief annoyed me. "He did. I was there."

"No, I believe you, I just wish I didn't. All right. I'm going to go have a talk with Janus and Finn." He said their names like they tasted bad. "Don't worry. We'll get you your pizza. Meet me by the trees. Okay?" Galen watched him until he disappeared behind a cabin, then looked up at me. I tried not to think about the fact that my dog didn't look to me until Tony was out of sight.

I didn't need anything from the cabin, so I took Galen to wait for Tony by the trees. I watched my dog, watched the play of light on his fur, rememorized his coloring, the curve of his tail, the perfect triangle of his ears, his square blocky head. It soothed me, took the starch right out of my spine so I had to sit down. I dug my fingers in his coat and felt the muscle and bone that made my dog. He rested his head on my shoulder. I rested my cheek on his shoulder. That's how we were when Tony found us.

Galen trotted over to him for a pat. Feeling a little dazed, I studied the pair of them. Tony looked almost as familiar as Galen. But nowhere near as safe. Eventually, Tony might want things from me. Things that I wasn't sure I could be anymore. "What's the verdict?" I asked. My tongue felt thick, which made my words slur. I was so tired. Time to get up. I pushed to my feet. Spots danced in front of my eyes, but I held very still and they went away.

"Let's go order a pizza or five." Tony extended his hand in a "lead the way" gesture.

"Do you have a car?"

"I thought we'd take your truck." He held up the keys. "I'll drive, though, if that's okay. You don't look too steady."

My truck. My blades were in my truck. I could be armed again. I felt light-headed and tingly at the prospect. "Okay."

"And I thought we'd go through a drive-thru, get you some espresso. A latte or cappuccino or something. I'm guessing it's been a good long time since you had good coffee."

"Coffee?" Shit. I was so busy looking at my dog and trying to remember how to breathe, I never considered the healing effects of coffee. And Aza didn't know how much I loved the drink, so he didn't devise some strategy to ruin it for me. Coffee and blades and Galen? Maybe I would be okay, after all. "Yeah. Sure. Coffee."

My truck was in the Sankhain parking lot. I didn't even see it when I walked through here earlier. I wondered what else I missed. I walked to the driver's side door. "Um, I thought I was going to drive," Tony said.

I nodded. "I just need to…" I took the keys, opened the door and felt under the driver's seat, holding my breath until my fingers closed around a hilt. They were here. I pulled them out and hugged them to my chest. "All yours."

While Tony drove, I strapped on my knives. The forearm sheathes, the belly band with the throwing knives. I slid the remaining sheathed blades into the pocket of my sweatshirt, and held the two unsheathed blades in my lap. Galen, on the seat between me and Tony, leaned his hip against my hip. I made sure I held the blades tight so if the truck stopped suddenly, none of them would go flying and hurt my dog. Or Tony. But mostly, I was concerned about Galen. Tony could take care of himself. Galen needed me. And while I appreciated Tony and what he was doing for me — and I relaxed enough to actually feel appreciation — I needed Galen.

As promised, Tony went through the coffee shop drive-thru, and I got a giant latte that I had to hold with both hands. Reluctantly, I set the unsheathed blades on the floor. Out of the corner of my eye, I saw the drive-thru attendant's eyes widen at the sight of my knives. I didn't care. I felt better with them than without them. Even having them on the floor rather than my lap made me feel vulnerable and jumpy.

I took a sip of my coffee. It was like being kissed for the first time, or the way being kissed for the first time should be. The milk was foamy and a little sweet, and the espresso was bitter and so, so hot. It burned a path to my stomach, and my heart fluttered — no shit, actually fluttered — in anticipation of the caffeine hit that would follow.

I felt eyes on me and I froze, jerking my hands and spilling a little frothed milk. Who was watching me? Keeping my breathing quiet and as absolutely still as I could, I peeked out the corner of my eye to see who it was. When I saw Tony, my whole body flushed and I felt like an idiot. Of course, it was Tony. Of course, he was watching me. He wanted to see if I enjoyed my drink. Fuck. After bracing the cup between my legs, I dug in the glove box for a napkin and blotted at the spill on my jeans.

My hands shook. My stomach was too empty for coffee. Didn't matter. I took a long pull, scorching my tongue. It felt good. And then I felt nauseous. And then I took another drink, and slowly, the nausea went away. Maybe it was the milk in the latte. Maybe it was my body adjusting to its mother's milk again. Who cared? My hands weren't shaking anymore.

Tony drove in silence while I drank. When I set the empty cup on the floor and picked up my blades again, I started to think I should say something. Maybe he was waiting for me to talk. "That was good," I said. "Thank you."

He didn't look at me, but he smiled. "I'm glad."

I held the blades with my right hand and dug my left into the fur on Galen's back. I tried to do it so no one could see me move. And I held my breath as I moved. I noticed these things, like they were happening on the television. "What day is it?" I said, suddenly realizing I didn't know.

Tony's hands clenched on the steering wheel, then relaxed and rubbed the worn plastic. "Tuesday. October eighteenth."

That meant it was August eighteenth when Aza took me. When I went with him. My choice. I did it to myself. Always remember that. "I guess I lost track."

"Yeah, that'll happen." Tony rolled his shoulders, like he was trying to release tension.

"Could we —" I hesitated, not wanting to ask. It was better not to ask for anything. I shook my head, trying to shake away the thought and the memories that would follow. "Could we go by Darcy's apartment? Just to...see?"

Tony stiffened and finally looked at me. "Kellan, Darcy moved away."

I stopped breathing. Gone. He was gone? I felt a flash of pain, of anger, of sheer disbelief. During those two months, I didn't let myself think of Galen, but I thought of Darcy. Anytime I thought it was too much, anytime I wanted to back out, anytime I wanted to give up, I thought of Darcy and remembered why I was there. I thought about seeing him again, hugging him, being wrapped in his scent and his arms, skinnier than Tony's, but oh, so safe. And now he was gone.

I shoved the pain, the memories, the tattered image of that reunion, shoved it all behind a door in my head and slammed the door tight. What I felt didn't matter. Darcy was alive, and he was safe. Away from me. He might actually stay safe that way. Didn't matter. Nothing mattered. One breath at a time. That reminded me to start breathing again. "Did you — talk to him?" My voice sounded so even and cool. Like none of it really did matter.

"Yeah. I went to see him right after you —" he stumbled — "left. I told him what you did. He wasn't happy."

Keep that door closed. Don't feel. Don't think.

"He sent me a text about a week later. A friend of his found him a job at a library up north. He said it was time for a change. He asked me to let you know, if I ever saw you again."

If. My phone was in my pocket. Silent. No messages. The door in my head rattled, like something big and bad was trying to get out.

As we pulled into my parking lot, Galen turned and nuzzled the side of my neck. His cold nose made me jump. Pulled me out of numbness and forced me to feel something. And then to feel everything. I remembered that night in front of Darcy's building, the light in his apartment, the brief feeling of triumph as Aza agreed to my terms, then the dawning understanding of what my life was going to be. Aza didn't waste any time. He raped me that first night for the first time. He manipulated me into orgasm that night for the first time.

See? You like it. I chose to do that. It was my choice. My doing. Don't blame someone else for your choices.

I wrapped my hand around one of the blades, not the hilt but the blade itself, felt it slice into the flesh of my palm. I forced air past my lips, in and out, in and out. In and out, like that night. Fuck. I pushed open the door and fell out, the blades in my lap scattering. Galen jumped to the ground and pressed himself against my leg, eyes wide and ears pinned back. Tony came around the side of the truck. His hand twitched, not to hit me, I was pretty sure, but to touch me. He didn't, though.

I straightened my spine and pushed my hair out of my face. I picked up the blades I dropped and stuffed them in the front pouch of my sweatshirt. Clucking my tongue at Galen, I started walking. One foot in front of the other. I was sweaty and I felt so cold, but I walked away from the truck and toward what was next.

"You have blood on your face," Tony said quietly as he unlocked the front door. The cut on my hand, I must've smeared blood on my face. I wiped my forehead with my sleeve, glad that the hoodie was black.

I tugged my sleeves over my hands, in an attempt to get warm. I heard a throat clear behind us, and I whirled around. Raoul stood there. I stared at him, he stared at me, nobody said a damn thing, and then he started to walk away. I could practically hear him thinking, Dumb bitch, you actually went through with it. Or maybe that was me thinking that. "I survived," I yelled after him.

He turned back. "You sure?" I smelled something like sunshine on a hot summer day.

"I'm standing here, aren't I?" I was, right? This was real. Right?

"Yup, I guess you are." Raoul walked back to stand by the tree in the front yard. Galen waved his tail at the faery. At my father. Who looked at me like I was dumber than a rusty paint can. "Was he worth it? Your friend? Now that you know what happens to martyrs, was he still worth it?"

Even feeling like shit, even barely on my feet with shaky limbs and a self-destructing brain, I didn't hesitate. "Absolutely. I'd do it again and again to save someone else from having to — spend time with Aza."

Raoul nodded stiffly. "Your mother never woulda done that."

Starting to feel the warmth of anger, I said, "Then I guess it's a good thing for everyone that I'm not her."

Raoul laughed, startling me. I heard Tony shift his feet, like he was preparing to fight. But Raoul's laughter turned into a smile, and he smelled light, solid. Almost...proud. "Maybe not a good thing for you," he said. "But it's sure a good thing for your friend. Y'all have a good night now." He left, and my bravado left with him.

My legs felt too heavy to move. I moved them anyway. Tony didn't say anything about Raoul, or anything else. I couldn't take the quiet. "Have you been teaching?" I said as Tony and I climbed the stairs.

"Mm-hmm." Tony unlocked the apartment and we stepped inside. It smelled musty, and like old garlic. It wasn't a bad smell. It was warm. How could a smell be warm? How's the sky blue, I don't fucking know. Somewhere under the garlic smell was the scent of meat, but the garlic was so pungent that it didn't bother me the way it did outside the kitchen at camp. "I'm teaching hand-to-hand, marksmanship and archery," Tony said.

"Wow. Keeping busy."

"Well, I've had a lot of time on my hands." Since you left, he didn't say, but I heard it anyway. "Smack and Gina have been training with a bunch of the younger girls. I'm kinda their faculty advisor, I guess you could say, but it's their show. They, um, they call themselves the new Hycene."

What did that mean? None of the younglings were shape-shifters, so they couldn't be Hycene. Did it mean they wanted to be like me? That made no sense.

Tony pulled out his cell. "What do you want on the pizzas?" he said. Panic. I didn't even know how to order pizza anymore. I started clenching and unclenching the muscles in my calves. Tony studied me for a second, then said, "I like green peppers and mushrooms. The mushrooms don't add a ton of flavor, but they add texture, and the green peppers play well against the sweetness of the tomato sauce. How does that sound?"

"Sure." My fingers tapped, tapped, tapped against the leg of my jeans.

He ordered two pizzas, one with cheese and one with peppers and mushrooms. "You want to watch TV?" he said.

I nodded. I didn't care much about what we watched. I just wanted something to fill the quiet.

He turned on the television and flipped through the channels. We landed on a marathon of "The Walking Dead." "I've never seen this," I said.

We watched, and I got sucked in right away. Some of it was bloody, but a lot of it was quiet and calm, and most of the actors spoke with wonderful Southern accents. And it looked warm there. Halfway through the first episode, the pizzas arrived. Tony jumped up and said he'd go get them. I had a feeling he wasn't enjoying the show as much as I was.

He came back as a mob of zombies ripped into a horse. "Aw, man, that's nasty," he said as he set the boxes down on the card table. Suddenly ravenous, I opened one of the boxes and pulled out a piece, biting into it without even checking to see which pie it was. Tony watched with a funny look on his face. "So, I'm sorry, I wasn't going to say anything, but I just can't keep my mouth shut. You can't even stand the smell of meat, but you can eat while watching this show?"

I didn't want to think about it. Something was working, and I just wanted to go with it. But guilt tugged at me. Guilt because I was starting to enjoy myself, and that wasn't something that was supposed to happen. "You want to turn it off?"

"No." He chose a piece of pizza and sat down in the armchair. "Well, yeah, but not if you like it. I'm just wondering how you're okay with the show, but not with pot roast."

I swallowed, memories flaring in my mind too fast to extinguish. Tony's hand grabbed mine, and I leapt off the futon.

"Whoa. Sorry, Kellan. I should've warned you. But you were about to drop your pizza, and I didn't want Galen to eat it."

I looked at his hand. Sure enough, he held both his piece and my half-eaten piece. I didn't notice that he took mine. I just felt his hand and freaked. Get a grip, Kellan. You're supposed to be the one looking out for Galen. Pull yourself together. One breath at a time. I reached up and pushed my hair out of my face, because I could reach up. My hands weren't shackled. My feet weren't tied to stakes in the floor. The lamp by the door lit the room so I could see my surroundings. I was here, now. And He wasn't.

Never again. He was gone for good.

I sat down, still feeling shaky, but determined not to show it. "Thank you," I said, and took my pizza from Tony's outstretched hand. I didn't want to eat it, but I did it anyway. Then I made myself reach for another piece. I stared at the TV, grateful once again for the noise. "When do we have to go back?"

"What, to Camp?" Tony's voice capitalized it. "I promised I'd take you back after we ate."

"Oh." I stopped eating again, suddenly imagining the deafening silence of the cabin.

"So, want some coffee? Keep eating. As long as we're back before sun-up, we're good. But you gotta keep eating. Plausible deniability, you know." Tony went into the kitchen, and I heard the sequence of cupboards that meant he was preparing coffee.

I drew a blade and set it on my lap. The dull gleam of the steel drew my gaze like a naked guy streaking down the street. I couldn't look away. I felt stronger, looking at the blade.

Tony reentered the living room, pausing a few feet away from me. I figured he, like me, was probably staring at the knife, nude against my leg. "Everything okay?" he said.

"Yeah. Just dandy."

He picked out another piece of pizza and sat back down.

I looked at him. He held my gaze with obnoxiously steady, neutral eyes. He reminded me of Finn, all composure and coolness. And that pissed me off. One Finn in my life was more than enough. "He fed me raw flesh."

Tony blinked. That was better. "That sounds awful."

"Raw human flesh. And I ate it. I liked it." Not completely accurate, but I wanted to shock him out of neutral.

"Coffee's probably ready. At least one cup brewed, anyway." He got up and went into the kitchen.

I picked up the blade and followed, getting angrier. "Did you not hear me?"

"I heard you." He held out a full mug. I had a half-eaten piece of pizza in one hand and a dagger in the other. I had to put one down, so I set the pizza on the cutting board and took the coffee. Tony gingerly took hold of the blade of the dagger and pulled it from my hand. Then he handed me the pizza. "Keep eating. Or do you want to go back now?"

I tossed the pizza in the sink and grabbed the hilt of my blade. I keep my blades sharp. As I pulled it out of Tony's hand, which was still wrapped around the metal edge, the dagger slit his palm wide open.

Chapter 21

Shocked, I dropped the dagger on the floor. Tony caught my mug with his uninjured hand. "Shit," I said. "Shit, I'm sorry. I'm so sorry." I began to hyperventilate.

He wrapped a dish towel around his hand and raised his hand so it was alongside his face. Elevated, to staunch the bleeding. What did I do? Jesus god, what did I do? I was a horrible, horrible person. I hurt everyone that mattered.

"Kellan, breathe. It's just a cut. I'm okay."

"No. No, you — you — no."

"Kellan!" He didn't touch me, but his shout startled me almost as bad. "Get. A. Grip. It's my hand, and I say it's fine, so it's fucking fine. All right? Breathe, before you pass out." I dragged in a breath. "Good. Now keep doing that. Come on. Take your coffee and go watch your horrible zombie show. I'm going to pour myself a cup, then I'll join you. Just keep breathing, or you'll scare Galen."

Galen. The name shuddered through me like a sob. Breathe. Breathe for Galen. I could do that. I picked up the coffee mug. Then I set it back down and opened the cupboard, pulling out a mug for Tony. "I'll get the coffee. You go sit down."

He only hesitated for a second before he said, "That'd be great. Thanks." I knew he was wondering if I was steady enough to carry one mug, much less two. But he just left me in the kitchen, like he never doubted me. An enormous lump settled in my throat, threatening to choke me. The kindness felt surreal. I needed something real. I picked up the dagger and cut a long, neat line down my forearm. Blood welled and pain blossomed, and I felt real again. My cut was bigger than Tony's and at least as deep. That made it better. That was the way it should be. I should be the one who hurt.

I carried the coffee into the living room and set a mug on the end table on the side of Tony's uninjured hand. "Has it stopped bleeding yet?" I said.

"Ah, just about."

Galen tucked himself against my feet as I took a sip of coffee. "Don't lie. I can smell the fresh blood."

"Then why did you ask?" He sounded annoyed. That made me feel good, like I rediscovered some part of myself.

Instead of answering, I settled back to watch the show and drink my coffee. I began to feel warm. I should've cut myself hours ago.

There was something comforting about watching a zombie apocalypse. Like it put my situation in perspective. Maybe the last two months were, literally, torturous, but at least I wasn't being hunted down by rotting former humans. At least I wasn't running for my life, with none of the creature comforts like electricity, Mr. Coffee, and pizza delivery. I chose a new piece of pizza, then sat back down and pulled Galen into my lap. Galen watched the journey of the food from the box to my mouth, but he was on his best behavior and didn't try to snatch it from me. I tasted the pizza with such intensity, I wondered how I managed to not taste it before. Tony was right. The green peppers were really good. I told him so.

"Glad you like it." He watched me with a funny look on his face, like he was trying to read a language he didn't know. "What happened?"

Instantly, I tensed, all the warmth draining away. "What do you mean?" Could he really be asking about the time with Aza? Did he expect me to spill all the dirty details?

"A few minutes ago, you were having a panic attack. Now you're all zen. What happened?"

I froze for a second. He was watching me too closely. I didn't want to be watched, and I didn't want to tell him what made me feel better. But I got a lot better at lying recently. I unclenched my sphincter and said, "Must be the coffee, I guess."

"You don't want to tell me, that's fine. But I'd appreciate it if you didn't treat me like an idiot."

Already, the urge to cut myself again made a rushing sound in my ears. I craved the serenity that seeing my own blood gave me. I set my mug on the floor. "I gotta pee." Stuffing the remaining bite of pizza in my mouth, I pushed Galen out of my lap and stood up, aware of the blades in my pockets the way new lovers were aware of each other's nearness.

"Tell me what's going on with you first." Tony stood before me, the towel wrapped tight around his hand. Steady and immovable as a fucking tree.

I felt my face heat. Anger tickled my gut. "I have to pee."

He crossed his arms over his chest. "You're acting like a junkie sneakin' off for a fix."

Usually, anger felt warm. This time, it was cold, so cold I could barely feel my skin. I didn't need permission. I could go where I wanted now. "Fuck you," I breathed. I sidestepped, planning to go around him. He sidestepped with me. Anger flared to rage and I shoved him out of the way. He stumbled and I escaped.

I locked myself in the bathroom, breathing hard. I sat on the floor, my back against the door, my feet braced so that no matter how hard he shoved on the door, he couldn't get in. I was safe.

Safe? Of course, I was safe. I was with Tony. Not Aza. Just Tony and Galen. Where was Galen? I heard scratching on the other side of the door. I was shaking and sweating and I felt a bone-deep chill that coffee would never touch. What was wrong with me? I was supposed to be free now. I wasn't supposed to feel like I needed to run away, like I needed to bleed. Like if I wasn't hurting, then I must be dead.

I survived. I made it to the other side. So why did I feel like I was still locked in that cold, dark room?

"Kellan." On the other side of the door.

I jumped. Aza was here. No. It was Tony. Just Tony. Breathe. Breathe for Galen. One breath at a time. "Yeah?"

"You on something?"

"What?"

"Drugs. Are you on drugs?"

"No. Of course not."

"Good. Then what are you hiding?"

"I don't have to tell you." My voice sounded childish and small.

"No, you don't," Tony said. "But keeping secrets makes it worse. You could learn that lesson the hard way, like I did, or you could try taking my advice."

I thought about it. I thought about how, if I opened that door and showed Tony the new scar on my arm, he would know. I would lose that newfound comfort, because if he knew, it would become a shameful thing. It was okay to want something for myself.

"Kell, if you don't want to face me, that's fine. But could you at least open the door and let Galen in? He's a basket case out here."

I didn't want Galen to know about the cutting, either. It was weak. Not alpha wolf behavior. Maybe he would decide I was too weak. I was too diminished to be worth his time and affection. Maybe he would be right.

I stood up and pushed back my sleeves. Then I turned on the light and opened the door. Galen rushed in and sniffed up one of my legs and down the other, checking for injury. Taking me in. I forced myself to look up at Tony. I thrust out my arm. "There. Happy?"

He frowned at my forearm, and I realized he was having a hard time understanding what I was showing him. There were so many scars, old and new, that the one I made for myself didn't really stand out.

I pointed to The Scar. "That. I did that. And I felt better for a little while after. But then you wanted to know what happened and the afterglow wore off and I wanted to do it again, so I was going to come into the bathroom and cut myself again, but then you got in the way." I paused to catch my breath. "I'm not a junkie."

"Why did it feel better?"

"Jesus, I don't know." I tugged my sleeves down and shoved my hands in the front pocket of the hoodie. "It's not like I wrote out a pros and cons list. It just felt good."

He crossed his arms over his chest again. It made the muscles in his shoulders and arms bunch and bulge. My eyes shied away like a spooked horse. "Kellan, I'm trying to help. I'm not getting off on it. And I'm not trying to be an intrusive douche. I'm trying to help you understand, so maybe we can find something else that will help just as much without causing bloodshed."

"I don't mind bloodshed."

"Then why did you hide it?"

I scowled. I didn't want to be head-shrunk. "Fuck you, Dr. Phil."

He didn't even blink. "If it's something normal and healthy, then why hide it?"

"Since when have I claimed to be either normal or healthy?" I tried to glare at him, but direct eye contact made me shake. Tony sighed, but didn't move. I slumped a little, suddenly weary. The only way out of this conversation, apparently, was through it. "Fine. It's not healthy. But I'm not healthy. You might've noticed, I'm a little bit fuckered in the head right now."

"Really? I didn't notice a difference at all." He rubbed a hand over the back of his head. I wondered if that bare scalp got cold in the winter. I wondered what he would look like with more hair. Then I pictured him with Fabio-style hair — long, flowing locks, although I imagined Tony's locks would be black rather than Fabio-blond. And I started to snicker. Then I started to laugh. Tony and Galen both stared at me as my knees threatened to give out from under me for the ten thousandth time that day, but this time, it was from laughter. "Are you okay?" Tony said.

I swallowed a guffaw. "Have you ever thought about growing your hair out?" Then I dissolved into giggles again.

"You sure you're not on drugs?" But he smelled less worried now.

My laughter dissolved, but a smile lingered. "Is there any coffee left?"

"Yeah. I'll go get your mug. Why don't you feed Galen?"

It was a good idea, but I wished I thought of it myself. I opened the bin that held Galen's food, and was assaulted by the smell of meat. Venison. Galen's kibble had venison in it. I gagged, dropped Galen's dish, closed my eyes tight, dug my fingernails into my palms. Was nothing the same? Would I never be able to enjoy the things we used to love, hunting together and bringing down prey, or me sitting on the floor, watching him hoover up his food, enjoying the mingling scents of dog breath and kibble and knowing the joy that food brought him? Should I just give Galen to Tony for good, if I couldn't even dish out a bowl of kibble without a nervous breakdown? Was I any good to anyone?

I smelled a scent as homey as fresh-baked bread. Tears leaked out of the corners of my eyes as I remembered how good it used to feel to smell Tony's scent. So familiar. So safe. Breathe. Breathe for Galen. I could do this for Galen. Maybe I wasn't good for him, maybe I was useless in every way, but without Galen, I had nothing left. I opened my eyes, and while pretending Tony wasn't standing there, I picked up Galen's dish and measured out a cup of kibble. I dumped it in the dish and then set the dish on the floor. Then I walked back into the living room and stared at the TV without seeing it.

Tony brought me a full mug of coffee. "You want any more pizza?" he asked.

"Maybe in a minute." The coffee was hot. It brought me back to myself. I sipped and pictured Fabio-Tony flicking his hair over his shoulder. "Oh, no more zombies?" I said when I finally saw the nine o'clock news on the television.

"Guess not."

I squinted at him. "Did you change the channel?"

"Nope." He was lying. I let him. "So, you want to watch something else?"

Whatever we chose to watch would eventually end. A CD, however, could be put on repeat ad infinitum. "Music." I chose a Five Finger Death Punch album and turned the volume just a touch too loud for polite company.

After a few seconds, Tony said, "Suddenly, I'm missing the zombies."

I laughed and he looked pleased. He sat down at the folding table in the breakfast nook, and I felt obligated to join him. Galen sat between my right leg and Tony's left.

I had coffee, loud rock music and my dog. Peace might be possible after all.

Of course, Tony had to talk. "So, about what we were talking about earlier."

I sighed. "What?"

"You need to talk about this stuff. To someone. If you don't want to talk to me, there are women you can talk to. Or, you know, Finn." His face twisted like Finn's name tasted bad. "But, like I said, hiding it is just going to make it worse."

I chose to focus on the easiest part of his unsolicited advice. "Why the hell would I talk to Finn?"

He shrugged. "I don't know. I just wanted to give you some extra options."

"Yeah, but Finn? Yeesh."

"He's an impartial ear."

"Yeah, because he doesn't actually listen when I talk."

"Oh, he listens. He heard what you said in Janus's office that night." Neither of us needed to clarify which night he referred to. "He was probably the only one who heard. Janus and I were too busy hating the idea to listen."

"You never talk about what happened to you," I pointed out, "before you came to the Sankhain."

"Well, I don't talk about it to you." At my furrowed brow, he shrugged. "I don't want you to see me that way. To think of me that way. But I talk about it. To Simone, mostly. I also talk to some of the younglings, the ones I trained with. Cat. Ryder."

I wasn't friends with the younglings I trained with. I had Mal. Why would I need friends when I had a relationship that went all the way back to the womb?

He studied me. "My pimp used to give us drugs. Uppers if we were too tired to work, downers if we tried to fight back. When I came to Camp, everything was so goddamn normal. Invisible forest aside, I mean. I went through a little withdrawal, but it was more than that. I didn't know how to just go to sleep all on my own. And when I did sleep, the nightmares...well, anyway. I decided that sobriety was for shit, and I snuck into the infirmary, looking for pills. Anything to numb me out a little."

I clenched my jaw to keep it from dropping. Tony did drugs? Real drugs? I was almost afraid of what he might reveal next. But curiosity won out. "So what happened?"

"What do you think?" His mouth tilted with a small smile. "Simone caught me. She sat me down and told me that we had two options. I could start talking about what happened to me and dealing with it, or she could tell Finn and Janus that I was trying to steal pills and they'd kill me."

He meant that literally, I knew. The Sankhain leadership had a zero-tolerance policy for the younglings. Drug and alcohol use were cause for elimination. They trusted recovering junkies with sharp objects and firearms. Junkies who were still using, not so much with the weaponry.

He wasn't dead, so I knew which option he chose. "So I tell my war stories and poof, I'm cured?"

"No." His scent heated with frustration. "There's no cure. But it helps. And eating good food and exercising, so you can feel strong. It helps, and you get better at it."

"Better at what?"

He pinned me down with his gaze, like a dead butterfly pinned to some creepy kid's foamboard display. "Better at coping. At living with it."

I couldn't breathe. The room was too crowded. I shoved back from the table and stumbled toward Mr. Coffee, whose green light shone like a beacon. Okay, maybe more like a nightlight. But Mr. Coffee aimed for beacon. It wasn't his fault he was just too small.

Relating to Mr. Coffee's identity crisis calmed me down. I had a wound I couldn't heal. That's what Tony was saying. It would never heal. My job was to learn to live with it.

That was bullshit.

Even if I couldn't heal it, I could improve it. I knew just how to do that. Aza needed to die.

Chapter 22

I turned back to Tony. "I'm tired. I'd like to go home." I had some thinking to do.

He studied me. "You did it again."

"What?"

"You went from panic to calm," he said. "What changed?"

I shrugged. "What difference does it make? I feel better."

"Yeah, last time, you felt better because you made yourself bleed. You gonna tell me you're thinking about something wholesome this time?"

He was harshing my buzz. "What do you care?"

"Because I care, Kellan! I care about you." He stared at his hands.

I didn't want to hear this. Tony needed to understand that what he wanted was never going to happen. I decided to lie. Tony didn't know anything about faeries, so I could tell him whatever I wanted to make this easier for both of us. "I don't even know if I can do it anymore."

"Do what?"

"Aza's penis was barbed. All along the shaft. He literally ripped me apart, over and over again, and the scar tissue is bad. I know that because he had to slice his way back in there the last couple weeks." It was a good lie. Graphic and disgusting enough that no one would ask for more details. "I have nothing to offer you. Absolutely nothing."

He was quiet for such a long time. I imagined he was disappointed and wondering how to get out of here without causing a scene, and that made me sad. Not surprised, but sad. I flipped Mr. Coffee's switch to off, and told Galen it was time to go.

Tony's voice startled me. "When I said I care about you, I wasn't talking about sex."

I pretended not to hear. I dumped the remaining coffee down the drain and rinsed the carafe, setting it upside down in the dish drainer.

"Look, the sex we had was amazing," he said. "And if you ever want to try again, I'm game, believe me. But that's about the farthest thing from my mind right now."

I snorted. "You're a man. It's never that far from your mind."

"I'm not that kind of man, Kellan." His tone and the deep, dark sadness in his scent drew my gaze. His arms were once again crossed over his chest, but this time, he gripped his shoulders, like he was trying to hold himself together. He stared at the floor and the overhead light threw shadows under his eyes, around his mouth.

I hurt his feelings. Galen walked over to him, leaned against him. To comfort him. The way my dog usually comforted me. I found a whole new reason to forget how to breathe.

Why did it never occur to me that Tony and Galen would form a bond? Why did it take me by surprise? Because I was stupid, that's why. I shoved Galen on Tony. I walked away and didn't look back. Of course, Galen bonded with him. That wouldn't go away just because I came home.

I left the kitchen, heading for the front door. I should've said something to Tony. I should've apologized for implying that he was a sex-crazed walking penis. I should've taken a deep breath and thanked him for taking such good care of my dog that Galen felt compelled to comfort Tony. But I had coffee and pizza in me, which meant I could run for a little while at least. Of course, if I ran with this much pizza in my gut, I'd probably puke it up. But not right away.

I unlocked the deadbolt, but as I opened the apartment door, Tony came up behind me and closed it. I froze. I wanted to fight, but fighting just made the beatings worse. He liked it when I fought. Don't move. Don't move and he won't see you. He'll lose interest. Just don't move. Don't feel. Don't think. Don't. Don't. Don't. And whatever you do, don't fucking cry out or he'll never stop.

Slowly, their scents trickled past the memories and the panic. Galen. Tony. Not Aza. Not that room. My face heated and I tugged on the doorknob again. Tony held the door closed. "God fucking damn it, let me out!" My voice was so shrill, it hurt me to hear it.

"You can leave. But not without Galen and me."

I could do this. I could pull it together and fake it. All I needed to do was get home, so I could think. Plan. And then hunt. But not if I was hysterical, because then they wouldn't leave me alone. And not if I was too calm, for the same reason. I clenched my teeth and spoke through them. "Fine. Then let's go."

"All right. I'm going to box up the leftovers and take them back to camp. You can eat them yourself, or if you don't want them, I'm sure the younglings will make short work of them. You promise you're not going to bolt the second I turn my back?"

"Yeah. Sure."

He looked at me like he had his doubts, but he dropped his hand from the door and walked back to the kitchen. While Tony messed with the pizza boxes, I snapped the harness on Galen. Tony returned, carrying one box that must've contained the remains of both pizzas. "You didn't pack up any clothes," he said suddenly.

I don't care, I almost said. If I said that, he'd ask questions, and questions would delay my return to the cabin. That quiet, quiet cabin. Too quiet. But at least there, I could think and feel without anyone watching me for signs of crazy. Going into the bedroom, I picked up a grocery sack from the floor, and stuffed a few items from each drawer into it. Then I picked up another, bigger bag and stuffed it with all knives from my knife drawer.

When I returned to the living room, Tony looked at the two bags, taking in their contents. "That's all you want?"

"Well, I don't own any more knives."

"Uh-huh. All right. Let's go." He didn't seem happy.

I sighed. "You think I need more underwear?"

"Well, I don't think you need more knives."

I glanced at the bags. "Fine." I set the bag of blades on the floor and went back into the bedroom, where I grabbed two handfuls of underwear. I didn't care about underwear. Surprising, given how excited I got about socks a few hours ago. But if underwear was normal and got Tony to stop watching me, I'd pretend to give a shit. "You want to inspect the contents?" I said when I stood yet again by the front door.

"No. Jeez." Tony led the way out the door, leaving Galen and the bags to me.

Galen nudged my hand as I picked up his leash. Like he was apologizing. Didn't mean to get attached to him, I imagined him saying. Sorry, sis. "Don't worry about it, big dog. None of this is your fault." I closed and locked the apartment behind us.

In the truck, Tony surprised me by turning the wrong way out of my driveway. "Where are we going?" I asked, feeling panic start to curdle inside me.

"Wal-Mart," he said, then refused to answer any further questions.

It was after ten, but apparently, some Wal-Marts were open twenty-four hours. The world was just full of exciting truths. Tony pulled into the parking lot and turned off the truck.

I turned to him. "If you think I'm going in there with you, you are so very fucking wrong."

"What makes you think you're invited? Stay here and keep Galen company. I'll be right back." And he was gone before I could come up with a snappy response.

I started fidgeting almost right away. Galen and I got out of the truck, and started jogging in circles around the truck. Technically, I wasn't going against Tony's order, because we never really left the truck. We were just around it, instead of inside its stifling confines. Testing the limits of an order made me sweat a cold, scared sweat, because cleverness and arguing semantics were both punishable offenses. But I was free, and as Kellan Faolanni, my job was to test the limits of orders. I remembered that much.

Tony didn't punish me for getting out of the truck, of course. Instead, he saw us jogging and he smiled. "I guess you've got some energy back. Yay, pizza."

"Ah, yeah. Yay."

"Here." He thrust a new plastic bag at me and got into the truck.

By the dome light, I took in the bag's contents. "The Walking Dead. Season one, two…there are four seasons here."

"Yup. I was going to get season five, too, but I figured it would take you a while to get through the first four. Maybe by then, you won't like it anymore." He sounded hopeful.

"I don't — are we going to drop these back at the apartment before we go to camp?"

"No. We've got TVs and DVD players at camp. You've got electricity in your cabin. We maybe can't get you cable," Janus had a strict "no cable" rule in the cabins, "but we can at least set you up with the DVDs."

"We're not supposed to have TVs in the cabins, either," I said.

"I'll explain it to them. They'll be okay with it." He sounded awfully sure, which surprised me, considering we were talking about Finn and Janus, who refused to bend in order to take a shit.

I was still struggling with the logistics of my not-bending imagery as Tony put the truck in gear and started for camp. Finally, I decided that as much as I liked how it sounded, everybody had to bend in order to take a shit. It just wasn't possible to do it any other way.

——— «» ———

By the time we arrived at the forest, I was nodding off. My body wanted to sleep. My brain knew that I had work to do. Tony turned off the truck and looked at me. "You never told me what you were thinking about before."

"What do you mean?" I didn't really have to ask, because I was still thinking about it. But I couldn't let him know that.

"In the kitchen. When you went all calm. What made you do that?"

I looked him in the eye and lied easily. "I was thinking about cutting myself again."

He studied me and it took all my self-control to hold still. "No, you weren't. If that's what it was, you wouldn't've been all secretive. You already told me that secret, no point in keeping it anymore."

If I told him, he would shoot down my idea faster than if it was a clay pigeon. "I don't have to tell you. I don't have to do anything anymore."

"You don't have to. But I'm asking you to tell me. For your own sake." His tone was so gentle, his voice so low and soft. Part of me wanted to sink into that voice and rest there. But the rest of me couldn't let my guard down enough to rest anywhere.

"I can take care of my own sake, my own self. Thanks." I opened the truck door and stepped to the ground.

The sound of Tony's door slamming shut made me jump. Again. I was sick of jumping. Maybe after I killed Aza, I could stop.

Tony rounded the front of the truck and stood before me. Close. Too close. I didn't have room to breathe. "You're going to hunt him down," Tony said. "You want to kill him."

How did he know? Fuck him and his fucking intuition. "Kill who?" I tried to hedge.

"Aza. You're planning a way to hunt him down. That's why you got so calm. That's the only thing that could make you this fucking okay. After everything you went through, after —" He punched the side of the truck. "You did this so you didn't have to kill him."

"I did this to save Darcy's life," I hissed. "Darcy's safe. But nobody else is. Sure, he's not supposed to come back here. But he came back once before. And what about all the other fucking people in the world? You really think it's okay to let Aza run rabid across the planet? I can't let him — I can't."

"So what, you're going after him? And then what? You're going to fight a faery war?"

"No, dumbass," I said. I could tell by the heat in his scent that Tony didn't appreciate the nomenclature. I didn't care. "I'm going to lure him back here to Madison. Maybe not even to Madison, maybe somewhere else in the Midwest. He'll be the one to break the contract. Then I can kill him, free and clear."

Tony stared at me. "That's the stupidest fucking thing I've ever heard, and I grew up in a crack den. Aza's not going to fall for that."

"I'll figure out a way."

"And don't try to tell me that you want to do this for the good of mankind," he went on, like I never spoke. "You want revenge. That's all you want. You want to make him bleed, because he made you bleed."

"I wish that's all he did!" I heard my voice, heard how shrill and brittle it sounded. I forced it down to a hoarse whisper. "I can handle a little blood. I can handle a lot of blood. I can handle my own fucking sister trying to kill me and almost succeeding. But I want my life back! I want my — me back."

Tony's scent was cold and dead. "Killing Aza won't get you anything. He took what he took. That's done. The nightmares are there already. Revenge won't make them go away."

I felt my last hope slip away. "It's something. It's a plan, something that I can hold onto." My voice cracked and I was ashamed to realize I was begging him. Begging Tony not to take away the one thing that made me feel strong.

"You got plenty of things to hold onto," Tony said quietly. "Like that dog that already watched you walk away once and it almost killed him. He wouldn't eat for a week and a half. I had to hand-feed him. You gonna do that to him again? What about Janus? You're like his own daughter. What about — what about me?" He paused, like there was more he wanted to say, but then didn't. "You have people who care about you. Who know what it's like to go through shit, who can support you without pitying you. Don't throw us all away so that you can maybe possibly kill some lowlife faery."

Don't think. Don't feel. Shut it off, shut it off, shutitoffshutitoffshutitoff. Galen brushed up against me and I crumbled. I knelt and buried my face in his fur. "Fuck you," I mumbled.

Despite my faceful of dog hair, Tony seemed to understand what I said. "Yeah, you, too. Can we go home now? I'm really fucking tired."

I pushed to my feet. "I'm not saying I'm giving up."

"Of course not." He sneezed. "Shit. I'm out of pills. Can we please go?"

"Go ahead." I was testing the water.

"Not without you. Those're the rules." Apparently, the water was colder than the Atlantic.

"Fine." I felt so shaky. So cold. Like I was suffering from emotional hypothermia. I put one foot in front of the other, and we walked through the forest. I carried the bags, Tony carried the pizza. At my cabin door, I said, "Are you going to sleep outside my window all night?"

"Shit, no. It's cold." He sniffed. "I'll see about hunting down a TV and a DVD player for you in the morning. For now, how about a radio?"

He was leaving. I was going to be alone. In the dark. In the quiet. As a human, because I couldn't risk trying to shape-shift and finding that... And no dream of killing Aza to keep me occupied. Because the fact was, no matter what I said, I was giving up, at least for now. I couldn't walk away from Galen again. And that left me with a whole lotta baggage and nothing to distract me from the weight of it. The muscles in my neck tightened to the point that my head twitched around, like I was having some sort of fit. "Yeah. Sure. A radio."

He was quiet. "Do you want me to sleep outside your window?"

Yes. "No. Of course not. That's stupid."

"Do you want me to find Gina or Cat? Get them to spend the night with you?"

This conversation was getting on my nerves. "I'm not a child."

"Don't have to be a child to be scared. Nothing wrong with being scared, either."

"Fuck you."

"You said that already." He sneezed, then crossed his arms over his chest, a sign that he wasn't going anywhere anytime soon.

"You need pills."

"Yup, I do. So maybe you could tell me what will help you feel better."

Maybe... "You could stay. Inside. If you wanted. Not to sleep together. Just to sleep separately, together." It sounded so ridiculous, but I was being honest. I used to be honest. I used to like that about myself.

His expression never changed. "All right. I'm gonna drop this —" he indicated the pizza — "in the fridge in the kitchens. Then I gotta go see Simone and get some more Benadryl. I'll find a radio. Then I'll be back. Or you can come with me, if you want."

I shook my head. I didn't want to go near the kitchen, and the infirmary was so bright and sterile, and there would almost certainly be younglings around. And Simone might want to examine me. The truth was, if I couldn't heal it for myself, nothing Simone did could help.

Tony left, and Galen and I walked around outside until he lifted his leg thirteen times. That seemed like a number he could be content with, so we went into the cabin. Whoever stocked the cabin with clothes and running shoes also left a giant Rubbermaid full of Galen's kibble, along with dog dishes I didn't recognize.

I gave Galen fresh water, and while he slurped up his fill, I opened the bin of food.

Face it. I could do this. I needed to do this. At the scent of the venison, I felt the now-familiar bile rise, but this time, I ignored it and dug out a few pieces. I raised them to my nose, then dumped them in the dog dish. I set the dish on the floor and snapped the lid back on the bin. After the initial onslaught of meat-scent, I was able to take in the entire scent. And the entire scent was okay.

I sat down on the bed, shaken. Galen walked over and nudged my hands. I automatically ran my hands over the top of his head, rubbed his ears, and ran my fingers down the back of his neck and into the thick fur over his shoulder blades. I was suddenly so exhausted, I couldn't hold my head up. Someone chose that moment to knock on the door.

I bolted off the bed and then stood stock-still, listening. Carefully, I checked the air. The door of the cabin was drafty. I could smell Tony on the other side. Not trusting my legs to carry me, I called softly, "Come in."

"Hey." He held up a small CD player/radio combo. "Simone had this in her office, so it was one-stop shopping."

I looked around the cabin, at its one bed. This was a bad idea. "I'll sleep on the floor," I said.

"That's okay, I can —"

"I said, I'll take the floor." My voice was too loud. Galen once again looked from me to Tony. I was giving my dog tennis neck. I needed to pull myself together, and now.

"Okay." Tony set the CD player on the bedside table and plugged it in. He seemed to be pretending I wasn't acting like a crazy person. "You want me to go get CDs from the truck, or should we turn on the radio?"

I studied him. He looked tired and allergy-ridden. I couldn't ask him to go back to the truck, especially since most of the CDs in there were pretty hard core rock that he would hate. "Um, radio."

He nodded and started fiddling with the dial. "I suppose you want to listen to rock music."

"Did you have something else in mind?"

"Maybe some blues?" he said hopefully.

I made a face. But he was being really nice to me. It didn't feel right to force him to listen to music he didn't like. "If you want, we could try blues."

He considered me for a second. "Nah. This time of night, they'd probably be playing experimental jazz. That shit sounds like dying cats."

I laughed. "At this time of night, the rock music probably isn't much better."

"How about classic rock? A little less screechy for my ears, but still noisy enough to make you happy."

"All right." I found a station. Zeppelin was playing, "Ramblin' On." That was one of my favorite Zeppelin songs, and I felt myself relax a little.

I curled up on the floor with a blanket and a pillow. Galen looked at Tony, then curled up beside me, his back pressed to my belly. I tried not to think about that brief hesitation on Galen's part.

The floor was hard and a little chilly. But I was spooning with Galen. I was safe. Music played in the background. I could sleep like this.

"Are you sure you don't want the bed?" Tony said. He yawned loudly.

"I'm sure. Good night." I waited for him to argue some more, but he didn't. Instead, footsteps approached, and though I tensed, I managed not to jump when Tony set two more blankets beside me. I waited unmoving until I heard the springs of the bed creak, and then I heard Tony sigh the way Galen did when he was settling in to sleep. I wondered if Tony always sighed like that, or if he picked up the habit over the last two months of living with Galen. Pulling the blankets around my dog and me, I listened to Tony's breathing, and knew he was asleep when he started to snore. Galen started snoring shortly after. Tony's snores were louder, more strident, while Galen sounded like a soft rumble. I felt a smile curve my mouth. The expression felt foreign, like someone else's face settled on top of my own. But it was there, and it was mine.

Chapter 23

The next thing I knew, bright sunlight poured through the windows. It was disorienting. I couldn't figure out where I was. I lay on a cold floor, which was familiar. But the sunlight and the blankets were strange. Then I heard rustling, and smelled soap and men's deodorant. Aza didn't have to wear deodorant. Faeries didn't sweat, he told me. But he liked his cologne. This wasn't Aza. These were Tony smells.

I sat up, feeling as old as I was.

"Hey, good morning," Tony said. He was dressed in fresh clothes. When did he get fresh clothes? Did he shower here or in his cabin when he went to get clothes? I felt panic creep into my chest at the thought of him being naked so nearby.

Don't be stupid, I told myself. You invited him to stay. Use of the bathroom was implied. "Good morning," I finally replied.

Galen was sitting by Tony. Now, my dog trotted over to me to say hi. I petted him, trying not to resent the fact that he got up when Tony got up, rather than staying cuddled with me. It made me wonder if he spent the whole night with me, or if after I fell asleep, he went and slept in the bed with Tony. Don't be stupid, I thought again. Maybe that should be my new mantra. It seemed to apply to more situations than "One breath at a time."

"How'd you sleep?" Tony asked. He pulled on a hoodie over his t-shirt.

"Fine. Good."

"Good. I was out. Benadryl is great that way." He sat down on the bed and pulled on his boots. I watched his hands lace and tie them, then when he looked up, I looked away. "Well. I gotta go teach. Beginner's gun class. Can't be late, or the younglings try to break into the gun safe. Gina's going to stop by in a little bit with some stuff for you. Okay?"

I nodded, wondering vaguely when he talked to Gina. Did he leave and I slept through it?

"All right. See you." Tony left and Galen got up to go with him. Then Galen looked at me and sat down, but closer to the door than to me. I stared at the door, because I couldn't look at him. It hurt. It was my fault, my choice that pushed him at Tony. But it still hurt.

It's not about you. I heard my mother's voice, clear as if she was standing over me. She lectured me once, in her hypocritical way, after I got mad at Mal for besting me at blades. When you make it about you, the world gets too small. So get off your butt, shake your sister's hand, and go practice. Watch what she does. Then learn to do it better.

I wasn't sure how the advice applied to her initial point, which seemed to be the need to be less self-centered. But most of my mom's wisdom didn't bear a lot of logical scrutiny. It was better to either forget it all, or take it piecemeal, like some religious fanatics use bits of their bible to support their hatred. So I took the bits that were helpful to me in that moment. First, that Galen's feelings weren't about me, and second, to get off my butt.

After a shower, I corralled my hair into a sloppy braid and dressed in a hoodie and a pair of yoga pants. I disliked the principle of yoga pants, because they were so damn yuppie. But they were incredibly comfortable.

I gradually became aware that my stomach was empty. Which meant Galen's stomach was empty, and he probably needed to pee. At first, I wanted to beat myself up for neglecting him. Basically, I forgot that he had needs. But I shut down the judgy voice in my head and took Galen outside, because that would do him more good than hearing me berate myself. As I waited for him to empty out, I saw Gina walking toward us, carrying a paper sack.

Watching her walk, she had more grace, more confidence than I ever saw in her. She looked grown-up and strong. I hated my body even more, looking at her.

"Hi. Tony said you might not want to go to the mess hall for a while. So I brought you some stuff." She hitched up the bag. "Grab the door for me?"

"Sure." When I held the door open, Galen trotted inside after Gina. I trailed behind.

"I've got breakfast, first off. Eggs and toast, and a thermos of coffee." Last night, the kitchen was out of eggs. When did they get more? "Plus food for you to keep here, some protein bars, peanut butter and bread. I've got a spare coffee maker in the kitchen that Finn said you can have in your cabin. But I couldn't carry it this trip."

Tears welled up before I could stop them. Why was I tearing up? Another sign of weakness.

"You should eat," Gina said, looking at me. "You need to build your strength back up. You'll get your strength back in no time,

Sankha Kellan. You're the strongest woman I've ever met. But to do that, you need to eat."

Gina smelled like meat. How could she not, spending all that time in the kitchen? The sack she brought smelled like meat. It was never going away. I could never escape it. I felt so tired. How could I possibly get strong if all I wanted was to curl up in a ball and disappear?

I cleared my throat. Walked over to the box of tissues on the nightstand, blew my nose. "Thank you," I said. I accepted the Tupperware filled with scrambled eggs, the thermos that smelled of coffee strong enough that it drowned out the meat scent in the room. I huffed coffee fumes while I ate, so that I could swallow without gagging. I gathered up my courage, then asked, "What did Tony tell you?"

"Not much." She sat down on the bed, clearly planning to stay awhile. "Just that you don't want to eat meat anymore. That the smell of it sickens you. That's okay. We can work with that pretty easily. I'll just prepare your meals separately and bring them here. Some of the younglings prefer meatless meals, too, even a couple of the Sankhain. Finn prefers vegetable-based proteins for most of his meals."

"They make vegetable-based protein?"

She laughed. "Sure. Beans. Black beans are very high in protein, but I like edamame best. Soybeans. They don't have much of a flavor or a scent, so they take on whatever flavor you add to them. Sauces or dressings. They have a little bit of a crunch, too, which I like."

"Soybeans." I tried to picture my mother's daughter living on soybeans. "I'm not eating tofu."

"No, I don't think tofu would be a good option for you. I think it would be too close to meat, texture-wise. But you know, nuts are a good source of protein, no relation to meat. And eggs, of course, and yogurt and other dairy. You can get a good, balanced diet without ever having to touch meat again." She fiddled with the hem of her shirt.

"You haven't told me how awful I look." I drank coffee and watched her face.

The corners of her mouth dipped before she firmed up her expression again. "You don't need me to tell you how you look. But I think you look pretty good, considering what you've been through."

Anger flared. "So Tony did tell you more."

She shook her head quickly. "No. He didn't. But I mean, come on. When you left, you loved meat more than air. You must've gone through some pretty awful things to change so drastically."

Anger abandoned me as quickly as it arrived. I was left with shaky hands and a plastic mug full of coffee. "I guess."

"I'll stop by later with the coffee maker." Gina bounded out of the cabin.

When I fed Galen, I was pleased to note that the smell of his food barely made me gag. I finished the coffee while he ate. I started to pace before he was even finished. Sitting still was hard. While I was with Aza, I became very practiced at being still to avoid attracting attention. Now that I was home, I wanted to move. So he couldn't catch up to me.

I used to be a rational person. I'm pretty sure I was one, once.

I turned up the volume on the radio. Sitting on the floor, I ran my hands over Galen for possibly the eighty-second time since I got back. I studied him, memorized him, breathed him in. When the anxiety grew too strong, I clipped Galen's harness on him and we went for a walk in the trees.

We ended up running loops around the camp. As it turned out, eating two good meals worked wonders for stamina. I still wasn't my old self, but I stayed on my feet for twelve loops. Galen was actually panting by the time we stopped. He wagged his tail at me. Just like old times.

I wanted cold water. Not cold out of the tap, but cold out of the fridge. All of a sudden, that sounded like the ultimate in luxury. And I knew just where to find some.

I made my way to the weight room. A small dorm refrigerator in the weight room was filled with large bottles of water. I was relieved to see that the room was empty. I didn't really want an audience for what I knew I needed to do next.

First, though, I found the dog bowl that lived in the weight room and filled it with water for Galen. I got myself a bottle from the fridge, then turned to the weight equipment.

By the time I did all the upper-body machines, I felt like I was made entirely of spaghetti noodles. It wasn't an unpleasant feeling. I actually felt more powerful than before. Like I might not be able to lift my own arm right now, but very soon, I would be able to bench-press a car. Or at least a Prius.

Galen and I were walking toward the cabin when Tony came running over to us. "Janus said it was okay, so I found you a TV and DVD player," he said, only slightly out of breath. "Wanna help me haul them to the cabin?"

I hesitated. I felt like I couldn't haul a bag of marshmallows, much less an appliance. "Um, I just finished a workout." I stopped there, hoping he would fill in the blanks.

"Oh, that's great. The DVD player's pretty light. Or I could get a youngling to help me," he said, like it was a ground-breaking idea. Why the hell didn't he just get a youngling to help him from the start?

I felt like I should at least try to lift the DVD player. Because if Tony got a youngling to help him, then all the rest of the younglings would know that I was too weak to carry a "pretty light" appliance. My ego begged me to prevent such a travesty. I said, "No, that's okay, I can help."

"Great. They're in the rec room." The rec room was basically a shed, positioned between the youngling bunkhouses and the infirmary. It contained a couple couches, some card tables, a collection of board games and books, and what Finn called "the entertainment center." It was an old hutch. Someone took out a couple of the shelves to make room for a TV and it held a VCR/ DVD combo down below.

"I'm not stealing the rec room's TV," I said.

"No, no, this one's smaller and older. Ryder's been tinkering with it, and he got it working again."

As we started walking, I gave Tony a skeptical look. "Is it going to burn down my cabin? Because I don't need a TV that bad."

"No, Ryder's great with electronics. He resurrected that radio I put in your cabin last night, too." Apparently, my expression revealed that I was less than convinced. "Seriously. I know he's not the best at reading or talking, but he's a whiz with wires."

Ryder was a big guy, almost as tall as Tony and easily as broad. He was sweet, strong, an excellent fighter, a decent marksman, and good with a blade. But he had the vocabulary of a five-year old, due to a blow to the head that left a permanent dent in his skull. The dent happened before he joined us, long enough before that Simone couldn't heal it. It didn't seem to bother him, other than the occasional killer migraine. But words would never be his thing. Sounded like he had a different thing going for him, though.

Ryder was actually in the rec room when Tony and I entered. He was reading a picture book. He nodded at me and said to Tony, "I think I just about got this one, sir."

"That's great, Ryder," Tony said. "Sankha Kellan and I are just here to pick up your TV. She's going to use it in her cabin for a while."

Ryder jumped to his feet. "Really? Oh, good. He needs a place to go. Thank you, Sankha Kellan."

I didn't know what to say to that. The TV was a he? "Uh, no, thank you, Ryder. Tony says you've got a real talent for electrical work."

Ryder blushed, ducked his head, and abruptly left the room.

"Did I say something wrong?" I asked Tony.

He smiled. "No. But I don't think Ryder's had a whole lot of opportunity to be complimented in his life. He'll probably end up with a crush on you."

Somehow, that made me feel worse. Like from here, my only option was to let Ryder down. "So where's this TV?"

Tony opened a closet that appeared to be the place electronics went to die. Radios, alarm clocks, alarm clock radios, CD players, DVD players, toasters, a microwave, and at least four small TVs.

"Jesus Christ," I said. "Who's the hoarder in the family?"

"Ah, I believe that would be Finn. I think he hopes that someday, they'll find a cure for broken-down shit."

"You think you know a guy," I said, seeing a toaster that was still covered in bread crumbs. "Ick. Can we get on with our shopping? This is depressing."

"Here." Tony picked up a small black box that I assumed was the DVD player. Then he hefted up a twenty-inch TV that looked like it weighed more than I did.

"You sure you've got that?" I felt a little silly, clutching the itty-bitty DVD player while the man did all the heavy lifting.

"Yup, I'm good. Let's go."

I didn't point out how crushed Ryder would be if Tony dropped his resurrected television in the middle of the yard. I just tightened my grip on Galen's leash and made sure he wouldn't trip Tony as we made our way to my cabin.

I held the door open for Tony. My stupid, flighty gaze settled on his hands. Large, blunt-fingered, strong, calloused. And, I knew, the gentlest touch. I didn't want to notice — or remember — any of that.

Except I did, and that brought the memory of a feeling, a feeling that now I could only associate with Aza. Now I was back in the dark room, the smells of earth and blood and sex surrounding me, soaking into my very pores. I couldn't take a deep breath, just short gasps that slowly made my vision go spotty. Part of me wanted that. Wanted to pass out, so I wouldn't have to see. Sometimes passing out was a gift. But the rest of me rose up in terror, because I needed to know. Needed to know what happened, what caused all the pains, the bruises, the scars that remained after he was done.

I dropped the DVD player and ran to the bathroom. I knelt in front of the toilet, waiting to vomit. It didn't happen. I was shaking, sweating profusely, but not vomiting. So I guess I was in good shape.

I leaned back against the wall and listened to Galen whine outside the door. I couldn't move. If I moved, if I opened the door, then it wouldn't just be Galen on the other side. Tony would be there, too. I watched my hand shake, studied it. A lot of the time with Aza, I would only process one body part at a time. He wasn't a whole person, he was just that hand. Or just that nose. Or just that...well. I could stare at that one body part and see how odd it looked, because if you look close enough at anything, even something you've seen a thousand times, it looks odd in ways you never realized before. And it helped to do that.

My hands were shaped funny. The palms were almost square, the fingers long, skinny, bony. The knuckles were a little too big for the fingers. The nails were short and ragged. The shaking slowed. I could breathe a little deeper. I crawled to the door and opened it a crack.

Galen burst through. I marshalled my courage and looked through the doorway at Tony. He wasn't there. The TV sat on the floor opposite the bed. Right next to the outlet. Right where I would've put it. It should've been nice that he figured out where to put it, but instead it made me feel like my lungs got sucked out of my body.

A few minutes later, I heard a knock on the door. It was Tony, carrying a small table this time. Without a word, I stepped back and let him in.

He set the table next to the TV, then brushed off his hands. "Want me to set it up for you?"

I was suddenly aware of how much I sweated this morning. All I wanted was to get in the shower and stay there until I felt clean, which would probably take a few years. "No. I can do it. Thanks, though."

He cocked his head slightly, like he was thinking of pursuing something. Finally, all he said was, "Okay. Give a shout if you need anything."

"Yeah. Sure. Okay. Thanks." I just strung small words on a chain, hoping to give him enough trinkets that he would leave. He did.

And then the cabin was so quiet, so still. Silence like that only meant bad things. I went over to the TV, plugged it in, hooked up the DVD player, and ripped into the Walking Dead DVDs. Once the cabin was sufficiently noisy again, I stripped and took a shower. I stayed under the spray and scrubbed until my skin was a bright, angry red, and when I turned off the water, steam rose from my skin. Then Galen let out a bark. Naturally, I panicked.

I threw on the clean clothes I brought into the bathroom with me. Then I stood at the bathroom door and listened, trying to distinguish which sounds came from the TV and which didn't belong. Finally, I discerned that someone was knocking on the cabin door.

I left the bathroom, trying to breathe and realizing how my clothes were growing damp because I put them on before I toweled off. Feeling like an idiot, an all-too-familiar feeling, I shoved my wet hair out of my face and opened the door. Gina stood on the other side, holding another big paper sack. "I brought the coffeemaker and some lunch," she said, smiling broadly, obviously unaware that my lungs were seizing up.

"Um, great. Thanks." Caffeine was the last thing my over-adrenalized system needed, but maybe the lunch would help calm the shakes that were just starting again.

I took the bag from her, thanked her again, and barely managed to shut the door like a normal person rather than slamming it in her face. Then I leaned against the door, slid down to the floor and closed my eyes. Hate. I hated that a simple bark, a simple knock, could completely unhinge me.

I couldn't take it. I carefully chose a blade and then rolled up my sleeve, choosing a spot free of tattoos or other scars. Then I sliced open my skin and watched the blood bloom. Not a deep cut, just enough to hurt, to leave a lingering sting behind. I felt my muscles and bones turn to jello, and a pleasant buzzing started in my head. Then Galen and I curled up in a ball on the bed and watched zombies attack a motor home.

I never realized just how flimsy motor homes were, until I watched the woman on screen try to keep the bathroom door closed as the zombie fought to get inside. Really, a motor home isn't the place to be in the event of a zombie apocalypse. Sure, you can move around for a while, but they use so much gasoline, and they're not built to withstand any sort of sustained attack. Although the motor home wasn't anywhere near as ridiculous as the people sleeping in tents. Those people were just cannon fodder.

I must've dozed off, because the next thing I knew, I was jolting awake. Galen sat up, too, looking at me, trying to understand what happened. I didn't remember the nightmare, but I knew it happened. As my heart pounded, I stared at the TV screen. The DVD was done, and the menu lingered on the screen, replaying the same few strains of the theme music. Ryder's TV actually worked really well. It hadn't started a fire, and the picture was pretty nice. I focused on that, and on restarting the DVD rather than putting in a new one. Getting a fresh disc would've taken precious time, and I needed some noise and dialogue to fill the room.

Galen and I sat on the bed a while longer, until the aftermath of the dream faded. When I felt like I could work my lungs without the owner's manual, I got up, brewed some coffee, and stood with a mug, looking out the window. I realized I never ate lunch, and I dug around in the bag. There was a large Tupperware container, along with another small one. I opened the big one and found a salad. I made a face and poked at the contents. Some kind of leafy green stuff that was probably spinach. I wasn't sure what the little green beans were. They looked like green navy beans. Rabbit food. I was a wolf, not a rabbit. Except a wolf didn't jump at every little sound. Maybe Aza turned me into a rabbit. A little faery magick trick.

The small container had salad dressing in it. With a resigned sigh, I poured all the dressing over the salad and grabbed a fork. I ate standing, because it felt good to move around. I was feeling stronger already.

The green beans were a little crunchy, which teased a memory out from the back of my brain. "Soybeans, probably," I told Galen. He sat by my foot, swishing his tail back and forth over the floor like a whisk broom. "Don't tell anybody, but they're actually kinda good."

After I ate, I fed Galen, and barely even reacted to the smell of his kibble. It didn't appeal to me, but I didn't gag, either. Progress.

Despite the progress, despite the zombies, I quickly reached a point where I needed to get out and move again. Galen and I headed into the forest. My feet took me on a familiar path.

The Spring looked like a pond. It was small and fairly shallow, but the water was cold and clean and, I knew from experience, delicious. Younglings didn't drink from the Spring until they passed their tests. It was part of the oath-taking ceremony. And once a Sankha drank from the Spring, we never drank from it again. Janus believed that multiple drinks from the Spring would make a Sankha feel like she owned it. Like we were entitled to it. We didn't own it, we were merely caretakers. Because of this, the Spring always had two guards on duty. Finn had a talent for picking guards who didn't like each other. One guard could be bribed or turned, two guards who were friendly could be turned at the same time. But with two guards who didn't get along, one of them would inevitably be willing to fink on the other, making it difficult to sneak past them both.

I spotted the two guards in trees on opposite sides of the Spring. They nodded to me. I tried to remember their names. One of them was called Celine, I was pretty sure. The other one was a scrawny boy who always looked like he just finished rummaging through someone's underwear drawer. I nodded back at them and sat down a few feet from the water's edge. The place itself was peaceful. A good spot to sit.

Why was it okay to sit still and quiet here and not in the cabin? Hell if I knew. Maybe it was the sunlight that snuck in between the leaves overhead. Maybe it was the fact that the woods were never actually quiet, but full of rustlings and snufflings and chirpings, all of which needed to be recognized, identified and enjoyed for their absolute rightness. Or maybe it was because wolves didn't belong inside walls. Maybe out here, I finally felt more like a wolf than a rabbit.

My body relaxed as I absorbed the sounds and smells. I felt the same boneless buzz that I got from cutting, but without the nagging feeling of brokenness. No matter how good the cutting felt, it also felt wrong. Shameful. Something born out of an inability to cope. This, however, felt clean.

I closed my eyes and raised my face to the sky, feeling the dapple of sunlight dance across my eyelids. When I opened my eyes, I saw Galen drinking from the Spring. I stared, dumbstruck, and then I started laughing.

Scrawny Underwear Boy shifted his position in the tree like he was trying to decide whether to shoot my dog or not.

I glared at the boy. "Shoot him and you'll be dead. I've been wanting to kill someone all day. Just give me a reason," I said. Finn was going to be furious. He told me that under no circumstances was I to give Galen water from the Spring. That it wasn't meant for people to grant their pets immortality, just because they have an unhealthy attachment to them. Of course, the animals in the forest drank from it all the time, granting them immortality, which meant we needed to hunt regularly. But Finn wasn't afraid of the forest animals. He was afraid of Galen.

Oh, well. Nothing I could do about it now. With a final chuckle, I stood and picked up Galen's leash. We began walking back toward camp.

When we stepped out of the trees, the first thing I saw was Tony standing by my cabin door, looking around. Like he was looking for someone. Like he was looking for me. When he saw us, I could tell by the set of his mouth and the unibrow-frown he wore that something was wrong.

Chapter 24

My first thought was, Finn already knows I let Galen drink from the Spring. Then I smacked myself upside the head for being a moron, and I squared my shoulders, which had gone all concave without my permission. Galen and I marched over to Tony. "Hi. What's up, frowny face?"

Tony's scent was thick with adrenaline. And something else — sadness? "I — I asked Finn if I could be the one to tell you."

All the air rushed out of my lungs as a horrible thought occurred to me. "Darcy?"

Tony blinked. "What? No. No, it's not Darcy. Why don't we go inside?"

"Why don't you tell me what the fuck it is you don't want me to know?"

I watched his expression as his scent went through a tug-of-war between frustration and worry. Like he was debating whether to press the issue about going inside or just tell me the bad news. Because it was bad news, obviously. "It's Mal," he said finally.

That was so not what I was expecting, I couldn't quite make the turn. "What's Mal?"

He was watching me so closely, it made me a little self-conscious. "Finn thinks he's found her."

JUST TELL ME THE GODDAMN STORY! I clenched my fists and my jaw to avoid screaming, managing to eke out, "How about, instead of dribbling little bits and fucking pieces, you just dump out the whole story?"

"There's been a rash of suicides in the UP." Michigan's Upper Peninsula, known as the UP, pronounced You-Pee. "Finn thinks the nocturnes are gathering there. And if the nocturnes are there..."

Then Mal was probably with them. I took a moment to absorb. Then, "I'll go pack some things. I assume Finn's sending a baby-sitter along with me? Is that you or someone else?"

Tony widened his stance, flexed his knees. Probably unconscious movements. He was bracing himself, because he was expecting me to hit him. "Kellan, you're not going."

At first, I thought I heard wrong. But it only took a few seconds for the reality to set in. "The fuck I'm not going!" Then, because Tony wasn't the one I needed to have this conversation with, I blew past him and ran for Janus's cabin. I heard Tony calling after me, and I didn't even blink. No fucking way they were taking this hunt away from me, too.

With Galen at my heels, I burst through the front door, out of breath even though I only ran about twenty yards. Smack sat at the desk outside Janus's office. Her eyes widened slightly when she saw me, but her voice showed nothing. "Hello, Sankha Kellan. Is he expecting you?"

"Unless he's a total moron, yes, he's expecting me." I started for the door to the office.

"Please allow me to announce you." Smack stood up and placed herself between me and the door.

"Move." I heard the deep-seated growl in my voice that human vocal chords just didn't make, the sort of sound that reminded people that I was other.

Smack didn't flinch. "I'm sorry, ma'am. But I'm supposed to announce any visitors. Please have a seat and I'll be right back."

I didn't have to comply. I knew it and so did she. I could throw her across the room. I could rip out her throat. I could shape-shift and howl loud enough to pop her eardrums. I pictured all these things in my mind and instantly started to tremble. I couldn't believe I just imagined hurting Smack. I took a deep breath, then took a step back, then another, until there was enough space between us that we both understood I wasn't going to do any of those things. I didn't sit down, though.

"Thank you, ma'am." Again, no indication in Smack's voice that anything was amiss. The only sign that she was upset was that she only said the appropriate words. No sarcasm, no muttering under her breath. She knocked on the door, then slipped through. I scared her.

One more reason to hate myself.

My breathing was harsh. I didn't want to hurt Smack. I never wanted to hurt her. I liked her. But those pictures in my mind were so vivid, I almost felt like they actually happened.

I slapped my palms against my temples a few times in an effort to shake the images loose. Make them fall out one of my ears, maybe. Stupid, sure, but what else was I supposed to do?

Smack opened the door and held it for me. I could see Finn and Janus both standing by the fireplace. As I walked past Smack, I made a point of thanking her. I waited for a comment, a mutter, but she didn't say anything. My body shrank in on itself as my face heated with shame.

Janus's expression was completely blank. Which told me he was the sort of angry that required him to control every little muscle, because if he relaxed for just a second, he would make the whole world explode. Maybe that was an exaggeration, but I figured he had at least enough power to make a few cabins explode, including the one we were standing in.

Was he angry because of Smack? Or because he knew I was there to defy him?

The door opened and Tony's scent walked in. I noticed that Smack didn't announce him first. Then I pushed the thought away, because I needed to be calm. I needed to be rational, because I needed to convince these men that they should let me hunt my sister.

If I couldn't hunt Aza, then I would hunt Mal. Because, goddamnit, I needed to kill someone.

I forced my chin down, gazing at the floor as I said, "Good afternoon, sirs."

"Leave us," Janus said. I peeked. He was looking at Finn and Tony, not me. Good. Maybe.

"Sir," Finn began, but Janus cut him off.

"Leave us." His voice was whisper-soft, but it surrounded us. Vibrated the air and made my knees want to give way.

I passed Galen's leash to Tony. My dog struggled to stay with me, nails scrabbling on the wood floor as Tony dragged him out. Galen was unhappy, but safe. One less thing to worry about. Secure in the knowledge that I was the only one left for him to hurt, I waited for Janus to make a move.

"You charge in here like —" He cut himself off. "Who am I?"

Look at me. Who am I? I am Aza. I am Master. The flashback was so solid, so real, I could smell his cologne. It took such a very long time to realize who was asking the question. "You're Janus. Sir."

"Am I? Well, that is a comfort to know."

"Um," I said.

"Yes, quite," he replied. "Sit."

Sit. Stay. Good dog. Followed by a laugh, a horrible, tuneless laugh like fingernails on an evil chalkboard.

I sat. In a chair, although I felt a deep-down desire to plop my butt on the floor. Like the good dog I was. I shook my head violently.

"Who," Janus said again, "am I?"

He didn't smell quite so angry anymore. He didn't smell happy, but at least not as angry. I felt secure enough to string a few more words together. "You're the leader of the Sankhain. The Guardian of the forest and the Spring."

"And who are you?"

I wasn't going to get my way. Someone would hunt my sister, but it wouldn't be me. I tried to be angry, but all I felt was defeat.

"I'm no one," I murmured, believing it.

I couldn't hunt my sister. I couldn't even hunt a rabbit. I was the rabbit. I was a frightened piece of prey now. That's all I was.

I never left that underground room that smelled of semen, blood, and other awful things. I would never really leave it. I carried it with me inside my head, along with the sound of his voice. I was no one and nothing. As he molded me.

"And that is why you will not hunt Amalea now." Janus was the only one who ever called my sister by her full name. It was a Gaachail name. It meant red sister, because she had auburn hair.

I should get up. I should just leave. Go back to my little cabin and watch my little TV. Wait for what came next. Survive one captivity. Land in another.

"Not because you are no one. But because you believe you are no one." His voice was right beside me. He rested his hand on my shoulder. I jumped, but didn't pull away. "For better or worse, you are Kellan Alastrina Faolanni. You do not make my life easy. But you make my life more. And I will not lose you."

No. Don't take this away. Please, please, don't take this away. "I need to do this."

"I believe that you believe that," Janus said softly. "But what I see when I look at you is a wounded animal. You must heal before you go back into battle, Kellan."

"I already healed. I'm whole again. Getting stronger."

"You know that I do not speak of your physical wounds."

"Then let me do something!" Suddenly energized — gotta love those mood swings — I burst up from my chair. "Let me hunt her to prove to myself and everyone else that I'm not just that girl who got tortured for the last two months. Let me be me again!"

He looked at me, and I knew what he saw. Eyes too bright, hair too wild, skin too pale.

I was that girl who got tortured for two months. The prey. That's all I was.

"Never mind," I said. "May I be dismissed?"

"No."

I didn't move. I just waited for the next command. I felt so tired.

"Perhaps you are right," Janus said.

I was so surprised, I forgot how heavy my head was. I raised it and looked at him instead of the floor. "What?"

"But if I allow you to go, it must be on my terms. If you — step off the line —"

"Out of line," I corrected automatically.

"Out of line," he picked up where he left off, "you will be forced to return here. Do you understand?"

"Uh, yes, sir." Then, because curiosity probably killed the wolf long before it did the cat in, I said, "What are your terms?"

Not that it mattered. I was going to get to hunt. Maybe not my first choice of prey, but better than nothing. Better than sitting here on my ass, waiting for my butt cheeks to go numb.

"Please retrieve Antony and Finlay. They will wish to hear our agreement and I do not care to repeat myself."

I was so thrilled, I would've retrieved a fucking Frisbee if he asked. I opened the door and Finn almost fell through the doorway. Apparently, he didn't want to miss anything good.

"Where's Tony?" I asked.

"Off somewhere with your — dog." I had a feeling Finn omitted a word or two between "your" and "dog." "It would not stop clawing at him, trying to get back inside to you."

I glared at Finn, my happy-happy-joy-joy fading quickly. "He, not 'it.' Don't be an ass. Do me a favor and go find Tony, would you? Janus wants to speak to all of us."

The sharp crease of anger in Finn's scent as I ordered him to do something made the whole day worth it. But the fact that he turned on his heel and did what I told him to do, well, that was the whipped cream, the fudge and caramel sauce, the pecans and the cherry on top. When I turned back and looked at Janus, he smelled like fresh-cut grass drying in the sun. "That was not precisely what I asked you to do," he said.

"Yeah, well. That was more fun." It was already working. I already felt more like me.

Something changed in his eyes, in his posture as he studied me. Like he was happy, but that wasn't quite it. His scent grew thicker, heavier, but no less bright. I struggled to interpret it. Could it be pride? Directed at me? But I didn't do anything particularly noteworthy. Still, I liked the smell.

When Tony and Galen burst through the door, their scents of sour anxiety drowned out Janus's whatever scent, which was a bummer. Tony stood, barely breathing, as I knelt to greet Galen and he sniffed me all over, checking for injury. When I stood up, he glued himself to my side and glared at the men in the room, like it was their fault he got separated from me.

"I have decided," Janus said, and we all snapped to attention, "that Kellan should, in fact, accompany you north to inquire about Amalea."

He made it sound like we were going to the North Pole to check on one of Santa's reindeer.

"Sir?" Finn seemed unable to go beyond that word.

Tony didn't have any trouble with words. "Sir, with all due respect —"

"I find," Janus said, "that when a subordinate begins a sentence with those words, he is almost certainly intending to be disrespectful."

Tony swallowed, adam's apple bobbing visibly. But he didn't back down. "I really have no intention of being anything but respectful, sir. But if I may speak my mind?"

Janus made him wait a long moment before nodding.

"Thank you," Tony said. "Kellan has been through a terrible ordeal. She has only just begun to heal. And seeing Mal again could be a very painful experience. Her presence could jeopardize our safety if she becomes distracted or distressed."

I was starting to get a little pissed by being talked about as if I wasn't standing right there. Not to mention, Tony's words were careful insults. "I'm awake, right?" I said.

All three men looked at me like I finally tipped off my rocker. "What?" Tony said.

"I'm awake. I'm not in a coma, or dreaming this, or otherwise incapacitated?"

The look on Tony's face told me he knew where I was going with this. "Yes, you're awake."

"Good. So stop talking about me like I'm Helen fucking Keller. Include me in the fucking conversation."

Janus raised his eyebrows, probably at my language, but he didn't say anything and I didn't apologize. It was Tony who spoke next. "I didn't mean anything by it."

"Right," I said, "just like you're not intending any disrespect by completely questioning Janus's decision-making capability. Glad we cleared that up. But how about we let the big guy say what he wants to say? Since he already made his decision and you're simply being informed of the terms of our agreement."

Finn made a noise that, from a less controlled man, I would've called a snort. Tony glared at him. And Janus beamed at me, once again smelling like that unidentified emotion. If it was pride, this time, I knew what I did to earn it.

"Thank you, Kellan," Janus said. "As I was saying, I have decided you will be part of the search. Under certain conditions. First, Antony will be in charge." Tony looked surprised, but managed not to say anything. "He will have the power to — seat you on the bench."

I frowned. "You mean, bench me?"

"Yes, that is what I said. If at any time your behavior puts at risk your well-being or his, he will order you to stand down and you will obey. Second..."

You will obey. I flashed on a dark room, a spiked choke collar tight around my neck, fresh wounds on my back stinging in the cold air. When I returned to the here-and-now, I was still standing, which was a nice surprise. Unfortunately, I missed Janus's second and third conditions, and I had to ask him to repeat himself, which made all three men look at one another like maybe this was a bad idea, after all.

"I'm fine," I said, which was obviously a lie, but I hoped that saying it with extra vehemence might convince them to believe me. "I'm just trying to absorb everything. I don't want to violate your terms because I missed something."

Janus hesitated, then nodded. "Very well. Second, you will go nowhere alone. And no, Galen does not count as an escort. You will be accompanied by Antony at all times."

Janus waited until I said, "Okay," before continuing. "Third, you will communicate with Finlay via phone every day. When he calls, you will answer. No exceptions. If at any time, he expresses dissatisfaction with your apparent state of mind, he will communicate to Tony to — bench you."

I gave Finn a look that promised him immense pain if he abused this power. He didn't look worried. "Fine," I said. "Anything else?"

"Yes." Janus walked over and stood with his nose two inches from mine. "If at any time you feel that you are not able to continue with your assignment, you WILL inform Antony and remove yourself from the situation."

Not asking much, was he?

"The purpose of this trip is to ascertain if Amalea is indeed in the Upper Peninsula. That is all. If it is so, then we will decide what the next step will be. You will not approach her. You will not kill her until you receive the order. You will not engage with her in any way, until such a time as I deem appropriate." Janus was big on gathering intel first and then taking his time deciding on a course of action. "Do you understand?" He wasn't just looking at me. He was looking at Tony, too. But I knew that my answer was the one everyone was waiting for.

Tony nodded. "Yes, sir."

Basically, I was going on the trip, but I had no rights whatsoever. My hands weren't just tied, they were chopped off and tossed down the incinerator chute. But I needed to go. If this was the only way, I guess I'd have to agree to it. "Yes, sir."

"Very well. Now, I am of the opinion that the team should be small, just the two..." Janus kept on talking, but I stopped listening. I felt cold, numb, despite the raging fire in the hearth. Absorbing Janus's terms was taking a lot out of me, like healing a mortal wound. I wanted to sit down, but I didn't dare do anything that might be construed as a sign of weakness. I steeled myself and daydreamed about zombies.

It took a while, but finally the voices around me stopped yammering. Janus dismissed us, and Finn walked out with us before turning for the mess hall. Tony kept walking with me toward my cabin. I just wanted to go to bed while listening to the dulcet tones of zombie warfare.

"Are you okay?" Tony stopped. I stopped, too, because I didn't want him to know how badly I needed to lie down.

"I'm fine. How many fucking times do I have to say it?"

"Well, I guess until you actually mean it. Or you could try a real answer instead." Tony so seldom got riled by my vulgar language. It was really annoying, and it made me want to try harder.

"Fuck you. And fuck your questions. If I wasn't okay, Janus wouldn't be sending me with you. He would listen when you called me incompetent and broken-down."

"I didn't call you incompetent or broken down. I called you wounded. Which you are, no matter how many fucking times you say you're fine. I'm glad you're up and moving, I'm glad you're lifting weights and finding ways to cope. But you're hurting too, and if you think we don't see it, you're an idiot. So get over yourself. And I'm not going to apologize for thinking you shouldn't be putting yourself in Mal's path right now. She's another trauma for you and the last thing you need is another trauma."

Trauma. I hated the word. I hated the sound of it, the pretentious way the "au" tried to make it into a bigger word than it was. And I hated that it was attaching itself to me like a leech, feeding on me, weakening me, changing me into something less than what I used to be. I had trauma. I had a scarlet letter T tattooed on my forehead.

I took a deep breath. I counted to ten. I dug my fingernails into my palms, until the stinging pain reminded me that I might have trauma, but that didn't mean I was trauma. "Who's coming with us?"

Tony didn't ask why I didn't know, when I was standing right there when the decisions were made. Instead, he told me that he and I would be going alone.

Me and Tony. Alone. In a car, in a motel, in god knows how many other situations.

Alone. Together.

That scared me more than the thought of Aza, more than the thought of Mal.

"Okay. Great. See you," I said, and turned once again toward my cabin.

Tony kept walking with me.

It started to piss me off, his seemingly infallible companionship. "Don't you have someplace better to be?"

"Do you want me to leave?"

I started to say yes, but once again my mouth betrayed me. "No." Then I tried to backpedal. "Well, I guess I don't care. I mean, if you want to go, or you have better places to be, then you should go. I guess."

He studied me, which was when I realized we stopped walking again. "Tell you what," he said. "I'm going to get some dinner. I'll stop by after I eat, see how you're doing. If you don't want to see me, just don't answer the door. But if you want company for a while, you can let me in. All right?"

I nodded and he turned to go. Then I said, "Wait!" He stopped and looked at me. "When are we leaving?"

I thought I saw something in his expression, but his scent never changed, so maybe I imagined it. "Tomorrow, at dawn. These days, we're talking five or so."

Fan-freaking-tastic. "Sounds great. Thanks." I turned and went into my cabin like none of it mattered.

———— «» ————

I found that Gina left my dinner in the cabin sometime while I was gone. I guess it didn't take all that long to prepare a meatless salad. As I ate, I felt some of the heavy exhaustion slide off my shoulders. My brain churned slowly, laboriously. Maybe the plant protein couldn't keep my body running as well as animal protein. I could eat more. Even if food held little or no appeal. It could be a job, like scrubbing the toilet. Something on the list of things to do.

I started to think about how different I was now, before I shoved the thought aside and started a pot of coffee. After eating, feeding Galen, drinking half the pot of coffee and watching almost an entire episode of zombie mania, I felt less different. More like the me that might or might not still be inside.

I was just starting to doze when the door knocked, and I jumped twelve feet in the air. I spilled my coffee all over the bed. Galen stared at me, apparently torn between defending me from the unseen foe and retreating to safer territory. Swearing up a storm, I stomped to the door and yanked it open. "What?"

Tony stared at me, his scent a yeasty bewildered. "I told you if you didn't want company, just don't answer the door," he reminded me.

"I — you — startled me. That's all. Come on in. But I'm watching Walking Dead, and I don't want to hear any protests."

"No protests. Can I have a cup of coffee?" He closed the door behind him.

"Yeah. Whatever. Help yourself. Just don't sit on the bed. I spilled coffee on it."

"You were drinking coffee in bed?"

"I wasn't in bed, I was on the bed. It's the most comfortable place to sit."

He seemed to consider that. "I could go get another chair."

I found myself struggling for words. He was just so damn easygoing. Nonjudgmental.

"I'll go get a chair. Maybe you want to change the sheets? But save me some coffee, okay?" He left, and I still couldn't speak.

I changed the sheets and hung them over the shower curtain rod to dry. I pulled out the assortment of protein bars, in case Tony wanted something with his coffee. Then I rewound the DVD to the point I left it, and sat down beside Galen on the bed. This time, I went coffeeless, because Tony would be returning and I didn't want to have to change the sheets a second time after he startled me again.

Sure enough, when I heard him outside, I jumped, then felt myself blush because I knew who it was. He entered, gripping a padded chair in each arm.

I pictured those arms carrying several bags of groceries because I was being a bitch and wouldn't help him. I pictured his hands stirring pasta on my stove. I pictured him above me, propped up on his arms, laughing at something I said. And then I pictured Aza above me, laughing because he was on top of me, because he got me to scream in pain and then climax. I found myself bent over at the waist, hands on my knees, panting.

I couldn't hold Tony in my now-head. My now-head held too many other things. Too many other memories that were vying for attention that I refused to give. If I let Tony memories in, then I had to let all the memories in, and I could not allow that.

"Kellan? Kellan?"

I don't know how many times Tony said my name before I heard him. When his voice suddenly penetrated the panicked haze, I realized my eyes were squeezed shut and I was saying, "No, no, no," over and over again. I understood how awful a sight I must be. And I forced my spine straight and my eyes open.

Tony was inches away. I could smell his toothpaste, count his eyelashes. I knew he was wearing cherry lip balm, because I could smell that, too. Too close. Much, much too close. I gulped, took a step back, and said, "Thank you for not touching me."

"Yeah, well. If you don't want the chairs, I'll put them back. I just thought these would be more comfortable than the crappy old wooden chair you've got over there."

I started to laugh, then clamped my jaws down on my tongue because laughter was the gateway to crazy. A cold feeling washed over me, and I had a sickening suspicion it was named self-doubt. I pushed all such thoughts away and focused on the moment before me. "It's not the chairs."

I studied the floor and waited for him to finish thinking. "Do you want me to leave?" he said.

"You keep asking me that." I felt someone should point it out.

"Because you keep doing shit that makes me think you don't want me around. But then I ask you, and you say no."

"I never promised to make sense."

"Kellan, you have the power now to tell me to get lost. Do you want me to get lost, or do you want some company? It's your call." Tony had a waiting smell, I realized. How did I never notice that before? It was an almost empty smell, but around the edges, there was a faint sweetness, like hope.

I unclenched fists that I didn't remember clenching. "I promised you a cup of coffee. Wouldn't want to deprive you of that."

"All right. Thanks." He hauled the chairs over by the TV.

"Actually —" I began, then choked. The thought that pressed down on my brain like an intrusive weight wasn't something I wanted to give voice to. But it appeared to be growing stronger, rather than fading away. Tony looked at me, the waiting smell filling the room again. One foot in front of the other. One breath at a time. "How about if we don't watch TV?" I said. "How about if we, you know, talk a little?"

He blinked, surprise taking the place of the waiting smell. "Yeah. Sure."

When we were both seated, both with a cup of coffee in our hands, but with the DVD on in the background because I found that silence was still too hard on my ears, I blurted out, "You might be right."

"Always good to hear. About what?"

"About...me. About being...not up for going. Going after Mal, I mean."

Tony leaned back in his chair, stretched his legs out in front of him. He took a sip of coffee, then finally answered. "Yeah, maybe."

I kicked his foot. "Yeah, maybe? That's the best you've got?"

He laughed and took another sip of coffee. "What I meant was, maybe you're not up for it. But what worries me is that you're starting to doubt yourself. So what changed?"

"You mean other than the last two months when Aza used me as a pincushion?"

"I mean, what changed from the moment we were standing in Janus's office and you refused to take no for an answer or hear any alternate viewpoints?"

The truth just spilled out of my mouth like marbles. "I fell apart because I couldn't hold the sight of you in my head. That's what happened."

He was quiet for a while. "When I brought the chairs in? That's what you're talking about?"

"Yes, that's what I'm talking about," I said in a tone designed to tell him how stupid he was.

The corners of his mouth twitched. "And you're worried if looking at me does that to you, then looking at Mal will break you into pieces?"

As usual, he was absolutely right. So annoying. "Yeah. I guess. I wouldn't put it like that, but something along those lines."

"You know that you can't actually pull a Humpty-Dumpty, right? I mean, some people do, I guess. Some people break into little pieces that can't be glued back together. But that's not going to happen to you."

"How the hell could you possibly know that?"

"Because you're talking to me."

I let out a frustrated shriek. "Why can't you just make sense?"

"You could've chosen to withdraw." He motioned at the TV. "To escape to zombie land. That's a good way to become more brittle. Don't get me wrong, escapes are important. But abuse them, and they'll make you as weak as any other drug. You're not doing that. You had a bad five minutes, and instead of letting it shut you down, you decided to talk about it. That makes you stronger. Less brittle. Less Humpty-Dumptyish."

"A bad five minutes? More like a bad two months and two days." Or maybe longer. Probably better not to start counting.

"It's easier if you only worry about small increments. If you say you're having a bad day — and you will have those — then the rest of the day is doomed, and it's impossible to turn it around. But if you had a bad five minutes, it's passed, and now you have a new five minutes and maybe it'll be better."

I scowled. "All this touchy-feely crap is making me nauseous. I just threw up a little in my mouth." But as much as I hated to admit it, what he said made sense, and I wasn't going to forget it as quickly as I might like.

He cradled his mug. "If you want to back out, I'll tell Janus for you. But it wouldn't hurt to take a few deep breaths and think about it some more. If you back out now, they're never going to let you change your mind. Be sure it's what you want."

My stomach twisted into several different types of pretzel as we sat in silence. "Galen can come, right?"

Tony leaned back again. "Didn't you hear? That was one of Janus's conditions — that you bring him along."

"Oh. Well. Good." Galen would be there. My hand connected with Galen's shoulder, and I dug my fingers into his fur. Slowly, I relaxed and began to feel more solid.

If it was really bad, I could always just throw myself off an overpass.

"All right," I said. "I'll go."

We spent a couple hours watching zombies, then fell asleep on the bed. All three of us. Galen lay between Tony and me, a living breathing fur-and-bone barrier to prevent any accidental touching. But I was able to fall asleep like that. When I woke up and realized what I'd done, I felt better than any moment since Aza took my hand and disappeared me to his underground torture chamber.

Maybe I would be okay, after all.

Chapter 25

We stood in the Sankhain parking lot, beside one of the younger vehicles. It was a Toyota Corolla that only looked about twenty years old. Versus the Pinto next door, which looked like it remembered Reagan's middle name, or my truck, which was older than the both of them put together. Finn wanted us to take the Corolla and hopefully avoid breaking down before we even drove an hour.

Tony didn't look like he slept very well, and he was sneezing and sniffling a lot. He was wearing a black ski cap, a hoodie and jeans. "All right. Let's pack up," he said. As he unlocked the trunk of the Corolla, Gina appeared out of the forest, carrying a giant travel mug and a paper bag.

"Give me a minute?" I said. Tony nodded and threw his duffel bag in the trunk.

Gina smiled at me as I approached. I smiled at the giant mug. "I brought you some road food," she said.

I took the bag first, because once I accepted that mug, the bag would cease to matter. When I looked inside, I saw bags of cookies. They looked homemade. I glanced back at Gina. The kid thought homemade cookies were road food. It made me want to invite her on the trip just so she could understand the joys of living off convenience store junk food.

"Um, thank you. These smell amazing." I could see chocolate chip and something else that smelled sweet and spicy. "Are those ginger snaps?"

She nodded. "I also stuck in an egg sandwich for you. Tony came to the mess hall with the first wave of younglings, but you haven't eaten yet."

"Thank you," I said again.

She stood there like there was something more she wanted to say. I took the mug and drank, then expressed further gratitude for the extra-strong coffee inside. "You're welcome," she said. She hesitated. "Please be careful. We only just got you back."

I swallowed hard and felt the coffee go down my esophagus in a big lump. Clenching my fist on the bag, I nodded. "I will. See you."

"Bye." She gave me a quick hug and vanished back into the forest.

Very aware that Gina could still be watching from inside the trees, I raised the bag over my head as I walked back to Tony. "Gina brought treats." Galen's ears perked up at the T word, but I was busy studying Tony's red puffy eyes and angry-looking nose. "Are you all right?"

"Yeah. I forgot to take my pills last night." He opened the driver's side door and slid behind the wheel.

"So take them now." I let Galen hop in first, then lowered myself into the passenger seat.

"They'll make me too sleepy to drive. I'll be fine."

As we pulled out of the lot, I said, "I can drive."

"I'm not supposed to let you."

"Another one of Janus's conditions?"

He shook his head and sniffed. "No. Finn told me when I went to pick up the keys this morning. He's concerned that you're not acclimated to the world yet."

I swallowed a growl and rolled my shoulders to release the annoyance that gathered there. "He'd rather have you drive when you're sneezing every five minutes and you don't even remember what it's like to be able to breathe through your nose. Sure. Makes perfect sense."

Tony sighed. "Can we talk about last night, by the way?"

I loved my ginormous travel mug. I did not love the prospect of discussing any part of last night. "Want some coffee? I'll never drink it all before it gets cold."

"Sure. Pass it over." He took a gulp, then winced. "It's already not that warm."

"Shit. Can we stop at Starbucks before we hit the road?" I took the mug back. I still loved the mug, but now it smelled like Tony's chapstick.

"Sure." He seemed to be making an effort to breathe through his nose. I felt bad for him.

"And while we're at it, we can pick up some antihistamines for you."

He shifted his shoulders like he had an itch between his shoulder blades. "Fine. Backseat, in the front pocket of my backpack. There's a bottle of pills."

Feeling relieved and not really knowing why, since I wasn't the one who was miserable, I shook two pills from the bottle and gave them to Tony. I also gave him my travel mug to wash them down.

I loved drive-thru. I loved being able to order and receive complicated coffee drinks without ever leaving my dog. I savored my cappuccino while Tony gulped his like it was water.

I pulled out my collection of CDs. "What do you want to listen to?"

"Got any blues?" he said.

"Yeah, sure, right next to my Dixie Chicks collection." I thumbed through the discs. "So I'm guessing Metallica's not first on your list."

He coughed.

I chose Shinedown. Far from blues, but at least most of the songs had a discernable melody and the lead singer could really sing. Sticking *Sound of Madness* into the CD player, I leaned back and finished my cappuccino.

After a couple songs, Tony said, "This doesn't suck."

"I'm sure they'd be happy to hear it." But I smiled, inexplicably pleased that I chose well.

The sneezing tapered off after a while, and in the absence of the sudden bursts of noise, I found myself nodding off. "When's the next Starbucks?" I asked.

He laughed. "I checked our route last night. There's one in Oshkosh. About another half hour."

Half hour. The CD finished and I chose another Shinedown album, *Amaryllis* this time. I caught myself staring at Tony's hands and told myself to stop it. But as we approached Oshkosh, I couldn't stop wondering what would happen if I touched him. If I just reached out and brushed my fingers across his knuckles. If it was my choice, rather than a surprise. But if I opened that door, would he expect me to keep taking steps through it?

No. No, no, no. I was not going to think about this. I was going to listen to the music and look out the window and enjoy the feel of sunlight. But it wasn't enough to just think that. I needed to say no out loud. The word begged to burst out of my mouth in a repetitive stream, to drown out all thoughts and feelings. Nonononononono. I clamped my teeth together and glued my tongue to the roof of my mouth, and felt my vocal chords hum with the need to speak.

By the time we pulled into the Starbucks parking lot, I was so twisted in knots that I opened my door before the car stopped. Tony called my name, but I ignored him, bolting for coffee-scented sanctuary. I ducked into the bathroom, locking the door and sliding to the floor. I was sweating and breathing fast, and a bathroom floor wasn't the best place to hyperventilate with a sense of smell like mine.

I pushed to my feet and stumbled over to the sink. I washed my hands, splashed water on my face, then realized that, like all Starbucks bathrooms, this one didn't have paper towels, just the forced-air dryer. I sighed, wiped my face with the hem of my shirt, and opened the bathroom door. On my way to the counter, I passed a guy carrying a ham and cheese sandwich, and I bolted again.

Tony stared at me as I sank coffeeless into the passenger seat next to Galen. My dog snuffled my hair and made me feel a little bit whole again.

"Didn't you want coffee?" Tony intruded on our moment.

I didn't say a word, just grunted something that might've sounded like a word in some language. The car smelled like Tony. I gathered up the empty coffee cups and, with Galen in tow, walked to a trash can. Then I led him to a shrub on the outskirts of the parking lot where he could relieve himself.

When we returned to the car, Tony was there, holding two to-go cups. "I got you a latte this time."

I was too wrung out to manage more than one syllable. "'Kay."

Tony frowned. "Kellan —"

"Galen needs to pee again," I said and ran away. After Galen peed on every scraggly bit of brush and weeds in the parking lot, I got into the passenger seat of the car, while Galen sprawled out in that backseat. Tony sat in the driver's seat, head back and eyes closed. "Better now?" he said, not specifying if he meant me or Galen. His voice was the warm, low rumble of almost asleep.

Before I knew what I was doing, I reached over and touched his hand. He jumped, which made me jump, which made Galen sit up with a grunt. "Sorry," I said, and almost ran from the car again.

"Kell?" That was all he said, and it riveted me in place. He smelled so confused.

I couldn't look at him. "Yes?"

"What — what was that?"

My cheeks were on fire, and a baseball lodged itself in my throat. "I — don't know. I guess I wanted to see what it felt like."

"Oh." He was quiet for sixteen mississippis. "What did it feel like?"

I squeezed my eyes shut, because I could feel moisture gathering there. I couldn't answer, because I didn't know what to say and even if I did, my voice would be so shaky. Galen started licking the side of my face. "Coffee?" I whispered, because volume felt wrong.

Somehow, Tony managed to press the cup in my hands without touching my skin. His effort to avoid touching me dragged my eyes open. I forced myself to look at him. He looked like something broke inside him. "You don't have to," he said. "We don't have to talk about it. We can just pretend it didn't happen."

I nodded. Pretend that none of it happened. Pretend that the Easter bunny was real, and lost dogs always found their way home, and "no" actually meant what it used to mean. I wrapped my hands around the paper cup. "It felt nice," I said, whispering again.

"Oh. Okay."

We drove off, and I asked if I could change the music to Metallica. Tony said sure, so I put in the black album because that was my favorite. I lost myself in *Enter, Sandman*, and hit the "back" button three times to listen to my favorite song over and over.

During the fourth round of the same song, Tony cleared his throat. "What made you do it?" he said, quickly and a little loud, like he'd been holding in the words and just couldn't for one more second.

I looked out the window. We were back on the highway, traveling about seventy miles an hour. I might survive if I threw myself from the car, but I couldn't guarantee that Galen wouldn't follow me, or that Tony wouldn't panic and cause an accident that killed him and dozens of other innocent people. Too high a price for my crazy. I settled for wrapping my arms around my ribcage, holding myself tight as I answered the best I could. "I've been thinking about it for a while."

His breath sounded rough, like he'd been running. "A while like since Beaver Dam, or a while like since last night?"

I thought about it. "Yes."

He laughed, a strangled, mutilated sound. "I'm sorry. I know you don't want to talk about it, but shit, Kell. I never thought you'd do that again. Shit."

This was just what I feared. That if I opened that door, if I touched him, he'd expect me to continue to do stuff like that. Next he'd want me to kiss him, or give him a blow job, or — fuck, I was going to puke. "Pull over."

He glanced at me, and whatever he saw made him pull the car over real quick. I opened my door and threw up my coffee, my breakfast, and at least six inches of intestine. *Kiss it, little wolf. Suck. Oh, you are so very good at this.* The sickening reel of memories prompted more dry-heaving. I could taste him in my mouth. Feel him there, brushing the back of my throat. Oh, god. I gagged, coughed. Spat. I was sweating, shaking, and I could feel just how pale my face was. I barely had the strength to pull myself out of my hunched position, back into my seat. Leaning my head back, I closed my eyes and prayed for death, or at least for the solitude of my cabin. While I was at it, I might as well pray for my very own unicorn to take me there.

Grabbing a bottle of water from a bag in the back seat, I took a swig and rinsed my mouth. I spat, then closed the car door and stubbornly refused to look at Tony. "Are you taking me back to camp now?"

"Why would I do that?" He pulled back into traffic.

My stomach felt sickeningly empty. I remembered Gina's ginger snaps. Ginger settles the stomach. I pulled one out, then offered the bag to Tony. "I thought you would, because I lost it."

"Yeah, and then some. That was gross. Though I have to say, it was made even grosser by the fact that I had to restrain Galen from hopping out of the car and cleaning it up."

I took a shaky breath. "Thanks for that."

"But I don't think you need to be sidelined over a little puke."

"I —" What I was about to say was absurd, but I needed to say it. I needed to be clear. "I can't give you a blow job. Not now. Possibly not ever."

"WHAT?" He swung his head around to look at me, and he actually smelled a little angry. "Why the fuck would you even say that? Did I ask you to give me a blow job? Shit, I would never — after what you've been through...What kind of a jackass do you think I am?"

Not the reaction I anticipated. "I don't think you're a jackass."

"Then why did you — oh." He glanced at me. "That's why you threw up."

Great. Now he thought I threw up because I thought about giving him — that he was what made me vomit. "No. I didn't throw up because of you."

"But how did you get there? I mean, I said I was happy you touched my hand. Interactions don't get much more G-rated."

It wasn't bad enough I could still feel the bile in the back of my throat, now I was going to have to talk about my feelings? But it was Tony, and I couldn't seem to turn away from a question from him. "Okay, see, you said that — and I thought — and...Shit. I thought, now you're going to want more. Like, you know, blow jobs. And then I was back there, and —"

He listened. Then he shook his head and his scent was both sour and sweet, like sadness, worry and affection all rolled into one. I knew that scent. It was pity.

The pity was worse than the anger. So much worse. "Fuck you. Don't fucking pity me."

"I don't — well, I don't think pity's the right word, exactly. But I know what that particular flashback feels like. I've been there."

Was that supposed to make me feel better? Oddly enough, *My Friend of Misery* was now playing on the CD player. *Misery loves company.* Misery might, but I didn't want any company on this one. I didn't want anyone else, especially Tony, to have felt what I just felt. "Fuck off. I just wanted you to know where we stand. That's all."

"Well, since we're sharing, I'd like you to know that was pretty fucking fantastic that you touched me. But I don't expect anything from you. And I would never make demands on you. So fuck off yourself."

I needed to be smaller. I pulled my legs up, wrapped my arms around them so I was a tight N of a person. But instead of easing the tightness in my chest, the posture made it worse. Until that tightness poured out of me, tears running down my cheeks, sobs erupting from nowhere, snot, a little drool, and a lot of rocking back and forth. Galen crowded his way into the front seat, rubbing up against me like a cat so that his fur mixed with the assortment of bodily fluids on my face. I thought it would never stop, but eventually, it did. I blew my nose in Starbucks napkins and wiped my face off on my shirt for the second time in one morning.

"There's a restaurant up there," I said, my voice a foreign object in my mouth.

He nodded and took the next exit.

"Is this the part where we pretend it never happened?" I said.

Tony cleared his throat. "Probably."

"All right."

———— ‹› ————

It was cool enough that I could've left Galen in the car, but I didn't want to leave him unattended. As a big, beautiful purebred dog, he might just prove too tempting, should someone with nefarious intentions happen by. And besides, I could smell fried meat from outside the diner. I didn't want to know what it smelled like on the inside. The last thing I needed was to puke again. Tony went in and got the food. Grilled cheese and French fries for both of us, along with two big-ass bottles of ice-cold water. He handed me one of the bottles, then took a big swig from the other one.

I thanked him again. I figured I probably uttered the words "thank you" more times in the last seventy-two hours than I did in the last seventy-two years, but it kept being necessary. That was starting to annoy me.

We rode in silence —well, silence with a Metallica soundtrack — over the border into the U.P. Tony didn't complain about the music, which strangely made me feel guilty for subjecting him to it. But I was still pretty wrung out from my bout of tears and I needed the noise. I settled for turning down the volume.

Around one o'clock Michigan time, we pulled into the parking lot of a motel that looked like it belonged on an episode of Criminal Minds. I gazed up at the second story, absent-mindedly checking that my blades were loosened in their sheaths. Tony sniffled. "I know it looks like Motel Hell, but I gotta get some sleep," he said.

"No problem." I tried to inject confidence into my voice. "I've stayed in worse places." Not by much, though.

He went to check us in. The motel was an open-air layout, which somehow seemed to make it all the more murder-friendly. When Tony came back out, I held out my hand for my room key.

"You're staying with me," he said. He glanced at the number on the key and walked to the corresponding door.

I knew Janus wanted me to have a chaperone, but damn it all, I wasn't a kid. Anger started to warm my extremities. "Why? Maybe I'd rather stay in a room of my own. Maybe after two months in a dungeon, I'm craving a little privacy."

Tony looked at me with red-rimmed, bleary eyes. His pills must be wearing off. "The room has two beds. And besides, I'm gonna pass out the second I hit the pillow. It'll be like a room to yourself."

"Yeah, except for the snoring." I was being a snot and I didn't care.

"I told Janus that I'd watch you. I told Finn I'd keep you safe. I can't do that if you're in another room. Please, just come inside. Maybe we can find you a nice zombie show to binge on."

Finn wanted him to keep me safe? I didn't know what to think about that. "Galen needs to go for a walk." I led my dog in the direction of the scraggly evergreens that lined the parking lot.

I heard a thump and a sigh, then footfalls behind me. "Kellan," Tony began when he caught up to us, but I didn't let him finish.

"What do you think is going to happen to me in the next room?" Galen chose a tree and dragged me to it, then sniffed all around the trunk and circled back and forth before choosing a leg to lift and finally lifting it.

"Those were the conditions, Kellan." Tony sneezed. "We can turn around and go back if you want, but not until I get some sleep."

Galen finished with the tree and assumed the position that reminded me I didn't have a plastic bag. "Shit. You got a bag?"

"Just leave it. We'll say a moose came by." Tony turned to Galen. "You done, big dog?" Galen wagged his tail and trotted over to Tony. "Great. Now sleep." We started back toward the motel room.

I was suddenly exhausted. So tired that picking up my feet was too hard, so I started shuffling zombie-style. "I'm sorry," I said, so quiet, I barely heard it. "About the room."

Tony stopped walking, so Galen and I stopped and looked at him. "Sometimes it's really hard not touching you," he said, also very, very quiet.

Heart suddenly pounding with fear, I took a step back, then stopped, clenched my jaw and my fists, clenched everything so that it was hard to breathe. Tony had a look on his face like I slapped him. I hated myself so much that I pulled a blade and sliced my wrist open. He inhaled sharply, but he didn't touch me, didn't take the blade away, didn't say don't do that. "You should get some sleep," I said, my voice tinny in the stillness created by all the things Tony didn't do. "Come on."

Galen walked between us. Tony leaned down and scratched the top of Galen's head. I clutched the leash, which felt warmer than my hands. "I'm sorry you have to share a room with me," Tony said. "And I'm sorry about the snoring."

I considered telling him that I didn't really mind the snoring. That it was a comfortable sound, like the wind in the trees of the forest outside my cabin window. I didn't want him to be self-conscious, I decided, so I told him. He looked at me funny, his cheeks growing red, which made me think he felt self-conscious after all. I sighed, tired of this awkward dance. Just give me something to kill already.

True to his word, Tony fell asleep as soon as his head hit the pillow. And as I predicted, he snored louder than a Metallica concert. But the TV was on, and like I said, I didn't really mind. Snoring was a wonderfully human sound. Aza didn't snore. Aza didn't really sleep, at least not with me. He wasn't with me all the time, though, so maybe he slept somewhere else. I pushed the thought away. Regardless, snoring was all right. Especially when, after a meal of kibble and a large helping of water, Galen joined Tony's chorus.

There weren't any zombie shows on, but I found another show that I saw a few times before, about two brothers who hunted supernatural beings. I got sucked in and soon relaxed enough that I dozed off.

When I woke, the room was dim. I glanced at the clock. It was five o'clock. I slept for about three hours. Tony and Galen were still snoring, though Galen opened his eyes when I stirred. I shushed him and told him to go back to sleep, then I crept to the small, dingy bathroom. While I sat on the toilet, I stared at a hole in the wall that was about the right size for a bullet hole. A .22, maybe. It was about shoulder-height. Ambiance.

Now that I was rested and a little less shocky, I picked up on some of the older smells that lingered in the room, and just like in that Starbucks' bathroom, I was really wishing I possessed a less sensitive nose. The smells of sex weren't surprising, but the urine on the bedspread and the vomit smell rising from the carpet really didn't do much for me. It wasn't long before I couldn't take it anymore and I slipped outside.

Boy, it sure was a good thing Tony and I were staying in the same room so he could keep an eye on me. I gulped the chilly air. The sky was overcast, making it seem closer to twilight than it actually was. The area was quiet, the most prominent sounds the TVs in the other motel rooms and the scurrying of small animals in the grass. But there was something else, a scent in the air that sent a thrill down my spine.

"Ballsy, showing up here," I said quietly. I reached for my left cargo pocket, where my iron blade was housed, but I didn't pull it. Not yet. I watched my sister step out of the shadows of the trees.

"Not really," she said. "From the sounds of things, your male companion isn't going to wake up unless we make more noise than him. I'm not sure that's possible."

"Are you alone?" There were so many smells in the parking lot, I couldn't tell if she had back-up. I should've been worried. I should've called out to Tony. I should've probably done any number of things. But curiosity could be a real bitch, and I was awfully curious about the bitch standing in front of me.

"No, I'm not alone. But I didn't bring any nocturnes, if that's what you're wondering. We've...parted ways. They're a tedious species."

"But they were here in Michigan."

"Well, yes. They were a convenient way to draw the Sankhain here. I'm surprised they sent you. I understand that you were detained."

"You know?" How could she possibly know about Aza?

"I have friends, Kellan. Was it — why would you — how are you?"

Friends? Did that mean she was still in contact with someone in the Sankhain? That she had an ally there? I shook my head. Too many confusing things going on at once. I forced myself to focus on the problem in front of me.

She was close enough now that I could smell the subtleties of her emotions. She was trying to hide it, but she was worried. Like the time I fell out of a tree and couldn't move for several minutes and she stood over me, holding her breath, wringing her hands. I didn't like it. She didn't have the right to be worried about me anymore.

When I didn't respond, she repeated herself. "How — how are you?"

It was an incredibly stupid question. Like asking the woman on her deathbed, How are you feeling today? "I'm fine," I lied. I lied because I didn't want her to know anything. Didn't want her to possess the truth.

She sniffed and shook her head. "Why do you bother trying to lie to me?"

"I don't know. Probably the same reason you bother trying to hide your emotions from me." I felt slight tremors start in my arms and legs. I wanted to go back inside. I wanted to pet my dog and forget that my sister still worried about me. I needed the world to make more sense, not less.

"Come with me." Mal held out her hand.

I stared at her hand, torn between wanting to take it and wanting to cut it off. "Fuck you."

She grabbed my hand, taking away my choice. Which naturally made me fight. But I was still weaker than I used to be and now she was stronger than me and I couldn't escape her grasp. "Bloody hell," Mal said. "Help me with her, would you?"

Before I could see who Mal was talking to, before I could scream for Tony, before I could anything, something hit me on the back of the head and the world went dark.

Chapter 26

When I woke up, I heard the most god-awful caterwauling and smelled wet hair. It was dark and my hands were bound. My heart pounded, but I forced my breathing to quiet while I listened for Aza's footsteps. Then I heard my sister saying, "Oh, for pete's sake, it's just a bath, Abby."

Slowly, recent events trickled back into my conscious mind. But remembering just led to more questions. Where was I? Who else was here? Who was Abby? Was Abby the one who hit me on the head?

I saw a digital clock that read 7:28. As a shape-shifter, I regained consciousness much quicker than a human. I was in a room, not too dissimilar from the room I left Tony and Galen in. Another motel, maybe? Probably not the same motel. I didn't think Mal was stupid enough to bed down in the same establishment as the Sankhain hunting party. I lay on one of the beds. Another person, a woman, from what I could see of her build, was stretched out on the other bed. I felt my eyes begin to burn as my night-vision kicked in.

"Oh, you're awake." That voice. I knew that voice. But that was impossible. Magda was dead. Someone clicked on a light and pain exploded inside my skull. Whoever this was that sounded like Magda would soon be joining her in deadness. If only I could get my hands free. When my eyes were able to focus again, I stared disbelieving at the woman who also looked exactly like Magda.

Magda was a Sankha — former Sankha — who, while on assignment in British Columbia, stopped checking in, stopped sending updates, stopped doing her Sankhainly duties. At first, we thought she was dead, but when Janus sent Mal to check, she caught sight of Magda. She just…defected. I never knew why. The why didn't matter. You don't retire from the Sankhain. Secrets don't stay secret for long if you allow that. That was what Janus told Mal when he assigned her the task of killing Magda. Mal almost refused. Magda was only a couple years older than we were. When we were younglings, she was almost as good as I was at climbing trees and we were both better than Mal.

I was there when Janus gave the order, listened to the silence on the other end of the line. Mal was going to say no. I grabbed the phone and told my only living sister that if Janus made me kill her for disobeying an order, I would make her suffer. Magda made her choice, I told her. Don't make the same mistake.

Mal agreed to kill her, but obviously, something didn't go as planned. Unless, of course, this was a nocturne wearing Magda's face, but she didn't have a nocturne's rotten-from-the-inside-out scent. She smelled like my old friend. Maybe she was a faery doing glamour, like Raoul. My brain rifled through the possibilities, as my mouth hung open like a Venus fly trap.

"Poor kid," Magda said. "Yes, it's me. Stop staring at me like I'm a bloody mermaid. How's your head?"

I closed my mouth, swallowed, and forced out words. "It hurts."

"Yeah, well, she did ask you to stop struggling."

"Oh, so it's my own fault? Fuck her, fuck you, and fuck the horse you rode in on." I didn't consent to falling through the looking glass. Not this time. I wanted to go home. I wanted Galen and maybe Tony, and my Walking Dead DVDs.

"You shouldn't say that word."

I froze. The voice was young, but that wasn't what stopped me cold. What made my heart shudder to a stop and my limbs freeze up was the fact that I could've sworn the voice belonged to my sister. Not my sister now, but my sister a century and a half ago. I sat up and twisted around to stare at the girl standing behind me with a very judgmental look on her face.

Her hair was the same as Mal's, thick and auburn with the slightest wave. Otherwise, she looked nothing like Mal. She looked like me. The same big, hawkish nose, the same wide mouth, high sharp cheekbones, and amber eyes. What the fuck?

I didn't realize I spoke out loud until she said again, "You shouldn't say that word."

I looked at Magda the dead woman, then at my sister standing behind the child that could only be a Faolanni cub. Mal had a strange flavor to her scent as she shied away from my gaze. It smelled like burning hair. Shame?

"Alabhan, this is your aunt. Kellan, this is my daughter, Abby." Mal still wouldn't look at me.

Alabhan. Gaachail for little cub. Why, if Mal hated the Sankhain so much, would she give her daughter a Gaachail name?

Fuck. Why did Mal have a daughter that I didn't know about? Why was Magda alive rather than dead? Why was I alive rather than dead? Why show me these people? Why not kill me?

A daughter. I closed my eyes and clamped my lips shut as my head throbbed viciously.

"Magda, will you take Abby and get her something to eat? Give us a moment."

I heard a door open and shut. The squeal of hinges, the click of a lock. Details. Focus on one thing at a time and maybe you won't have to feel the whole of it, just the parts. I started to struggle to free my hands. Quietly, so maybe she wouldn't see until it was too late.

"I suppose you want an explanation." The bed dipped as Mal sat next to me.

I opened my eyes. "That's a bitch of an understatement." Hold her gaze so she doesn't notice your hands.

"Please stop trying to free yourself." So much for that. I paused in my efforts for the moment. "You might remember Magda's rope-tying skills have always been excellent."

"All right, sure, we can start there before we talk about how the fuck you had a kid without telling me. Magda. Why is she alive?"

"Because she didn't deserve to die. She fell in love. That's a capital crime? It's ridiculous." She was so composed, so controlled. I hated that about her, when I felt like I wanted to start spinning in mad circles like the cartoon Tasmanian devil. "And as for Abby... well. That's complicated."

"Yes, I've heard child-bearing can be awfully complicated. Doesn't explain why you DIDN'T TELL ME." Since she didn't seem inclined to explain herself, I asked another question. "Are you going to kill me?"

Mal's eyes flashed, and I smelled another rare scent from her — hurt. "Of course I'm not going to kill you. If I wanted to kill you, you'd be dead. You're my sister. I wanted you to see that I didn't really betray you. I just couldn't live that way anymore."

"Live what way? Honestly? Openly?"

"Obediently!" We were both on our feet, noses inches from each other. I didn't remember moving.

I took a step back, feeling a little dizzy. "What?"

She pressed her palms to her thighs, spreading her fingers as if wiping them dry. "I wanted a daughter. But I didn't want to condemn her to the same life we were forced into. I wanted her to be able to choose her own path. I tried to raise her without them knowing about her, but hiding in motel rooms is no life for a child, either. I needed to free myself."

"So you stuck a sword in my side and joined up with the nocturnes? That's the best plan you could come up with?"

"It was the fastest plan I could come up with. And I did ask you to join me."

Why did every answer just create more questions? "That's stupid. It's the stupidest thing I've ever heard. You could've just fallen off the map, gone to Costa Rica and lived in a hut on the beach. Instead, you ensured that you were Public Enemy number one and we would never stop hunting you."

"Actually, I intended to fake my own death. Convince one of the nocturnes to put on my face and then let whomever they sent after me kill it." She paused. "That's what we were doing here. I let the nocturnes kill as much as they pleased to draw the attention of Janus and Finlay, force them to send someone. Then a nocturne would assume my form, the Sankhain would see the nocturne me, kill the nocturne me, think I was dead…and we would be free."

I felt sick. And tired. I was literally sick and tired of this conversation. Of this segment of my life. Could we please go to commercial break? "Me. You were going to let me kill you. Or think I killed you."

"No. I assumed that they wouldn't send you. That they wouldn't trust you to follow through. I assumed they would send someone else. When I learned you were here…that changed things."

All I wanted was to curl up in a ball and go to sleep so I could wake up from this nightmare. "Well, nice to know someone has faith in me. Sorry to spoil your plans."

She ignored my sarcasm, which was a shame, since I had to dig awfully deep to pull it off. "I broke ties with the nocturnes, sent them on their way. I had to kill five of them to convince them that our alliance was over. They're not as smart as they look." She stared at her hands, then met my eyes again. "Once I found out you were here, I knew I had to see you. To introduce you to Abby. To explain."

I didn't bother answering. I decided to just let her talk. A daughter. Mal hid her in motel rooms so we wouldn't know about her. So I wouldn't know about her. And now she decided to introduce us? Nothing made sense.

"And here we are," Mal continued. "This is why I had to leave. So my daughter could have a path of her choosing." She hesitated. It was strange, seeing my confident, capable sister so hesitant. "You could join us now. The nocturnes are gone. It's just us. Please, Kellan. I miss you."

And just like that, my resolve to stay silent shattered. "Why?"

She smelled genuinely confused. It smelled like mud on fur. "What do you mean?"

"Why do you miss me? You spent — how many years? How old is she, your daughter?"

Mal lowered her gaze for a second. "Five."

Five. My vision started to go gray. Five years that she lied to me. Hid from me this life-altering shift. My words caught in my throat and I had to use extra air to push them out. "You spent five years lying. What do you miss, exactly? All the conversations where you didn't tell me the most important thing in your life? All the times you came to visit and left your daughter with — who, Magda?" Mal nodded. For five years — five years — every time Mal came to Madison to check in with the Sankhain, she left her daughter with a woman who was supposed to be dead. "And when I called you? All the times we talked on the phone? What, did you gag her and lock her in the bathroom?"

She shook her head. "I would —" She faltered. Finally, her composure seemed to slip and her voice trembled slightly. "I would go outside, or out to the car, somewhere I could keep an eye on her room, but be out of earshot."

"And Magda?"

She started to say something, then stopped.

Rage and a deep, dark pain caused me to shake. "Why? Why trust her and not me?" I instantly regretted allowing her to see how much it hurt, so I tried to redirect the conversation. "Who was the father?"

She shrugged. "Some guy in some bar. He didn't matter. He was a means to an end."

I watched her shrug a second time, a motion as familiar to me as my own breath. And just like that, my brain shut down. My legs didn't want to hold me anymore, so I sat down hard on the bed. My brain didn't want to hold me anymore, either. I stopped looking at my sister, staring instead at the ugly still life on the wall. What was the bloody fascination with painting bowls of fruit?

I heard Mal's voice, but I didn't care about her words any more than I cared about the stupid pear in the painting. The pear was a charming shade of booger green. I wanted my dog. I wanted my hands free. Aza tied me up. I couldn't be tied up anymore. I got out. I survived. I wasn't going to be this person anymore. "Untie me," I said, as I felt panic begin to rise, filling me. Making my skin tingle and my chest feel icy cold.

"Kellan —"

I pushed to my feet and bared my teeth at her in a snarl. The wolf was pushing her way to the surface. Usually, I had more control than this, but I was out of practice. Aza broke my self-control. I felt spit dribble down my chin, but it didn't matter, because my brain wasn't so human anymore. "Untie me now." My voice was a low growl, an animal noise.

I was close to shape-shifting, but I couldn't shape-shift with my hands bound behind my back. The bones wouldn't be able to align themselves properly, and I'd end up with torn muscles, serious injuries that took precious time to heal. I knew this, because Aza made me shape-shift while I was hog-tied. He figured out that if he inflicted enough pain for a long enough duration, he could force the shift. I would lose all control, and he could make me change forms no matter the position I was in. It caused a lot of pain, but it was possible. I needed to keep my shape. The logical human side knew that. Unfortunately, the wolf side wanted to rip Mal's throat out, and the panic of having my hands restrained was making it harder to control myself.

"All right," Mal said, rising slowly and putting her hands out in front of her. A placating gesture. "I understand that you want me to untie you. But first, you need to understand why I did what I did, and you can't do that when you're angry. I'm sorry, Kellan, but I can't let you loose."

I couldn't breathe. I had to get free. I had to move. I had to get out. Out, out, out, out, like a drum beat in my head. I felt the change start inside me, and I knew I wasn't going to be able to stop myself. Despair mingled with panic until I didn't know if I wanted to scream or cry. I collapsed to my knees and howled.

I might've been weaker than I was before Him, but I was still a shape-shifter. I wrenched my arms, and felt the rope begin to give. My sister's face swam before my eyes. Her face was wet. Why was it wet?

"At least now you know," she said. Then another sharp pain, this time on the side of my head, and for a second time, the world went dark.

Chapter 27

Someone was holding me. Carrying me. I didn't know where I was, when I was — hell, I barely knew who I was. But I knew I didn't want to be carried. "Put me down."

"Oh. You're awake." Tony.

"My head hurts and I think I'm gonna hurl. Put me down." That worked. Tony set me down, I fell to my knees, dry-heaved a few times, and then just sat there, catching my breath and remembering.

It was still dark. I glanced up at the moon. Not even midnight, judging from its position. Such a short time span for the world to change so drastically.

Tony crouched down. "Galen's in the car. He'd really like to see you."

I nodded, and Tony left. When he returned, Galen knocked me over and I almost blacked out again at the sudden movement.

I pushed myself up into a sitting position. "How'd you find me?" My tongue felt thicker than it should have.

"Finn showed me how to track the GPS on your phone." I felt a surge of anger so strong, I heaved again. They were tracking me. "How are you feeling?" Tony asked.

I almost told him not to ask stupid questions, but I figured he probably didn't know that my sister kidnapped me so she could introduce me to her kid and the supposed-to-be-dead woman she'd been toting around, so to call his question stupid would be unkind. "I feel like a bucket full of shit."

"You were out cold and your head wound bled a lot. Was it Mal?"

"Yeah, um...was anyone else around when you got here?" I asked. "What time is it?" Maybe they were still in the area.

"About eleven. And no, the place was empty. I had to pick the locks on six rooms before I found you."

"Did you search the rest of the motel?" Damn. More than three hours since Mal knocked me out the second time. "What took you so long to get here?" Maybe they were hiding out somewhere. Maybe I could find their scent, track them. I started sniffing the air.

"I was sleeping," Tony said. He sounded annoyed that I asked. "I'm sorry I didn't get the memo that you were going to get kidnapped. I would've set my alarm."

Ignoring his tone, I put my nose to the ground, not caring how strange I looked. Nothing. I crawled a few paces, heading back to the motel. Galen sniffed along side me. Still nothing.

Disappointment flooded me. Why? Did I want to find her so I could ask her more questions? Or so I could kill her? I pushed the questions away as I realized Tony was saying something.

"This was on the floor next to you." All trace of annoyance gone, his tone turned soft. He held out a small white square. A folded piece of paper with my name written on it. His eyes were searching, asking all kinds of silent questions.

I turned away from those eyes and their questions, taking the note and shoving it in my pocket without a second glance. I didn't want to talk. I didn't want to tell Tony that my sister had a cub, a daughter that she never told me about. Or that my sister shared this part of her life with a woman that she was ordered to kill years ago. Or why my sister really joined forces with the nocturnes. But all that knowledge sat in my stomach like a dozen rotten eggs, and I couldn't hold it in.

I told him everything. He only interrupted a few times. He was good that way. I finished with, "I guess knocking me out stopped the shape-shifting before I got too far into it."

All he said was, "Wow. You're really having a shitty night."

I started laughing, then clamped my mouth shut because I felt hysteria closing in. Burying my face in Galen's coat, I inhaled his scent and felt clarity return. I didn't know what to do about Mal or her cub or her friends in the Sankhain or Magda or the nocturnes or any of it. While I was at it, I didn't have a damn clue what to do about Aza, either. But I knew where we needed to go next.

I looked up at Tony. "Where does Darcy live?"

"Um..." He smelled surprised — sort of like half-risen dough.

I waited, but he didn't say anything else. "I thought you knew where he moved to."

"I do, but it's some weird little town that nobody's ever heard of. Give me a minute. Jeez." He frowned, then said, "Elk Mound."

"How does some weird little town that nobody's ever heard of manage to have a library?"

"They don't, he works in Eau Claire, but he lives in Elk Mound."

"Why?" Why would anyone choose to live in a place called Elk Mound? It sounded like a euphemism for elk shit.

"Why are you asking me these questions?" Tony's scent finally shifted from surprise to suspicion.

I ignored him and stood up, pulling out my phone. "Can you show me how to use the GPS on this thing?" He studied me, and I could imagine what he saw. Blood-smeared face, wild hair, crazy eyes. My hands were shaking a little, too. Yeah, I was six shades of nutballs, but I didn't care. "Can you show me or not?"

"I can." But he didn't reach for my phone.

"My dog and I are driving to Elk fucking Mound. Show me how to find it on the GPS."

"No, you're not." He said it so calmly that I stomped on his foot. He was wearing steel-toed boots, so it didn't do much damage, but he still took a step back. "Kellan, let's just go back to the motel. We'll call Finn and Janus, see what they say. The nocturnes are still out there —"

"The nocturnes are gone! Haven't you been listening? They're all gone. Mal, Magda, the cub. All of them. They ran. There's nothing left." I felt the note in my pocket like a cartoon anvil, weighing me down. Push it away. "But I'm enjoying this goddamn road trip so much that I want to go to Elk Mound to ask Darcy why the fuck he abandoned me. And so that's what I'm going to do. And I'm not asking Janus and Finn what they think, because they'll say no and I don't want to hear it. I spent the last two months with Aza shoving god knows what up my —" I broke off, my breath heaving, rasping. "I'm going to see Darcy. Now fucking show me how to fucking use the fucking GPS," I yelled.

"Jeez, Kell, you're going to get us arrested." Tony held out his hand. "GPS is easy."

I stared at him, sure it was a trick. He didn't want me to go. He wanted to call Finn and follow the rules, and I was so tired of rules and having my hands tied behind my back and being forced to be a good little wolf. All of a sudden, my legs gave out and I was on the ground again. Galen shoved his nose in my face, but I pushed him aside. "What if she was right?" I whispered. "What if everything she said was right? That obedience is for schmucks? And this life is something you get condemned to?"

"How hard did you hit your head, Kell?" Tony knelt before me, his voice gentle, but his hands at his sides, not touching, never touching.

I considered his question. "Which time?" I said. Then I focused on Tony's face. "I need to go. She left again, don't you understand?

She had a kid and she left, over and over and over again. She's always going to leave me. Why did she leave me?"

"I don't know," Tony said. "I can't seem to do that, even when you scream in my face."

"But Darcy left, too. All my pack does is leave." I needed to see Darcy. I needed to talk to him and find out why he left. I needed to ask him because I couldn't ask Mal. I needed — "I need an energy bar." I was feeling woozy, that out-of-body feeling that meant my blood sugar was dangerously low.

He disappeared from my line of sight. I heard rummaging, then the crinkle of a wrapper. He pressed the bar into my hand.

"Thank you." I gave a tiny piece to Galen, an apology for pushing him away. He swallowed it whole. Then I ate the rest and felt marginally better, at least physically. My whole being seemed to sag, though. Even my voice was saggy. "I have to go. I have to see him. I have to know if there's still — anything there."

Tony looked away and he smelled sad. Why? "All right," he said. "We'll go."

"No. I'm going alone. I don't want you to get in trouble. Just tell them I stole the car and —"

Tony interrupted. "I'm not going to lie. And if you think I'm letting you drive after being conked on the head, not once, but twice, you're more fucked up than I thought. Besides, how would I get home if I let you take the car?"

"I SAID I'M GOING ALONE!" I didn't even swear. That showed how serious I was.

Tony turned and glared at me. "And I said I'm going with you. You can listen to whatever god-awful shit you call music. You can sit in the backseat and ignore me the whole way there. You can call me names and punch me in the 'nads if you feel you have to, but I'm going with you."

"I —" I said, but I guess he wasn't done. He smelled angry. It was a familiar, spicy smell. So much nicer than sad.

"When we stop to get food, you can sit at a table by yourself. When we get there, you can talk to Darcy by yourself. But I'm going to be there in the fucking car, waiting outside so that when you're done, you don't have to be alone. Because if that dumbass rejects you, I'm not going to let you go through it alone."

If he rejects you...Because that could happen. I didn't want to believe it, but it was true, and Tony was brave enough to give me a reality check. And as much as I didn't want to hear it, I could appreciate the no-pussyfooting honesty. "When we stop to get food, I'd rather wait in the car while you go in and get it," I said. "Most restaurants smell like meat."

He was quiet for a while, like he was waiting for the roundhouse punch to blindside him. Finally, he said, "Okay."

We went back to the motel to get our things. It didn't take long, since we never took the time to unpack.

As I fed Galen, I felt something in the center of my chest. Something light and airy and not at all like anything I felt over the last two months. If I put a name to it, I'd call it hope.

Tony and I got in the car. He started to flip on the radio, but I stopped him. "I need to call Finn first," I said.

"Why don't you let me —"

"No. My decision. My turn to listen to the lecture. I promise not to swear at him or hang up on him." I hoped I managed to get through most of the necessary conversation before I broke either promise.

Tony sighed. "Sometimes I think it would've been easier to be a junkie."

"No, you don't."

"No, I don't." He glanced at me. "Try not to say anything that'll get us beheaded, okay?"

"I'll do my best."

"To not get us beheaded. Right?"

"Yeah, okay." This was familiar. I was messing with him. It felt foreign, but good.

Despite my bravado, my stomach churned as I listened to the phone ring on the other end. It was now a little past eleven-thirty. Maybe Finn was asleep and it would go into voicemail. "Hello?" His voice almost made me drop the phone.

"Um, hi."

"Kellan? Is that you?"

"Yeah, who'd you think it was? Don't you have caller ID?"

"Yes, but you don't sound like yourself. What's wrong?"

"Well, it's been kind of an eventful evening." I told him what happened. Finn never interrupted, not once. I think I would've preferred it if he interrupted. Then I would've known what he was thinking. "And now I've decided that I need to go see Darcy Jamison. So that's where we're going."

He was quiet for so long, I checked to make sure the connection hadn't dropped. "We?" was all he said.

"Yes. Me and Tony and Galen." Even though Finn wouldn't consider Galen an important member of the party, I didn't want to leave him out. Dogs understood more than people gave them credit for.

"Antony is still accompanying you."

It wasn't a question, but I answered. "Yeah. He's following orders. He's not supposed to leave me alone, remember?"

"You saw Mal? And her — child?" The way he hesitated before saying "child" made me wonder what other word choices flitted through his mind before he settled on that one.

"Yes." For some reason, I didn't tell Finn about Magda. Maybe I just couldn't stand to be the one to condemn her a second time.

"That's —" But he never said what it was. Apparently, I wasn't the only one flummoxed by the revelation that was my niece. I slipped my hand in my pocket and touched the note. "I will speak to Janus. For now, assume that the same rules are in place. You will remain in contact with us and take no unnecessary risks."

I waited. There had to be more. Where was the belittling, the tongue-lashing? The "wait until you get home" speech? "We aren't in trouble?" To ask the question took more courage than I cared to admit.

"I said I would speak to Janus." Finn's way of saying, don't count on it.

"Okay, well, thanks. Talk to you later." And I hung up before he recovered his wits and decided a tongue-lashing was required after all. "He's going to talk to Janus," I told Tony. "So for now, I think we're kind of in trouble-limbo."

"All right." Tony turned on music, but left the volume low. "Want to talk about it?"

I was digging into another protein bar. "Talk about what?" I said around a mouthful. I knew what he wanted to talk about. I was stalling.

He shot me a look, well-illuminated by oncoming headlights. "You know what."

"If I say no, will you let it go?"

He was quiet for a beat, the time it took him to consider and decide. "For now."

"Then no."

This time, he was quiet for a verse. "Can I ask you a question?"

"Well, that didn't last long. Okay, I guess."

"Why is Darcy part of your pack?" *And not me.* I could hear those last three words loud and clear, even though he didn't say them. The sad scent flickered through the car again before Tony's scent went empty, blank. Like he was hiding what he was feeling from both of us.

I swallowed, my throat suddenly dry. "He wore my clothes."

"Uh, excuse me?"

"Last spring, when he showered at my apartment, he had blood and puke all over his clothes, so he borrowed some sweats.

And he used my soap and my shampoo. So, you know, he smelled like me."

"That's it?" Now he smelled annoyed, not quite as spicy as anger but a kissing cousin.

"Pretty much."

"The guy's a human, an outsider, someone you barely know, but he wears your sweatpants and, all of a sudden, he's family?"

See, this was why it sucked trying to explain wolf things to humans. They didn't understand how huge a scent connection could be. "It's — you asked. Why did you ask if you didn't want to know the answer?"

"Jesus, Kellan, people ask questions they don't want the answers to all the fucking time. But that's probably the first time in the history of the world that the answer was so fucking illogical."

"I don't know, I'm guessing Hitler had some real doozies in his day."

"Sure, the Nazi defense. At least you're not as bad as Hitler." His scent was inching toward anger.

"Why are you mad?"

"Because —" The word exploded out of his mouth, but nothing followed.

I dug my fingernails into my palms. I inhaled, focusing on Galen's earthy scent. And I tried to be brave. I wasn't scared of dying, but damn, I was scared of talking. "You're — you're special in a different way." I swallowed again, my spit feeling like it bumped along down my dry esophagus. "He might be family, but you're…" Say it. Say it, Kellan. "You're my mate." I felt cold and burning, all at the same time. It wasn't fair to say that to him, when I could never be the person I was before. "Or at least, you know, if you wanted to be, I mean, I can't do the things that —"

"Shut up, Kellan." But he didn't smell mad anymore. In fact, I could smell the saline of tears, though his cheeks looked dry. Thank the goddess for that.

I stuck Shinedown back in the CD player. I would've preferred Metallica or maybe Five Finger Death Punch, but I had a feeling Tony would hate 5FDP even more than he hated Metallica. And I wanted to show my gratitude that he didn't cry, because boy, would that have made an awful night so much worse.

"How long does it take to get to Elk Mound?" I said.

"You're the one with the GPS, Navigator."

"Oh, yeah." I fiddled with my phone. "Five and a half hours. I'm gonna need some coffee."

"And food that doesn't come in a foil wrapper," Tony said.

"Yeah, that would be nice."

Tony found a 24-hour truck stop and bought us grilled cheese sandwiches, French fries and half a dozen apples.

I stared at him. "Apples?"

"You're going to turn into a ball of grease if you don't eat something in an actual food group."

"You're very judgy about food, you know." I ate French fries, which were potatoes, which I was pretty sure was part of a food group.

"So Mal has a kid, huh?" He finished his apple, tossed the core out the window and started the car.

"You said we didn't have to talk about it." My coffee smelled like diesel fuel and I considered tossing it out the window after Tony's apple core. It was quite possibly The Worst in the history of coffee, and I sampled extensively, so I felt qualified to make that judgment.

"We're going to be in the car for five hours. What else do you want to talk about?"

Nothing. "I'm going to sleep a little," I said abruptly, and set my coffee between my feet where it couldn't hurt anybody. Leaning back, I closed my eyes and focused on breathing slowly. I really had no desire to sleep, having just regained consciousness, but pretending to sleep was a lot more attractive than discussing my sister's progeny.

Tony turned down the radio, but didn't turn it off. He was a nice guy that way. I felt heat gathering behind my eyes, and turned my face toward the window. If I started to cry, I didn't want him to see.

I didn't cry, but it was a narrow miss. And I must've been more tired than I thought, because the next thing I knew, I was jolting awake. Tony, mid-yawn, looked over at me. I could see bags under his eyes and his mouth seemed to sag at the corners.

"Why don't I drive for a while?" What I wanted to say was, pull the fuck over before you crash the car and kill my dog, but he'd been nice to me, so I made an effort.

"You're feeling up to it?" He didn't even try to argue, didn't mention Finn and Janus's rule about me not driving. Poor guy must be exhausted.

"More up to it than you are." I regretted the harsh tone as soon as I opened my mouth.

"I'm fine." His hands tightened on the wheel, like a tighter grip would keep him awake.

"Tony..." I didn't know what to say to make things better. My talents lay more in the making things worse department.

"We've only got about another two hours. I'll be fine."

I was so sick of being human. Of saying the wrong thing, doing the wrong thing, hurting people, feeling shit. Looking out the window, I suddenly needed to move. To run. "Tony, pull over."

"Kellan, I said I'm fine." Then he looked at me. "Your eyes are glowing."

"Pull. Over."

He obeyed. Then he reached over to grab Galen's collar.

"No," I said. "I want him to come with me." Tossing the bad coffee on the side of the road, I left Tony in the car. We were on a quiet stretch of country highway, no guard rails or buildings, nothing between us and the fields around us. We took off at a run, and when I was far enough from the road that Tony's headlights no longer interfered with my view of the stars, I stopped. I stripped and shifted, and I was free. I howled, and my brother howled with me.

We ran. We raced and I tackled him, and we wrestled. I won — I always won, I was bigger and stronger, but as soon as I wrapped my jaws around his throat, I let go with a nip and started running again. We chased down a rabbit and when I caught it, I shook it, snapping its neck. Then Galen and I shared the rabbit, and it tasted good. It tasted normal. I didn't feel sick or scared or lost. I felt like me.

I threw my head back and howled again. The chill in the night air thrilled me. I looked at Galen, and we agreed — time to run again.

Hours weren't really a big concern for a wolf, but I knew we ran for a long time because when I shifted back, the sky was growing light. I didn't vomit up the kill this time — I stayed a wolf long enough to digest the rabbit. I knew we should get back to the car, I figured Tony would be worried. But after shifting, I lay on the ground with Galen stretched out beside me. We stared up at the sky — well, I stared at the sky and Galen stared at me.

"I didn't know I could do that anymore," I said quietly. I never admitted that, not even in my head. It felt scary to say it out loud, but easier knowing Galen was the only one listening. "Aza figured out that if he electrocuted me, he could force me to shift, and I had no control. No joy. I didn't know if it could feel like that anymore."

Galen nuzzled my hand and I obligingly dug my fingers into his fur. "Thanks for coming with me," I said. "Thanks for sharing the rabbit. Shit, I ate meat." I felt a grin overwhelm my face.

Chapter 28

It was getting a little too light out to be laying naked in a field, so I dressed and walked with Galen back to the road. Tony was snoring in the driver's seat. I almost hated to wake him, but now that I was human again, I was starting to shiver in the cold air. It felt like it was forty degrees, tops. The car looked awfully inviting.

Still, I hesitated for one last second. There were conversations that we needed to have. I needed to tell Tony what I told Galen. I needed to talk about it, because the other members of the PTSD club told me that would help. I needed to talk about Mal, too. I couldn't just keep shape-shifting every time the emotions got intense, because intense seemed to be all I had in me lately. Tilting my head back like a child studying the shapes of clouds, I took one last look at the brightening sky and took a deep breath.

I opened the passenger door and stuck my head in the car. It was warmer inside the car than out, but not by a lot. "Tony?"

He jerked, wiped his mouth and blinked at me. "Cold."

"Yeah. Start the car, then scootch over. I'm driving."

Again, no protest, no mention of Finn's rules of the road. He slid over to the passenger seat, and I walked around to the driver's side. After letting Galen into the backseat, I got in. As my hands closed around the steering wheel, an involuntary grin spread across my face.

"You look better," Tony said.

I had dirt smeared all over me and I had grass in my hair. Made me wonder just how bad I looked before. "Thanks? I feel better. You hungry?"

"Starving."

"Have an apple."

"Kellan?"

He sounded hesitant, which made me nervous. "Yeah?"

"I'm sorry your sister let you down."

And just like that, I wanted to run again. But I didn't. I took a deep breath and said, "Okay. I ate a rabbit."

That earned me a few minutes of quiet. "That's, um, that's good. Or — I guess."

"I shared it with Galen."

"Oh. Well, that was nice of you." Poor Tony smelled very distressed. Humans never knew how to respond when I talked about wolfy things.

"But I wouldn't mind eating again. And I need some coffee that isn't older than me. That diesel coffee was awful last night."

"Diesel coffee?" He rubbed his face. "Coffee sounds good."

I was babbling, and it felt so good, I kept going. I told Tony about Aza, about the electrocution, the shape-shifting, the fear that I'd never know that joy again. "I feel...amazing."

His scent relaxed as he listened until he just smelled like himself. "You won."

I considered that. I didn't know what was going to happen with Mal. I didn't know what to do with the knowledge that I had a niece or that my sister wasn't a nocturne. I didn't know much of anything, but, for now at least, my body was mine again. A victory, maybe, but... "No. Not yet. Not until I talk to Darcy."

"Kellan..."

I didn't want to hear whatever he was about to say. "I know, okay? I know he's not going to want to see me. He's going to hate that I showed up without calling. He's going to be pissed and hurt and all those things that drive me crazy. But I have to see him. I have to say — I don't know, something. I have to." We were entering a more populated area, and I pulled into a drive-thru.

Tony didn't say anything except, "I'll have an egg sandwich and some hashbrowns."

I parked the car and we ate in silence. I served Galen some kibble from the supply in the trunk, and then we got on the road again. Not long after, Tony started sneezing. I got a bad feeling. "I was running through the grass. Weeds, pollen."

"Uh-huh." He sounded like he thought of this a long time ago.

"Galen did, too."

"Uh-huh."

I glanced at him. His eyes were red, his nose already looked raw from blowing. As I watched, he rubbed his eyes so hard that I was sure they'd pop like overripe tomatoes. "I should find a shower."

"I'm okay." He sneezed and pulled a couple pills from his pocket.

Twenty minutes later, when the antihistamines still didn't appear to be working, I pulled into a motel.

"Bedbugs don't even slum it here," Tony said, looking around.

I shuddered. "Yuck. Shut up. You don't have to come inside, but I'm going in long enough to shower and rinse Galen off."

Tony opted to stay out in the car. After showering, I put on clean clothes and transferred the contents of my pockets. And I found the note from Mal. I forgot about it. I glanced at Galen. If I was going to read the note, this was as good a spot as any. At least here, Galen would be the only witness to my latest nervous breakdown.

Kellan,

I'm sorry. I'm sorry for hitting you on the head, for running. For lying. For all of it. I'd take you with me if I thought you wanted me to, but you obviously don't, if the thought of accompanying us made you involuntarily shift. I love you, little sister. I'm sorry for being mushy, but I don't know when I'll have the chance to say it again. I hope someday, you and Abby will get to know each other. I hope someday, you'll forgive me. — Mal

I didn't cry. I also didn't breathe. Part of me wanted to throw the note away, but instead, I carefully folded it and slipped it back in my pocket. Then I gathered up my wits and my wet dog and left this latest no-tell motel.

When we got back to the car, Tony was sleeping again. I didn't know how to wake him gently, so I just opened the back door and let Galen jump in and shake water all over the interior of the car. Tony blinked at us. I slid into the driver's seat and turned up the heater. My hair was wet and I felt chilled.

I didn't drive, though. "I read the note. From Mal." That was all I said, and Tony didn't ask me to elaborate. I shuddered through a breath. "Is this a bad idea? Visiting Darcy?"

"Did you even brush your hair?"

"Yes. Tony, please."

He took a deep breath. "I don't know. But you said it's what you've gotta do, so let's do it."

I hesitated, then asked, "How do I look?"

Tony waited a beat before answering. He smelled a little like the jalapeno of anger, but more like the sourdough of fear. I smelled that combination on other people before — jealousy. "You look fine," he said, his voice sounding tight.

I didn't know how I felt about him being jealous. "I mean, do I look like I just escaped a sex torture dungeon? Because I'm guessing if I look really bad, Darcy's going to feel worse about me taking a beating for him."

"Oh." His scent shifted to something more neutral. "No. You look like you just got out of the shower. That's about all."

"Okay." I pulled out of the parking lot and we drove to Elk Mound.

We found Darcy's address. He was living in a little house with a fenced-in yard. It looked very quiet, very domestic. "No car," Tony said.

"Maybe he's at work." I sat there, not sure what to do. I didn't want to ambush Darcy at work. But the idea of waiting until he got home made me feel claustrophobic and creepy at the same time.

"There's no good way to do this," Tony said. "If we show up at his work, he'll feel put on the spot. But if we lurk around here until he gets home, he probably won't appreciate that, either."

"I can't call," I said with certainty. "He could hang up on me, he could tell me not to come, he could have the cops on hand when I do show up."

"Go to his work." When I looked at him, Tony nodded. Thankfully, he didn't address the insanity of my hypothetical scenarios. He just offered his opinion. "It'll be easier on you than sitting around here all day, drinking coffee and stewing. It might be easier on him, if he's in a place where he's got a role to play. And he can't run away."

Not for the first time, I felt both gratitude and envy at Tony's ability to boil down a situation to a swallowable size. We drove to Eau Claire. When we arrived at the library, Tony stayed outside in the car with Galen, as he promised he would. I walked inside, feeling like my guts were trembling. The library was huge and beautiful. Lots of windows, lots of wood paneling and big armchairs. And one familiarly pasty librarian.

He was right there, behind the desk, talking to a young woman with a death grip on a screeching child. She smiled, nodded at whatever he was saying, and turned away with the kid, her smile morphing into a distinctly homicidal-looking grimace. She walked past me. I inhaled, making sure that she was just human. Nothing monstery about her. Hopefully, the kid would be okay.

When Darcy saw me, he went blank. "You," he said.

"Me." I took one step toward him, then stopped. "I, um, I wanted to see you."

He stared at me. For a long time. I almost chickened out, almost turned and followed the footsteps of Homicidal Mommy.

But then I saw the tears. We both started walking and collided in a huge bear hug. He wasn't mad at me. Relief made me giddy, and I greedily inhaled his scent. *Pack.*

"I'm sorry," I said. "I'm so, so sorry."

He tightened his arms around me. "Why are you sorry? You should be sorry. How could you do that?"

I laughed a little as I listened to the Darcy stream-of-consciousness interrogation. Happiness bubbled up inside me like I was a walking can of 7-Up.

"Are you okay?" he asked next. "No, of course not. What happened? When did you get out? Is that the right term, get out? Probably not. Are you —"

"Shit, Darcy, give it a rest." I pulled back, dried my cheeks and smiled up at him. "I'm okayer. Okayish." I looked at him, really looked at him. He lost weight. He looked hollowed out. "How are you?"

"I'm, um..." He pushed his fingers through his hair, a sure sign of nerves since he never showed any trace of vanity before. "I'm fine."

I narrowed my eyes, sudden fear gripping me. His sister died of cancer, after all. "Are you sick?"

"What? No. No, I'm not sick. I'm all right. It's just been a rough couple months." He smiled, wan, but overall a valiant effort. "That's stupid. It's been a lot rougher on you than on me."

I wasn't sure about that. PTSD and all, I seemed to be recovering. Darcy, not so much. He smelled a little sour, the way a person does when they've been drinking regularly enough to start taxing their liver. One of the perks of being half-wolf — I could smell an alcoholic from across the room.

I saw another young woman hovering around the desk, watching us, looking like she needed librarian-type help. "Should I let you get back to work?" I said, not wanting to, but also not wanting to get Darcy fired.

He blinked, looked around as if he forgot where we were. "Yeah, I guess so. Do you have to get back right away? Or could you stick around for dinner?"

"I could stick around," I blurted before he even finished the question. Then I remembered I wasn't alone. "Tony and Galen are here, too."

"Well, if you don't mind driving out to Elk Mound, we could eat at my house. That way, Galen could be there, too."

I didn't mention that we already visited his house. I figured he didn't need to know that I was in full-on stalker mode. "That sounds perfect."

He gave me directions to his house and asked if six o'clock would work, before hurrying off to help the girl at the desk, who was starting to fidget and sigh. And I showed tremendous personal growth by refraining from sticking my tongue out at her.

As I walked back to the car, I could feel a smile stretching my face in a way that used to be familiar. And maybe could be familiar again. Tony wasn't sleeping this time. Instead, he closely watched me as I slid behind the wheel. "I take it he didn't scream and throw heavy books at you?" he said.

Galen nuzzled the back of my neck, and I reached back to scratch his head. "No. He invited us to dinner."

"All of us?" I tried to read Tony's scent. He didn't smell jealous, just surprised.

"Yup. Galen too."

"Well, all right." He leaned back and closed his eyes. "We should probably find a place to stay. I'd kind of like a shower, too."

"Do you mind if —" I hesitated, feeling silly for what I was about to suggest. "Do you mind if we take a walk first? It's so pretty here." And it was. All kinds of hills, and trees everywhere, most of which already lost their leaves, but bare trees had their own kind of beauty. And there was a river, too. "Plus, Galen could use a break from the car. You don't have to come if you don't want to." But I'd like you to, I finished silently.

"Are you kidding? I'd love a break from the car." He was already opening his door and getting out.

He was coming with me. I had a sneaking suspicion that, no matter what I suggested, Tony would've said yes. And maybe it was the residue of Darcy's bear hug, maybe it was lack of sleep and OD'ing on complicated emotions over the last twenty-four hours. But I felt something burst open in my chest, and I started crying again.

Already standing, Tony leaned back into the car. "What? I don't have to come. Would you rather walk alone? Or have dinner with Darcy alone? I told you, I'll wait in the car while you two —"

"Oh, shut up." I wiped my eyes and blew my nose. "I just... feel...good."

"Okay." He said it slowly, like he was prompting me to keep going.

"And part of me doesn't know how to feel this way anymore. And part of me is waiting for the other fucking shoe. And part of me just..." I started crying again.

Tony sat back down in his seat. "Part of you just really, really wants it to be real?"

It shouldn't surprise me that he figured it out. It was what he did, figured out what I wasn't saying. It was really annoying, and kind of helpful. And always surprising, despite knowing him as well as I did. I managed to stop crying, and when it felt like I could speak normally, I said, "Let's go for a walk."

We got out of the car and started up a hill. "At the risk of being punched in the nose for making you cry again," Tony said.

"That's a hell of a lead-in."

He smiled, but continued on like I never spoke. "The good is just as real as the bad."

I was having trouble breathing, so I picked up the pace as we climbed the slope, forcing my lungs into action. "I won't punch you in the nose, but let's stop talking about this."

"All right." We walked in silence. It was nice. It was like life. The sort of life that other people got to live. People who didn't swear oaths and battle their siblings and spend two months in a faery's torture dungeon. It was sunlight and a leash in my hand and a friend beside me.

Of course, I couldn't let it last. "The bad's going to come back, right?"

"Sure." He said it so matter-of-fact, like I asked him if he wanted a donut. I appreciated that. He didn't add any padding to his answers. "That's always going to happen. You can spend your life thinking about that, or you can, you know, not."

"I'm not sure I can. Not, I mean."

He laughed a little. "You already did, for a few minutes there. Even if you just let the good in for a little while, that's something."

I was getting sick of Guru Tony. "All right. We can go back to not talking now."

He glanced at me. "Race you to that footbridge." And he took off before I could protest that we were both wearing boots and jeans. What choice did I have but catch up to him and beat him to the bridge?

When we skidded to a stop, we were all laughing, even Galen. His mouth hung open and his tail waved maniacally. And before I thought about it, I threw my arms around Tony.

He stiffened, which made me stiffen and pull back. "Sorry," I said.

"No." He put his hands gently on my back and pulled me toward him, questioningly. Giving me the chance to say no. "You just surprised me."

I hesitated a little, because now I was thinking about it. Remembering why I didn't like to be touched. But I didn't want the moment to be over, so I leaned in again. It was much more awkward than the first hug, but it felt okay. His scent was so close, so strong and homey and familiar. *Mate.* The word rang through my mind, and, suddenly, I relaxed into the hug.

I heard a little shudder in his intake of breath, but other than that, his only reaction was to relax along with me.

"My sister's an asshole," I said as we pulled apart again. "But you're pretty all right, Gigantor."

"You're an asshole," he said, and I punched him in the shoulder. He laughed. "But you're pretty all right, anyway."

We started walking again. I wanted to tell him that Darcy was drinking too much. What I wanted was Tony's advice on how to handle it. But since it wasn't my secret to tell, and since Darcy didn't actually tell me, I just smelled it on him, which is kind of cheating, I didn't feel like I could divulge it.

"If somebody was doing something," I said, "and you know they're doing it but you're not supposed to know because you only know because you can smell things on them that humans can't smell, but you want to help them because they're going to end up hurting themselves because humans are really fragile, do you think it's okay to talk to them about it?"

Tony was quiet for a beat. "Huh?" he said.

I sighed, frustrated. "Darcy's — there's something going on. And I don't feel like I should tell you, and I don't know if I should say anything to him because he didn't tell me, I just smelled it on him. But I don't know if I can let it go, either."

"Okay, that's slightly less convoluted." Tony rubbed the back of his neck. "He knows you're a shape-shifter, right?"

"Not exactly."

He cocked an eyebrow. "Well, if he's going to be your friend for long, he's probably going to learn that. He's been able to handle some pretty weird shit. I think he'll be okay. But he might not be ready to get a reality check about — what it is he's doing."

What did that mean? "So I shouldn't say anything?"

"Shit, Kell, I don't know." He glanced at me. "I can't tell you what to do. Mostly because if it goes bad, I don't want you to blame me. But also because you know him better than I do. And you're the one who has to live with your decision."

"I take it back. You're not all right. You suck."

He snorted. "Well, you're still an asshole, but you're not going to make me decide for you."

Galen put on the brakes and started circling. "Shit, I didn't bring a bag," I said.

Tony glanced around. "No one's watching. When he's done, we can sprint back to the car."

I glared at him. "We can't do that. It'll look like an elephant made a pile here."

"Well, you can't expect an elephant to clean up after himself."

I sighed. I didn't have a better option. When Galen finished, we took off. We clamored back into the car and sat there for a minute. Part of me was waiting for someone to yell at us to go back and clean up after my dog. But of course, no one did.

"You want to stay in town here or back in Elk Mound?" Tony asked.

"Is there any place to stay in Elk Mound?" I didn't remember seeing a gas station, much less a motel.

"No idea." But he waited for me to choose.

"Let's find a place here." I wouldn't mind resting in an actual bed for a little while.

Chapter 29

I didn't ask for my own room this time. I decided it would be simpler just to share. We got a room at a small motel that allowed dogs, and while Tony was in the shower, I changed my clothes, opting for a pair of yoga pants and a baggy t-shirt. Once again, I transferred the note to the pocket of my current pants. By the time Tony came out of the bathroom, I'd already settled on one of the beds with Galen stretched out beside me. The TV was tuned to a movie that I wasn't watching, but the noise helped me relax.

Tony studied the screen with his head cocked to the side. "What are those? Giant ants?"

"Huh?" I looked at the TV, really looked for the first time. "I don't know. I didn't feel like channel flipping."

"Mind if I do?"

"You're not into apocalyptic giant insect movies?"

"Sure. They're right up there with zombies." He lay down on the other bed. "What time are we going to Darcy's?"

"He said six."

Tony made a sound at the back of his throat and looked at the clock. "Are you hungry? We didn't get lunch."

I was feeling pretty sleepy. If I ate a big meal, it would just wake me back up. "I think I'll just have another protein bar. I want a nap."

"All right. Mind if I go out and get something? I can pick something up for you if you want."

"Um, sure." My stomach rumbled. "Just whatever. Meatless whatever," I amended.

"So the rabbit didn't change that?"

I didn't even have to think about it. "No. It's different as a human."

"Okay." He stuck his wallet in his pocket and paused by the door. "You gonna be okay here by yourself?"

"I'm not by myself. I've got Galen. And the giant ants."

He smiled. "Good."

I fell asleep before the door closed behind him.

———— 《 》 ————

I woke up to something dripping on my face. Galen's head was two inches above mine, and as he panted, he dribbled drool on me. "Ugh," I said, and shoved him away.

As I wiped my face, I looked at Tony in the other bed. He was snoring softly. The clock said it was quarter to five. We'd need to leave by five-thirty if we were going to get to Darcy's by six. I turned to Galen. "Go drool on his face. Wake him up for me."

Akitas were notorious for being one-person dogs, so it didn't surprise me when Galen lay down and put his big head in my lap instead of obliging my request. I played with his ears for a minute, then decided that I could probably use another quick shower before dinner. I dressed in jeans, a t-shirt and an oversized flannel, performing the now-familiar ritual of transferring the note. I was getting good at moving it from one pocket to another with minimal touching and looking. I felt a pull to keep it with me, but that didn't mean I wanted to acknowledge it. When I emerged from the bathroom, Tony was awake, but still lying in bed.

"Hey," he said, stretching the word out into multiple syllables. He sounded like he was still mostly asleep. "I brought you mac-n-cheese."

"Oh. Thanks." I forgot he went for food.

"It's in the fridge."

I glanced at the clock again. Five-ten. "We should probably leave in twenty minutes or so."

"Yeah, I was thinking about that." He pushed himself into a sitting position. "I'm pretty beat. I feel like I haven't slept in a month."

"Uh-huh." I waited to see where he was going with this.

"So why don't I stay here with Galen and you can go to Darcy's on your own? You two need some time together and I don't want to fall asleep on my plate."

What happened to not leaving me alone? Apparently, being tortured made me incapable of anything, but getting hit on the head, kidnapped by my sister and discovering a secret niece qualified me to handle myself. I sniffed, checking his scent. No tension or worry, nothing to indicate hesitation. "You're sure?" I said.

"Yup. If I get hungry, I'll just eat the mac-n-cheese." He smiled, looking slightly more awake, but not much.

"All right." I felt a flutter of nervousness at the thought of spending so much time with Darcy without a buffer. But maybe it would be good. Maybe it would be just what we needed. "Wait — that mac-n-cheese is mine."

His smile widened, showing off his remarkably straight, white teeth. For the kid of a junkie, he had a great smile. "I'll try to restrain myself, but I make no promises."

I stuck my tongue out at him. "I'll take Galen out before I go. That way you don't have to get up."

Tony thanked me, then slid back under the covers and closed his eyes. He was snoring again before I finished buckling Galen's harness. I looked into Galen's eyes, and he stared back at me. And I knew that as nice as it was for Tony to offer to keep him while I had dinner with Darcy, there was no way I was leaving my little bro behind this time.

I wrote Tony a note, telling him that I took Galen with me. Then we left. I pulled up the directions to Darcy's on my phone and managed to follow the directions with ease. GPS was remarkably useful. Most technology seemed more trouble than it was worth, but this actually fell into the good idea category. When I told Galen that, he wagged his tail in agreement.

Darcy opened the front door before I had a chance to knock, like he'd been watching from the window. I felt the same sense of well-being when I saw him again. *Pack. Feels right.* Welcome home, wolf.

I gave him a hug and we went inside. Darcy apologized, said he got home late and didn't have time to cook. Was it all right with me if we ordered pizza?

"Only if you let me pay," I said. I didn't know how much librarians made, but every Sankha had a company credit card. I was much more comfortable with Finn paying for the pizza than Darcy.

After a small argument, he agreed to the arrangement and pulled out his phone. "What do you want? Extra meat?"

I realized Darcy didn't know. I didn't have a chance to tell him earlier. Good thing he didn't cook. "Uh, no, actually. I'm off meat."

Darcy's mouth drooped open for a second, but he recovered quickly. "When we went out for curry, you called the rice the clutter crowding out the chicken."

"Uh-huh." I didn't want to talk about it. I didn't want to think about it. He must've seen something on my face, because in a very un-Darcy-like move, he let the subject drop.

"Okay, well, what would you like?"

I remembered the green pepper and mushroom pizza from my first night back. I asked him if that sounded all right.

"Sounds great!" His enthusiasm sounded a tad forced, but I still didn't want to talk about it, so instead I studied the room around me.

Like Darcy's apartment in Madison, the living room of the little house was crammed full of books. Unlike Darcy's apartment, the books all looked tattered, second-hand. What was with the yard sale volumes? He owned the biggest collection of antique books I'd ever seen.

When he hung up the phone, I asked. "Where are your books?"

"These are my books."

"No, I mean the good ones. The ones your mom collected."

He fidgeted with the phone, pressing the volume button over and over again, causing it to beep over and over again.

"Darcy, Jesus, stop that or I'll take it away."

He set it on the coffee table, which looked like the product of a desperate dumpster dive. It looked like my coffee table, actually. "They're still in Madison," he said finally. "I couldn't risk moving them. I was so scared something would happen to them. So I kept my apartment when I moved here."

Madison rent was ridiculously high, compared to other Wisconsin areas. "Awfully expensive storage unit."

He shrugged, looking and smelling like discomfort — sweaty with a hint of adrenaline. "I guess — I guess I wasn't ready to admit that I wasn't going back."

"So why did you move?" I said.

"We should sit. Do you want something to drink? I made coffee." So that's what that smell was. I guessed either bad coffee or compost pile.

It wasn't Darcy's fault that he was a tea drinker. But tea drinkers should never, ever make coffee. I knew it would be a struggle to pretend it was good, but I couldn't think of a good reason to refuse the coffee. "Sure, coffee sounds great." I let him serve me a beverage. I forced myself to take a sip, then made a sound something like, "Mmmm." Oh, yeah, it was bad coffee. Not only was it weak, but I could taste the poor quality of the grounds. Tea drinkers. I struggled through another sip, then repeated my question. "Why'd you move, Darcy?"

"I couldn't bear it."

The words stopped me short. I choked on my coffee because my esophagus forgot how to work. I knew the answer would hurt. I just didn't know how bad.

In another un-Darcy-like move, he didn't come over and try to save me from drowning in a mouthful of coffee. He just watched and waited and when I was breathing normally again, he went on. "When he — when I watched him take you, it was like..." He picked at a cuticle for a moment. "Like watching my sister die all over again."

Oh, god. He saw. Darcy watched Aza take me. He saw. My body went still. It felt like even my blood froze in my veins.

Darcy kept talking. "I was so mad at you when Tony told me you volunteered to take my place. And then I was so mad at me. Because it was my fault you were in this mess at all. I asked you for help. I should've — I don't know. But, well, I just couldn't stand to keep being there. To keep seeing the same sights and know that you weren't going to see them. You were — it felt like you were all I had left, and in a split second, you were gone. Too. You were gone, too. So I left."

I tried so hard to find a word. To think of something. All I came up with was, "Fuck, Darcy."

"I know. I'm sorry."

That loosed my tongue. "Why are you sorry? Shit. I'm sorry I couldn't tell you the plan first. I'm sorry I left you alone. I'm sorry I caused you even more pain. Fuck, Darcy." I was crying. He was crying. It was like a goddamn sorority house in here.

As always, Galen saved me. He shoved his head in my lap, then looked toward the door. Just before the doorbell rang. "Pizza?" I said. I fumbled in my back pocket for my wallet and managed to stop crying as I walked to the door.

I handed the delivery girl my Kelly O'Connell credit card, then waited while she swiped it through the doohickey on her phone. I didn't look back at Darcy the whole time. I could hear him still sniffling, and if I looked at him, I knew I'd start crying again.

Pizza gave us something to occupy ourselves while the emotional debris settled around us. We didn't talk much as we ate. He only ate a piece and a half. I ate most of the rest.

When the plates were piled in the sink and we were once again settled in the living room, Darcy said, "So what's new with you?"

The question was so absurd, I started laughing, and Darcy joined me. And it felt a little better. Not a lot. But a little normalcy returned. "Oh, you know. Pretty much the same old stuff. Evil sister kidnapped me so she could introduce me to her spawn."

His eyes bugged so wide, I thought they'd fall out of the sockets. "What?"

I told him the whole story. It got the topic off Aza, and off us, which helped with the normalcy.

Darcy sat quietly as I told the story, only interrupting with murmured exclamations like, "What?" and "Oh, no." I even told him about Magda. I didn't tell Finn about her, but I told Darcy. When I was done, he sat quietly a little while longer. "Well, that's that, then," he said finally.

I frowned. "That's what?" He smelled determined. Like English breakfast tea — black and strong. It was a new scent for him. New scents always threw me for a loop.

"I have to move back to Madison. I can't expect you to deal with all this on your own."

I should've felt indignant that he assumed I couldn't handle it. I should've pointed out that I was two hundred-plus years old, thank you very much, and I managed to tie my shoes every morning for at least the last hundred and fifty. But I didn't. Because I felt all warm and tingly and glowy. Like a hundred-watt bulb lit me up from just behind my sternum and turned me into a human glow stick.

Despite the glow, I forced myself to say, "You just moved. You really think you should quit your job again?"

"Oh, I didn't quit my job. Well, I sort of did, but my boss said I could take more of a leave of absence. I think she was hoping I'd come back. Now I think it's best if I do."

"But —"

"My job here was just temporary. The reference librarian went on maternity leave. The head librarian here is good friends with my boss, they were talking, and I got hired as a temp. I'll have to stay until Susanne gets back, but..."

I walked over to him, plopped down next to him, and threw my arms around him in an awkward sideways embrace. "Yes," I said, dangerously close to tears again. Time to shift the focus before things got snot-filled. "So that's me. What about you?"

"What do you mean?"

"How have you been?"

He shrugged. "I'm fine." Even Galen didn't buy the attempt at nonchalance. My dog gave a little whumpf of disbelief.

"Darcy..." It wasn't like I never had the hey-I-can-smell-the-lie conversation before. I just wasn't sure I ever needed the other person to accept me the way I needed Darcy to accept me. "I know you're not fine."

"Well, you know, it's been hard, but I'm coping."

The scent was faint, but it was there. "How much have you had to drink today?"

"I — what? What are you talking about? You've been here this whole time. I drank water."

"I know you haven't had anything for a few hours. But you did earlier. And yesterday, too." I felt my own anxiety rise as he began to smell angry. It was a dark, bitter smell that I could feel coating the back of my tongue.

"What — what —" He just kept sputtering that one word over and over. Galen shifted restlessly at the change in the mood.

"I'm a shape-shifter, Darcy. I can smell it on you." When I realized I was holding my breath, I forced a gulp of air down my throat.

"You — you're a shape-shifter? Like them?" Like the monsters.

I steeled myself. I wasn't a monster. But I wasn't human, either. At least I didn't tell him I was half faery. That would probably send him over the edge.

"I'm a different sort of shifter than nocturnes, but yes, I guess in some ways I am like them. My sense of smell, for one." I hesitated, then pushed forward. "I don't just smell the alcohol. I can smell the changes it's making in your body. It's hurting you, Darcy."

Nostrils flaring, almost like he was scenting the air, he stood up and turned his back to me. He crossed his arms over his chest and stood so tense, he almost vibrated. "You have no right to judge me," he said in a voice so tight and raw, he sounded like a completely different person.

How did he feel judged by what I just said? I felt him pulling away from me like a sudden rush of cold air. Don't think. Don't feel. The familiar mantra helped steady my voice. "I'm not judging. But I am worried about you."

"You left!" He whirled around. "You were gone. My sister's gone. Everyone's gone. I'm alone. And don't tell me you know what that feels like." Rage radiated from him. I only smelled him like this once before. Right after his sister died. "You have your Sankhain. All your people. You have no idea what it's like to lose EVERYONE!"

I wrapped my hand around Galen's collar. Don't think. Don't feel. But I did feel. I wanted my friend back. "You're right. I suck. It's my fault you're a drunk now."

"I'm not a drunk." He spat the words.

"Whatever. But people who drink occasionally for fun don't go all Incredible Hulk when you ask them about it. And they don't stink of alcohol at ten in the morning." I took a deep breath. I didn't want to say the next words, because they left me too vulnerable. But unless I wanted to walk away forever, I needed to say them. "And you didn't lose me. I'm here now. I can't make up for what you lost. But I, you know..." I swallowed hard. "I love you. And stuff."

"You — what?" Darcy stared at me like I just spoke in tongues.

"Not like a romantic something. But like a — like a brother something." Fuck, I hated emotional scenes.

And just like that, the tornado faded, the storm clouds broke apart and the sun shone almost too bright to see. Darcy smiled. "Like a brother something?"

"Fuck you. Forget it. I take it back." But I was smiling, too.

"Nope, too late. You can't take it back." He hesitated, then sat down beside me. Galen watched him closely, but didn't try to kill him, so I let go of the collar. "I like to drink. It feels better."

That simple statement felt much bigger than the words. Because he didn't say all the things that the drinking felt better than. "I'm sorry you're hurting."

He put his hand over mine. "You're right, though. It is a little better now."

I knew enough about dependency to know that this wasn't the end of the conversation. But at least he wasn't angry at me anymore. "Good. Now, as much as I love you and all, this is getting a little too touchy-feely. So what do you call an anorexic with a yeast infection?"

He stared at me.

"A quarter pounder with cheese." And I bared my teeth in a grin.

"That's offensive," Darcy said. He shook his head. "And disgusting."

"I know, that's what makes it so good." I chuckled a little, then took a deep breath. "You're really coming home?"

He hesitated and my heart stopped. But then he nodded. "I will. I'll have to finish this job and get my old job back. I'll get right on it." His mouth half-curved in a sorry attempt at a smile. "You probably need to go. Tony will be missing you."

I missed you. The memory intruded on the moment, and I hated Aza for being in my head as my gag reflex triggered. "I guess."

Darcy looked so lost and so sad.

"Do you want me to stay?" I said very, very quietly.

He swallowed and I could almost hear his spit grating on the dryness of his throat. "No. I'll be all right. But thank you." He almost-smiled a little better this time. "I'll see you soon."

"And you'll call me sooner. Right?"

"Of course."

"All right." I snapped Galen into his harness, grateful to have an excuse to look away. Part of me wanted to escape, but the rest of me couldn't resist saying, "Don't drink."

His face shut down. "What?"

"Just for tonight. Just try it. Go for a walk. Cook something. Surf internet porn. Anything. Just don't drink tonight. If it sucks, you can go back to normal tomorrow. But for tonight, just...don't."

His jaw clenched, but his scent didn't go to anger. It smelled unbelievably sad. "You're neither my mother nor my sponsor. I'm not your responsibility."

"You don't get it, do you?" I stepped closer. "I saved your life twice now. I'd do it again in a second. You are my responsibility."

"No, Kellan, I'm not." He stared over my head. "I never asked you to save me even once."

"Of course not, because this isn't a Disney movie and you're not wearing a ball gown. But you didn't have to ask. It's what I do."

He managed to meet my eyes. "And at what cost to you? You've lost your sister. Your mental health. Your ability to eat meat."

I felt like something was slipping away and I didn't understand why. "Okay, first of all, losing my sister was her doing, not yours. And second, vegetarianism is very in right now."

"Kellan." It was a Finn tone of voice and I didn't like it coming from Darcy's mouth.

"Well, it is." It was a petulant Kellan tone of voice and I didn't like that much, either. "Fine. Bottom line is, I didn't lose you. And I don't want to know what that would cost me. So as far as I'm concerned, I'm still coming out ahead. But if you die of cirrhosis, then all that shit was for nothing. So flush the vodka!"

He blinked rapidly for a really long time. "I'll try. For tonight."

"Okay, then." My lungs were too tight to take a deep breath, and I wanted to get out of here before the impending hysterics began. "I told Tony I'd be back by ten," I lied, "so I'm going to go. I'll talk to you later. I'll call you when I get back to the motel. Okay?"

Darcy nodded and I bolted.

———— «» ————

I managed to make it to the car, door firmly shut, before I started to hyperventilate. But of course I couldn't just sit there in Darcy's driveway, so even though I probably shouldn't have been operating a Matchbox car, I started to drive. I pulled into the first open gas station that I passed, promised Galen I'd be right back, and went in to buy coffee. I thought the coffee last night was bad. This was so much worse. But it was hot, so hot, it burned the tears from the back of my throat, and the caffeine made me feel like myself again. And at least it was stronger than Darcy's coffee. I spent the rest of the drive forcibly not thinking about Darcy and whether he was taking a drink right now.

When we reached the motel, I shut off the car and sat in the dark with my dog, feeling the coffee eat a hole in my stomach. Eau Claire was surprisingly quiet for a college town, or at least, this particular parking lot was. I closed my eyes and pretended that I was surrounded by trees. I pretended that the scents I smelled, rather than old leather and motor oil, were those of damp earth, scurrying critters, rotting leaves — a forest at night. And I realized the coffee didn't burn the tears away, because there they were, flowing down my cheeks.

Galen crawled in my lap, no small feat considering he weighed more than most first graders and the steering wheel dug into his spine. But he did it, and I wrapped my arms around him and buried my face in his fur. And I said to him what I couldn't say to anyone else — "I can't lose any more. Don't take away anything more."

I prided myself on being tough. On being the one who could take the punishment. On being the survivor. But being a survivor meant being willing to lose everything, to watch all that you loved and all that you were fall away, and to keep going into the unfamiliar, all alone. Darcy was the survivor, not me. I was lost.

—— «» ——

I tried to wipe my face, but when Galen and I walked into the motel room, Tony must've seen that I'd been crying. He leapt off the bed and started to walk toward me. He stopped himself a few feet away. "What happened?"

I shook my head. I couldn't talk. I needed a drink of water to clear my throat, so I could call Darcy and tell him all was well. If I started talking to Tony, I'd just start crying again. I hated this new crybaby version of myself more than any other version.

After gulping two glasses of water, I called Darcy's cell. He answered. Our conversation was brief and awkward, but at least I didn't cry. He promised to call me in the morning. He said he flushed all his alcohol. I didn't know if I believed him.

When I hung up, I sat down on my bed, setting the phone on the little bedside table. Tony sat on his bed, facing me. "Kellan?" The gentleness in his voice made me feel so tired.

I couldn't look at him. I didn't trust my tear ducts to hold still. "He never wanted me to save him."

The words surprised me. Of all the things to hold onto from that conversation, I chose that? But saying them made me all choked up again.

"I'll make some coffee." The bedsprings creaked as Tony stood and walked over to the counter by the bathroom where the sad little four-cup coffee maker lived. I watched him put two of the tiny coffee bags into the basket and fill it with water. After hitting the on-button, he came back to the bed, and my gaze returned to the floor. "Kell, whether he wanted it or not, he's grateful you did."

"You don't know that." My voice was almost accusing, like it was Tony's fault that it might not be true.

"I do know it, because I've met Darcy. He's a good guy, and he appreciates other good people. And you're good people."

"No, I'm not. I'm selfish. I saved him for me. Because I couldn't let go. I should've asked him what he wanted."

I smelled the shift in his mood, and the anger that rapidly filled the air surprised me enough to look up at him. "Kell, I know it's been an emotional couple of days, but that's just stupid."

He got up, poured us both a mug of coffee, draining the pot. I didn't take the offered cup, I just stared at it. "Stupid? You're the emotionally evolved one here, and you're telling me I'm stupid?"

"I didn't call you stupid, I called what you said stupid. Now take your damn coffee." I obeyed, but only because it smelled so strong and fresh. "You think you should've asked his opinion before offering yourself up to save him? Do you hear these things as they come out of your mouth? Fuck, Kell."

"He wanted me to stay. Maybe I should've stayed. Fought Aza. It would've been better to kill him anyway."

"And start a war? Alienate Finn and Janus? Bring a world of faery magick down on our heads? Given that Raoul managed to fool you and your nose for years with a simple spell, I don't really want to think about what they can do when they're pissed off. Do you?"

He had a point. "Well —"

"And say you did start that war. You think the Sankhain would be the only ones to suffer? Please. Every war has collateral damage. How many innocent people would've been hurt in the crossfire? And even if it was just the Sankhain, who would you be willing to sacrifice so Darcy could have a say in the matter? Gina? Cat? Smack?" He paused. "Me?"

I remembered that mental image, the thought of Tony eviscerated like the dead guy behind my apartment building. "No," I said, although I couldn't remember if he asked a yes-or-no question in all that.

"You're alive. Darcy's alive. You've got time to figure things out between you." Tony leaned closer, and I could smell the coffee on his breath. "And just so we're clear — I'm not willing to sacrifice you, either. Not that you asked me what I wanted, but I'm telling you anyway."

Darcy was alive. Darcy and I had time. Time to figure things out. Tony's words swirled around like my brain was a blender. And when the whirring stopped, I held something totally different between my ears. "Mal has a kid."

"Okay." He sounded a little confused, but of course, he didn't know about the brain-blender.

"Darcy and I have time, but what about Mal and me? She has a kid. A kid. That she never told me about. And then she expected me to just run away with her and join the rebellion? She never killed Magda. She told me she did, but she didn't. What else did she lie about? She has a kid!"

At my ever-rising voice, Galen stood and pressed himself against my legs, trying to push me back, back to safety. He was trying to protect me from a foe he couldn't see, but knew must be there if it was upsetting me this much.

Tony said something, but I couldn't hear him around the rushing in my ears. I needed to breathe. I needed to soothe Galen. I needed to not pass out from hyperventilating. But when I breathed, all I could smell were awful motel smells, dirty feet and mold and old pee. I stumbled over to the window, pushed it open and drew cold, exhaust-tinted air into my lungs. A hint of wood smoke mingled with the rest, and that one scent grounded me, made me feel like the world was a familiar place after all.

I turned and looked at Tony. "I want to go home."

He frowned. "But Darcy -"

"Is moving back to Madison. You're right. We'll be okay. But I want to go home. I want to go back to my cabin and my DVDs and my trees and my weight room. And my — my pack. Gina and Smack and Cat and Ryder and Janus. That's why I did all this. Right? Why I let him ra-rape me," I stumbled over the word, but I managed to say it, "for two months. So I could go home and be with them." I clenched my fists because the next words were hard. "So I could be with you. Not Mal. She left and she lied. You didn't."

I noticed his fists were clenched, too. "What's wrong?" I said. "Am I being stupid again?"

"No." He unclenched his fists and shook his arms out, looking away. "Sometimes it's harder than others not to touch you."

One foot in front of the other. One breath at a time. I didn't want to be touched, but I did believe it wouldn't hurt me. I went to him and slowly, awkwardly put my arms around him. It was different from the hug on the street earlier that day. This time, it was on purpose.

He didn't move. I waited for what seemed like a long time, then said, "Are you going to hug me back? Because this is getting weird."

He gently wrapped his arms around me. And then, like he wanted to make the most of this chance, like he was scared it might never happen again, he hugged me so tight that I couldn't breathe.

And about two seconds in, I started to feel scared. I started to worry that he would try to keep going. He'd kiss me, stick his tongue in my mouth, touch me, below the waist, and —

I wriggled a little and his arms loosened. I took a deep breath, and his arms loosened a little more. Tony's scent filled me, and a little of the fear faded. Not much, but a little. I put my hands between us, placed them on his shoulders, pushed back gently. And he stepped away. He didn't look or smell disappointed. He smelled like fresh-baked cinnamon rolls. I didn't know that scent. But if I had to guess, it was a scent of child-like happiness. Not the sort of scent that led to tongues and stuff.

"Are you ready to go home?" I asked.

He walked away, going into the bathroom. And returned with his shaving kit and my little bag with shampoo and toothpaste. "How fast can you pack?"

"Well, considering I didn't unpack, probably pretty fast." After sticking my toiletry bag in my duffel, I fed Galen. While he ate, I sent Darcy a text, telling him we were heading back to Madison, that I would see him soon and he should call me anytime. I held my breath until his reply came: "Drive safe." Then two seconds later, another text: "If it's not too much trouble, could you text me when you get home?" I smiled. I never had someone who wanted to know if I got home safe. It was kind of nice. I replied that I would, then gathered my duffel and Galen's bag.

Tony left the keys on the dresser and we walked outside. The wood smoke was a little stronger — someone had a bonfire going, was my bet. The smell seemed stronger than smoke from a chimney. This was an open-air fire. I breathed deep.

"You want to drive?" Tony asked.

"Actually, if you're up to driving, I was thinking I might sleep a little."

"Sure."

He was probably expecting me to lean the passenger seat back and sleep half-sitting up the way a human would. I didn't. Instead, I crawled into the backseat, took off my clothes, and shape-shifted. I noticed Tony twitch as he watched, and I realized this was the first time he saw me shift. A human moment of discomfort, almost embarrassment, passed through me, but then I completed the shift. I was a wolf. Even when I was a human, I was a wolf, and sooner or later, Tony needed to see that. Still, I watched him, studied him for a reaction. His eyes widened slightly, then he smiled, started the car and pulled out of the parking space.

Relief shuddered through me. He accepted me. My mate.

Galen and I curled up together, and I slept like the dead all the way home.

If you enjoyed this read...
Please leave a review.
It takes less than five minutes, and it really does make a difference.

Reviews should answer at least three basic questions.
(But won't give the story away.):

- Did you like the book? *("Loved the book! Can't wait for the Next!")*
- What was your favorite part? *(Characters, plot, location, scenes.)*
- Would you recommend the book?

Your review will help other readers discover this book. Consider leaving your review on Amazon, Barnes and Noble, Apple iBooks, KOBO, Goodreads, BookBub, Facebook, Instagram and/or your own website.

Brian Hades, publisher

To leave a review on Amazon
~ Even if the book was not purchased on Amazon ~

1. Go to amazon.com. Sign into your Amazon account. If you do not have an Amazon account, you need to create one and activate it by making a purchase. Amazon will check to see that your account is active before allowing you to leave a review. Amazon has some restrictions, such as not leaving a bias review. For more information on Amazon's policies please read Amazon's Community Guidelines for book reviews:

   https://www.amazon.com/gp/help/customer/display.html?nodeId=GLHXEX85MENUE4XF

2. Search for Wolf is a Four-letter Word by Carrie Newberry and when you see it, click on it and then click on the details page.

3. Scroll down to find the Write a Customer R Write a customer review eview button. Click it.

4. Select your star rating. A rating of 5 is best, 1 is worst.

5. If you have a photo or video to share, add it to the upload box.

6. Add a headline.

7. Write your review.

8. Press the SUBMIT button

To leave a review on Barnes and Noble
~ Even if the book was not purchased on BN.com ~

1. Go to barnesandnoble.com and sign up for an account.

2. Search for and find Wolf is a Four-letter Word by Carrie Newberry, then click on the book's details page.

3. Scroll down to the review section and click on the Write a Review button.

4. Select your star rating. A rating of 5 is best, 1 is worst.

5. Add a review title.

6. Write your review.

7. Add a photo if you wish.

8. Select if you would recommend this book to a friend.

9. Select appropriate TAGs.

10. Indicate if your review contains spoilers.

11. Select the type of reader that best describes you (optional).

12. Enter your location (optional).

13. Enter your email address.

14. Checkmark that you agree to the terms and conditions.

15. Press the POST REVIEW button.

About the Author

Carrie Newberry studied creative writing at both the University of Wisconsin-Madison and UW-Eau Claire. But when she realized they would no longer let her take writing workshops for credit, she left academia and started work full time at a dog grooming shop. She lives in Madison with a dog who sings along with the radio, a cat who talks in her sleep, and an enormous collection of books. Also the author of *Pick Your Teeth With My Bones*, the first book in the Eternal Spring, Invisible Forest series, Carrie is hard at work writing Kellan's next adventure.

Need something new to read?

If you liked Wolf is a Four-letter Word, you should also consider these other EDGE-Lite titles...

Pick Your Teeth with my Bones
(Book One of the Eternal Spring, Invisible Forest series)

by Carrie Newberry

The Fountain of Youth is at Risk...

A secret society of warriors has protected the Fountain of Youth for centuries.

Its location is a closely guarded secret and the society itself is shrouded in mystery. They are invisible. They are unknown. They blend in with the urban environment. For all anyone knows, the woods near Madison, Wisconsin could be their home!

On any given day, if you look hard enough, you might spot Kellan Faolanni, a single, lives-alone, drives-a-truck kind of woman. She's the girl-next-door type. Innocent looking and easy to get along with. You'd never know she's a battle-scarred shapeshifter.

That's until the existence of a traitor is revealed, and a leaked document containing the history of her people threatens to expose her, her fellow Sankhain guardians, and the secrets they keep. Secrets the warriors have sworn to defend with their lives. With a fellow protector (and her faithful dog Galen), Kellan sets out to unravel the mystery of the compromising documents.

By using the unique sense of smell that has kept her alive and fighting for two hundred years, Kellan follows the trail deep into the dark heart of the forest. But the truth she uncovers – both about the Sankhain and about herself – challenges everything she thought she knew and forces her to choose between her role as a weapon in the hands of her leaders and the dictates of her own conscience.

Everything they've sworn to protect is in jeopardy. Failure to locate the traitor is not an option.

Pawns and Phantoms
(An Everland Mystery)

by Misha Handman

Todd Malcolm would be the first person to tell you that

he's no Basil Stark. He's just a bouncer, part-time detective's assistant, and brawler who does his best to get by on the mean streets of 1950s Everland. But when Todd gets mixed up in an arson one night, he's thrown in over his head.

With his friends Glimmer and Vance Carson, Everland's 'other detective', Todd will have to contend with federal agents, angry tigers, murderous mermaids, and shadowy threats at every turn. Does Todd have what it takes to handle this case, or is he just a pawn in a dangerous plot?

About Misha Handman

Misha Handman Born on Vancouver Island, Canada, Misha Handman spent his early life immersed in the arts, with one parent a teacher and the other a manager of theatre and opera. Moving across the country to Ottawa, and then Toronto, he began writing at a young age – first writing comics and designing card games for his closest friends and then, buoyed by their approval, gradually expanding out to submissions to magazines and short story collections, and graduating from the University of Toronto with a classic English degree.

The Rosetta Mind
(Book Two of the Rosetta Series)

by Claire McCague

Estlin Hume was living off-grid on 12 acres outside of Twin Butte, Alberta when he got snagged into being translator for first contact. Home again, he wakes to find himself surrounded by aliens, affectionate squirrels, government representatives, and military personnel. That's nothing new. But he hadn't planned on hosting one thousand three hundred and sixty-one cuttlefish in a massive saltwater tank suspended above his house!

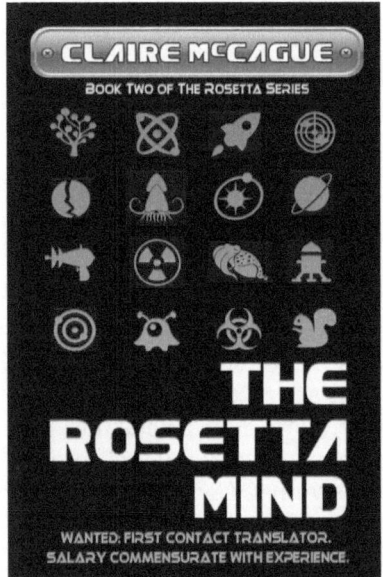

Stuck at the center of the alien contact crisis, Estlin is challenged by ill-advised directives from government officials, trenchant military interference, and random acts of violence from unknown nefarious agents— all of whom are determined to find out for themselves what the aliens really want. No matter the cost! No matter the outcome!

About Claire McCague

Claire McCague is a Canadian writer, scientist, musician, and science fiction fan. She works on sustainable energy systems, plays with words, and owns an excessive number of musical instruments. She's performed with dance bands for decades. As a theatre director and playwright, she's had productions on stages and in fields from the Fraser Common Farm in BC to the Manhattan Theatre Source.

For more EDGE titles and information about upcoming speculative fiction please visit us at:

www.edgewebsite.com

Don't forget to sign-up for our Special Offers

www.ingramcontent.com/pod-product-compliance
Lightning Source LLC
Chambersburg PA
CBHW030808210726
48290CB00002B/479